GRAPHITE

THE MARKS MADE BY A GRAPHITE PENCIL CAN BE ERASED

GRAPHITE

BUT THOSE MADE BY A DIAMOND ARE MORE LASTING

Book 2

A S J WELLS

Copyright © 2024 A S J Wells

The moral right of the author has been asserted.

Apart from any fair dealing for the purposes of research or private study, or criticism or review, as permitted under the Copyright, Designs and Patents Act 1988, this publication may only be reproduced, stored or transmitted, in any form or by any means, with the prior permission in writing of the publishers, or in the case of reprographic reproduction in accordance with the terms of licences issued by the Copyright Licensing Agency. Enquiries concerning reproduction outside those terms should be sent to the publishers.

This is a work of fiction. Names, characters, businesses, places, events and incidents are either the products of the author's imagination or used in a fictitious manner. Any resemblance to actual persons, living or dead, or actual events is purely coincidental.

Troubador Publishing Ltd
Unit E2 Airfield Business Park,
Harrison Road, Market Harborough,
Leicestershire LE16 7UL
Tel: 0116 279 2299
Email: books@troubador.co.uk
Web: www.troubador.co.uk

ISBN 978 1 83628 005 7

British Library Cataloguing in Publication Data.
A catalogue record for this book is available from the British Library.

Printed and bound by CPI Group (UK) Ltd, Croydon, CR0 4YY
Typeset in 11pt Minion Pro by Troubador Publishing Ltd, Leicester, UK

My sister, Elizabeth Ward, & my grandchildren,
Molly & Albie Bird, & Ben & Hayley Vonka.

CHAPTER 1

A quiet morning in Houghbury in the heart of southwest England. The ripples had faded from the mistaken incarceration of Maurice Jenkins for saving a toddler's life. It led to the disgrace of a Catholic priest and the arrest of the town's biggest hoodlum by a small London policewoman. The hoodlum, Sidney Cracken, had been befriended by Maurice while in prison, and proved to be a gifted artist. He was currently being tutored by Judith, mother of the boy Maurice saved, as compensation for the trouble she caused the latter.

Sergeant Bob Pollock was examining an item of post exceptionally carefully. It was addressed to Maurice Jenkins c/o Houghbury Police Station, and it had a Ugandan stamp. He was reading the details of the sender when he was rudely interrupted.

"What've you got there, Pollock?" Inspector Banbury demanded as he snatched the large envelope.

"It's for—"

"I can read! I'll see that he gets it." Banbury marched away to his office, leaving Bob open-mouthed, about to protest. He was still gaping when Detective Chief Inspector Basil Watson passed his desk.

"Seen a ghost, Bob?" he quipped as he walked by.

"Sir! Can you spare a moment?" Bob called after him. The DCI returned.

"A moment, yes. What's the matter?" He placed the thick file of papers he had been carrying on the sergeant's desk and arched his back to relieve the morning's tension.

"A new man delivered the post today and just dumped it on my desk and left. I rang for the mail team, who were delayed. I noticed an unusual stamp in the bundle and was examining the item when Inspector Banbury grabbed it. He took it away before I could protest," Bob narrated.

"Strange! Did you notice anything else about the letter?" Basil frowned.

"Yes, it wasn't for us at all. It was addressed to Maurice Jenkins c/o Houghbury Police Station. I was looking at the sender's details when the inspector seized it. It's from Sean Anderson. You know, sir. The Catholic priest who went from here to Africa to join some charity organisation," Bob explained at length.

"George Banbury interfered with the mail, did he? **Right**! Look after this file, Bob, I won't be long." He disappeared in the direction of Banbury's office. Basil knew of Banbury's antipathy for Jenkins. Basil did not like Banbury, and nor did most of his colleagues. The inspector was suspected of malpractice, but he was never caught crossing the line. Though he was not of a vindictive nature, Basil saw this as an opportunity to chastise Banbury. He strode into the inspector's room and caught him about to put a large envelope into his paper shredder.

"I'll have that, Inspector, thank you!" he demanded.

"It's nothing to do with you, Watson!" Banbury glowered at his superior.

"**Do not shred that envelope**! At present, you're only guilty of not following postal procedures. You shred it and there will still be enough to charge you with breaking postal laws by destroying someone else's mail." He tried to sound coldly official even though he was relishing the changed expression on Banbury's face.

"Pollock's a **liar**!" Banbury struggled to regain some standing.

"**That does it**! Unless you hand me the letter **right now**, the next person I speak to will be the chief constable." All pretence of impartiality was gone, and he strode across the room, seized the letter and left. Banbury kicked the shredder and slumped in his chair, grinding his teeth. When Basil returned to the front desk, he found the mail team and Bob waiting with expectant smiles.

"Here's the missing letter. Sergeant Pollock, phone Jenkins and ask him to collect it as soon as possible." He looked at the other two and added, "We don't want any *more* mishaps, do we? No need to say any more about this unfortunate mistake. Make sure you book the letter **in** to us and **out** to Jenkins." The mail team tried to hide their smiles of satisfaction as they agreed. Bob replaced his phone.

"Jenkins was in and will be here soon to collect his letter," Bob explained, and gave the cause of the morning's excitement back to the DCI.

"I think it would be best if you gave it to him, sir." Basil took the letter and studied it.

Something will have to be done about Banbury's attitude. He makes little attempt to hide his extreme views, yet in this more enlightened age he somehow manages to get away with it. I have overheard officers gossiping about Banbury twisting the rules. Possibly they are too frightened of him or the consequences to actually stand up and accuse him. If it had not been that the letter was for Jenkins, I would have let him destroy it, giving me hard ... or rather, shredded ...evidence against him. I hope I am not being too malicious when I wish for such evidence. He is a disgrace to the service, thought the chief inspector as Bob waited patiently for him to speak.

"No, Sergeant. You saved it, so you should give it to him. Make sure you get a receipt from Jenkins."

When Maurice arrived, he was handed the letter by Bob Pollock, who tried to suppress a smile of satisfaction as he filed the receipt. Back in his car, Maurice opened the letter from Sean and found another inside, which was for Helen Phillips. Sean explained how he had lost his address book during his move. He gave some details of his experiences so far. It was interesting work and should have fitted him like a glove. Unfortunately, his mind was in even deeper turmoil over the loss of Maria, as he had no social relaxation there. Maria was the nurse he had become infatuated with during his enforced sabbatical in Spain. His bishop had ordered him to have a month's leave to sort out his questionable religious beliefs after he was seen on TV venting his anger at a suspect paedophile, Maurice. Prior to his departure, he had found some empathy – perhaps it was even a mutual attraction – with Helen Phillips. He would like Maurice to deliver the enclosed letter to her.

Maurice knew that Arnold Phillips had lived in the village of Rudton, but didn't know the exact address. Arnold was the binman who cheered up Maurice and died later when they were due to meet again. He had been anxious to see where the family of his late friend lived, and this was a golden opportunity. He could deliver the letter immediately, and he might even catch a glimpse of the family. With his new beard and cropped hair, he felt reasonably safe from recognition by the woman who blamed him for her husband's death. Leaving his car at the start of the village, he enquired about the Phillipses' address from an elderly man working in his front garden. It was Harold Brown, whose wife, Rachel, was currently childminding for Helen.

The clash of a school holiday with one of Helen's cleaning jobs had obliged her to ask Rachel to look after Nicola and Roger for the morning. The friends they would normally have gone to for the day were all away on vacation. It was at times like this that the loss of Arnold was amplified for the children as, unlike their friends, they had no father to take them out for trips or play with them.

Harold Brown left his gardening and walked down to the Phillipses' house with Maurice, as he was due to join his wife and the kids for lunch. Helen would not be back until later. As they approached the house, they heard a cry of pain.

"It sounds like Nicola!" exclaimed Harold, who quickened his pace. Maurice ran ahead and saw a girl writhing in pain in the front garden, with her frightened brother standing over her. Dashing to the children, Maurice was met by Rachel Brown.

"What's happened?" she cried.

"She trod on the ball and twisted her leg," Roger gasped as he cleared his throat.

"Let me see." Maurice knelt beside the crying girl and gingerly ran his hand along her ankle and up her leg until she cried out. He noticed a small patch of blood appearing on her shorts.

"I think it's a serious break," he announced worriedly.

"Better call an ambulance!" puffed Harold as he arrived on the scene.

"Take too long! I'll get my car and take her direct to hospital. Your wife can come with me and you stay here with the boy, and wait for Mrs Phillips." Maurice took charge with his newfound confidence.

"Who are you?" Mrs Brown queried, reluctant to take instructions from a stranger.

"I'm an old friend of their father, Arnold. I'll only be a minute. Give her a paracetamol," he shouted as he dashed off.

"Do you know that man?" Rachel asked the children.

"No" was the joint answer.

"He seems genuine and caring, and I think he's right. We must trust him. Anyway, you'll be with him, won't you, dear?" Harold could not stand the sight of the little girl in such pain.

"I think he's nice," Roger said to Rachel.

"There you are, dear. Out of the mouths… as they say." Harold smiled.

"Oh, all right! You'll have to explain to Helen if we're not back." She reluctantly accepted and got a glass of water for Nicola to have with paracetamol. Violent braking announced Maurice's return by the garden gate. He opened the rear door of the car and dashed to Nicola.

"Can you hold her bad leg while I lift her, Mrs…?" He gently put his hands under the girl's body.

"Brown. Mrs Brown. Yes, I've got it." Slowly, to prevent further injury or pain, they raised Nicola and placed her on the back seat of the car. Mrs Brown squeezed in and held the girl's head in her lap. Maurice drove as fast as he could without disturbing Nicola. At the hospital, he parked at A&E and called for assistance from some paramedics who were nearby. They took Nicola on a stretcher and Mrs Brown went with them. Maurice checked for the appropriate phone number and returned to the Phillipses' house. He parked nearby and was met by an anxious Roger as he walked to the front door.

"What's happened to Nic? Where have you left her?" he beseeched Maurice. His face was a mixture of worry and fear.

"Don't pester the poor man, Roger," Harold instructed.

"No, it's okay, Mr Brown." Maurice knelt in front of the worried boy and placed his hands on his shoulders. "She's in the Emergency ward at the hospital, and the doctors are treating her right now. You've been a *very* brave boy and you are going to have to be brave for your mummy when she gets back."

"I didn't mean to push her." Roger suddenly sobbed, revealing the reason for his frightened look when Maurice had first arrived. Maurice gently squeezed the boy's shoulders.

"Of course you didn't. We all have accidents when we're having fun playing," he reassured Roger, who wiped his eyes.

"Do you like to play?" Roger gulped.

"Now don't be silly, Roger," Mr Brown intervened. Maurice looked up at him and smiled appreciatively.

"No, it's all right, Mr Brown. Roger's right to ask." He looked back at the boy's troubled face. "I haven't got any children of my own, but I **do** go and play in the park with two French kids who live next door to me."

"How can you understand them?" Roger queried.

"I know some French and I've been teaching them English," Maurice explained, and stood up.

"Was there a particular reason you came today?" Mr Brown asked.

"Oh yes. In the rush, I'd forgotten." He reached into his pocket and withdrew the envelope.

"I've got this letter for Mrs Phillips from a friend in Africa. He didn't know her address and asked me to deliver it." He handed it to Mr Brown.

"I bet it's from that priest who gave us his computer," Roger butted in.

"Yes, it is from the Reverend Anderson," Maurice replied very formally. "Now I've delivered it, I'd better be going." He shook hands with Mr Brown, who thanked him for all his help.

"Why have you got to go? Mummy will be back soon, and I'm sure she'll want to thank you too," Roger pleaded.

"I'd better not, Roger. She'll be too concerned about your sister to bother with me." He headed for the gate in their overgrown hedge. Roger ran after him.

"Don't be a pest, Roger," Mr Brown called out.

"**Please**! Please stay. **I** can make you a cup of tea or we could play football." As Maurice turned to grin at the youngster's idea of hospitality, a firm yet musical woman's voice came from the other side of the hedge.

"**Roger**! Who are you talking to?" As Helen Phillips came through the gate, she saw Mr Brown first. "Oh, hello, Harold. Rachel and Nicola indoors, are they?" Then she noticed Maurice. "Sorry. Didn't see you there."

Before either man could speak, Roger blurted out, "It's Nic, Mummy. She fell and went to hospital." Maurice kept quiet, unsure of the reception she would give him.

"We think she's broken her leg!" Harold explained as Helen's jaw dropped. "This kind gentleman came to give you a letter, and he took her and Rachel to Emergency at Houghbury Hospital," Harold continued. Helen was visibly shocked, and a dozen questions ran through her mind as she looked at each of the men and her son in turn. Nicola in hospital became her paramount concern.

Almost sensing what this lovely young woman was thinking, Maurice spoke up. *Apart from a feeling of obligation, I would like to spend more time with her.* "You're **too** distressed to drive, Mrs Phillips. I can easily run you and Roger to the hospital. I know **where** Nicola is **and** where I can park. While you visit her, I can bring Mrs Brown home," he suggested.

Helen stared at Maurice and said, "Don't I know you?"

"We've never actually met. Sean Anderson asked me to deliver a letter to you." He hedged the issue, and Harold helped by butting in.

"Don't bother with Rachel. We were going shopping this afternoon anyway, so I'll pick her up at the hospital. You and Roger go with this young man. Nicola will be wanting her mummy desperately." Helen looked from Harold back to her helpful stranger. She dashed into the house to fetch Roger's coat and to lock up. Maurice put them in his car and they waved to Harold as he drove off.

When she had calmed down, Helen turned her attention to the stranger driving them.

"Why did you have a letter from Sean for me?" It did not seem quite proper to use the priest's Christian name, but the stranger had and she did not want to be outdone.

"We were sort of acquaintances who helped each other. He lost his address book when he went to Uganda but knew how to contact me. As I had nothing more important to do today, I brought your letter straight here," he explained as best he could, without revealing either his identity or how keen he was to come.

"What's your name?" The question he had been dreading came more from polite curiosity than from a serious need to know. He did not wish to lie so he gave her his middle name.

"My friends call me Antony."

Peering through the windscreen and clutching the door handle as if urging the car to go faster, Helen's subconscious produced the retort Arnold would have used. "What do your enemies call you?" Maurice momentarily took his foot off the accelerator in his surprise.

"Jammy is the most polite one of many names." At his

school, the kids had reversed his initials, MAJ, and it had stuck in his mind.

"Jammy! Jammy! Jammy!" Roger called out.

"Roger, don't be rude! I'm sorry about that… Antony." She added his name with some reluctance, as it felt most odd addressing a stranger by his first name.

"That's okay, Mrs Phillips. Roger… the dodger… and I are good friends," he laughed.

"Roger the dodger, that's me!" the boy chanted with delight, forcing Helen to take her mind off Nicola for a few moments. Her attention turned to her driver again and she glanced at him.

"I have a feeling I should know you," she mused.

"I hope you will. If I look familiar, it's probably because I've lived in the Houghbury area all my life," he suggested, hoping to delay the inevitable.

"Will we take Nic home with us, Mummy?" Roger's timely interruption relieved Maurice's identification fears.

"I don't know. It depends what the doctors say."

With her anxiety about Nicola foremost once more, their conversation ceased. Luck was with them and they found a parking space close to the hospital entrance. Maurice took them to A&E and enquired about Nicola. Then he had a hospital volunteer take them to her.

"I'll be waiting with the car when you need me, Mrs Phillips," Maurice said as he left them. Helen and Roger were left with Rachel in a waiting area. On her neighbour's advice, Helen spoke to a senior nurse.

"Ah, Mrs Phillips. Your daughter's had a complicated fracture of her thigh. The surgeons are trying to fix it right now. They should be finished soon, but she won't be in any condition to talk for some time as she's had a general anaesthetic," the nurse explained very calmly, to reassure the worried mother.

Satisfied that her Nicola was not in a life-threatening situation, Helen allowed the dam of her pent-up emotions to burst, and she started to weep. Rachel sat beside her and tried to provide some comfort. Roger became restless and started jumping on and off the chairs.

"Stop that!" Helen almost shrieked at him, and immediately felt sorry. "Harold will be here any moment now to take you shopping, Rachel. I'm deeply grateful for all the two of you have done for us. I don't know how I'd have survived without you since Arnold went. Could you ask Antony to come up here, please? He's in the front row of the car park." Helen wiped her eyes and held Roger's hand tightly.

"You do know the young man with the beard then?" Rachel announced.

"Not really. I've never met him before," Helen admitted.

"Blow me! The way he came to the rescue and handled your children, I thought he had to be an old friend. I bet he will be now," she suggested to Helen.

"He's my friend too," piped up Roger.

"Yes, dear." Helen squeezed his hand. "I think we can call him a friend."

Mrs Brown kissed both of them on the forehead and left. Roger instantly wiped his forehead and said, "Yuck!"

Rachel found the car with Maurice dozing in it while listening to Classic FM. She tapped on the window and called out, "Antony!"

"Eh! Who?" Then he saw Mrs Brown and realised she was talking to him. "Oh, Mrs Brown! Sorry, I was miles away."

"Helen wants you to go and see her now, please."

"Okay." He got out of the car and locked it. "Aren't you going back?"

"No. I'll wait at the entrance for Harold," she told him.

"I'll say cheerio then, Mrs Brown. Here's my phone number in case I can help Mrs Phillips or her kids in the future." He handed her an old parking ticket on which he had written 'Antony' and the number.

"Why don't you give it to Helen?"

"She might not... er... find it in an emergency." He sidestepped the real issue. Rachel gave him directions to find them.

"How is she?" Maurice asked as he approached Helen in the waiting area.

"She's in the operating theatre at present." She went on to give him as much detail as she could remember. "Roger is very restless and I wondered if you would be kind enough to take him to the hospital café for a snack. It is nearly his teatime and I believe he didn't have any lunch." She opened her purse from her bag.

"I'd love to. Don't bother about money, it'll be my treat for my friend Roger the..." He paused and looked at the boy, who filled in the rest of his new nickname.

"Dodger!" Roger said with pride.

What sort of thing do you like to eat?" Maurice asked as he took the boy's hand and left.

Several minutes later, Nicola was brought out on a trolley and Helen accompanied her to a ward. The porter gave her a chair, while the nurse told her that Nicola might not wake up for some time. Helen sat beside the bed, gazing at her daughter and listening to her heavy breathing. She reached in her bag for a tissue to wipe her eyes and found the letter from Sean. Aimlessly, she opened it and started to read. 'Dear Helen, I

have asked Maurice Jenkins to deliver this to you in the...'
She read no further! With a partially suppressed cry of horror, she rushed out of the ward. In her highly emotive condition, she forgot Maurice had been fully exonerated. All she could think was that a convicted child molester and the cause of her husband's death had got her Roger. The café was about to close and was empty of customers when she arrived there.

"Have you seen a bearded man with a small boy?" she demanded of the person shutting the doors.

"Yes. They bought some sandwiches and soft drinks. I think they went outside for—" She heard no more as she ran to the exit. Running outside, she saw them seated in a small garden area.

She grabbed the astonished Roger and shouted at Maurice, "Liar! Liar! You're not Antony. You're Maurice Jenkins!" She spat the words at the person who had been the object of her hate since Arnold died. She pulled the struggling boy away as Maurice got to his feet and tried to explain. Helen was deaf to his words and marched her protesting son back into the hospital.

One moment, Maurice was the happiest he had been for a long time, eating and playing word games with a young boy. The next moment, he was plunged into the very depths of despair. *What should I do? I guess her overreaction to learning my true identity is due to the strain she is currently under. I did purchase an extra sandwich and drink for her, but I guess it will be refused now. Unless something drastic happens, she will not want a lift home with me. It will be best for me to leave, as she can always get a taxi or ring the Browns.*

Back at the ward, the nurse in charge had seen Helen run out in panic, and she approached her.

"Is there something wrong, Mrs Phillips?"

"Yes! I just found out the man with my Roger was that Maurice Jenkins!" she exclaimed, as if his very name was horrible.

"Jenkins?" the nurse queried. "**Oh**, he's the brave man who saved a child's life and spent months in prison before the truth was known. Fancy you knowing him. He's a **real** hero!" Helen gaped at her. She was still considering the nurse's words when a doctor entered to check on Nicola.

"How is she, Doctor? Will she be all right?" she asked, her maternal concern dominant once more.

"She's going to be fine. She's extremely fortunate to have been brought in so quickly after the accident. Any later and there could have been permanent damage. Mrs Brown told us how lucky it was that your friend was there to help," he assured her.

"Um… er… yes. Very lucky. How long before she comes round?" She guiltily changed the subject.

"Don't worry about that. We kept her in the recovery room until she came round. Once we knew she was okay, we let her go back to sleep. She is very young for such major surgery and will probably sleep all night. I suggest you let her be and come back early in the morning. You could probably do with a good night's sleep, and I'm quite sure this fine young man has had enough of hanging around in the hospital." He patted Roger on the head, and the boy immediately ran his hand over his hair in disgust. As the doctor was leaving the ward, he turned and pointed at Helen. "Your husband was Arnold?" he said hesitantly.

"Yes," she replied sadly.

"Have you got transport here?" he asked, remembering where she lived.

"I did have, but now I'm not so sure."

"But, Mummy, there's Antony," Roger protested.

"I think he may have left now," she remarked soulfully.

"It's shift changeover time, so let us know if you want a lift. We may have someone going your way." The doctor left.

Helen gently kissed Nicola on her cheek while thinking, '*If only I hadn't been so hasty! Jenkins could have taken Roger to the Browns and I could have stayed all night.*

She came out of the hospital in time to see Maurice arrive back in the car park. Going over to his car, she steeled herself for the apology she would have to make. He got out of the car and spread his hands towards her.

"I am so sorry. I should've been honest with you from the start." She tried to get her own apology out, but he continued. "When you were angry with me, I felt I had to leave. I was so depressed that I stopped in a lay-by. Then I remembered one of the last times I felt so down, your Arnold gave me new hope. I owed it to him to return, so here I am, at your service, madam." He made a sweeping bow. This was a gesture he would never have made prior to his incarceration, when his shyness had been the subject of ridicule at work. Now he was determined to throw off that old shy and retiring persona. Unfortunately, it was over the top for Helen, who decided he was too good to be true. She hesitantly held out her hand.

"Truce then. I want to apologise for my rudeness and ingratitude earlier." He took her hand and gently yet firmly shook it. It was only a hand, but its touch sent a shiver of pure ecstasy down his spine. It took all his willpower to release her hand. She sensed something too and peered into his eyes. They seemed very genuine to her; perhaps she was misjudging him. The look changed as he let go of her.

"Are you all right?" she asked softly.

"I-I-I-I" he stammered, before donning his new character. "I've never been better in my whole life." Though spoken flamboyantly, it was meant genuinely.

He is a regular Casanova, she thought. *If I was a single girl again, I can imagine being swept off my feet by him. He is taller than I supposed.* The new beard helped cover his prison pallor and with his short hair gave him a fashionable appearance. *Not nearly as handsome as my Arnold*, she thought, *yet he has a charm and a bearing which make him attractive.* He was aware of her studying him and was temporarily lost for words. Then he remembered where they were.

"How did you find out who I am?" He cast his mind back.

"It was in the letter you gave me. It was from my very good friend Sean," she stated dreamily, as if mesmerised by the very sound of his name on her lips. He noted her manner with considerable disappointment.

"How is Nicola?" His concern was real.

"She's going to be fine, thanks to you. The doctor said she had to have major surgery and she probably won't awake until the morning. He told me to take Roger home and get some sleep. Now you are here, I would ask you to take Roger to the Browns' for the night, please, and I will stay with Nicola," she asked submissively.

"**No!**" was Maurice's shock answer. She was dumbfounded. "I will take you **both** home! There's nothing you can do for Nicola for a while, and your son needs you too. He has had a terrible experience for one so young." He put the boy on the back seat of the car and closed the door. Then he took her hands as if to stop her from doing anything silly and continued with his instructions. "I did not want to say any more in front of Roger, and you must promise me never to mention this…"

"I'm promising nothing until I know what it's about!" She had a feeling of *déjà vu*. She could remember Arnold doing exactly what this strange man was doing now. *He seems so serious now, like somebody I could totally depend on. Yet, moments ago, he was flippant.*

"It's about Roger. He let slip to me that Nicola's fall was his fault because he pushed her. I told him not to worry as accidents always happen when people are having fun playing. I think it cheered him up a trifle. He may still be worried and I think he will eventually want to tell you. I just want you to be prepared when he does. I don't want to undermine your authority, but I think he's suffered enough." He kept his voice low and confidential. She looked at him in wonderment. He **must** be a father to have such consideration for a child, she reasoned.

"Have you got kids of your own?" She hadn't meant to be nosy; it was more of a reaction to his dialogue.

"No," he said sadly. "I've never been married. I've always liked playing with kids, though, and I've spent quite a bit of time with the two French kids who live next door to me. Perhaps that's why I'm still single."

"I don't understand." She frowned at him.

"Perhaps I've never grown up. Women don't want an overgrown kid," he replied dismally.

She was about to reply that **she** would, and the thought made her frightened.

"I'm sure some day your Miss Right will come along," she managed to suggest.

He gazed at her and thought, *She already has and she's a Mrs.*

Unsettled by his look, she got into the front seat of his car. "We'd better get going or Roger won't have time to eat or get rid of some of his energy before bedtime."

"What were you talking about?" Roger asked as they drove off.

"M… Antony's been telling me what a brave boy you've been," she told him, and then played a game of 'I Spy' the rest of the way. Maurice joined in when he could. He left them at their home, with an almost casual farewell and Helen's promise she would contact him if she needed further assistance. Reluctantly, Maurice drove home, wishing there was some way he could get to know her more intimately.

When Helen finally got to bed herself, she read Sean's letter:

Dear Helen, I have asked Maurice Jenkins to deliver this to you in the hope you will understand that you are wrong to think ill of him. I found him to be a kind and considerate person who has suffered a great injustice. I now consider him to be a friend as I also consider you to be. I trust this is not presumptuous. As such, I would like to think that you two could be friends as well. Work here keeps me fully occupied and is interesting. However, the climate does not favour me and I will not extend my current term. There is little social life here, not that I had much at Houghbury. I feel I need more to ease my loss and my separation from you and my other friends in England. I realise you are busy with your family and work, but I wondered if you could find time to write to me about the local news… (He went on to describe his work more fully and the area he lived in.)

Fond regards, Sean

Helen lay back and pictured him in his hot country, and decided she would reply immediately to her **fond**, presumptuous friend. When her alarm clock sounded, she awoke with a start, her bedside light still on and Sean's crumpled letter under her head. *I will reply later*, she thought. *Now I have to get Roger ready and go to the hospital. Nicola will need me.*

CHAPTER 2

Sergeant Birdie Lee of the Metropolitan Police had become involved with Houghbury when she was asked to check details for Maurice's appeal for wrongful imprisonment by her stepbrother, Derek, clerk to Terry Schott, the solicitor. This had thrown the spotlight on master criminal Masood, whose car was the one that nearly killed Judith's boy. It had been driven by a Malayan lad who had subsequently died mysteriously in prison. The lad had driven down to Dorset in an old Ford, wrongly taking his sister with him, and had returned in a new Audi through Houghbury.

At a Met police station, DI John Langley was delighted with the request from Chief Inspector Ron Bennett and Birdie's Inspector Phil Tyler to check on a Ford car that got burnt out with its driver in Dorset at that very time. Also to check on any missing enemies and associates of Masood and to discuss it with Doug Evans. Doug was one of the first to be contacted after Sergeant Lee's torture by suspected henchmen of Masood. This had strengthened further Doug's obsession with Masood. John knew he would keep an eye on the criminal even outside of his normal duties. At six feet and built like an athlete, he often took risks, overconfident of his ability. His colleagues envied his good looks and easy-going charm, although he was never considered a ladies' man. Given the scent of evidence, Doug couldn't wait to track it down.

Dorset Police were cagey to start with. They resented what looked like interference from London. Once John had asked the Dorset inspector to keep his enquiry secret as it concerned a master criminal with international implications, Doug received cooperation. He found that the car was almost certainly a Ford Escort! There were no traces of blood or fingerprints anywhere. The driver was just blackened remains due to the intense heat of the fire, which must have been caused by a tank full of petrol. The autopsy on the remains of the driver showed it to be a male, about 1.68 metres tall, and aged between forty and fifty. The body had been so badly broken by the fall that there was no way of knowing the man's state of health beforehand. Doug thanked the inspector and assured him they would let him know as soon as they had something positive to report.

Sometimes, Doug regretted the fact that the office he had been given since being assigned to the Masood case was in a corner, giving him limited views of the rest of the office. He compensated by placing noticeboards on almost every spare piece of wall. One of these boards had a lockable cover and he started using it as his 'shrine' to Masood, to maintain some degree of secrecy from any remaining mole in the office. The other boards were very different. Doug used them for official notices interspersed with personal, unusual or humorous pictures; a combination that broke the monotony and caught the attention of the rest of the team when they were allowed in. His love of privacy when working alone was one of the qualities about him John, Ron and Phil valued at this time. They knew he would be able to work discreetly on the problem they had posed him.

I've never been more grateful for the qualities of modern computers, thought Doug. He set up a spreadsheet to check all known or suspected criminals in the London region, who were about 1.68 metres tall and aged between forty and fifty. There were quite a few, but none had been reported missing. The check from the opposite angle on missing men produced a few; none within both parameters. Remembering that Interpol had added Masood to an international list, he asked John to contact them. It was a slender hope, he realised, as they could not know all the movements of all their listed criminals in all countries.

It was two days before they were able to reply. All were accounted for, even down to the four who had travelled to other countries on or about the 17th of October. Two of those had returned to their own countries; one from Turkey was still in the UK and one from France still in Cuba. One of the two who had returned had visited Spain and then the UK; he was also from Turkey. This intrigued John and he asked for more information. The Turkish authorities were keen to assist, as their country was anxious to do everything possible to aid their application to join the EU.

The UK visitor, Babur Demir, was head of a fairly new and particularly ruthless gang. They were suspected of drug and girl smuggling. It was estimated that they had links to prostitution organisations throughout Europe. The man who went to Spain first, Hakan Kaplan, was the second-in-command of the same gang! John's imagination worked overtime as he tried to find a reason for the two heads of a modern criminal gang to be visiting different countries at the same time. Why should Kaplan leave the day after Demir and return from England while the other was still there?

Contacting Interpol again, he asked for any pictures and details of both men. These arrived via the internet within an hour on his secure website. Kaplan was aged thirty-one and was 1.83 metres tall. Demir was forty-four years old and 1.71 metres tall, nearly what he was looking for. John asked Doug to check the facts with his Dorset contacts. Doug contacted the Dorset pathologist who had examined the body in the burnt-out Escort. He explained the case he was interested in and asked how accurate the height of 1.68 metres was.

"Accurate to within about a half of one percent. Why are you interested?" the pathologist asked bluntly.

"I'm trying to find the dead man's identity as it could well have a bearing on a case I'm handling. I've a possible suspect, but he's 1.71 metres tall, which is more than one percent over your figure," Doug explained.

"That could be him then!" announced the pathologist.

"How can it be?" queried Doug.

"My measurement was based on a straight projection for the skeleton and… er… bits. The combination of the crash and the intense heat, depending on how long it burned, could've shrunk the bones. He could've been up to 1.72 metres tall," was the reply.

"Is there anything else about the body that could make the identification more certain?"

"It's too late for a complete forensic check without disinterring the body."

"**No!** I don't want that as it would alert interested criminals," Doug hastily requested.

"One thing I did notice was his teeth."

"His teeth?"

"Yes. At a rough guess, and it is only a guess, I'd say they'd not been fixed in the UK. Is that any use to you?" He offered the information in a flat voice.

Doug thanked him and agreed to let him know how good his guess was. *I've a gut feeling we're on the right track, but there is no concrete evidence, and I still don't know exactly where it is all leading.* He promptly sent the information to John via the internet.

John ran his fingers through his hair, roughly combing back his unruly mass of thick grey hair. He stretched his whole body as he got to his feet and stifled a yawn. He had been sitting at his computer and phone for hours without standing. Easing his limbs, he paced around the room. A quick trip to the bathroom to refresh and back to his personal grindstone. Well, it was certainly personal, but that intimate involvement made it less of a grind.

It had always been a joke at the police station that Ron Bennett and John Langley had become inspectors because of their doodles. Neither minded the witticisms, as between themselves they agreed there was some truth in it. Both had used doodling as a means of clarifying their thoughts. Now, more than ever, John felt compelled to doodle. First, he sketched a very crude map of Europe. Then he gave each character a symbol, placed at their normal locations. Finally, he drew dotted lines for their movements, with the appropriate dates. It was like a slap in the face! *Why has Demir not returned to Turkey after all this time? Unless… unless he is the man in the burnt Escort. Interpol has no record of him leaving the UK.* John sent an urgent enquiry to UK Immigration in the vague hope Demir had definitely not left the country.

The next day, he received an urgent message confirming Demir had never left and was on a large list of other temporary immigrants who had failed to leave. *Success*! It now looked certain that Demir was the body in the burnt Escort. More local information was needed, so he contacted Doug Evans again. John gave him the photos of the two Turks and asked him to check CCTV coverage near Masood's usual haunts.

After hours of fruitless, head-aching staring at tapes, Doug spotted Kaplan. The Turk had met Masood in a restaurant. There was no sign of the other one. He suggested he show it in a multiple-photos ID to Fellows, Birdie's torturer, who did not get shot during her rescue. John agreed and reminded Doug to keep the operation as secret as possible.

John Langley was not a patient man, as members of his team often found to their cost. He could not wait for Doug's results, so he contacted the Turkish police and requested more details about Demir. Had he returned from England? If not, where was he? Could he have any details of Demir's medical or dental history? What was his number two, Kaplan, doing now?

The following day, Doug Evans visited Fellows in prison. After explaining the purpose of his visit, he was given the assistance of a prison officer.

"My colleague will show you a series of photographs," he explained to the thug when they were seated in the interrogation room. "I want you to study each one carefully in turn and tell me which ones you know or recognise." The prison officer placed the first one on the table.

"Never seen 'im before!" the convict growled.

Doug got to his feet, walked round the table and stood over Fellows. He picked up the photo and stared at it, while the convict grinned. Then he bent over the man very slowly, placing one hand gently on his shoulder, and slowly but imperceptibly tightened his grip. He held the photo about 15 centimetres in front of the thug and asked in a smooth yet threatening voice,

"I suggest you do as requested and look very closely at each photo, before making a decision. Some of these photos are of people we know that you know. If we catch you telling lies, we'll make sure it's entered on your record and will be taken into consideration when you seek remission." Fellows hunched his shoulders, partly from worry and partly to relieve the pain of Doug's iron grip.

"Oh! It's a woman!" Genuine surprise showed on his hard face.

"Very good! I was beginning to have doubts about your basic knowledge of biology. It's a start, but do you recognise her?" Doug persisted. Fellows stared at her again.

"Yeah! It's that one we didn't know was a cop. She's the one wot got us in 'ere."

"Good. That's correct. Next photo, please," Doug requested as he returned to his seat.

The prison officer took the second photo from the file and placed it on top of the first one.

"Nah! Ne..." A deep growl-like cough came from Doug. "Oh yeah! It's me mate Bill."

Doug was staring intently at Fellows and made no attempt to confirm or deny the man's statement. After a few seconds, he had the third photo placed in position, never taking his eyes from Fellows's face. This time, the thug studied it closely then looked at Doug as if seeking a sign, then back at the photo.

"No, I don't think I know this one." Doug still watched him carefully without any expression or movement.

"Next one, please." Doug was like a robot; all he ever said was "Next one, please," in the same flat voice; his only movement was making marks on a list concealed from the convict. Even the prison officer could detect no signs to distinguish between the photos. There were two more negative responses and then Fellows correctly identified one as a policeman. Then there was Masood...

"Know 'is face. Can't think 'ow. Probably lives near me." It was only slight, but Doug detected a faint pause before he had answered, and again when Fellows tried to explain further.

He continued with the photos like some timed slide show. There were three more Fellows had to know and three he didn't. Meticulously presented among the six were the two Turks. Kaplan's picture brought a totally negative response, visually as well as verbally. However, with Demir, there was a longer pause and a bit of forced coughing, then,

"Never seen 'im before." Doug noted the pause and the badly disguised startled look in Fellows's eyes. Even then, Doug was a blank canvas; the sort of frozen expression that women see as a challenge to melt.

When he was finished, Doug collected up the photos and the file into his briefcase. With a wink at the prison officer, he walked round the table, and as he approached him, Fellows stood up and backed away. Doug held out his hand and allowed the trace of a smile on his face.

"I'd just like to thank you for all your cooperation, Mr Fellows. You've been most helpful."

Fellows shook Doug's hand reluctantly and shook his head.

"I never said nuffink! They can't blame me!" he blurted out.

Still smiling, Doug raised his eyebrows. "Can't blame you for what, Mr Fellows?"

"Nuffink! They can't blame me for nuffink! I've said nuffink!" Doug indicated to the prison officer and they left the room for a moment so he could explain a dangerous ruse he'd planned.

Then they escorted Fellows back to his cell. When they were nearly there, Doug thanked the thug for all his vital assistance, knowing other prisoners would hear.

Back at the police station, he quickly gave his results to John Langley.

"So you feel certain he did know Demir and not Kaplan?" John slapped his desk as he spoke.

"Yes. And... comparing his reaction with the one for Masood, I consider they were generated by different emotions. With Masood's photo, he was frightened to admit he actually knew him. With Demir's picture, his fear was more aligned to guilt. Therefore, I think you are right. Fellows and his mate do contract work for Masood and could well have killed Demir. Masood would not want the body identified or even found in the London area, which is why it would be disposed off and disfigured well away from there."

"Thanks, Doug. We still have to keep this under wraps in case Masood has any more 'associates' working here." He made inverted comma signs as he said associates. Beckoning Doug closer, he pointed at an email he had received from Turkey. "I had this come today on my personal internet address. Demir has not returned to Turkey. He left for the UK and has not been heard of since last October. Kaplan seems to have taken charge of their gang now. Fortunately, there are two unusual things known about Demir, although the Turkish police do not have his proper records. The big toe on his left foot was badly deformed due to some accident, and he is known for his golden smile. His top middle tooth is pure gold. I've rechecked with the Dorset pathologist and both items match the body in the burnt Escort!"

John left the office at his usual time and took his normal tube train to go home. On the way, he changed trains twice and then caught a bus, lest someone was trying to follow him. At Ron and Phil's temporary home, where they were safer from Masood, who had already tried to kill them, he showed them the results of his endeavours. They had set up a board with all the known facts of the case, and now added the new ones. Sitting with their tea and biscuits in front of the board, they studied it in silence for several minutes.

"Why did Kaplan go to Spain first before coming to England?" Phil suddenly thought aloud.

"If he has taken over the Turkish gang and had to get rid of Demir, why didn't he come direct to London where Demir was visiting Masood?" John amplified Phil's question.

"Yes! If he wanted Masood to kill Demir, why not ask him direct?" Phil nodded thoughtfully.

"We've been too parochial in our outlook!" Ron exclaimed. "We know Masood is part of a large international crime syndicate, believed to be trading under the name of Zebec. What if Masood didn't have the authority to eliminate the head of the Turkish branch?"

"Kaplan would have to get that authority from the very top man!" John suggested.

"Which is why," all three spoke as one, "**he went to Spain first**." They gave each other a high five.

"Why couldn't Kaplan just get rid of Demir in Turkey?" John asked.

"Well, John, the Turkish gang is fairly new, and it could've caused trouble among the other members. The way it was done makes it look as if Demir left for the UK and just disappeared. The other gang members could not blame Kaplan, who had simply visited the big cheese in Spain. That's why the body had to be unidentifiable," Ron explained, and watched as Phil added a piece of card with a large question mark to the very top of their board.

"So you got some useful information from Interpol then," John remarked.

"They were helpful. Perhaps we should reciprocate and tell them what we've discovered?" Phil looked at Ron.

"You're right. At the same time, they might advise us if they have any reason to believe the top man lives in Spain."

Ron made a few notes. He thanked John for all his support and asked him to thank Doug. They would be returning to normal life in a couple of days and wondered how best to do it.

"I'd love to see the expression on Masood's face when you two return from the dead. How about we have him brought to the station on some pretext and you just happen to pass him?" John suggested, with a look of relish at the possible outcomes.

"I've never met him, so I don't suppose he would react at my presence," Phil commented.

"I've met him a few times in the past and he should recognise me," Ron affirmed.

"Right. I'll get Doug Evans to bring Masood in tomorrow afternoon to be in a line-up for Fellows to identify. This will put the heat on both of them. Meanwhile, you two come into work a bit later, so all our staff can acknowledge you, and any mole won't have had time to warn Masood. Then we can arrange it for him to meet Phil first and then you, Ron, and we can note his reactions." John became excited over his plan, which the others agreed to.

"Meanwhile, we'll contact Interpol again to our mutual benefit, we hope," Ron said to the departing John.

"One thing more, John. Could you find out from our Manchester colleagues if there have been any suspicious people or activities around the bombed car area?" Phil added, referring to the car in which they transported the Malayan's sister for safety to an RAF base where Ron's brother was. The bomb had been detected and sent on a crazy route to a quarry near Manchester for detonation.

"It's already done. Some of us are hard at work while you two layabouts are having a luxury ho… liday!" He ducked just in time for the soggy dishcloth thrown by Ron to miss his head by inches. Giving a two-finger sign, he left rapidly.

The exchange of information with Interpol proved mutually beneficial. The happenings with the Turkish gang filled some gaps for them, and the possible existence of a mastermind in Spain substantiated their theories about the ZEBEC organisation. In return, Ron and Phil were given the likely whereabouts of the top criminal; it was the Andalusia region of Spain. The problem was, it was both a very busy tourist area and thousands of foreigners had homes there. Foreigners from all over Europe, particularly the northern countries, and even from the rest of the world. For the majority, it was the climate and way of life that attracted them. For the criminal element, it was the proximity to Africa.

Thus, the head of the crime syndicate could be of any nationality and living in any size premises in any location, inside or even outside Andalusia. Furthermore, Interpol had not been able to establish if their target was a permanent or temporary resident. The influx of foreigners was year-round, and there were hundreds of legitimate businessmen who stayed there intermittently. They had not discarded the thought that the man they sought could be a local, and had a long list of those who had had regular contact with foreigners.

Kaplan had flown into Madrid and had been picked up by a suspect in a black BMW, which headed south. The next time the occupants of the car were seen, in Toledo, Kaplan was not there. The Spanish police were not surprised, as members of the syndicate were known to change cars regularly to avoid being followed. Even if they had managed to trace him to Andalusia, the syndicate had several premises and numerous other places for secret meetings. Masood had been in the Granada area of Andalusia for a while between his time as a minor brothel-keeper and illegal immigrant in London, and his return legally and as head of his gang. Hindsight is a wonderful thing! The two inspectors could see now that Masood may be quite a clever operator, but the syndicate had assisted his rise to power. Keeping him in the limelight protected the others.

John's plan did not work as expected. Masood objected strongly to attending the station and insisted on having his lawyer present. Fellows broke out in a cold sweat when he was given an 'accidental' glimpse of Masood, before he joined the line-up. Naturally, Fellows identified no one. As Masood was leaving, he was asked to sign a statement by Phil at the reception desk. This done, without a glimmer of recognition of Phil, he turned to leave and bumped into Ron.

"Oh, hello, Chief Inspector. Still in your old job then?" He smiled, as if taunting Ron.

"Any reason I shouldn't be, Mr Masood?" Ron fired back at him.

"After all the years I've known you chasing moonbeams instead of real criminals, I would've thought you would've moved on to higher things." He laughed; was it a sinister sound or just his natural laugh?

"Oh? And what higher things would they be?" Ron parried.

"Well, it's quite a list of possibilities."

"Try me with some," Ron demanded.

"Well, you've been a chief inspector for some time now, so why haven't you been promoted?"

"Because of your friend Thwaite, of course!"

"I'm sure I don't know what you mean." He smiled and forced a look of surprised innocence on his face.

"Any other higher things, **Mr** Masood?" Ron was exasperated by this evil man he was unable to arrest.

Masood stepped back, as if expecting Ron to get violent, and spoke with an insulting laugh. "Why, cloud cuckoo land, where they put all the folks what spend their lives chasing moonbeams!"

When Masood had finished, Ron stared into his eyes carefully before he replied. "Moonbeams aren't only very attractive, but they can also illuminate one's path from the cliffs of Dorset to the rest of Europe," he rejoined confidently.

"Don't you mean the cliffs of Dover?" Masood's jovial expression faded slightly.

"No. Dorset cliffs are not as white as those at Dover, but they are equally dangerous for foreigners in old Ford cars who are unsure of their route!" Ron frowned at Masood, who turned abruptly to his lawyer.

"We've wasted enough time on these busybodies." Masood said and left hurriedly.

CHAPTER 3

Ivor Kowalski made a slow and painful recovery from the shooting he had suffered while trying to rescue Birdie Lee. It was weeks after he became fully conscious before he could accept that he was crippled. Once, after a particularly pleasant repartee with an attractive nurse, he tried to advance his desires only to find he was totally incapable. Physiotherapists paid him daily visits to demonstrate what he was capable of, and to increase his movements. Little by little, he began to concur with the medical staff's diagnosis, unpalatable as he found it. From the very depths of despair, they gave him the confidence to try things. Colleagues and other friends visited him regularly, but their barely disguised sympathy annoyed him.

One ray of hope was his most frequent physiotherapist, who he named Jumping Jean because of the way she always bounded into his room. It was not just her attitude that enlivened him; she could be described as a veritable blonde goddess. Unable to make any physical advances towards her, he resorted to a form of oral interplay. Every time she came to give him therapy and asked how he was feeling, he gave the same answer.

"I can't wait to get into Jeans!" To which she had various ripostes. His favourite was when she said, "Naughty boy! I'll put you over my knee and smack your bottom!" She tried to look serious.

"Ooh, **yes please**, miss. I'm sure a bit of flagellation could work wonders for me. And I'm **sure** you would enjoy it." He licked his lips suggestively. On one occasion, she actually started to move him, as if to carry out her threat, and only ceased when he gave a barely disguised grunt of pain.

He was relieved to know Birdie, who he treated as his little sister and not one of his many conquests, was recovering fast and was being kept somewhere safe. The other news about the team's progress on the Masood case pleased him and made him wish he was still a part of it. Some reading and TV filled his waking hours and helped to slightly relieve the boredom of lying so still all day. When Jean intercepted a stranger attempting to get into his room, his security was maintained at a high-risk level, though how anyone could see him as a threat was a mystery.

"I'm not safe here," he stated in a plaintive voice. "You'd better lie on the bed with me tonight, Jean, and then I will feel safe."

"I'm sure you'd like that, but there are a couple of reasons I can't." She shook her head as if addressing a wayward child.

"I know it's my legs! However, I won't mind being submissive, and you're very fit," he replied cheekily.

"That's another reason! The ones I meant were the hospital management would not approve, and…" she gave a long pause, placing her hands on his shoulders and gazing into his eyes "…I would not feel safe."

It had been a long-standing assertion that patients fell in love with their nurses. Ivor could understand why, and from his current experience he classified other carers in that category. Though his innuendo with Jean was somewhat risqué, it disguised the things he really wanted to say to her. He longed to tell her what he thought of her, and the words never came. One bullet had changed him from a superfit sex machine (his own view), full of confidence in every situation, to a weak cripple who had replaced confidence with venom. His visitors tired him completely because of his struggle to be diplomatic and welcoming. The longer he was in the hospital, the more brittle he became with everyone, except Jean.

Unclothing her with his mind's eye, he concluded that she was everything he had wanted out of life. Blonde, trim and beautiful, a true English rose, though he noticed when others had entered at the same time as her that she was very petite. *How on earth can she hope to manhandle lumps like me?* he thought.

"Ah! Here's my blonde bombshell," he greeted her one day.

"Yes, Ivor. I've come to blow you up!" As soon as she said it, she knew it was the wrong thing.

"Great! A blow job! I didn't know you could get one on the NHS." He pursed his lips and waggled his eyebrows. She blushed faintly as she put some of her equipment on the table in the corner of his room.

"Look, buddy!" She adopted an American drawl. "You may think you're dynamite, but I ain't gonna light your fuse." She turned towards him with a metre-long elastic band in her hands.

"Ooh! I didn't know you had a rubber fetish." Ivor gave a lascivious belly laugh. "Flagellation then. You're into S and M?" he queried.

"Wrong again. It's to develop your muscles." She approached him threateningly.

"Any particular muscle?" Ivor asked suggestively.

"Yes!" She placed the band in his hands. "Your arm muscles." She was used to banter with her patients, and most of it she had heard many times before. Somehow, this one was different. Was it because he was the only one she had ever had who was partially paralysed due to a bullet wound? Or was it because of his age and appearance? She too knew of the danger of hospital romances. Nonetheless, she had a distinctly hollow feeling when Admin advised her that he was to leave.

"Leave?" Ivor was flabbergasted. "Why the **hell** should I leave here now? I'm not cured yet, and *who's* going to look after me?" he ranted, when Ron Bennett gave him the news.

"Calm down, Ivor! You have to accept that there is no quick cure for your problem. If you're lucky, you may have movement in your legs in a year or so. Meanwhile, you do not need to be in a hospital occupying a valuable bed. We are moving you to a secure locality and have got someone there who can act as your carer, and—"

"**Act! Act as my carer?**" All his pent up-frustration surfaced. "What happens if I need medical attention?" He raised his head as far as he could.

"I can't tell you the location yet, as walls can have ears. Though we can't think why Masood should want to harm you further. At this secure house, you will have Suzy Ramas, a qualified nurse to attend to you," Ron whispered in Ivor's ear. Ivor's eyes opened wide.

"You mean that wog driver's sister?" he protested between his teeth. Suzy's brother was the one who died in prison, and she was being kept at an RAF base for safety. She was the prime witness in getting Maurice released from prison. Now she was posing as sister to Bennett's sister-in-law; his brother was an officer at the base.

"There's no need to be racist, Ivor!" Ron warned him.

"**Forget racism. I've seen some of these Asian nurses, or alleged nurses. Some have dubious qualifications, and they're all tiny and ugly, or at best plain. And you expect**

me to share some safe house with some god's gift to Frankenstein?" His temper was getting worse by the minute as he trawled the depths of insulting speech. The gallant, courteous ladies' man had transformed into an obscene bigot. Ron stared at him in horror. He realised it was useless to try and reason with Ivor while he was in this frame of mind.

"I'll ignore your remarks. The move is tomorrow, and I don't think you'll find Suzy unpleasant. Goodbye!" Ron turned and left to prevent a further tirade.

"Don't think! That's the trouble with you lot. You just don't think," Ivor muttered to the closing door.

Outside the door, Ron bumped into Jean and, not knowing her affinity for Ivor, warned her.

"I shouldn't go in to see Kowalski for a few minutes, miss. He's in a foul mood because I told him he has to be moved." Had he known she had a special relationship with him, he would have explained that the outburst she may have overheard was most unlike Ivor.

Jean **had** heard! Her earlier hollow feeling had now been filled with a mixture of regret and relief. Regret that a budding relationship had been destroyed, and relief that she had found out his true nature in time. It proved to her how wise management was to warn of the danger of hospital romances. When she did visit him next, for his final session, she maintained a formality he had not seen since her first visit. He tried to express his sadness at leaving her, and it was received with a coldness he could never have believed her capable of.

"These are the plans for your future exercises." She showed him a file. "I will see that your new carer gets it and understands the importance—"

"**Jean!**" Ivor interrupted her set speech with an impassioned plea.

"...importance of continuing with your recovery regime. With your current rate of progress—"

"**Jean**! How can you be like this after all we've been to each other?" he interjected.

"Mr Kowalski! Please stop interrupting. I'm sorry if you think I've been unprofessional in our relationship. You've been a most pleasant patient and I've enjoyed working with you. But now I must say goodbye." There was a pressure building in her chest, and she knew that if she did not leave immediately she would burst into tears. He held out his arms as if to embrace her, but she fled from the room. As Shakespeare said in *Richard II*, 'Sweet love, I see, changing his property, Turns to the sourest and most deadly hate…' So it was with Ivor. This supposed rejection by the one bright light in his drastically curtailed lifestyle made him resentful towards everyone.

"It's not like him." Ron had seen the doctor and made arrangements for Ivor's move. As he returned to tell Ivor, he met Jean leaving his room, with a long face and close to tears.

"What's not like him?" Her response was forced.

"Ivor has never been a racist as long as I've known him. He's just very bitter about being so… handicapped and having to move." Ron tried his best to compensate for Ivor's outburst.

"They say a person's true worth is shown in a crisis," she argued. "And why wouldn't he want to move to a more private place with a personal carer?"

"His **true** worth in a crisis! I'm sorry to disagree with you, but I think he showed his *true* worth when he risked his life for a colleague, which is why he's in the condition he is in right now. **You** must know the reason he doesn't want to move. He was desperate to stay here, and gave even the most vile excuses to stay. I know he is as comfortable as he could be here, but it's much more than that. Although I know he is a philanderer where women are concerned, **this** is something I've not seen in him before."

"**What**? Tell me what you've seen and I haven't!" she retorted, trying to walk past him.

"Yes, you have seen it but are afraid to admit it. He's besotted with **you**!" Ron sidestepped to block her path once more.

"He's got a funny way of showing it." She sighed and stepped back again. Ron put a hand on her arm.

"Give him a chance, you'll see. He would have welcomed this move if you were to go with him." Ron had always avoided interfering in colleagues' personal affairs until now; here, the circumstances were exceptional.

"I'll think about it. I'm too upset at present." She shook off his hand and fled.

Extra security was provided for Ivor's move, and Jean was compelled to notice it despite the distractions of her other duties. The more she mulled over Ron's words, the more she knew it was the truth. Yes, he was only a patient and she had only known him for a few weeks, yet it was more than sympathy she felt for him. She had had many boyfriends, and few were more than ships passing in the night. Most treated her like a dumb blonde, and none had raised her spirits as Ivor had. She now understood how, after his unfortunate outburst, he had tried to show his feelings for her. Many thoughts flashed through her mind as she carried out her assigned tasks like a robot. *He loves me, or not; he could be crippled for life, or not; he's going to be alone with a beautiful oriental carer, or not; he'll soon forget me, or not; I'll soon forget him, or…* Then it struck her! *I am no longer a schoolgirl or even an inexperienced student physiotherapist. I am a mature woman who should make my own mind up. To hell with common sense! I do love him! I will take a chance on him, as they say in the song.* She finished what she was doing and dashed to his room. A junior was stripping the bed.

"Where's Kowalski?" Jean asked anxiously.

"They took him about five minutes ago. If you want to see him, you'll have to hurry," the surprised girl said.

Ignoring all the rules about running in the corridors, Jean tore down to the front entrance, brushing staff and visitors aside as she went. They had his trolley close to the ambulance when she dashed up. Ignoring all the bystanders, she ran to his side.

"I'm sorry, Ivor. I do love you," she puffed hurriedly, to the astonishment of both the police guard and the medical staff. He turned to look at her and gave her a smile that spoke volumes.

Before he could speak, two shots were heard. She fell to the ground and he slumped back.

Immediately, the armed police guarding him returned fire in the direction of the shots, high on one corner of the main hospital building. The nurse and doctor who had accompanied Ivor to the ambulance leapt into action. They were too late to save Ivor. They rushed to help Jean, who had been hit in her shoulder. The force of the bullet had knocked her to the ground and she was unconscious. With the hospital porters, they hoisted her up and ran with her back through the entrance.

CHAPTER 4

"Quick, Steve! Turn left! Follow that blue VW Golf MAP or D 986 or 5 W!" Detective Sergeant Doug Evans instructed the driver of the unmarked police car.

"We can't do that! We'll be late for Kowalski's funeral," replied the driver.

"**Do it!**" shouted Doug. The surprised Steve cut across the traffic with some difficulty and did as instructed.

"Which would Ivor want most, lads, us at his funeral or catching the scum that killed him?"

The three officers in their best uniforms nodded in unspoken agreement.

"Who's in the Golf, Doug?" one asked.

"Keep it in sight but don't let him see us. These uniforms are a dead giveaway," Doug urged.

"Very droll, Doug. Wearing uniforms to a funeral really is a **dead** giveaway." One backseat officer broke the sombre mood. There was a smile from the others, who were too angry about Ivor's death to laugh out loud.

"**Who** is in the Golf?" the questioner demanded.

"I'm sure it's Judge Reynolds. The bastard who's in Masood's pocket, and let Thwaite off," Doug replied, without taking his eyes off the disappearing VW.

"That's not his car and I didn't notice that the driver even looked like him," argued Steve.

"I was reflecting over happier times with Ivor when that car passed in front of us and I noticed the twitch. Reynolds is noted for the nervous twitch he has under his left eye. I've been following him on and off for weeks now. A couple of times, I thought he was acting strangely, and I lost him in the same multi-storey car park. The reason I never found him, just his empty car, must be because he switched to that Golf. It may even have passed me and I wouldn't have known it was him. He's wearing a baseball cap and thick-rimmed glasses, and seems to have more and darker hair than usual." Doug was solving the mystery piece by piece, and aloud. Understanding the need to keep a low profile, all four policemen removed their hats.

"You may find this useful, Doug. It's got a 20-times zoom." A backseat officer, Geoff, passed a compact camera to Doug, who reached over his shoulder to accept it, without losing sight of the Golf.

"We're going to get hell for missing the funeral," the quiet one in the back, Vic, reminded the others.

"Which is all the more reason for getting positive evidence against Masood's judge. Without him and Thwaite, Masood will be *very* vulnerable," Doug advised them. The Golf turned down a side road.

"Slow at the corner, Steve. I recognise this road from my time in Vice. If Reynolds is the sex fanatic you say he is, he's probably going to pick up a girl there," the camera owner suggested. Steve slowed the car to a crawl and moved forward far enough for them to see down the side road. The Golf had stopped opposite a very young girl on the pavement at the far end of the road. Steve gently took the police car round the corner, and Doug opened his side window and prepared the camera. All four kept quiet and still, although there was enough traffic and pedestrians there to make their presence unremarkable.

Through the telephoto ability of the camera, Doug was able to see the girl but not the driver, and he took a couple of photos. The girl got into the back of the car, and Doug could just make out that she put on some form of blindfold. When the Golf moved off, the police car followed at a distance. After nearly ten minutes, they were forced to crouch down and drive past the Golf, which suddenly turned into the underground car park of a run-down block of flats. Steve parked their car round the corner.

"What do we do now, Doug?" asked the reluctant Vic. Doug peered into space and concentrated, trying to block out the thought that he may have brought them all on a wild goose chase.

"Here's how I see it. He's committed no crime so far, and it could just be wishful thinking on my part. However, I would like you all to consider this. If he's simply picked up a girl for sex, that's not a crime, although—"

"…unless she's under age!" Steve interrupted, as he had a better view of the girl than the two in the back.

"Yes, Steve. She could well be. I was going to say that at the very least it would besmirch the reputation of one of Her Majesty's judges," Doug added. There was a prolonged silence.

"We can hardly go into the building in our uniforms," Vic muttered.

I can see why he's still a desk jockey and not in CID like the rest of us, but he's right, mused Doug.

"Thanks for that, Vic. I'll take my jacket off and put on my civvy mac, which I always carry just in case. I could wander around in the flats building and pretend I'm looking for a Stephen Crosby."

"That's my name," protested Steve. "Anyway, two can play at that game. If Geoff pulls down the other bit of their seat back, he'll find my mac in the boot."

He reached back to collect the garment, but Geoff was quickly out of the car, saying, "I'll wear it over *my* uniform and go walkabout outside while you and Vic get on the radio and check on the Golf—"

"...and the ownership of these flats," Vic interrupted Geoff. The three from the CID looked at him in amazement.

"We might make a detective out of him yet, lads." Doug laughed as he got out of the car.

"Meet back here in twenty minutes. That should be long enough for His Lordship, and we'll be ready to follow."

"It's as seedy inside as it is outside," Doug announced as he got back into the car. "I think most of the flats are empty, although the absence of cobwebs on many doors shows they must have been opened fairly recently."

Geoff climbed into the back with a broad grin of satisfaction. "I met an old woman who lives nearly opposite the flats and pretended I was thinking of moving in," he declared with some amusement.

"She assured me she liked to keep to herself and didn't like to spread gossip, and *then* told me more than I could've hoped for. It seems the building has very few tenants and was due to be replaced some years ago. She keeps thinking there are people moving in when she sees vans unloading packing cases into the block, but nobody else seems to actually live there. She has just happened to notice, and purely by chance as she adjusts her curtains, some couples going inside the block for short visits. She thinks they must have been prospective buyers." He mimicked an old woman opening curtains to snoop.

"We've been busy too, haven't we, Vic? The building belongs to a David Winchester, a true blue Englishman with no known record or known fortune, but he has a magnificent moustache. Cross-checking with Masood, the only known link is that they are both supporters of the same charity."

"Let me guess," said Steve. "Drugs for the poor."

"Not quite! Are you all sitting comfortably? It's HHI."

"What's that, a disease?" joked Geoff.

"No!" scowled Doug. "I remember tracking Masood to one of their functions. It's Help for Homeless Immigrants."

"You are joking?" Geoff was dumbfounded. The other three shook their heads. Doug searched his memory.

"Did you say Winchester has a grand moustache?" he asked Steve.

"Yes. It's his pride and joy," Steve replied.

"I thought it rang a bell. At the HHI charity dinner, Winchester was seated next to Masood. They nodded at each other, and I was mystified as to why they did not talk to each other. At the time, I presumed it was because the proper English gentleman did not wish to communicate with some upstart 'wog'! Now I believe it was because they did not want their clandestine association to be known. They could've been passing messages or money under the table," Doug recalled slowly.

"The car is registered to Reynolds's gardener. I think it is so that it's not linked with the judge directly. The licensing authority has it addressed as care of a private post box, which belongs to the judge. It's—"

"Keep down!" Doug ordered. "Here he comes!" The Golf appeared from the underground car park and they could not see any sign of the girl in it.

"Follow him!" Doug instructed Steve. "If he's left the girl in the flat, we can always come back. If she's in the car and we can't see her, she may need assistance," he explained.

"How can she need help? She's a whore who's just been providing her services," Vic queried.

"Tell him, Geoff," Doug said, with a hint of exasperation.

"You're still a bit of an innocent, aren't you, Vic? Men like Reynolds have strange needs. Normal sex is not enough for them. I won't go into detail, but suffice to say the women in these encounters can be abused and hurt or even killed. That is why some people advocate licensed brothels to eliminate such dangers and avoid health complications."

Vic looked at Geoff open-mouthed. The Golf stopped in a deserted cul-de-sac between some warehouses. The heavily disguised Reynolds got out, opened the rear door and pulled out the limp girl. He propped her against a wall and removed her blindfold, and then drove off. The four policemen, who had ducked out of sight, went to the girl's aid as soon as the judge was gone. She was obviously in some pain and protested as they lifted her up and carried her to their car.

"*NU MAI!*" she screamed. Geoff and Vic explained who they were as Steve put up a flashing light and sped to the nearest A&E. Still struggling, she was carried inside. Doug showed his ID to the doctor in charge and explained what had occurred, without naming the offender.

"It is vital that you check her for all types of injuries, and if there is any semen on her, it must be sent for DNA analysis immediately. I will need a complete list of her injuries and all her personal details. I can't impress upon you strongly enough how important this is. We can't reveal the name of the perpetrator, as it is highly political. Nobody outside of your known staff can have access to her unless I am there in person. We will stand guard for her until we are relieved."

He paused for breath and continued. "It would be best if you could keep her in a single room. To illustrate the danger she may be in, I can tell you we had to divert from the funeral of a colleague murdered by the associates of her molester."

Doug spoke quietly, so others could not hear, but his tone left the doctor in no doubt about the risks involved. Once the girl had been placed in a single room, Doug remained on his own while the other three returned to the police station to face the music.

The doctor approached Doug confidentially nearly an hour later. "Did you have trouble making the poor girl understand you?"

"Yes. When we went to pick her up, she cried out in a foreign language. Have you had any success with her?" Doug got up from his seat by the door to her room. The doctor gestured for him to sit again and he sat next to him.

"One of my nurses has spent time in Romania with a charity, and has learnt enough of their language to question the girl. Her name is Anica Vasile and she's only just turned fifteen. She only arrived in England last week and was told by her mentors to earn her fare by standing on that corner and being nice to gentlemen in cars. She doesn't know where she was taken because her client blindfolded her. It seemed to be a deserted building, because she didn't hear anybody else and their footsteps echoed a lot. She anticipated having to have sex but was horrified when the man tied her face down on a bed. He whipped her and then had anal sex. He hurt her very much, which the bruising testifies to. We've taken semen samples as you requested and sent them for DNA analysis, and I've kept duplicates in my safe. You will have to get a sample from the brute who did this to her, for comparison." He kept his voice low so nobody could overhear him.

Doug had made a few notes as his confidant spoke. "How is she now? Will she be kept in overnight?" Doug was concerned for her, both as a person and as a crucial witness.

"She's still in a state of shock and has been given painkillers, which will probably make her sleep all night. Then, I'm afraid we will need the bed," the doctor said reluctantly.

"Thank you, Doctor. I'm sure I can rely on your discretion to keep this under wraps. I will be on guard here for a bit longer and then there should be a replacement for me."

The next morning, Doug reported to DI John Langley and gave him both a verbal and a written report, including the facts presented to him by the doctor. John told him about Ivor's funeral. It had been carried out with full honours, and even the most hardened policeman found it moving. Everyone felt the void left by Sergeant Birdie Lee's absence, particularly when newly promoted Superintendent Ron Bennett read out a eulogy that she had sent him. It had been decided that it was too great a risk for her to attend. There were many questions asked and many suppositions about the mini-sized Marilyn Monroe, in the wheelchair, with her shoulder swathed in bandages. Jean insisted on going, and her hospital felt obliged to help her.

"I'd like to think that some beautiful woman would shed as many tears at my funeral!" one clown at the funeral said.

"In your case, they'll probably be laughing!" retorted an annoyed colleague.

Then John and Doug went to the hospital and formally interviewed Anica Vasile with an official interpreter. Her statement corroborated what the doctor had said, plus some more lurid details she had been too terrified to talk about before. After she had been discharged, she was taken from the hospital by a circuitous route to stay with Suzy. Peter Bennett thought of protesting that his fake relation was being used excessively when he realised she would have less to do with an abused girl than with a crippled man. It also meant that one of his fellow officers, Flight Lieutenant Cassidy, would not have a rival for Susan's affections, just when they were really bonding.

Doug went to see Judge Reynolds in his chambers and adopted the friendliest approach he was capable of.

"I know this is ridiculous, Your Lordship, but I have to take a sample of your DNA."

"**You what! How dare you!**" Reynolds erupted.

"It's for the Kowalski case. The whole force is up in arms about the murder of one of their own and is insisting every single person who had any dealings with him must be checked."

He paused for effect. "The gunman was killed in an exchange of fire with our men and they found a letter on him from his employer, whose DNA we now hold," he explained apologetically.

"I've had **nothing** to do with the poor man," the judge protested.

"No, not directly, but he was upset at your decision in the matter of former Superintendent Thwaite, and the men think there could have been something personal in it. I've assured them that it's not possible, and reminded them that you are a judge of the highest standing, but they think nobody should be above the law. What do you think, Your Honour?" *And nobody is above being buttered up*, thought Doug.

"They're quite right, and I must set an example."

"Thank you for being so understanding, Your Honour. Naturally, the sample will be destroyed once the case is closed," he reassured Reynolds as he returned the sample to its container and carefully labelled it.

The sample was rushed to the laboratory and proved to be a perfect match. Despite the reservations of the Crown Prosecution Service, Reynolds was promptly arrested. He was allowed out on bail and promptly fled the country. In one way, it saved embarrassment for the judicial system. In another, it meant a hideous crime had gone unpunished, a sex monster was at large somewhere, and the CID did not have the information they needed against Masood. The speed and secrecy of Reynolds's departure made John Langley and Doug Evans very suspicious. It obviously benefitted Masood to have him leave the country before he gave any incriminating information about him, but it meant the crime boss had lost his leverage in the police, and now the courts.

"We keep whittling away at his organisation, but it flourishes because Masood is still there. At this rate, we could be retired before he gets his comeuppance," Doug moaned to John, who was deep in thought.

"Unless…" John started.

"Unless what, John?"

"Unless he really is part of a larger Europe-wide organisation, in which case." He paused meaningfully.

"In which case, without his inside contacts and with us closing in, he could be surplus to requirements." Doug snapped his fingers with delight. John held his hands wide, with the palms uppermost.

"If I'm right, on the one hand, he could disappear abroad, and on the other, he could be the next one for the chop." He brought his hands together in a silent clap.

"And who will they send to replace him, if he does go?" Doug wondered.

"Let's wait and see," John advised him, and changed the subject. "Have you heard the latest about Phil Tyler?"

"No! Up to his neck again, is he?"

"In a manner of speaking, yes. You know the trouble he had with his wife after he collected Suzy Ramas. Well, she heard from some anonymous source that the woman was extremely attractive, and has been getting at him ever since. The result is that he has finally agreed to adopt a child, which she has been pestering him for over the years." John said it with such relish that Doug thought he must be the anonymous source. Seeing his expression, John continued.

"**No**, it wasn't me! It's just that the boot is on the other foot. For years, he has bragged how he's been as good as single because he had no kids to tie him down. And now…!"

CHAPTER 5

Birdie had spent the time of Ivor's funeral alone in her apartment, wallowing in self-pity over his demise. Terry had told her to get out and mingle with the crowds in the nearby shopping mall, and she used the excuse of her security to stay put. Derek had warned him to give a hint to his sister and not to try and instruct her about being more sociable at a time of obvious stress for her.

"I didn't instruct her, Derek. I just told her to get out more!" Terry exonerated himself.

"Uh-uh! No wonder she wouldn't go. I'm her big brother and I gave up trying to tell her what to do when she was only ten years old. If you are really serious about her, you will have to train her a little at a time or she will dig her heels in." Derek enjoyed telling his employer what to do.

The pleasure of the moment soon passed, and Terry, whose thoughts were constantly on Birdie, noticed the worry lines on Derek's face.

"Enough of your lectures for now, Mr Lee. A problem shared, as they say, so tell me what your problem is." He got to his feet and walked round his desk to Derek's side. Derek's whole bearing sagged.

"It's Sonia!" He gasped, as if the pressure of his worry for his wife exploded within him. He took a deep breath, sighed and continued. "She's... got... a... tumour!" The words came with difficulty and he started to shake. Terry made him sit down and gave him a glass of water from the decanter he always had on his desk. The slick lawyer now understood how shameful guilt could be in certain circumstances. He had been worrying about Birdie not following his advice, and here was her brother with some potentially life-threatening news.

"Where is it?" Terry asked with a slight croak.

"It's in her right breast," Derek said simply, looking with surprise at his boss. He had never heard him speak in such a tone before.

"How serious is it?" Terry cleared his throat before asking.

"They're not sure. She's going in for further tests tomorrow. As they're doing it so quickly, I assume they think it could be serious."

Derek inhaled and exhaled as if the action would relieve the pressure he was under.

"Is there anything I can do?" He placed a hand on Derek's arm.

Rather than ease Derek's stress, the touch increased it, as he knew Terry was not one for unnecessary social or physical contact among humans.

"There is one thing you could do for me, please, Terry. It might sound cowardly of me, but I would like you to let my sister know."

"Of course I will. If the right moment comes, I could tell her tonight. You'd better tell our 'Miss Perfect Secretary' you won't be in tomorrow." He grinned as he said it, anticipating Derek's reaction.

"**No way! You** can tell 'Miss Nosey Parker' when I don't turn up." Derek put on a high-pitched voice as he impersonated their well-meaning and very efficient secretary. "Really, Mr

Schott! **Why** won't Mr Lee be at work today, Mr Schott?" Terry laughed and clapped.

"Very good! I'll use my mini recorder tomorrow so you can see how accurate you've been," he said, praising Derek, who managed a faint smile. "Give Sonia our love and best wishes. We'll keep our fingers crossed for her," Terry added more sombrely.

"Not going to say a prayer then?" Derek faked a look of disappointment.

"I don't know about Birdie, but if I said I was going to pray, you'd think I meant like an eagle!" he explained. Derek nodded his agreement and departed.

Earlier that fateful day, Terry had called on Birdie to ensure she was going to handle Ivor's funeral without too much distress. When he was unable to persuade her to go out and mingle, he asked her to do him a special meal.

"What's the special occasion?" she demanded.

"Do we **need** one?" he retorted.

"If I'm to do a special meal for you, then yes."

"It's your birthday?"

"No!"

"It's someone you knows birthday?"

"No!"

"An anniversary?"

"No!"

"We're going to have sex?" he suggested hopefully.

"**No!**" She laughed this time.

"That's it then! We've a hundred and one reasons to celebrate," he announced triumphantly.

"**Now** what are you on about?" She feigned annoyance at his word games, though she enjoyed the challenge they presented.

"Between us, we must know a hundred people who do not have a birthday today. That is one hundred reasons for celebrating that none of them is a year older today. And… to cap it all, to pop the champagne cork, we are not going to have sex!" She laughed and gave him a hug.

"There are times when I really love you." She acted a girlish giggle.

"So we can have sex?" He hugged her back, and she decided to play him at his own game.

"Beans on toast tonight then," she declared.

"What about our special meal?" he protested.

"Well, you said it! One of the reasons we should have a special meal is because we were not going to have sex." She was more than pleased at putting one over on him. He held her at arm's length and gazed lovingly into her eyes.

"So we are going to have sex?" The very thought lit him up.

"Do you want a special meal?"

"Yes, please," he replied automatically, thinking of the ecstatic promise of the night to come.

"Oh! So you don't want sex?" She fired back at him.

"**Yes! Yes! I do!**" His animal instincts were aroused.

"But you'd like a special meal?" she asked sensuously, fluttering her eyelashes at him.

Oh yes!" He was completely besotted by her look and envisaged a glorious evening with a wonderful feast followed by more-than-wonderful lovemaking.

She pushed him away and walked towards her kitchen. "That's decided then. I'm going to provide a special meal for you here, this evening, and then you're going to bed in your own apartment."

"What about our sex?" he begged.

"You made your choice. You chose the meal rather than

me. I'm deeply hurt. I thought you loved me, but it seems you love your food more." She pretended she was about to cry. He was going to protest at being hoodwinked; instead, he walked after her and put a comforting arm around her. He knew from the few weeks that they had been together what she expected him to say, and thought two could play at that game.

"Don't cry, my darling. You know you are right."

"What! You love your food more than me?" She turned to face him, waiting for a rebuttal.

"Yes. Of course I do," he declared earnestly, and smirked. She pushed him away, grabbed the wet dishcloth and threw it at him. Quick as he was, her speed caught him out and it hit the top of his head as he ducked.

"Aargh!" he cried, and stood up clutching his eye. "There was something on it that's gone in my eye." He kept blinking in pain. Birdie came over to him and pulled his hand away. She moved close to look in the eye and he pounced. He wrapped his arms around her tightly and kissed her as if he was going to eat her. She went limp and returned the passion. They remained like that – two persons in a single shape – for a long time. Suddenly she broke off.

"I've just heard the pips on the radio. You'd better go to work. Don't worry about me being alone with my sorrow. After all, I've got preparing your special meal to keep me busy." She sang the last statement. To some extent, it was true. She watched an old film on TV and then tried the news. Cue item about ceremonial funeral for a murdered policeman! It transfixed her, and the memories of her dear friend and saviour hit her like a tsunami.

She got the tears out of her system and started on the meal. Cutting the onions found her tear glands empty and simply irritated her eyes. She tried to refresh her face and also put on a more alluring dress, hoping it would distract Terry. It didn't!

He could see she had been crying and longed to comfort her. *I will have to wait for the right moment, as I expect uncalled-for or excessive sympathy could affect her adversely. Another problem I have is telling her about Sonia some time during the evening. Where and when and how?* The food smelled, looked and tasted delicious – a real gourmet repast. A cool, crisp New Zealand sauvignon blanc with the fish starter and a vintage Rioja with the main course helped him relax slightly, but the choice of the right moment handicapped him.

"What's wrong?" Birdie demanded loudly, overcoming her intense sadness of earlier. "You've hardly eaten, and you've only sipped at your wine, **and** you've not said a word!" Her voice had a life not emulated in her dried eyes. "You were full of possibilities this morning, and I'm the one who has had to face up to a personal loss. I'm very disappointed in you. I go to a lot of trouble for you and you show no appreciation. You could at least have shown me a little sympathy." She finished her tirade and burst into non-existent tears.

In his haste to reach her, Terry spilt his wine on his trousers. He knelt beside her and held her tight.

"That's the second time today that I've been thoughtless!" He kissed her dry cheek and turned her face towards him. "You mean the world to me, and I did feel the pain you must have been having today. I just didn't know how much sympathy to show you, as I understand how some people find it hurts rather than helps." Her dry sobs died away and her police training took over, despite the unaccustomed amount of wine she had imbibed.

"The second time? I knew there must be something troubling you. Tell me about it. Perhaps it's me that's been thoughtless." She wiped her tired eyes on her serviette.

This has to be the moment, reasoned Terry.

"My worries for you being alone today were enhanced by criticism from Derek, and I failed to notice for several minutes how worried he was. I felt very selfish for not seeing it earlier."

"What's Derek worried about?" Birdie interrupted.

"Sonia!" Terry said bluntly. Birdie stared at him.

"Don't tell me she's having an affair?" She laughed at the improbability of such a thing.

"No. She's got a tumour!" Birdie's laughter forced it out of him.

Her face dropped like a stone. "Oh my god!" She slapped her forehead. "I'm the one who's been thoughtless. No wonder you lost your appetite. You've been wondering how to tell me, haven't you? How serious is it?"

"She's going in for tests tomorrow, so there must be a strong chance it **is** serious." He watched her whole being slump, as if another nail had been driven into her coffin. He continued holding her close as he lifted her and placed her on her sofa. She was very vulnerable at that moment. First, the funeral she was not allowed to attend. Then the meal she had prepared so carefully for him and he scarcely touched it. **Now** the added worry of her sister-in-law's health.

The ice maiden had been melting slowly as her love for Terry grew stronger. At first, she was in a poor physical condition and he respected it. During that period, a meeting of minds enhanced their mutual physical attraction. He knew this was not to be a case of ships that pass in the night. Their ultimate physical consummation was going to be very special, and all the conditions would have to be right. Much as he desired her, he could not abuse her current state, so he held her close and gently rocked her until he sensed she was very tranquil. Then he put a comedy film on the TV, cleared the table and washed up. When he noticed she was asleep, he covered her with a blanket and quietly left for his own apartment.

CHAPTER 6

Reconciliation with her parents enabled Judith Donnelly to visit them and show them their grandson, Charlie. An overnight stay with them was relaxing for Judith, and she told them all about the incident with Maurice Jenkins. She narrated the more exciting aspects of her life, including helping Sid.

"Aren't you frightened, being alone with a man convicted for common assault?" said her mother, worriedly.

"I was at first. Then I realised his autism had made society reject him, and that had made him aggressive. He is really just a child trying to survive in an adult world. A child, that is, in most things except art. He has an ability that **has** to be seen. He's due out soon with maximum remission from his sentence." She smiled at the thought of being able to develop Sid outside the oppressive prison walls.

"What about Tom, dear?" Her mother was anxious. There had been no mention of Judith's husband throughout her stay, and she had a specific reason for asking. Judith regarded her quizzically. Despite their years of separation, she could still sense that there was something behind the question.

"He's all right, I suppose. I hardly see him these days. He's always working away from home. It's been the same ever since Charlie was born. I speak to him on the phone every few days and try to keep him up to date with our news. I'm not sure if he really pays any attention." She reflected for a moment and admitted, "I'm not sure whether he's just not interested in our son or me or both of us. I'm beginning to feel like a single parent raising a son on my own. I do miss Tom's company, and perhaps that is another reason I enjoy working with Sid. **There**! Now you know! Now **you** can tell me why you asked as you did." She poured out her troubles to her mother and finished rather rudely.

"There's no need to snap at me, dear. There is a reason I asked, and I wasn't sure how to tell you."

"Come on, Mummy. I'm a grown woman now, so spit it out, for goodness' sake."

"Well, you know our friend Zena, who used to visit us when you were a child."

"Y-e-s." Judith was getting fed up with the delays.

"Well, she now lives in Nottingham." She paused as if she had made an earth-shattering announcement.

"Nottingham? That's where Tom goes to work." *I don't like the way this is heading.*

"Zena has seen Tom in the town centre on several occasions with his arms wrapped around the same young woman. She only told me because she assumed you two had been divorced!" She spoke rapidly, as if the barrier to her worst fears had been breached. Judith had known deep down that he was probably having an affair but had refused to accept it, for Charlie's sake. Her shock at having to face up to the reality of the situation turned to ire.

"**Satisfied now**!" She fired the words at the one person she had always worshipped until she went to college; the one person she knew she could always trust and lean on. "You **said** our marriage would end in disaster, and **now** you've been proved right." Her emotions grew even faster than her tirade, and she burst into tears.

"No, my darling. I'm not satisfied! You made your choice and it has resulted in a wonderful grandson for me… I nearly made the same mistake when I was at college." She cradled her formerly little girl as best she could. There was an interminable pause as Judith fought to regain her composure.

"You, Mummy? I always thought you and Daddy were made for each other. You never mentioned any hiccups before." She wiped her eyes and stared at her mother with renewed interest.

"It was the National Service that saved me," Mother declared.

"National Service? But that was for men," Judith queried.

"Yes… I was… or at least I thought I was… in love with this fellow student." She gazed into space as she remembered.

"We even started making plans for our life together. When our courses finished, we intended getting married despite the objections of both sets of parents. He got called up before we could consummate our union, as they say. I was going to wait for him forever. Next thing I learn, he's got some girl into trouble and has to marry her. Naturally, I was heartbroken for months, until my knight in shining armour came along." Judith's mother gazed into space, remembering.

"That **was** Daddy, I hope?" Judith looked at her mother reprovingly.

"Yes, dear. It was your father. We have our arguments now and again, but I wouldn't swap him for anyone else. You'll see. Someone will come along, or may have already, who will make you a good, loving husband, and a good father for Charles."

Judith smiled at the 'Charles'. Her mother had never been able to accept that a boy could be officially named Charlie and not Charles. Apart from enlightening her, her mother's dissertation had softened the blow about Tom's philandering.

She slept in the guest room with her son, who was in a foldaway bed.

Looking at her dormant offspring, she thought about her mother's words – *may have already* met **someone**. *Perhaps I have! The man I thought was a pervert trying to kidnap my boy has turned out to be the very opposite. He's kind and considerate and wonderful with children.* And *he's not bad-looking! As I've heard men say about a woman,* en passant, *I wouldn't kick him out of bed! I'll not think of Tom! He's history and he's going to pay for his deceit. I'll think of Maurice Jenkins. Judith Jenkins. Even the name sounds right. The Tate is proud to present an exhibition of paintings by the renowned Judith Jenkins.* It was at this stage that she went to sleep, clutching a pillow tightly between her thighs and picturing Maurice by her side as she signed autographs at the Tate.

The next morning, she discussed her marital problems with her father. On his advice, she contacted Terry Schott, who accepted her divorce case, although it was outside his normal field. It made a refreshing change from his criminal cases, and he knew Derek would do most of the work for him. It would give Derek the fresh challenge he needed to occupy his mind while waiting for the results of Sonia's tests. To prevent any awkward meetings, and having made certain she wished to proceed, he had Tom Donnelly formally advised.

The emailed reply astounded Derek and Terry. Please proceed with all haste. I will not contest the matter, and will admit to adultery. However, as I am already somewhat impoverished and have another woman to support, I will strongly contest any excessive demands for alimony. Derek immediately printed the whole page, to show the statement of intention and confession by Tom, and the email address of the sender.

Judith returned home to a house that seemed even emptier than of late. *Tom was no real comfort to me when I thought Charlie had nearly been abducted. Now I realise I was so preoccupied with the boy that I failed to notice Tom's increasing lack of affection. Did I drive him away? I don't think so. I remember his behaviour during our time with his relations, and he has made no attempt to come home during the school year. In fact, he couldn't wait to get back to Nottingham, and I thought it was his enthusiasm for his new job! What a fool I've been!*

Spurred on by the icy blast of reality, she threw herself into her painting and teaching Sid Cracken. The latter had been making such good progress with more mature social skills that the prison psychiatrist decided it was time for a 'perpetrator and victim' encounter. He knew Derek had already met the new Sid and decided there should be a meeting with Birdie, if possible.

When Derek suggested it to her, she was intrigued, and after some careful consideration she agreed. To help someone else and change her surroundings, even briefly, would take her mind off her woes. Naturally, Terry was completely against it. He held very liberal views about society but was less relaxed when it came to the possibility of danger for the woman he loved. Birdie could not be seen at the prison, as it was almost certain Masood had contacts there. They needed a place out of town, and Sid would have to be away from the prison all day to make any informers think he may have been on a long journey.

When she heard their problem, Judith volunteered her house. It was promulgated on the grapevine that Sid was going for a whole day's tuition with Judith. This worked so successfully that many were the ribald comments flying around the prison about Sid enjoying his teacher's favours. Judith's proposal for Birdie to stay with her for a couple of nights was quickly accepted. Judith longed for adult company in her own home, and Birdie welcomed the thought of female company for a change. A couple of nights later, Terry dropped Birdie at Judith's house after dark. He placed her overnight bag in the entrance and left.

"He's a lovely man," Judith declared longingly. Birdie observed the faraway look on her hostess's face.

"You'd better not be thinking what I think you are! He's *my* lovely man!" Birdie grinned and adopted a fighting stance. Judith lost her dreamy look and held up her arms as if to protect herself.

"Alas, sweet maiden, pray desist. May not a poor betrayed and abandoned wench cast her eyes and thoughts about for fresh male company?" She pretended to tremble.

"Forsooth, thou mayest. But set not thy trap for... Oh, to heck with it! Don't get fresh with my Terry!" They both giggled like schoolgirls and embraced, cementing what was to be an enduring friendship.

The evening passed all too quickly as they drank wine with a few nibbles and chatted for hours. One dark woman and one fair, but both extremely attractive in their own way. They discussed their lives and their hopes, and Birdie confided her current situation to Judith. She also asked her about the man that she was there to meet.

"I was secretly terrified when I was to meet him for the first time. I only went because I felt I owed it to Maurice after all I'd put him through. I needn't have worried. He's just an overgrown pussycat really. And, despite Maurice's analysis of him, he can and has learnt a great deal since I started working with him. Not just about art. When he is not being bullied or harassed by others, he has an enquiring mind. He's been a godsend for me. I was devoting my entire existence to Charlie, which was no good for either of us. My work with Sid began with me treating him like a child."

She smiled at her own analysis. "Now he is much more mature, though he still needs to develop his social skills." Judith's pride in progress with Sid was very obvious.

Birdie gazed at her new friend and wickedly raised one suggestive eyebrow. "I thought you visited him to help him with his art. How come you've helped him in other ways?" Judith failed to notice and innocently continued.

"It just sort of happened. While he was drawing or painting, he began asking questions, mostly about art and artists and galleries and such like. So I took him some books on the subject and had to help him understand them. Slowly, his questions became more complex, and I found myself having to do homework to keep up with him. As I said before, his biggest handicap now is trying to deal with people. Previously, he did it by acting like the monster you'll remember. I'm worried about how he will react when he meets you tomorrow—"

"**You're** worried! How do you think **I** feel? He may try to attack me again!" Birdie interrupted.

"Unless I'm very much mistaken, the boot's on the other foot. He doesn't think of you as the woman he tried to attack, but as the one who floored him and put him inside. I think—" She was interrupted again. This time by Charlie, who had had a bad dream. That finished their women's night in, and they both retired.

The plentiful imbibing of quality wine had its effect on both of them. Having been instructed, however whimsically, **not** to cast her net for Terry, Judith's thoughts kept being drawn back to him. Forcing her mind on to other matters made her dream of romantic liaisons with the lawyer. She slept so soundly that she remained in one position until a cloudburst rattled her window. She awoke with a start and nearly screamed when she found a hand between her legs. She rolled out of bed as fast as her drowsy state would allow. Then the numbness in the arm she had been lying on eased with some tingling, and she comprehended that the 'molesting' hand was her own.

Birdie had a similar experience. Subconsciously, she had some trepidation about meeting Sid, so she kept her drowsy rumination concentrated on Terry. Once asleep, her subconscious took over and a tattooed ogre was leaning over her threateningly. Influenced by the stories learnt during childhood, she kissed him and he disappeared. There was **no** handsome prince replacing him. Instinctively, she stretched her legs and felt something on the end of her bed. She lifted her head and peered through sleep-laden eyes. It was a frog! She screamed loudly. When she was fully awake, she was always in command of her emotions. Now she was still under the influence of the previous evening's alcohol and not fully alert.

Judith entered the room in a hurry. "What's wrong? I heard you scream!" She advanced towards the bed and put the light on. Birdie sat up.

"Oh my god! It's a toy!" She laughed frantically, pointing at the small cloth frog at the end of her bed.

"What did you **think** it was? Charlie likes to put his animals on the beds. I should have warned you. I might not be a detective like you, but I suspect there was something else behind your scream." She sat on the edge of the bed and comforted the shaking Birdie. When she was more composed, Birdie told her the details of her nightmare, then they both had a laugh. Now there was a strong kinship between them,

Judith realised she would have to reciprocate and divulge her recent fantasy.

"It's all your fault, young Birdie! If you hadn't warned me that you and Terry have a serious relationship, I wouldn't have tried to suppress all thoughts of him before drifting off. Net result, of course, I did dream of him, and very romantically. Boy, he's hot stuff!"

Birdie turned towards her and pretended to slap her face. "You hussy! Leading my man astray, and he's not even proposed yet. How was he?" she coyly asked at the end of her outburst.

"You mean you don't know? I thought you two were living together," Judith exclaimed.

"We live in separate apartments, and the right moment has not come up. I suppose it's my fault really. In my profession, I'm surrounded by a crowd of oversexed policemen and have built up barriers to avoid anything distracting me from my career. Then there are all the evil sides of sex, which I encounter in my work. I did relax my guard once and he was too honourable to take advantage of me, and now he's dead!" she confessed.

"Was he the one whose funeral was on TV recently?"

"Yes," Birdie replied softly.

"Since you're being so frank with me, I must tell you the end of my dream tonight."

"Don't tell me you've had sex with Terry!" Birdie had pangs of jealousy even though it was only in a dream.

"That's what's so disappointing! Things were really getting passionate when something rattled my window and woke me up. I jumped out of bed because there was a hand between my legs! It was my own! My arm had gone numb because I'd been lying on it." They both chuckled in a salacious manner.

"Just a minute, Jezebel Judith! What do you mean you were disappointed? Do you mean you **want** to have sex with **my** Terry?" She frowned menacingly.

"I wouldn't mind. Though I couldn't now I know you and we're friends. No, it's just that I've not had a man for what seems like years. I thought it was my dedication to Charlie that put Tom off, but now I realise it was because he was getting his oats elsewhere." She looked so depressed that Birdie was obliged to exhilarate her.

"Terry's not the only fish in the sea! You're young and beautiful and Mr Right is bound to come along soon. In the meantime, you could always get yourself a toy boy without any strings." The flattery worked and Judith roused herself from her stupor, sat up very straight, paused, and then began pacing the room like some professor, deep in thought.

"Pinocchio won't do then?" she announced with an air of disappointment.

"Pinocchio?" Birdie was mystified.

"Yes. He's a toy boy, but he did have strings," Judith explained merrily.

"What a shame! He did have a really long…" Birdie stopped to have a forced fit of coughing, while Judith regarded her in shock. "A really long nose!" Birdie concluded. Their merriment woke Charlie and they all went to their respective beds.

Judith's house was a small detached one with three bedrooms and a tiny garage. It was at the end of the road on a small estate, next to farmland. The sales blurb had described it as an executive country development. At the end of her narrow-yet-long back garden there was a small brick and flint barn. The farmer had used it for storing various implements, but now most of these had grown too large and expensive to be kept remote from the main farm. Its roof was in good condition, the walls very solid, but the doors were decaying. Being end on to, and providing half of, Judith's rear boundary, she had often cast a longing eye over it as a suitable place for a studio for herself. Tom's reaction had always been highly negative.

The prison psychiatrist brought Sid to Judith's in his own car to prevent problems with the neighbours. After reminding Sid that he would be released soon, provided his good behaviour continued, they went into the house. Birdie kept out of sight until they were settled in the lounge, and Charlie was being cared for by a neighbour for a couple of hours. When Birdie entered, Sid jumped to his feet, tried to take a step back and collapsed back on the sofa. She stared at the shy, distressed man as he tried to rise again. *Is this truly the thug who tried to attack me? How could anyone fear him now? I cannot believe it, but I really feel as if I should help him out of his current predicament!* The thoughts raced through Birdie's mind, and she found herself stepping forward briskly and helping him to regain his balance. Gripping his hand, she noticed he was shaking with nervousness.

"Sorry if I startled you, Mr Cracken. I'm Birdie Lee. You may remember me? We met under unusual circumstances before." She tried to shake his hand as he loomed over her, and failed, as he was as rigid as iron.

"I-I-" he stammered, gaping at the smiling face of the little female holding his great paw.

How the hell did this slight woman manage to floor me? How can she be so pleasant after what I tried to do to her? What should I say? What should I do? He continued to stare at her and was at a complete loss as to what should happen. The psychiatrist said nothing and scribbled some notes. Judith stood up and took control.

"Oh, for goodness' sake, you two. Sit down, both of you! You look like a couple of lovebirds. Who wants tea and who wants coffee?" They did as instructed after hastily dropping their hands to their sides.

"Coffee, please," Birdie answered, with a look that was half guilty and half humorous.

"I'd rather 'ave tea, Miss Judith, if it's not too much trouble," Sid requested, smiling at her.

"What would you like?" She addressed Sid's therapist, who was still writing notes.

"I don't mind. Tea or coffee will be satisfactory," he stated in a matter-of-fact way.

"Ah yes. You must be the psychiatrist." Judith looked at Birdie and winked as she left the room. The jest was lost on its subject, who frowned momentarily before continuing with his copious and no doubt world-shattering record of the occasion.

Birdie turned to Sid and was about to pass on the wink when she noticed their observer was watching her like a hawk. Seated beside a man that she had sent to prison, she wondered where to start.

"Judith tells me you are a gifted artist, Mr Cracken." She turned towards him.

"Please, miss, call me Sid… I do like drawing and Miss Judith's teaching me to paint and… and she gives me confidence. I… I'm sorry for what I did to you, miss." He tried to repeat the last words as he had been instructed, but they came as a flood. The former ice maiden abruptly found a maternal feeling she had not encountered previously, and placed a comforting hand on his arm.

"Perhaps I should be the one to apologise. After all, I think you got the worst of our encounter." He looked puzzled until he saw the look of merriment on her face. Then he too grinned, and very gently, as if she were made of priceless china, he patted her on the back and spoke with a new confidence.

"Yes. And you're the only woman what I've fallen for!" he announced boldly, just as Judith returned.

"What, Sid? Are you getting fresh with this hussy the moment my back's turned? I thought I was your special friend!" The tray she was carrying vibrated as she acted out her jealousy.

Sid blushed profusely, removed his hand from Birdie's shoulder and tried to think of an explanation. The psychiatrist got so excited with his writing that he broke the lead in his pencil. Birdie held her hands together as if to pray.

"Oh dear, Sid. She's found out our little secret. What are we to do?" Birdie strained to keep a serious visage.

"But-but!" Sid tried to protest. The 'expert' searched frantically through his case for a pen or sharpened pencil. Judith placed the tray on the coffee table and stood over the pair on the sofa, with her hands on her hips. She looked from one to the other, waiting for an explanation. *I could take any real heat out of this situation quite easily. I don't wish to make this naïve man suffer, but now is a good opportunity to see how he handles himself in such an awkward situation*, Birdie reasoned to herself. Sid cleared his throat and tried to rise. Birdie held him down and spoke to him in a sensuous voice.

"You'd better tell her the truth, Sid. We can't go on hiding this from her." Judith now looked totally perplexed. The therapist found a pen, and in his animated condition, he managed to pour the entire contents of his case onto the floor.

"We ain't got no secret, Miss Judith! We ain't 'iding nuffink!" His manner of speech returned to his former style. "She 'ad me on my back before I met you." A double entendre to explain a double entendre was simply digging a deeper hole of confusion, so Birdie relented and assisted him.

"Take it slowly, Sid, and tell Judith what happened the last and only previous time that we met."

"Yes, miss, I **will**." He gripped the arm of the sofa as if putting the brakes on his dialogue. "We was on this 'ill outside of town and me mates told me to attack this lady. I wish I 'adn't, 'cos she threw me on me back and 'eld me down with 'er foot. No female 'as ever made me fall before, and I don't like to talk about it," he admitted reluctantly. Birdie clapped and patted him on the back. He turned to look at her in anguished surprise.

This can't be the same man, Birdie thought. *He's not the monster I recall. He's a real sweetie.* She noticed Judith's enlightened expression. *I'll teach her to have dreams about my man,* she decided.

She leant towards the timid, child-like man beside her, placed her hands on his cheeks and kissed him full on the mouth. He blushed again, but this time his eyes sparkled wide, and he pursed his lips for more.

"That's enough! Birdie, leave him alone! You go and sit next to what's-his-name and leave my poor Sidney alone, and drink your coffee or it'll be cold." Judith forcibly helped Birdie to change seats.

"Sigmund!" a strange voice announced. The women and Sid looked about for the source of the voice; they had all forgotten the presence of the psychiatrist.

"Eh?" "Pardon?" "What?" The three spoke at the same time.

"I'm not what's-his-name! My name is Sigmund," he declared proudly. The two women burst into laughter, which puzzled Sid.

"You **are** joking?" Judith suggested. The subject of their laughter glared at them. He had never seen the funny side of his name in relation to his occupation, or the funny side of anything else. No wonder his private practice had failed and he had finished up – well – in prison!

"I never joke!" he stated categorically.

Sid looked at Judith questioningly, and she waved to indicate she would explain later. They all settled down and spent the rest of the morning in constructive discussion, as dictated by Sigmund. His plan to allow some form of open chat had been torn up by the two wilful women's wicked sense of humour. He failed to realise that humour was one thing Sid **had** to learn if he was to integrate into normal society. He also failed to realise just how much Sid had grown in confidence during the meeting.

Time had flown for Sigmund, working in a totally different environment, and his machinations were further disrupted by the return of Charlie; this was another factor he hadn't allowed for. It could not have been foreseen how effective the presence of a small boy would be, and Sigmund wrote furiously as whole new rehabilitation methods occurred to his limited imagination.

There was an instant rapport between Sid and Charlie, which resulted eventually in the large man crawling around the floor on all fours with the small boy perched precariously on his back. *I have tried to compensate for Tom's long absences, but Charlie obviously needs male company as much as I do. Boys will be boys, and Sid is just a big kid at heart. I think this is why I've formed ideas about Maurice Jenkins. He's so good with children, and... well...* Her scheming thoughts made her believe the others in the room would notice a look of guilt, which was purely mental. *And I bet he's good in bed!* Her suppressed desires came to the fore. *I'm the mother of a wonderful boy and I must not have such thoughts. To hell with that! I'm still a young woman and I'm entitled to my desires. Judith Jenkins? It sounds like the name of some pop star.*

"Careful, Charlie, or you'll fall off!" The sight of him wobbling on Sid's back worried her and broke her train of thought.

"Don't worry. I've got him safe," Sid assured her.

After a light lunch, provided by Judith, Sid and Sigmund departed for the prison. As he went out of the room, Sid looked at Birdie and pursed his lips, and she took his hand and gave him a kiss on each cheek, to the disgust of Judith.

"What about me, Sid? Aren't I worth a kiss?" Judith went close to him.

"I never dared 'ope of kissing you. You must know I…" he leant towards her so the others could not hear "…I worship the ground you tread on. I'd do anything for you – Miss Judith." He whispered her name like some magic spell. It sent a shiver of delight up her spine. She hesitated and then grabbed him and gave him a kiss of an intensity he had not even imagined in his hitherto limited life. Her earlier salacious thoughts about Maurice had left her keyed up, and she released her passion on the innocent Sid. Sigmund was forced to intervene and separate them. Even Birdie was astounded.

"For goodness' sake, Sid, stop calling me Miss Judith. I am just plain Judith to you!" she instructed.

With his newfound confidence, Sid replied, "Er, all right, but to me you are anything but plain!" Even Sigmund was amazed. Sid blushed profusely as he realised what he had said.

While Sigmund returned a docile, lovesick Sidney to prison, the ladies discussed the events of the morning.

"What on earth possessed you to kiss him like that?" Birdie was intrigued.

"I don't know really. Perhaps it was because the only love or affection in my life is my son, and I'm not too old to have physical desires. The sight of you pecking that simple hulk of a man seemed to arouse the animal in me. I must admit I was dreaming of someone else when I first grabbed him, but there was dynamism between us, which astonished me." Judith glowed with the memory.

"I was told he was incapable of sex! It seems to me that you are arousing him physically as well as mentally. Just a minute! Who were you thinking of when you kissed him? Not my Terry, I hope!" Birdie demanded.

"No. Not Terry," Judith answered briefly, wishing to drop the subject.

"Who then? Come on, tell me!" Birdie pressed her.

"Oh, all right then. It was Maurice Jenkins. He's attractive he's good with kids **and** he's single!"

Charlie required attention, and the remainder of Birdie's day with Judith was occupied with amusing the boy or discussing some TV programmes, in which she had become a forced expert. They agreed to go on a shopping spree together as soon as Birdie was allowed.

CHAPTER 7

"Ali Masood, or Ali Parouk as he was formerly called, has put his house up for sale and has left the country by way of Dover," Doug Evans informed Inspector John Langley with some satisfaction. "I hate to lose him, but I've advised Interpol, who will keep an eye out for him. The problem as I see it, Guv, is that this European crime syndicate still has part of its organisation here. Now we've got to start afresh to find the new headman." He banged the desk in annoyance.

"Leave it with me, Doug. I've got a meeting this afternoon with 'Daddy' Tyler and Superintendent Bennett," John told him gleefully.

The police station was buzzing with the news of Phil Tyler's capitulation in agreeing to adopt a child. This had gained him the nickname 'Daddy', and John loved the sound of it. Everyone was delighted with Ron Bennett's promotion.

"Why do you two think Masood left?" Ron asked them as they sat round the conference table with their papers and obligatory mugs of tea.

Phil shuffled his papers before replying. "As I've not been so closely involved in the pursuit of Masood, perhaps I can give my opinion as an observer. I think it's down to a multitude of factors crowding him, and reducing his ability to operate so freely. This made him more vulnerable and of less use to the European syndicate. Those factors were…" He looked at a list in front of him. "In chronological order, the suspicious death in prison of Ramas; the kidnapping of Sergeant Lee; the uncovering of Thwaite, his police mole; the wounding and subsequent murder of Ivor Kowalski; the body in the burnt Escort, and, finally, the loss of Reynolds, his vital link in the judiciary." Phil read his list slowly, and his colleagues nodded their agreement at each point.

"There is one factor neither of you will know about, and it could affect Sergeant Lee. Doug Evans has only recently told me about it and I've double-checked the result." He paused for effect.

"Get on with it, John." Ron began to wonder if they were both vying for glory.

"When Doug interviewed that thug Fellows in prison, he made a great public show of thanking him for his invaluable assistance."

"**That** was somewhat irregular!" Ron said reprovingly.

"He did it mostly to put more pressure on Masood, and partly in revenge for what he did to Birdie Lee," John revealed confidentially. "I have given him a verbal warning. Though I admit I did congratulate him, unofficially, on his initiative," he announced proudly. Ron nodded approvingly, and Phil gave him the thumbs-up sign.

"What's happened to Fellows?" Phil asked.

"That's the beauty of it! **Nothing** has happened! Nobody has touched Fellows, and we know for certain that Masood has more of his cronies in the prison." John could not disguise his pleasure at the outcome.

"If they can't be bothered with one of their own grassing on them, and Masood has gone, they certainly can't be bothered about Birdie anymore. She can come out of hiding now." Phil was delighted for his top sergeant. He failed to notice Ron peering at him over the top of his reading glasses and arching one eyebrow.

"Very true, Phil. Good news for her, but a double whammy for you, I'm afraid. Chief Inspector Watson of Houghbury Police has asked for her to be assigned to him temporarily for an internal investigation, which needs an outsider. She will be put there for health reasons to cover the true purpose."

"Which is?" Phil requested.

"I'm afraid it's all very hush-hush at present."

"What's the second whammy for, Ron?" John's curiosity was aroused.

"You've both forgotten that there is someone else who can now come out of hiding," Ron hinted strongly.

"The Ramas girl!" John slapped his forehead. "How could you forget, Phil? You met her and I hear she's a real beauty!"

"That's the very reason he's trying to forget. He was quite taken with her and it's resulted in him becoming a father, if you know what I mean." Ron laughed in a friendly fashion at Phil's discomfort.

"Won't it be embarrassing for you when she returns to work locally, Daddy Tyler?" John joked.

"She is a real smasher, John, and you'd have fancied her if you'd ever met her. When you two have quite finished gloating, I think **you** should know she's engaged to some pilot. A friend of your brother, Ron."

"You're right. I did know, but I tried to keep it from you in case you got hurt." Ron laughed again, and continued in a more serious manner. "You may be interested to learn that Ivor's physio, Jean Sessions, has applied to join the police, when she has fully recovered from her bullet wound."

"Sessions! So that's her name. Now I understand that it

had a second meaning when Ivor told me he really loved his physio sessions!" John explained.

"One more piece of news concerning the Masood case. Bernard Thwaite, late of this parish, has moved from his Wimbledon house to one near Midhurst in West Sussex." Thwaite, their former superintendent, was a high flyer who had been dismissed for leaking information to Masood, thus helping his own progress in the police force. The meeting passed on to mundane administrative affairs.

Earlier in Houghbury, PC Joe Baxter had waylaid Chief Inspector Basil Watson for a confidential chat. Joe, the friendly overweight policeman who had arrested Maurice Jenkins, was the very epitome of 'PC Plod'. He explained how he had not believed that Jenkins was guilty, right from the start, and had suspected that the crucial evidence of the pornographic photos of the children had been planted. He had been admonished previously for expressing his opinions and had kept quiet. He had heard via the grapevine about Inspector George Banbury's misdemeanour and felt he could keep silent no longer. Basil thanked him and asked him to keep it under his hat until he had checked it out. Knowing that Birdie was being kept in the area, he had contacted her superintendent and asked for her assistance.

When he found she was no longer to be kept under wraps, and could be appointed to Houghbury on a temporary basis 'for health reasons', he was delighted. He knew her reputation as a high flyer and the rumour that she wanted to join the CID. He explained the suspicions to her regarding planted evidence in the Jenkins case, and said her cover to trace the guilty party would be sorting personnel files for any signs of bribery. Many of the staff knew from the grapevine of the mole that she had uncovered with the help of her dead partner, so her task would appear logical.

Sergeant Bob Pollock introduced her to everyone at the station and made sure they remembered that she was the one who captured Sid Cracken. Watson had told him that Joe could be spared to help her occasionally. Everyone assumed her task was just makeshift while she recovered, as dear old Joe was never given any critical tasks. It turned out to be a perfect partnership; Birdie was the hare, dashing after clues and things; Joe was the tortoise who used his long experience and cynicism to double-think things. They had converted a small storeroom for her to use as an office, complete with a computer terminal.

"I've made sure you'll have privacy here, Sergeant. You can set your own password for the computer, like this," Joe said, demonstrating methodically.

"Thanks, Joe. Is it all right if I call you Joe?" Birdie smiled at the rotund man, who was old enough to be her father.

"Of course, Sarge."

He smiled back and thought, *I like her! I think I'm going to enjoy working for her, and I'll show the others that I'm not quite over the hill yet!*

"While we're in here, you **must** call me Birdie. Sarge is okay when inquisitive ears are around. The chief inspector says you can give me the background I require, Joe."

The elderly constable related the Jenkins case from his arrival at the scene of the alleged crime up to the conviction. Then he gave her his opinion of the events, highlighting the suspicious discovery of the incriminating photos. "I know it was breaking the rules, but I made copies of all the items in the Jenkins file some time ago, lest there would be an investigation." He carefully revealed a file, which he placed on her desk.

"It's all in this box file, including the original photos; I put the copies I made in the official file." He looked at Birdie apprehensively.

"That was very reprehensible of you, Joe." She gave him a severe look. "**And** it was absolutely brilliant! I can't understand why you've never been promoted." She softly clapped her hands in delight. She spread out the personnel files she'd been given, to distract anyone who entered unexpectedly. Then she opened the box file and took out the photos. Joe sat next to her.

"My wife's a teacher and we have a comfortable life, so I've always taken the easy way at work. However, I'm nearly due for retirement, and I welcomed this as a final opportunity to show them what I'm **really** capable of."

"Away from the hustle and bustle of London, I can understand taking a more relaxed view to promotion. Can you get your hands on a magnifying glass for me, Joe?" She peered at the photos, trying to ignore the subjects and concentrate on the paper and printing. Joe reached in the briefcase he was carrying, fumbled around and produced a set of three magnifying glasses.

"Shazam! Your wish is my command, oh, great Birdie. These magnify three times, four times and five times. To get something more powerful, you can use any two or all three together, giving you seven and eight and nine and twelve times magnification," he expounded with pride.

"Shazam indeed, Sir Joe. You are truly a magician. I will test you and your magic bag later, I think." Examining the photos more intensely, one by one, she could find nothing unusual about the paper. Only a full forensic test might help, but this was not possible because they did not officially have the photos. There was nothing unusual about the ink as far as Birdie's untrained eye could see.

"What's that at the bottom left-hand corner of each photo?" Joe asked her as he peered at each one minutely. Birdie looked at them again and again, concentrating on the corner.

"Joe you're wonderful," she finally declared. "Each one has a very tiny but identical smudge there. Combined with the general quality, I'm pretty certain these were printed on someone's private computer printer and it has a very slight defect! These pics have been downloaded from the internet. All we need to do is find the actual printer."

"How do we do that? We can't do an official search as we don't officially have the photos," Joe said, dampening her enthusiasm. She looked at Joe without seeing him as her mind weighed up the alternatives.

"Without going public and alarming the culprit, we can eliminate Maurice Jenkins."

"How? Won't we need a search warrant to check his computer and printer – if he has one?"

"I'm friends with Terry Schott, his lawyer. He'll fix it for us, and Jenkins should be only too pleased to help find the person who framed him. This has to be kept absolutely secret. We mustn't alarm the culprit or he may dispose of the evidence." She carefully placed the photos back in the box file and returned the magnifying glasses to Joe. *If George Banbury found these, then he's the number one suspect for planting them. Did he just manage to find the appropriate website and print the pictures in time to plant them? Or did he already have some?*

"If Banbury planted the photos, he could've done so before." Joe voiced his thoughts, thus interrupting Birdie's. "I know it's only gossip, but there have been earlier cases where Banbury has amazingly found the incriminating evidence."

Birdie looked at him in awe and spread her arms wide. "I don't know why they wanted me on this case. You could easily have done it on your own, Joe."

"Oh no, Birdie! You're the one who gives me the confidence to voice my thoughts, and you're the one with the authority. And..." He hesitated.

"And what, Joe?" She smiled encouragingly at him.

"And it's a great pleasure to be working with such a beautiful sergeant," he mumbled, blushing.

"Why, Joe, you're quite the ladies' man. If you were single – and – I was free – who knows? You'd be a real catch!" she tutted, pretending to be shocked. Joe looked down at his feet.

"Aren't you free, miss?"

That's none of your business I would have said back in London, Birdie thought. "You could sound more disappointed, Joe!" She blinked sadly.

"Is it your friend Mr Schott?" Joe persisted.

"Not yet, Joe. Perhaps one day. Now! Back to the task at hand. I'll go and see Terry Schott for lunch and will try to get a check of Jenkins's appliances this afternoon. If you get time from any other duties, perhaps you could look at evidence in earlier cases to see if there were suspicious circumstances, particularly if they involved Banbury. I'll see you here tomorrow morning." She carefully locked the box file and the personnel papers in a filing cabinet she had been provided with. Then she advised DCI Watson of their progress and how they were proceeding. She also told him how excellent Joe had been.

Arriving at Terry's office, she was dreading seeing her brother. Keeping busy with the Cracken meeting and now with her investigation had eased her worries about his sick Sonia. As she entered the reception area, the usually prim secretary greeted her with a broad smile and announced her in a loud voice. *What's wrong with the woman?* thought Birdie. *Is she warning Terry because he's doing something that he shouldn't? Oh my god! I'm jealous! The sooner I possess him for myself, the better.*

"Birdie! How lovely to see you." Derek hurried up to her and gave her such a hug she feared he would break her recently mended ribs again. Then he held her at arm's length. "Isn't it a wonderful day, sister?"

"It might be if you would tell me why." She was bewildered by his sudden and overwhelming affection.

"You've not heard?" She shook her head, hoping for illumination. "Sonia's tumour is nothing more than a fatty cyst! She's perfectly all right!" He grabbed her again and kissed her on her cheek. Terry came from his office, drawn by the loud voices. He winked at the secretary and held his hand to his mouth in horror.

"Is this incest in my offices... or have you just given her the good news, Derek?" The secretary looked mortified at his suggestion and furiously continued with her typing.

Terry took Birdie into his room, closed the door and kissed her so passionately that she had to fight for air. He pressed her up against his desk with his leg between hers and ran his hands up and down her back suggestively. *I want him right now; my body is lusting for him. I don't care where we are. I have to have him now.* Her lecherous thoughts were nullified by a cold voice from the speaker on the desk.

"You buzzed me, Mr Schott? Do I need my notebook?"

They parted reluctantly and tried to suppress their mirth.

"Sorry, Mrs Cole, I was demonstrating something to Miss Lee and accidentally pressed the buzzer." He switched the appliance off and they both laughed.

"To what do I owe this pleasure, Miss Lee?" He bowed to her.

"But for the timely intervention of old King Cole's wife, you nearly did!" she jested.

"Nearly did what, miss?"

"Enjoy the pleasure!" She astounded him by gyrating her hips very sensuously. He started to reach for her once more.

"We still can." He got down onto his knees and held out his arms. "**Please!**"

"No, no, sir. Business before pleasure." She sat on the clients' chair and explained what she was doing at the police station, and why she needed his help.

"Maurice does have a computer and a printer. That I do know. Should I ring him for us to go and see it?"

"I'd rather you didn't. For me to conduct an impartial investigation, we can give him no warning. Can you take me to his place this afternoon?"

"Certainly, darling, though I'd rather take you to mine. He might be out, as I know he has some interview this week. Let me take you to lunch first." His expression of disappointment was genuine. They lunched at a smart bistro in a side street away from the melee of tourists the town attracted at that time of year. Managing to find a table away from the other diners, they were able to discuss the discovery of the photos and Maurice's reaction to them.

They each had one large glass of malbec to complement the light lunch they ordered. It relaxed them enough to keep holding hands under the table. A couple of times he gently walked his fingers along her thigh, and she did not protest or attempt to stop him. *She must have noticed and she has not tried to restrain me. Is she truly primed for the next step in our relationship? Or is it because she doesn't want to create any upset in public? Or is she playing with me because we will be seeing Maurice soon?* Terry's thoughts were as rampant as his body!

I dare not look at him. We're like a couple of kids on a first date. I've never had such strong feelings of… carnal desire. I hope he didn't notice how my fork shook in my hand when he caressed my thigh. Hell's bells! I didn't want him to stop, but we've got to visit... someone. I can't remember whom! Birdie was no longer the Ice Maiden as her libido took hold.

"This is exceedingly pleasant, but we'd better get going or we could miss Maurice." Terry rose from the table and paid the bill.

Oh yes, Maurice Jenkins. How could I forget? That's the reason I'm here. Although.... She looked at Terry standing at the cash desk and sighed. *I wish there was another reason!* She blinked hard to clear her lustful thoughts.

Ringing for Maurice on the apartment block entry phone produced no reply, so they buzzed Pru Gravillons. She confirmed he was going to be out all day as he had a series of interviews in Southampton.

"By the time we get back, there won't be much of the afternoon left. I've no more appointments for today. How about you?" Terry asked her in a soft voice, while he was running his fingers up and down her back in a stimulating manner. Birdie's whole body tingled and she was breathing more heavily than usual.

"No. Nothing that can't wait. Why? Where are we going?" She hoped she knew the answer.

"I'm taking you to paradise, my love."

He put his arm firmly around her waist and led her to his car.

The smell of the soft leather seats and the gentle vibration of the engine reinforced their mutual lust. Even the movement of the lift to his apartment was uplifting in more ways than one. His door had scarcely closed behind them before they assaulted each other. Gone was any restraint and any sign of maturity or civilisation. They were two rutting animals tearing each other's clothes off.

When their initial passion was spent, Terry left her side and went to the kitchen. Returning with two glasses and a bottle of champagne and some crackers with cream cheese on, he set them on the bedside table.

"How wonderful!" Birdie stretched euphorically and sat up. She reached for a glass and was stopped by Terry bending over her. "Can't I have some, please... lover?" She put on a dejected look. "Wasn't I worth it?" She pretended to cry and then stroked her beasts suggestively.

"You can only have some if you make me a promise, you shameless hussy, you." He wagged his finger at her.

"Anything, my lecherous lord of the bedchamber." She spread herself wide to his shocked gaze and wriggled around. He got down on the floor and reached under the bed. When he reappeared, he grasped her hand and looked at her very sternly.

"You can have a glass of champagne and anything else you desire, so long as you do promise."

She lifted her head and peered at him. *He's holding the* Kama Sutra *in his other hand and he wants to try something... kinky. I've heard of such things, but never thought my first experience would be with such a man. All this time he's only wanted me for my body.* Her face sharpened with her thoughts.

"I am not promising anything until I know what it is," she announced positively.

He noticed the sudden change in her attitude. *I wonder if I've misread her? She's turned quite remote. Perhaps this is the wrong time. Perhaps there will never be a right time. Bugger it! I'm all geared up, so it's now or never!*

"I want you to promise... to marry me as soon as possible."

It came like a tirade and hit her like a tornado. He held out his hidden hand and produced a simple ring with one large diamond, which he offered to her. She sat upright and burst out laughing, making his heart sink. "I'm sorry you find it funny. I am being very serious." He got to his feet.

"No, I'm laughing at my earlier thoughts. You were taking so long about this promise, I imagined you were going to produce the *Kama Sutra* and ask for kinky sex!" She laughed again and he looked astounded.

"So you don't want to marry me." He looked crestfallen. "All you want me for is sex."

"I do, if it's always going to be as good as that," she said bluntly. Now he was totally confused.

"Why won't you marry me?" The time for joking had passed. In the space of one afternoon, he had gone from seventh heaven to the very pits of hell. She bounced naked out of the bed and grabbed him, spilling some champagne over her hip.

"Of course I'll marry you. I thought you'd never ask. I said I do, meaning I'd marry you and expect every day to be like today." He kissed her passionately, starting with her forehead and working his way down – her nose, her lips, her shoulders, each of her breasts (causing her to gasp with pleasure), her stomach, and finally her hips, from which he licked the drops of champagne.

"Ooh yes! I love that. More, please. Much more!" He released her and reached for the bottle, which he proceeded to trickle slowly over her body and lick off at the same time.

"Remind me, my fiancée, to get more champagne in, and definitely the *Kama Sutra*." He spoke then paused for breath. *Ah, she has put my ring on.*

"Now you're properly dressed," he pointed to the ring, "we could have something to eat."

"**Me!** You eat me and I'll eat you." She could not believe she said it, as she dragged him back onto the bed. That night was one meal they never forgot.

CHAPTER 8

Perusing boxes of evidence, PC Joe Baxter started with enthusiasm and high hopes. After a couple of hours, when he found it entailed mostly standing on his pavement-pounded feet, he made a few notes and returned to his normal desk duties. The following day, he entered the police station weighed down by the thought of telling Birdie of his lack of success.

"Mornin', Joe." Sergeant Pollock's breezy greeting roused him from his worries.

"Yes. Mornin', Bob."

"If you've got a few minutes before your girlfriend arrives, I wonder if you'd mind putting these in the appropriate officers' pigeon holes." Bob held out an old shoebox.

"What! A pair of shoes? Can't you just give them to the owner when he or she arrives?"

"It's not shoes! It's full of those photos people entered for the chief constable's competition nearly three months ago. I've just got them back." His surprise at the change in Joe's attitude was palpable.

"I'd be delighted to help." Joe grabbed the box and broke his own speed limitations to his desk.

Each photo had the owner's name on the back. To ensure he was not biased by the names, Joe spread the photos face up on his desk and checked each one carefully with his magnifying glass. There were forty-five photos, and three had the mark he was looking for. He paused in disappointment before turning them over. *If there are three, it could mean more than one printer has the same fault, or that three members of staff have access to the same printer. So near, yet so far*, he thought. Slowly, he turned the first one over – *George Banbury! I wish this was the only one, then we would have all the evidence we need. But I am not about to start falsifying evidence by losing the other two.* He turned the next one – *George Banbury!* Joe had a eureka moment and swiftly turned the last one – *George Banbury!* He quickly piled up the photos and returned them to the shoebox, which he locked in his desk.

He had not entered the competition himself, and had no idea of the rules, so he checked with Bob Pollock. The latter said he could find a copy of the rules if necessary, but he remembered staff were allowed to enter up to three photos each.

"Your girlfriend has come in, Joe," Bob advised him on the internal phone.

"You're only jealous, Bob," Joe retorted as he put his phone down. He unlocked his drawer and took the shoebox to show Birdie.

As he entered her temporary office, she greeted him with such relish that he wondered if she was on drugs.

"You're the first here to know, Joe. I'm going to get married!" Instead of congratulating her immediately, he adopted a look of anguish and clutched his hand to his chest.

"What's wrong, Joe? You're not having a heart attack, are you?" She was concerned for her elderly assistant.

"No, Birdie, only a broken one. I was going to divorce my wife and propose to you myself." He could not maintain the pose any longer and grinned as he crossed the room to kiss her on the cheek.

"Heartiest congratulations. Is it anyone I know?" She put her hand to her cheek, regarding him with surprise.

"Why, Joe, I didn't know you felt like that or I might have turned him down." She winked at him. "It's Terry Schott, the local lawyer. You must know him."

"Yes. He's a good man. I don't mind losing you to him, but there's a drawback with your intended name. Some busybody might get the wrong idea and report the marriage to the RSPCA!" he suggested with a laugh.

"How do you work that out, Joe?"

"Can't you just see the headlines – *Birdie Schott* – as if someone has used a gun against one of our feathered friends."

"Enough of this ribaldry, PC Baxter! You could get shot for assaulting a superior officer." She wagged her finger at him and then chuckled. "Seriously, though, what did you discover yesterday? I got nowhere as Jenkins was away. How will we be able to check Banbury's computer and printer, if he has them?" She sat down and opened the Jenkins file.

"I'm sorry if my exuberance upset you, but age does have its excuses. Yesterday, I drew a blank, but this morning, our prayers were answered. Sergeant Pollock gave me some photos, entered in the chief constable's competition, to return to their owners. To prevent accusations of bias, and to have a second opinion, I would like you to study all the entries to see if you can pick any which match the Jenkins ones." He carefully spread them on her desk at random, concealing the names, and handed her a magnifying glass. It didn't take long for her younger eyes to select the same three entered by Banbury.

With such conclusive evidence, she was able to get a search warrant for Banbury's home. Birdie and Joe went to his home and waited for DCI Watson to arrive with Banbury, who was insisting that they had no right to interfere with his private life.

"Methinks he protesteth too much," Birdie whispered to Joe as they entered the house. Basil Watson sat with Banbury and his wife while the other two searched. They came to what was probably designed as a small bedroom and found the door locked. When they asked for the key, Banbury procrastinated with excuses ranging from "It's only a storeroom full of junk" to "I've lost the key."

DCI Watson had been making a few notes and finally lost his patience. He got to his feet and addressed Mrs Banbury directly.

"Where does your husband keep his computer, Mrs Banbury?" She looked nervously at her husband.

"I don't have one," he exclaimed loudly as she was about to answer. Watson wheeled on him angrily.

"We are not leaving without looking in that room! If you do not supply the key immediately, PC Baxter will break the door down." Banbury peered through his screwed-up eyes from Watson to Baxter, who was rubbing his hands at the very idea. With a countenance of complete dejection, Banbury collapsed onto his easy chair, fumbled in his pocket and produced a bunch of keys. He handed them to the DCI with reticence.

Inside the locked room the searchers found a computer and printer. Most damning was a locked cupboard full of pornographic magazines and – the jackpot – a whole collection of indecent photos of women and children. Nearly all the photos had the same mark as the ones in the photo competition and those used as evidence against Jenkins. Watson called for backup and a van to remove all the items, carefully bagged and labelled. He formally arrested Banbury and had him taken to the police station.

Birdie was concerned for their prisoner's wife, and Watson agreed to let her interview the frightened little woman. The DCI decided it would be best for a woman to ask the questions and possibly to have to comfort the distraught wife. Also, he had an ulterior motive – he wanted to judge her ability. He knew her impressive reputation from her superiors in London, and he had been told that she was going to marry Schott. Therefore, he reasoned that she would be looking for a posting to Houghbury.

Birdie dealt with Mrs Banbury in a confident yet kindly fashion and soon had her opening up, as if she was chatting to a close friend. She poured her heart out and told them more than they could ever need. Basically, she had been totally dominated by George. He had grown more dictatorial and obscene in his desires as their unfortunate marriage progressed. She had never been allowed in his study because he said he had official confidential work to do there. Her sister lived in Houghbury and had been telling her to leave George for years, but she had been too frightened to do so. Now she would stay with her sister until the matter was resolved.

"Well done, Sergeant Lee. You got more information than I could've hoped for, and you left the poor woman happier and more relaxed than when we arrived." Basil Watson was not one to give praise lightly.

"Hate to say this, sir, but I really enjoyed the challenge! It's rare that I get a chance to give a sympathetic interview in the big city. I've always seemed to be landed with rough low-lifers." She was physically drained after her night of passion but was on a mental high. As he drove her back to the station, Basil noticed her blinking and trying to hide a yawn.

"Are you all right? This morning's experience wasn't too much for you?" He expressed his concern.

"Sorry, sir. I'm fine. It's just that I was celebrating my engagement very late last night. I won't let it happen again."

"I should **damn** well hope not!" he declared.

"Pardon?" Birdie was astounded by the remark.

"I most certainly would not want a sergeant of mine getting engaged every night!" he chuckled.

"Nor would I want to, sir. But then I'm not really your sergeant."

"I didn't get to be a DCI without checking facts and keeping my senses primed. I've taken the liberty of checking on you and, unless I'm very much mistaken, you could be seeking a job with us." He had glanced at her and just stopped in time as the traffic lights went red. She remained silent until they reached the police station, then he spoke to her when they had parked.

"Sorry if I've been presumptuous. After what you've been through, I could understand if you decided to retire and lead a quiet wife's life. Joe is retiring soon and you could take over his duties!" he said, tongue in cheek, anticipating her answer. She noted the gesture and decided to reply in kind.

"Sorry, sir. I could never take Joe's place! The man is a genius! I'll never understand how he managed to avoid promotion all these years… however long I work here."

Basil was delighted at her delayed acceptance. With the growth of the local population, he had been allocated an extra detective sergeant post, which he formally offered her. She accepted without hesitation.

Banbury was charged with perverting the course of justice, which carried a maximum sentence of life imprisonment. During his time on remand, he reaped what he had sown over the years. None of his former colleagues visited him. In fact, the total lack of friends of any kind was so apparent that some even pitied him, until they remembered what others had suffered at his hands.

Maurice Jenkins contacted Terry Schott the next day to find out why he had to visit him. Terry invited him to join him for lunch, where he was introduced to Birdie.

"We want to thank you for bringing us together, Maurice. Without the miscarriage of justice that you suffered, Birdie and I might never have met, and now we're engaged to be married." He squeezed her hand. "As you know, she's Derek's sister and he'll be giving her away. I've no close surviving relatives, and because you were the bonding factor, I'd like *you* to be my best man." Birdie nodded in agreement.

"I'd be honoured to. I didn't think your bride-to-be would want me there as she suffered greatly due to me." He looked at her and frowned.

"Nonsense! Your case may have started the ball rolling, but it led to much greater things, which were not your fault. Thanks to Terry – and Derek's – persistence, a major criminal has fled the country and a corrupt policeman and a judge have been unmasked. So, indirectly, your miscarriage of justice has led to the actual strengthening of justice," she explained carefully.

"Don't forget yesterday!" Terry reminded her.

"Oh yes. We've uncovered the person who planted the evidence that largely resulted in your original guilty verdict. It was Inspector Banbury! It appears he was schizophrenic and transposed his perversions onto you. He's being held awaiting trial, and his unpopularity is shown by the fact not one person has visited or tried to contact him. In fact, there's such delight at his downfall in the police station, I could feel sorry for him but for the suffering he caused you."

The Ice Maiden had melted into a creature of much

empathy, and even had compassion for wrongdoers. Maurice looked mystified, so Terry changed the subject.

"How's the job hunting going, Maurice?"

"Not well, I'm afraid. I may have to adjust my requirements. The most favourable positions are too far away or don't want me. The others are too boring or too poorly paid." His world was returned to grey after their rays of sunshine had momentarily brightened it.

"I didn't think you were avaricious, Maurice. What's made you change?" Terry was surprised.

Maurice was taken aback by the direct question and thought for a few moments before deciding to confide in them. "Helen Phillips," he announced bluntly.

"Helen Phillips? Does she want money from you?" Terry was astounded.

"No. At first, I felt I owed her something for being the cause of Arnold's death. Then I met her and her children and, well, I fell in love with them all. Unfortunately, she is in love with someone else, and although she's forgiven me, she's a difficult person to try and help. I think I may be in a better position to assist the family if I was more financially secure." His lamentation began to affect them, so Birdie intervened.

"I've had recent experience of forgiveness. My experience may persuade you to have faith in the passage of time, the cure of all ills. Remember how Sid Cracken was in prison for trying to attack me. Well, thanks to your transformation of his character, I agreed to meet him. I was astonished at the change and forgave him. Although I now see him in a different light, only time can help me forget how I first met him. You must give this Helen time," she instructed him.

"You see what a wise woman I'm marrying." Terry gazed at her with pride.

"You're very lucky." Maurice sighed, reaching for his wallet as the waiter came with the bill.

"Don't you dare! We invited you, and we're paying." Terry got a nod of approval from his fiancée.

"We and we. I like the sound, **Mr Schott**. I hope you continue to say it when I'm Mrs Schott."

"Naturally, Miss Lee." They reached for each other's hands across the table and Maurice was the gooseberry.

"I'd better be going. I've got a suitable career to find. Thanks for the meal and also for the honour of being your best man. Even if I have no job and no love, at least I do now have something special to look forward to." He rose from the table and left the lovebirds in their own world.

"We'll let you know the date as soon as we can arrange one." Terry's attention was riveted on Birdie, and he was only vaguelyaware of the other person at the table departing. "When you get the post you want, you can treat us," he called after the departing Maurice.

CHAPTER 9

Tom Donnelly did not contest the divorce, and Derek Lee was able to process it rapidly. Little Charlie had been the innocent cause of two life-changing occurrences. The obvious one, which put Maurice in prison. The other was the disruption of his parents' marriage by his arrival. Tom did not want kids, and his heart was not in the duties of fatherhood he was expected to undertake. Despite some success in his job, he had failed to develop socially from his days as a rebellious student. He managed to suppress his immaturity when it affected his pocket or his standing with comparative strangers; not in his domestic life. Judith overcompensated by doting on her son to the exclusion of any affection for her husband. Thus, Tom welcomed the separation because he no longer had to contend with a child he never wanted and he had gained a new, younger, more passionate partner. She had yet to discover that his apparent youthfulness was a weakness, not a strength.

Judith's parents pretended they were helping her to overcome her loss of Tom, and visited her and their grandson regularly. She accepted the pretence, though she knew the real reason was they never liked Tom. They had some bonds mature and decided to spend the money on buying and renovating the barn at the end of Judith's garden. To her mother, it was a way of helping Judith; to her stern father, it was an investment in property. Instead of replacing some missing tiles on the roof, they had a skylight inserted. The old doors were changed for ones mostly of glass, and more light was gained with a couple of large windows. With a solid floor, electricity and water, and an access door from her garden, it became the studio Judith had always dreamt of. The work was completed quickly, as a friend of her father had a building company that fitted the work in between some major contracts.

One corner was sectioned off by a containing fence as a play area for Charlie, with decorative panels to cover the flint walls. There were toys, games, and a tiny table and chair, and it also had a small daybed for him to nap on. At first, he was a constant distraction as he resented being confined, and Judith had to steel herself to be stricter with him. This made her parents really welcome when they visited, as they were only too pleased to look after their grandson.

Inevitably, they eventually met Sid! On his release from prison, he had returned to his old lodgings, and the only thing keeping him from reverting to his former self were his visits to Judith for lessons. She noticed some change for the worse in him and was very concerned in case he met up with any of his former cronies. She was also worried in case he met her parents. When it did happen, she forgot about all the explanations she had considered earlier.

"This is Sid Cracken. He's the gifted artist I told you about, and I'm helping him." Her father gazed up at the large person in front of him in silence. Her mother smiled and approached Sid quickly, holding out her hand.

"Hello, Sid. I'm Judith's mother. How nice to meet you." She took his great hand in her own and tried to shake it. Sid stared at her in awe and then at her husband. He tried desperately to speak.

"Er... 'ello, I'm Sid." He blushed with confusion and meekly allowed his hand to be taken by the father. Judith came to his rescue and led him over to the desk where he worked.

"You carry on with that still life, Sid. I'd like you to try using some stronger colours, as I showed you earlier. I'll take Mummy and Daddy into the house to look after Charlie." On the way to the house, she thought, *How can I remind them who Sid really is? As they have actually met him, I'll sound them out on first impressions.*

"What do you think of Sid?" She looked at each of them in turn.

"He's very bashful for such a large person," her mother stated pleasantly.

"Wouldn't want to meet him on a dark night! Looks a bit simple to me. Is he the one you saw in prison?" her father added. *Oh dear. He's remembered! I'll give them the more technical diagnosis in the hope it'll blind them a bit until they get to know him well.*

"Yes, he is, but I must remind you about his illness. Basically, he's autistic, with an above- average level of brain dopamine. This has made him subject to fits of hyperactivity, anti-social behaviour and low levels of learning. He's now on a course of dopamine antagonists, which reduce the levels of hyperactivity and anti-social behaviour and increase his level of learning." She paused momentarily for breath. *I hope I got that right in case Dad checks.*

"He was treated as an idiot during his childhood and failed to mature properly. More seriously, the bad company he fell into easily led him astray. This resulted in him being imprisoned for an attempted assault on a woman, which is where I met him. A considerate fellow prisoner took him under his wing, and with the help of the psychiatrist, they've improved him to an almost normal level." She spoke as rapidly as she could.

"I knew there was something fishy about him. He's a nutter!" her father exclaimed, who had only understood the parts that fitted his pre-judgement of Sid.

"Aren't you in danger, dear?" her mother queried.

"I'm safer with him around, and so is Charlie, who loves him. Without his former friends [she made quotation signs with her hands], he's coming on in leaps and bounds. He's an excellent pupil and also very good company for me. I only told you about his past because I didn't want you to hear it from some malicious source."

"But you said he tried to attack a woman! How do you know he won't attack you?" her father persisted.

"I just know he won't. God help anyone who tries to harm us while he's around, as then he'd get rather angry. I hate to say this, but I feel safer with him than I did with Tom. He's already had a meeting with the woman he tried to attack, and she's forgiven him completely. One day soon, I think you could be proud to know him. When he's completed enough paintings for a representative portfolio, I intend to submit them to the Royal Academy. I'm quite sure they'll confirm my belief in his outstanding ability. Think it over carefully. I hope you'll be gracious to him when you meet him again – as you surely will." She left them with Charlie, obviously thinking different thoughts about what she had just told them, and returned to Sid in her studio.

"I'm sorry, miss. I didn't know your folks were 'ere. Should I go now?" Sid still showed signs of his earlier embarrassment, and rinsed his brushes in preparation for leaving.

"Nonsense! You carry on with your painting. I've explained everything to them, and they'll have to accept you as my student... and friend."

She held his arm bearing the brushes and forced it away

from the sink. *How could anyone think he'd harm me? He's putty in my hands*, she reasoned to herself as she looked into the flushed, adoring face of her protégé.

"Y-y-you called me your friend!" he stuttered, explaining his new complexion.

"Of course you're my friend, and…" she paused to give his arm a squeeze "…I'm proud to have you as a friend, but, for goodness' sake, call me Judith." Sid glanced at her and then looked the other way to hide the potential appearance of tears. Understanding his feelings, she released his arm and returned to the 'formal' lesson.

A few days later, Birdie spotted a face in the market she recalled with distaste. It was the young thug who had urged Sid to attack her! As he was behaving oddly, she decided to shadow him. Then she realised he was following someone else. It was Sid Cracken! Her task was made easier by the thug's whole attention being on Sid. Sid left the market with some shopping and went down an old narrow passageway. The thug caught up with him and grabbed at Sid's bag. Birdie slunk close enough to hear the conversation.

"Fuck me if it isn't me old mate Sid! What you bin stealing then?" He opened the bag to look, and Sid held his arm tight and retrieved the bag.

"Leave me alone, Bud. I don't want anything to do with you." Sid started to walk on.

"Oh no, you don't. We're old friends and you're comin' with me for a bit of fun like in the old days." He grabbed Sid's arm. As Sid tried to shake him off, a uniformed constable appeared at the other end of the passageway.

Bud threw himself on the ground and shouted out. "Help! Help! He's robbing me! Help!" It had the desired effect as the constable rushed up to try and grab Sid.

If he gets hold of Sid in his current stressed state, the officer'll get slaughtered, which is probably what Bud wants! Birdie's mind raced as she leapt from the doorway where she had been hiding and shouted, "Don't touch him, Officer!"

All three men froze at the surprise command echoing down the narrow alley.

"Don't move, Sid. I'll sort this out!" She reached the statues as the officer moved to get hold of Sid. Birdie lunged and caught his arm. As he tried to pull free, she twisted it behind his back.

"Let go! You're assaulting a policeman… and you're helping a mugger to escape," the very young constable protested.

Jeez! I must be getting old! This lad must be fresh from college! Birdie thought, with her back turned to the other two. A disturbance made her look round. Bud had got to his feet and was trying to hit her from behind. Not that he had any sympathy for a policeman, but because it would help his version of events. His fist never reached her as Sid grabbed him in a bear hug, pinning his arms to his sides.

"I've got him, Miss Birdie. I never hit him before," Sid almost pleaded.

"You're in league with the mugger," declared the young copper.

"I'll let you go now, Constable, if you promise to be a good boy." As she said it, she knew it had been wrong of her to patronise the poor officer. The raw official was so embarrassed he said nothing.

"We'll all go to the police station now and sort this out. Sid, you keep hold of Bud. Don't try anything, Officer, or I may have to march you in like this. Then what would your colleagues think?" She winked at Sid, who was about to disclose her identity.

"You're lucky to catch me off guard. So who's going to help you now?" He spun round as she released him.

"I shouldn't try, Officer. She floored me once!" Sid chuckled with pleasure at the sight of the flushed officer squaring up to Birdie. The forlorn constable looked from Birdie to the huge man towering over him, and thought desperately.

"Right, you're all coming with me to the police station!" He tried to gain control of the situation as other people appeared in the passageway, but his voice squeaked a bit. Birdie looked at Sid, winked again, and nodded.

"Yes, sir! We're coming, sir." She managed to suppress her laughter and sound deferential.

"Yes, sir, we're coming, **aren't** we, Bud?" Sid squeezed his captive, who gasped and nodded.

"Follow me and don't try to escape!" the constable commanded, in as deep a voice as he could manage, for the benefit of passers-by.

"Yes, sir." Birdie and Sid looked at each other and spoke in unison.

The strange procession caused many curious stares as they emerged from the alley and walked the few hundred metres to the police station. As they entered, Birdie kept behind Sid so Joe Baxter on the desk could not see her.

"Well! Well! What **have** you got here, Constable Floyd?" Joe recognised Sid immediately and wondered about the struggling youth he held.

"I'm arresting this man," he pointed at Sid, "for assaulting and trying to rob this man." He pointed at Bud. "And," he puffed out his chest with pride, "I'm arresting this woman for assaulting me!" He got hold of her arm and pulled Birdie forward. She smiled at Joe and gave him the biggest possible wink.

"You know who you've got here, son?" Joe started to blurt out. Birdie interrupted quickly.

"Yes, PC Baxter! He's caught me, Killer Birdie, Houghbury's master criminal." Sid could not restrain himself and laughed aloud.

"What are you laughing at, mugger?" Floyd asked angrily. Then he noticed Joe was laughing as well. "Will someone please let me in on the joke?"

"Constable Floyd! May I congratulate you on arresting Sergeant Birdie Lee," Joe announced. The poor lad's mouth dropped open and he visibly paled.

"You mean the one who…" He did not know where to start. Birdie had enjoyed her practical joke, something the old Ice Maiden would never have done, but now she felt sorry for Floyd.

"Constable, I'm sorry for tricking you. I admire your initiative and bravery in the circumstances. However, I hope you've learnt one valuable lesson as a result. Never jump to conclusions! I was following Bud, I think Sid called him, and saw him try to contaminate Sid as he used to. When Sid resisted, he tried to seize Sid's shopping and, seeing you, he flung himself on the ground. The rest you know. I had to stop you from grabbing Sid as he was already upset and might've hit you." Remembering Sid was holding Bud, she went over to them and stared into Bud's eyes. "You can let go of the naughty boy now, Sid. I don't think he'll give us any more trouble." She turned and walked towards Joe as Sid released his captive.

The frustrated, and now irate, Bud reached in his jacket pocket and shouted, "That's all you know, bitch," as he produced a pistol and fired at Birdie.

Sid twisted Bud's arm as he fired. PC Floyd leapt on Bud and knocked him to the ground. Three or four other police personnel came running and soon had Bud handcuffed. He was charged with attempted murder and locked up. The reception area was small and for several hectic minutes it was like a London railway station in the rush hour. When the crowd had thinned, Joe went through to the cells where Birdie had helped escort Bud and checked that she really was all right.

"Yes, Joe, I'm okay now, though I must admit I was a bit shaken by events. Perhaps this being engaged to be married has relaxed me too much and my reflexes and judgement aren't what they used to be." She smiled at his consideration.

"I can't see anything wrong with your judgement or your reflexes, B... Sergeant," he corrected himself as Floyd passed them. "You were proved right to trust Sid Cracken, weren't you?"

"Oh yes, Sid! I must thank him." As the commotion had completely subsided, they went to thank Sid for *his* bravery. He was slumped on a seat in the waiting area, and Birdie was the first to notice the blood oozing through the fingers he was clutching to his side.

"Oh shit! Quick, Joe, phone for an ambulance. Someone get the first aid kit." Using a rolled bandage, she did her best to stem the flow of blood until the paramedics arrived.

Sid was slowly losing consciousness and whispered to Birdie, as he was being stretchered out, "J... Judith."

"I'll tell her, Sid, don't worry." Later, when she was helping Floyd to fill out his report, omitting the embarrassing pieces, she commended him on his valour against such odds.

"How do you know Sid, Sergeant?" the grateful PC asked. She told him the story from the attempted rape, at the behest of Bud, to his redemption by Maurice Jenkins.

"Ironic, isn't it, Sarge? You put him in prison for trying to hurt you, and now he may've saved your life at the cost of his own."

Floyd's summation struck Birdie coldly and she thought –*Out of the mouths of babes and sucklings…!*

"You'll make a good copper, Floyd, and you've reminded me I've got a phone call to make."

She went to an empty office and phoned Judith. She gave her all the details of Sid and was amazed at the brief thanks she got before the line went dead. The news of Sid hit Judith harder than she could ever have imagined. Her parents were not available so she took Charlie with her when she dashed to the hospital. As she drove, she questioned her motives.

He's only a pupil; why am I concerned at all? He's not nature's gift to women; why should I have any feelings for him? He's not handsome or clever! He's not very graceful! Yet I do care. She swerved to avoid a loose dog. *Why? Yes, he's a brilliant artist and I admire him for that. Yes, he's wonderful with Charlie. There must be more. His simplicity and his enthusiasm to learn make him almost a blank page for me to write on. At times, I feel more like a mother than a tutor.* She fretted as she got stuck behind a slow convoy. *I know he likes – no – worships me. Is that why I feel responsible for him? Do I really want an adult child to look after? Is he capable of any form of civilised, mature action? Will he always be someone else's responsibility? I've great affection for him – as I would for another son – but as a man?* Her self-debate remained unresolved when she arrived at the hospital; her worry for Sid had not lessened. She found Birdie already in the waiting area.

"How is he? How did it happen? How did you find out?" Judith gabbled breathlessly at Birdie while Charlie stared at her in amazement. Having already confirmed that there would be no more news of Sid's condition for some time, Birdie carefully told Judith the whole episode.

"You mean the man who once tried to attack you saved your life?" Judith was astonished. Her immature pupil was a hero, and she explained this to Charlie.

"I'm as surprised as you. And – his bravery's proved he is capable of mature actions." Judith's eyes widened – *Has Birdie been reading my thoughts?*

"**And** it's removed his evil mentor from society. The one who tried to shoot me was the one who made Sid attack me, and landed him in prison," Birdie continued. They saw the unconscious Sid for a moment as he was being taken to a ward. The surgeon said he should make a full recovery and would need time to recuperate when he was discharged from hospital.

"I wish I could do something for him, but I'll probably be on my honeymoon when he comes out," Birdie said with a mixture of regret and pleasure as they were leaving.

"I **can** do something! He could stay with me. I've a spare room he could have. Oh dear! Does that sound a bit forward? What would the neighbours think?" Judith was voicing her thoughts.

"You've changed then. I'd heard that you used to be quite the bohemian once, and didn't care what others thought." Birdie laughed and continued. "It sounds like a good idea. You'd have a live-in pupil."

"It's my parents!" Judith explained. "I never used to care what they thought. Now they're back in my life and doing so much for me and for Charlie, I **have** to consider them," Judith explained.

"Leave it to me. You introduce me to them and I'll explain the dilemma. I'm sure they'll agree once they know I'm the one he tried to attack."

It worked! Judith's parents gave tentative approval, because they knew she would have gone ahead with her plan anyway. They also noted Charlie's enthusiasm and took into account that they would be visiting nearly every day. With only a few weeks to their wedding, Terry and Birdie helped Judith prepare for the impending arrival of Sid. To make it easier, they turned the small dining room into Sid's bedroom. This met with parental approval, as it provided a greater barrier between nurse and patient. Judith and Birdie were secretly amused by their attitude.

Sid was not the best of patients when he arrived there. Judith got great satisfaction from waiting on him and was impatient at his inability to remain inactive, as he desperately wanted to do things for his idol. He compensated for his injury by inventing games he could play with Charlie. He found painting while lying on his bed was not practical, as he kept dirtying the bedclothes. He resumed using his original skills and produced excellent sketches; many were of animals and other creatures for Charlie. He read books, which Judith provided, and amazed her with his questions and observations. Slowly, he began to accept her reprimands when he annoyed her. It was as if being in the home of the woman he adored gave him a protective shell, and nothing she said could upset him.

For her part, she became relaxed in his company and no longer felt guilt when she did tell him off. Having him there brought a new vitality to her life. On one embarrassing occasion, he tried to carry some washing for her and tripped. He dropped the washing and Judith made no attempt to catch it. She caught Sid gently and held him close until he regained his balance. *I want to hug the great teddy bear but I would hurt him.* She turned away lest he read her thoughts, as his eyes never left her face.

The emptiness I felt when Tom left has gone, so Sid is helping me without knowing it, she mused later.

CHAPTER 10

"Why don't we see that nice Antony any more, Mummy? I thought he'd come and play with me." Roger had questioned his mother more than once, and it annoyed her.

She had received more letters from Sean and had increasingly romantic notions about him. She assumed his letters were always a bit formal because of his calling. *He's not shown any indication of love for me, yet I've high hopes. He must have feelings for me that go beyond mere friendship, or why does he keep writing and telling me many of his innermost thoughts? He's indicated that he wishes to resign from the priesthood, and it could be because he wishes to make our association more... more intimate.* She peered into the washing-up water as if seeking an omen. *Maurice Jenkins was certainly a... a revelation to me, but I don't share Roger's cordiality towards him.*

"His proper name is Maurice, so stop calling him Antony. I'm sure he's much too busy to come out here and play with you," she scolded her son. *Actually, it'd be nice to have someone like him come here... occasionally... to help out, but I don't want to encourage him. He might start getting ideas... he'd only get hurt when Sean returns. As soon as I put him out of my mind, Roger puts him back. I must find out what Sean feels about kids.*

"Mr Brown's here, Mummy." Nicola dashed into the kitchen, interrupting her rambling thoughts. The Browns had been a true blessing to her, and had virtually assumed the role of grandparents.

"There's something you'd like me to do for you, Helen?" Harold asked politely as he met her in the hallway.

"Yes. Now that Nicola is well again, I'm worried about that old rockery in the front garden. The two of them can get over-boisterous and I think they'll hurt themselves on the part-hidden rocks. Do you know anybody who'd shift them for me? I can pay as long as it's not too much." *I realise Harold and I would not be strong enough.*

"Yes, I know just the person, and he'll be very cheap. I'll see if he can come tomorrow." Harold seized the opportunity to take Maurice up on his earlier offer, and he rang him as soon as he got home.

Only weeks until his lawyer friend's wedding and Maurice still had no job. His monetary reserves were almost depleted. But for the impending celebrations, he might have relapsed into the state of depression that had resulted in the past year being so eventful. Following Birdie's advice, he waited for time to heal Helen's opinion of him. That would have been more bearable if he had been fully employed. As it was, time for him dragged painfully slowly. The phone call from Harold Brown gave him some hope, and he eagerly agreed to undertake the work.

Helen answered the door, the next afternoon, to find Maurice there, and frowned heavily.

"What do you want?" she asked bluntly.

"Mr Brown told me you wanted some stones moving." He was disappointed by her reception, and then he understood Harold had not informed her that he was coming. "Sorry if I've got it wrong. Perhaps I'd better leave," he added.

"No, no. It's me that should be sorry. I did ask Harold to find someone to move the stones, but I *never* imagined it'd be you. You must be much too busy to bother with us." She felt ashamed.

He laughed. *I could never be too busy for you and yours.* "I wish I'd the choice, but I'm still looking for a job. I told the Browns to call me if you ever needed help and I'm glad they did." Encouraged by her apparent acceptance of his presence, he pressed on. "You may not welcome my attention, but I do still feel a sense of responsibility towards you and your kids. I'd like to help you... and Nicola and Roger... in any way I can. Before you get on your high horse, this *is* going to cost you." He turned and considered the amount of large stones. "Most definitely it's going to cost you three – perhaps even four – cups of tea. You're not going to get off scot-free!" He grinned as he swept aside the strained atmosphere, and she was forced to relax and smile at him.

The children were overjoyed to find Maurice labouring in their garden when they returned from school. He had nearly finished, so they changed out of their uniforms ready to play with him –they hoped. Helen insisted he have a shower when he did finish, to get rid of the dirt and sweat.

"I'm going to give you a bonus for all your hard work, Maurice." He loved the sound of his name on her lips. "I'll **not** take no for an answer. You **will** stay to dinner." She noticed his expression and hastily added, "Roger and Nicola **insist** that you stay. I have to warn you, though, they want you to play with them. I said you'd be too tired."

The way to a man's heart is through his stomach and, just maybe, the way to a woman's is through her children. I just have to give her time, he reminded himself.

"I'd love to play with them, however tired I am. I'll go outside with them until the meal's ready and try to tire them."

He was as good as his word, and it was three exhausted bodies that hauled themselves in to dinner.

This is nice; it's so good to have a man at the dinner table. Lots of men have flirted with me, particularly since Arnold passed away. I'm still young enough to have desires, and I haven't aged too badly. The only one I've met who I feel I could trust completely is Sean. This Maurice is very pleasant and the kids adore him. He'd make a good teacher... perhaps I'll suggest it to him. I wonder if it'd be too brash to have him round for a meal sometimes when Sean marries me? Should I mention to Maurice I'm going to Schott's wedding? Better not! It'd appear boastful or, worse, encouraging.

She took away the plates and brought in the desserts. *I can clearly envisage Sean sitting at the head of the table and saying prayers before the meals. As an experienced priest... well, he'll be an ex-priest when he marries me, and he'll be a wonderful mentor for Nicola and Roger. Ah! This imposing man with a beard – and ex-convict – has finished.* Maurice enjoyed eating with the children, though he would have preferred to dine with Helen alone.

Noticing that she was consumed with her own thoughts, he had entertained her offspring, hoping that she may be thinking of him. When he finally looked from the kids to her, she raised his hopes.

"I've been thinking, you'd make a good teacher."

She's been thinking about me! Maurice's heart raced.

"Have you considered it yourself? I'll find out what Sean thinks when I write to him next," she continued, and his soaring hopes plummeted to earth.

She writes to that damn priest! He told others to kick me in the crotch; now he's doing it by remote control! I was going to tell her about Terry's wedding, but I think it'd only start her off about Sean again.

"No, I've not considered it. I love kids, but I don't think I could handle dealing with a lot all at once." He paused, observing her closely as he continued. "You've replied to Sean then?"

"Oh yes! We've a weekly correspondence. He confides a great deal in me. I think he has strong feelings for me, and he's told me he's going to resign from the priesthood so he'll be free. Are you all right?" She noticed the look of anguish on Maurice's face. It was caused by the psychological blow he had just received.

"It's okay. I think I've eaten too much. It was such a fabulous meal that I couldn't resist anything. I'm not used to such rich living, and these two are very lucky to have such an excellent cook for a mother. I'd offer to wash up, but I think I'd better go before I get too settled into your wonderful domestic life."

"If you must go, it's probably the best time as these tearaways have got homework to do before bed. You've done more than I'd any right to expect today, and the meal was the least I could do to repay you." The children wanted him to stay. Helen wanted him to leave. *Her wish is my command*, he thought as he said his farewells.

With his renewed hopes dampened, he had a restless night, determined not to let depression seize him again. When he received an early call from Terry asking him to go to his office, he feared the worst. *What can it be but bad news if he has to see me? What can go wrong now?* he wondered as he climbed the stairs in the old building.

"Glad you could come, Maurice. I've a proposition that I need to put to you in person."

Oh no! Here it comes! He's found someone he'd rather have as his best man. He's going to suggest I take some boring, mind-

numbing job. Why is he pausing so long? The thoughts raced through his mind.

"How are you with stocks and shares?" Terry finally asked.

"Not very good at present as I've no money to save," Maurice replied dully.

"No, you misunderstood me. Do you have any knowledge of investing in the stock market?"

"Oh yes! I quite fancied myself at it. I never invested much myself. I kept an eye on the market while I worked for the insurance company, hoping I might get the opportunity to do it for them. Unfortunately, I was passed over for the posts, though I did get the mental satisfaction of theoretically doing better than the two who got the jobs," he reminisced enthusiastically.

"That's brilliant! I've a client, Jeremy Cook, who's a financial advisor. He's retiring in a couple of years and needs an assistant who he could trust to take over his clients. He has a lot of elderly people he invests for and is concerned that they'll continue to get good advice. I've told him about you, and he thinks you could be just the person he's looking for. What do you think?"

"Sounds ideal! I can show him the computer spreadsheet I developed in my spare time for checking the stock market. After the way they ignored me at work, I never told them about it."

When Maurice and Jeremy met, there was mutual empathy. Jeremy knew of Maurice's previous employment and his recent tribulations. Once he had been given the position, Maurice showed Jeremy his spreadsheet and how it could be used. Jeremy accepted it on a trial basis.

Time proved to be a slow healer for Helen. The loss of her lover and companion; her children's father; her advisor and handyman was constantly underlined. *I never realised all he did for us until he'd gone. It's fortunate we'd done several tasks in preparation for our courses. Now, though, there are repairs – and maintenance jobs– which I can't do. I'll get Maurice Jenkins to do them. After all, but for him, Arnold'd still be doing them. He can't have any illusions about me, because he knows I'm promised – well, almost – to Sean. I feel safe with Maurice, and the kids like him, and it'd protect me from the annoying attentions of other men.*

With his future looking secure, Maurice had less free time, but he was still able to help Helen whenever he could.

CHAPTER 11

Why has there been no communication of any kind from Sean since I got back from Madrid? In the short time I knew him, I'd never have believed him to be the sort to cut off all contact. Perhaps it was just a holiday romance for him, and he's decided to end it now he's returned to his religious duties. He did promise to let me know his decision. Something must have happened to him. I've sent emails to Sean without any replies. Something must be wrong! I'll check with his friend Miguel. Maria could not get Sean out of her mind, or heart.

I wonder how Sean's coping in Africa? Will he return to the Church or to me? These and many other such thoughts went through Miguel Santos's mind as he attended to the wealthier ladies in his hair salon. Normally, he would carry out polite conversation with his clients and had long ceased to be amazed at the secrets and gossip they divulged. It was during one such session that Sean entered his mind. The woman he was attending to was describing all her misdeeds since her last visit to him. *She's treating me as her confessor! Perhaps she gets some kind of absolution just by divulging her sins. Perhaps this is what it's like for Sean?*

"Yes, I was listening. It's just that I've got something in my eye. I'll be back in a moment," he answered the woman, as he wiped his hands and kept blinking one eye. *I could write a book about the stories we hear in my salon. It's lucky for our clients I've no need or desire to do such a thing. However, I've sometimes fancied writing a novel, and there'd be no harm in getting ideas from clients' gossip. I'll start recording the tales my girls recant during coffee break, though I'll have to be careful. One of my competitors did and was arrested for blackmail!*

Some months after last hearing from Sean, a pretty young woman came to the salon and specifically asked to speak to Miguel. This created many curious looks from both staff and regular customers. Something in her manner intrigued Miguel, and he agreed reluctantly to see her alone in his office.

"I'm Maria Caballeros," she stated, as if the name should mean something to him, and seated herself in the chair he offered.

"Hello, Maria. How can I help you?" he asked flatly, sitting down opposite her.

"Have you heard from Sean Anderson?" Her voice trembled as she spoke. His surprise showed.

"No. Not for months. How do you know him?" Maria then explained who she was and how she had become involved with Sean. The control over her emotions, which she had built over years of nursing, weakened as she talked, and tears crept down her cheeks. Miguel was at once distressed by the sight of the heartbroken woman and yet jealous of her relationship with Sean. He handed her a box of tissues and spoke as unemotionally as possible.

"You've come to see me at just the right time. I'm going to England next week to some friends' wedding. I'll have time to divert to Houghbury to check on him. *I'd* like some answers too."

So this was my rival for Sean's affections! He's handsome, charming and considerate. Had I known earlier, I could've been most jealous of him. As it is, he shares my concern. Perhaps everything Sean told me was a lie. Perhaps… "Do you think he really was a priest?" She voiced the thought aloud.

"Yes. Had he been a fake, trying to gain some advantage, he'd definitely have used it while he was in your hospital. Something's stopped him from contacting either of us, and I'll find out next week." He patted her arm as she prepared to leave.

"A senior doctor has asked me to marry him, and I've refused to give him an answer until I know what's happened to Sean." They received more enquiring looks as he led her to the salon door with his arm around her.

The wait for news of Sean was interminable for both of them. Miguel spent his spare moments, including the flight to Gatwick, England, making notes from his coffee break recordings. He enjoyed the celebrations at his gay friends' civil ceremony in Brighton and it took his mind off Sean. Then he hired a car and drove to Houghbury, booking in at a pub for a couple of nights.

The next day, he visited the priest at St Michael's Church. The new incumbent confirmed that Father Anderson had been the priest there. He referred Miguel to the bishop for more information.

The bishop was alarmed to find an obvious homosexual enquiring about Sean, and was secretly pleased that he was no longer one of his team. So, without hesitation, he referred him to the African Community ServiceAssociation. They explained what Sean Anderson had been doing for the past six months. They did not know his current whereabouts, as he was currently making his own way back to the UK now his tour of duty had finished. They suggested he speak to a Maurice Jenkins, who was the only contact they had listed.

Maurice was very surprised to be visited by an obviously gay Spaniard, asking about Sean Anderson. Miguel gave him little information to explain how he knew the priest.

"I met Father Anderson ven 'e was in Spain and thought I'd look 'im up vile I'm visiting oter friends ere in England. I'm told ' e's in Africa and wondered if you 'ad any news of 'm?"

"I have a lady friend he writes to regularly. She may be able to tell you where he is now and when he's due back. Funny thing, a celibate Catholic priest corresponding with a woman. Particularly as it's because of a woman he went to Africa in the first place."

Not knowing how much this foreigner knew about Sean's history, Maurice gave him a brief résumé of the part he had played in Sean's life and how the news of Maria's death had devastated him, causing him to go to Africa. Miguel noticed there was something in the way Maurice explained, as if he was withholding information. It made Miguel decide to say nothing about Maria.

As he was busy in his new position as a financial adviser, Maurice gave Miguel directions to Helen's house, and rang her about the impending visit. Afterwards, he wondered if he had an ulterior motive in sending her an obviously gay acquaintance of Sean.

The children were home when he arrived. "*Buenas tardes!*" the two kids greeted him with at the door, and he was delighted to reply in kind. Helen was a bit taken aback when she realised he was gay.

Have I been mistaken about Sean? There have been items in the press about the philandering of Catholic priests. Is Sean gay? Surely I couldn't be that wrong about him? Perhaps I'll find out from this Spaniard… when the kids have left.

Nicola and Roger were keen to try out the little Spanish they had learnt with this unusual man. They had not met anyone like him before. Helen had prepared a place for him at dinner and was anxious for any news he might have. When the kids had been relegated to their rooms to do their homework, Helen told Miguel all she knew about Sean's adventures in Africa and that he was due home soon. Then she asked for any information he might have. He explained how he had become friends with Sean and how they had debated on religion and other matters.

"I couldn't understand why 'e broke off contact vit me until today. It's obvious 'e's in love with Maria and 'eard about ze terrible crash of ze coach in which she was travelling. 'E must've read the names on ze internet of dose 'oo died. It didn't give ze names of ze few survivors. Maria's mother was also M Caballeros, and she's ze one 'oo died. I only learnt of ze existence of Maria last veek ven she came to my salon. She'll be overjoyed ven I tell 'er vat's 'appened. Ven Sean gets back, *you* can tell 'im ze good news. I understood zat your friend Maurice was ze reason for Sean coming to Málaga. I believe 'e not tell me everyting and like you very much, so I not tell 'im about Maria. Tank you for ze *sabroso*... er... tasty meal. I von't disturb ze children at zeir schoolvork, but I must get back to my lodgings as I leave early tomorrow."

When he had gone, Helen was still shocked by the news and saw her romantic dreams fading. *I wasn't wrong about Sean... he's not gay. If Miguel hasn't told anyone else in England about Maria being alive, then why should I? If I keep it to myself, Sean need never know and I can marry the man of my dreams. I don't fully understand why he didn't tell Maurice, but it's to my advantage. Maybe I'm not doing the right thing – why should I? I've lost the love of my life once and I don't intend letting it happen again.* The return of her kids prevented her from reasoning any further.

Back at the pub where he was staying, Miguel found Maurice sipping a pint of bitter while he read a work file. *When in Rome*, Miguel mused, and got himself a glass of the local brew. He sat in the corner, near the open fire, with Maurice and told him of his meeting with Helen.

He still omitted any mention of Maria. *Why can I talk about her to a woman and not to a man? Am I being 'macho' or just plain bitchy? I'd better change the subject before I say too much.*

"From ze bits of information I've gained vilst I've been 'ere, I tink zere's more I should know."

Maurice, relaxed by the beer and the warmth of the fire, was only too ready to narrate more fully the dramatic events set in motion by Charlie falling off his scooter. "It's strange how a normal, boring day in my life, interrupted by such a minor incident, should lead to me in prison and the involvement of the Met." Maurice lowered his voice as he related his time in the spotlight.

"Vy was ze opera interested in you?" Miguel was very puzzled.

"The opera? I don't understand you."

"You said ze Met was involved!"

"Yes. The Metropolitan Police of London."

"Ah! I thought you meant the opera as in the Met opera in New York. Zat explains one of ze t'ings I 'eard vich I vas going to use for a story. One of my rich clients boasted zat 'er new cleaner also vorked for a rich Arab. Ze cleaner knew little about ze man because 'e always spoke in Arabic to ozers. Once she 'eard 'im get very irate on ze phone and she gazered ze subject of his 'ate vas ze London Met. Apparently 'e 'as a nice apartment near ze top of a modern building in Málaga. My client told me it's very secret, as ze cleaner only knew from zat one conversation. I assumed it vas a famous opera singer 'oo'd lost a role. My client vouldn't pronounce ze man's name out loud, and wrote it down so I could check it against London opera stars." Miguel spoke like a conspirator.

"What did you discover?" Maurice played his part and looked around the room as if to check on any eavesdroppers.

"Nusing about ze man's status, and now I know vy. 'E must be a criminal 'oo's been forced to leave England as 'e spends most of 'is time in Málaga," he suggested. "'Is address is on one of my valk routes, so I checked it. Zat's vy I know it to be an expensive apartment tower. 'E must've been successful at vatever 'e did."

"I've a friend who was in the London police. If you tell me the name, I can see if she knew your mystery man."

Miguel pulled a pen from his pocket, scribbled on a beer mat and passed it to Maurice. "I've given you my email address as vell so you can tell me vat you find out."

Maurice glanced at the mat and put it in his pocket. He then continued briefly with his saga, omitting his true feelings for Helen but explaining how he helped her when possible out of respect for her late husband.

"I may be an ex-convict, but I do have a better job now. Thanks to my former interest in using a computer to study the stock market, I work as a financial adviser." Maurice felt obliged to finish his tale on a high note. Miguel offered to buy him another drink.

"No, thank you. I've enjoyed talking to you, but I've got a busy day tomorrow and I must get home. Enjoy the rest of your stay and have a good journey home. I'll let you know what my friend says about you-know-who." He winked as if they were sharing a dark secret, and Miguel tried to wink back. "Perhaps we'll all meet up with Sean again soon," Maurice concluded loudly.

He gathered his papers and shook Miguel's hand a little too strongly as he departed. Miguel flexed his crushed fingers and went through the archway to the bar. *It's totally different to my usual beer, yet I'll have another one as a nightcap.*

As he approached the bar, a man with his back towards Miguel got to his feet and accidentally knocked Miguel off balance. With amazing dexterity, the man grabbed Miguel's arm and held him erect.

"Oh, I'm so sorry! I was so wrapped up in my thoughts I didn't look before I leapt. Are you okay?" Doug Evans held on to Miguel's arm and peered into his eyes. There was a moment of uncertainty with a seemingly prolonged silence as they assiduously regarded each other.

There was no lightning strike, just the understanding of some kind of mutual bond. Miguel was first to break the intangible dimension that had engulfed them.

"Vat is zis leap you did?"

Doug realised his new… friend… was foreign. He'd come down to the bucolic charms of the provinces simply to interview Birdie Lee. Now he was confronted by a foreigner whose presence more than upset him; it derailed him mentally.

"It's an English expression – to look before you leap means to be careful before you do something. It doesn't really mean you jump. Let me buy you a drink. Do you live here, or are you just visiting?" Doug released Miguel and indicated for him to sit at his table. More used to giving orders than receiving them, Miguel surprised himself at how readily he obeyed. Unaccustomed to the local brew, he lowered his guard and willingly accepted the dominance of… of what?

"I'll 'ave a glass of ze local bitter, please."

As Doug went to the bar, Miguel studied him and sought the answer. *Of what indeed? Purely by chance I visit this town I'd never heard of before I met Sean. Purely by accident I meet what? All I'm aware of at the moment is this incredible man who's entered my life. He's the ultimate... what?* Unwittingly, he scratched his head as if to stimulate his brain cells. *Goodness, unless I'm very wrong, he's the ultimate alpha male I've always dreamt of. No! I'm behaving like some empty-'eaded teenage girl with a crush on her teacher. We're grown men and will pass on like ships in the night. He's coming back and I can feel my face glowing.*

Doug gave his order at the bar, and while he waited, he was able to observe his new companion's reflection in the glass behind the bar. *He's staring at me. Why? I've never met him before as far as I can remember. Yet... he seems familiar to me, as if I've known him for years! He disturbs me! In a nice way, he disturbs me because I find myself very attracted to him. But he's a man! How can I possibly be attracted to a man, unless...? No! It's not possible! Though, looking back, I've never been at ease with women socially.* He paid for the drinks and, as he returned to his seat, his professional investigative side took hold.

I must remember that the reason I deliberately bumped into this man was because I noticed him and the one who just left behaving suspiciously. Then I heard him call the other one Maurice! Vaguely, I recall the name in association with Houghbury. I'll just have the drink and a chat and see where the dust settles.

"I got you a pint. I hope that's okay." He handed one glass to Miguel.

"It's more zan I'd normally 'ave, but ven in Rome, as you English say."

"Cheers! As we say in England." Doug raised his drink to Miguel, who reciprocated. "What brings you to Houghbury?" Doug continued.

"I've been making enquiries about a friend, for myself and for a woman 'oo vas close to 'im." Miguel gulped some of his beer.

"Did you find him?" Doug nearly asked if the friend was the man he'd been with earlier. Then he realised it would reveal that he had noticed them.

"No, but I know vere 'e is, and vy ve lost touch viz 'im." He shook his head and took another swig of beer. Doug looked into his own drink, drank some, and spoke as nonchalantly as possible.

"Sounds fascinating! Are you some sort of detective?" Doug grinned and sat back on his chair.

Miguel shook his head and spread his hands wide. "No, I'm not. Can you guess vat my job is?" He too sat back, and then put his hands on his chest and tilted his head on one side. Doug studied him while he held his glass to his lips. Pausing as long as he thought it wise, he tried to look baffled, and suddenly clicked his fingers.

"From your good looks, your bearing and your fashionable clothes, I think you're either a film star or a fashion model." He said it with as much sincerity as he could muster. *It's all true, but it's not something I'd normally tell someone. However, I have always found a few well-aimed compliments can help people relax.*

"Tank you very much. I'm flattered by your opinion, but I'm only a 'umble 'airdresser." Miguel glowed almost coquettishly.

I'll have to let him guess about me now, thought Doug. "Now it's your turn to guess what I do."

Miguel appraised Doug from head to toe and narrowed his eyes in contemplation. "Vith your looks and build, *you* could be a model, but I t'ink you do something vich needs more brain vork. I t'ink you're a... TV presenter." Miguel had thought of many likely jobs. Then he realised he did not know the English words for them, so he picked at random one he did know.

"I wish I was. No, my job is not that attractive. I'm in IT. I work with computers, doing research for companies." *Mentioning research should help explain my enquiring mind.*

"Zat's a coincidence! Ze man I vas just talking to in 'ere uses computers to study ze stock market. You must play sport or some physical activity to keep in such good shape."

Is this man trying flattery on me now, or is it just part of him being gay? At least he's given me an opening about his earlier companion. "I go to the gym whenever I can. I do like to keep fit. That other man wasn't the one you were looking for?" *I know it wasn't, but hopefully he'll think I've a short memory or was paying more attention to my beer than him.*

"'E was not. I still 'aven't found 'im. Zat's ze one 'oo caused my friend to fall from grace, vizout intending to."

"Fall from grace? Sounds intriguing." Doug smiled and drank some more.

Whether it was his desire to produce stories or the effect of the beer, Miguel explained the events as first Sean and then Maurice had told him. He withheld the bit about the Met and the stranger in Málaga, because Maurice had seemed to consider it a secret.

Meanwhile, Doug was also being cautious about giving more information. *I really like this man. I'm very attracted to him, but my professional caution makes me hold back until I've verified his facts. I think he's not told me everything yet. I'll be able to check when I see Sergeant Lee tomorrow.*

"Fascinating! I vaguely remember an item in the newspaper about a man who was mistakenly sent to prison for a heroic act. Gosh! That was the one you talked to earlier! What did you think of him?" Doug's interest was genuine.

"'E seemed okay to me. 'E vas very open about 'is recent misadventures and ze people involved. I did notice 'e was a bit strained ven I told 'im about my visit to ze woman 'oo writes to my missing friend. I t'ink 'e may 'ave romantic feelings for 'er." Miguel sipped his beer.

"Now you intrigue me. This Maurice likes a woman who corresponds with a missing friend of yours who has fallen from grace! I don't wish to be impertinent, but are you and your missing friend gay?" Doug tapped the table with his index finger as if to enumerate the various points.

"You are part right. I freely admit I am gay. I 'ope you don't object!" Miguel paused for a reaction.

"Not at all. In fact homophobes annoy me."

"Zen I must ask you, are you gay?" The question unsettled Doug mentally.

"Not as far as I'm aware. I have an open mind on such subjects. You said I was partly right. So your friend is not gay? How did he fall from grace – as you put it?" Doug changed the subject to relieve the question of his own sexuality.

"'E was a Cat'olic priest in zis town. 'E was captured on TV saying somesing 'e later regretted. Ven I last saw 'im in Málaga, 'e vas trying to sort out 'is beliefs."

Miguel went on to explain about Maria. All the while, Doug was studying him, but *not* as he would a suspect. *This is ridiculous. I feel more than relaxed with this Spaniard. I really enjoy his company. Dare I even think it? I'm attracted to him more than I ever have been to a woman. Does this mean* I'm *gay? Enjoy his companionship for these few moments, then we will part as – good friends; him to Málaga and me back to London. No doubt his attitude'd change if he knew my real job. I must discipline myself!* "What a romantic tale, I'd love to know how it ends. Now I must leave you as I have to get a good night's sleep ready for work tomorrow."

"Yes. I've an early start so I must go too. 'Ere's my card. You must come and visit me in Málaga. I'll be able to show you ze sights and tell you 'ow my friend's tale finishes." They both stood up and shook hands slowly, with hidden sensations.

CHAPTER 12

Terry and Maurice stared at Birdie, who was still gazing in almost horror at the beer mat with the name Ali Parouk on it. She sat back down at the table where they had just been dining at Maurice's expense, and motioned for them to do the same. She checked nobody could hear her and then she spoke softly to them.

"Does anyone else know about this, Maurice?"

"Only I have seen the name, and Miguel never spoke it aloud." He was at once excited and yet frightened by her manner.

"Do you think this Miguel has told anyone else?" Birdie continued.

"No. I only met him yesterday, and although some people'd be prejudiced against a gay hairdresser, I'm pretty certain he's a discreet and trustworthy person. He only mentioned it to me because I explained that the London Met is not an opera house!" He gave a nervous laugh, which Birdie did not reciprocate.

"I may be making a mountain out of a molehill, but, to be on the safe side, I'd like you to keep this secret for the time being. If you *can* contact Miguel, impress upon him the need to not only keep this secret but also to avoid the person and anything to do with him. This man is known to be very, very dangerous. You know what his friends did to me, and had one of my colleagues killed." Her expression darkened as she remembered Ivor. She leant forward and placed her hand on Maurice's arm.

"This man was forced to leave the country because we were close to arresting him. He may be of no further use to the international crime organisation he worked for. On the other hand, he could still work for them. It's a shame I didn't know this morning. I had a meeting with a detective sergeant from the Met about the case that involves the very man you just told me about. I'll let him and my old boss know, and I'm sure he'll check it out quickly." As she withdrew her hand from Maurice's arm, Terry clutched it tightly.

"You're not to get involved, darling!" he instructed her anxiously. They became cocooned in their own private world and did not notice Maurice leave them as he went to pay the bill.

Maurice sent an email to Miguel that evening:

Warning! It may be a false alarm, but you are advised to keep clear of the person whose name you put on the beer mat. Do not mention him to anybody, ever! He is very dangerous, and has friends who have already killed a policeman. I will give you more definite news when I can. Good luck, Maurice

Birdie contacted her former boss, Phil Tyler, urgently on his mobile and gave him the information. He was particularly thrilled because it interrupted his worries about his new parental duties.

The next day, he had a meeting with Superintendent Ron Bennett, Chief Inspector John Langley and Detective Sergeant Doug Evans, insisting they have it in a nearby café.

"I've had a message from Birdie Lee. She's been informed that our friend Masood is spending a lot of time in Málaga. Well, we're pretty certain it's him. He's living under the name of Ali Parouk, the name he was known as when he first came to the UK." Phil kept his voice down so they could barely hear him, and looked around to check the few other customers.

"How come she never told me when I saw her?" Doug was irritated.

"Apparently, she was only told by this Maurice Jenkins yesterday."

"How did **he** know?" Doug was still upset at the belated news, which almost made his trip to Houghbury a minor event.

"It appears Jenkins was told by a Spanish hairdresser from Málaga—"

"Miguel!" Doug interjected.

"Yes, that was his name. How do you know?" Phil questioned, while the other two stared at Doug.

"I saw two men acting suspiciously in the pub where I was staying. Following my usual routine, I got into conversation with one when the other left," he remembered with a frown.

"He was Miguel and I discovered the one who left was Jenkins. During our chat, I found out quite a bit about Miguel and was satisfied he was there for genuine reasons. However, he never mentioned Masood."

"I find that very surprising! The reason the Spaniard told Jenkins was because he mentioned the Met, and the Spaniard thought the London Met was the opera, as in New York. Surely he should've told you once he realised you are in the Met?" Phil was baffled at what seemed to be a slip-up by a highly regarded detective.

"You've answered your own question, Inspector. I never told him I was in the Met. I said I was in computer research. I could kick myself, though! We got on well, and, although I decided he was… honest, I never told him I'm in the police."

Oops, I nearly said he was straight, which could be misconstrued depending on how much Jenkins told Birdie and she passed on to Tyler.

Phil frowned and was about to comment that Miguel was **gay** when he noticed Bennett and Langley nod in understanding. *No point in telling them that Miguel is gay. I get fed up with all the leg-pulling I'm suffering at present. It would only cause this young detective a lot of unnecessary and probably unwarranted harassment if it leaked out.*

"We should involve Interpol and the local police, but I'm concerned that this organisation could have plants in both of them. If the crooks can infiltrate us to such a high level, then I'm sure they'll have done so in other parts of Europe. Interpol's assistance in the past may have been genuine and we just struck lucky. Can we take the risk now we have a bigger fish to fry?" Ron Bennett looked at each of them in turn.

"Ali Parouk is probably a common name in the Arab world, and it may not be our Masood," Doug suggested.

"If it is Masood, the fact he is spending a lot of time in a region that is on the short list of areas suspected of housing the European criminal mastermind could be of interest. Of course, even that fact could be a red herring to throw us off the scent," Ron said, in almost a whisper.

"If it is him, is he still working for the criminals, or is he simply being rewarded for past services? He might be a link to bigger fish, or we could all be wasting time by pursuing him," Ron continued.

"There is one other possibility we should consider, Ron." John Langley was toying with his pencil as he looked at the notes he had been making.

"You mean it could be another Ali Parouk who is part of

the same crime organisation?" Phil ceased his doodling for a moment and looked at John triumphantly.

"No, that's not what I had in mind, but it's another possibility. My suggestion is that if it is our Masood, he could be the head of the whole lot!" John had hardly finished before both Ron and Phil scoffed at the idea.

"I agree! Masood **could** be top dog!" The two inspectors looked at Doug in astonishment.

"Okay, Doug. Tell us why you think that," Ron urged him.

"How many crooks in Western Europe manage to dictate to a police superintendent and a high court judge? Who would be the one in such a large organisation to decide to eliminate one of the local heads? I may be biased against Masood and regret that we never convicted him, but you must realise that it was only the freak incident in Houghbury that forced him to leave England. We've been after him for years and got precisely nowhere." Doug's fists were clenched hard to cover his emotions.

"Perhaps we'd have a better idea if we could find out if it is Masood *and* about the place he's living in while in Spain." Phil suggested. His new role as a father was very tiring, and it had made him only too conscious of property values.

"I agree. How can we check on him without involving Interpol or the local police?" Ron Bennett took charge.

"It means we **have** to do the work ourselves," Doug stated baldly.

"Is it really worth doing? It would also cause two more problems! One, how can we send someone without Masood getting wind of it? Two is the very real matter of the expense." Ron was busy doodling pound signs as he spoke.

"If I can volunteer, guv. I'm due some leave and could go there. As to the expense, it would just be down to me as normal holiday expenses. Also, I now have this contact, Miguel, which could be *very* useful as a reason for being there **and** as a source of local information. I can identify Masood and find out what he's up to. If he is still active in any way, you will then have to decide how to proceed." Bennett and Langley welcomed Doug's enthusiasm as the expected behaviour of the Hound of Masood.

Phil drank his coffee to hide any facial signs of disbelief in Doug's motives. *This is wrong of me to harbour such thoughts. Doug is a good detective and he is the right man for the job. So what if he has an ulterior motive? His private life is none of my concern unless it damages his position as a policeman. Anyway, I hope my mind is liberal enough to accept the fact he could be gay.* Doug's all-seeing eyes, from years of undercover work, noted Phil's part-hidden reaction. So it was agreed for Doug to have a week's leave starting the coming weekend. As they walked back to their offices, Doug waylaid Phil.

"Is there something you didn't tell the others, Inspector Tyler?"

"How do you mean, Doug?"

"I noticed your expression when I volunteered to go to Málaga."

"I didn't tell them that your Miguel is gay!" Phil decided to be blunt.

"Are you insinuating that I'm gay?"

"Are you?" Phil retorted, fighting fire with fire.

"Not that *I'm* aware, but what if I was? Are **you** homophobic?" The atmosphere became decidedly strained between them. Phil took a deep breath and relaxed his shoulders.

"I'm sorry, Doug. This seems to have gone down the wrong track. First, I am not homophobic. Secondly, it doesn't matter to me personally." He took a deep breath and continued.

"However, and this is the reason you may have seen me frown, it matters to the police force if it opens you up to blackmail. It may be an accepted part of today's society, but, as you know from your own reaction, it is not universally accepted. As long as it has no effect on the performance of your duties if you were to be gay, I will say nothing to any of our colleagues. As I've found to my cost recently, they love to gossip and get in digs, however hurtful." Phil gasped for breath when he finished his tirade. Doug looked at him in wonder. He had never seen this mild inspector so aroused before.

"Thanks for being honest with me, Phil. Is it okay if I call you Phil, as we **are** discussing private matters? I shall be equally honest with you on the basis that this goes no further. You've put your finger on the hub of the matter. It may be what happened to my sister has made me wary of any relations with women. It may be something in my genes. I don't know. I did have a sense of… empathy with Miguel. It came as a complete surprise to me – well, more of a shock really. I never let my guard down, as you realise that I never divulged my true identity to him. It has disturbed me and I have to find out my real feelings. I do not intend to let my personal quest interfere with my official duties. I'll let you personally know the outcome, because I'm glad to have this chat with you. This way, if there should be any slip-up, you at least know the full facts. One last thing," Doug grinned, "I will refrain from calling you Daddy, despite the… fatherly chat you've given me!"

Phil smiled back and patted Doug on the shoulder. "If you weren't so big, I should put you over my knee and render some fatherly punishment." They both burst out laughing, causing the other two to turn round just as they were entering the police station.

"Hello, hello. Sharing a joke in private with my sergeant, Daddy Tyler?" John grinned.

"Well, as I'm the daddy, I was just giving young Doug some fatherly advice to watch out for all those budding Carmens in Spain." He looked at Doug and winked.

"They could be as beautiful as a certain Malay girl we know, eh, Phil?" Ron jibed, and they all entered the building with much friendly banter.

Doug rang Miguel, explained that he had a week's leave starting Saturday and that he would like to visit him. Was there a hotel he could recommend? Miguel was overjoyed and insisted Doug stay with him as he had a nice villa on the edge of town, with only his maid to keep him company.

"Suppose Masood sees you in Málaga? Won't he be suspicious?" John Langley asked, when he knew the trip was booked.

"First, I will shave my head in the current fashion. Second, I'll let this moustache that I started while I was in Norwich grow longer. Third, I will give up shaving, hoping a little designer stubble will help, and, finally, I will wear outrageous beach-type clothing. I don't think Masood ever saw me in really sloppy gear. Of course, I could always walk with a stoop and a limp." He laughed at the thought of it.

"Of course, you will have the advantage that now he's abroad and no doubt enjoying the fruits of his former illegal enterprise, he'll not expect you to be there. We have to be careful in our dealings with other authorities in case they've been infiltrated. So, for goodness' sake, keep out of trouble," John urged him.

"Don't I always! I'm a good boy, remember, guv." Doug clasped his hands and raised his eyes to the ceiling as if praying.

"Huh! You're no choir boy, but as Phil said, watch out for those *señoritas!*" John laughed salaciously. Doug grinned back at him.

"Don't worry about me. If I can resist our sex-starved policewomen, I'm sure I'll be safe with these foreign wenches."

"We've got sex-starved policewomen? Who are they? How do you know?" John cocked his head on one side and wagged his finger at Doug.

"What?" exclaimed Doug. "Do you mean the rumours I've heard about you and, let me see… WPCs Blakey, Green, Curtis, Wade, Neil and McLintock, to name but a few, are not true?" He dodged just in time to avoid the ruler John threw at him. Coughing deeply, John prepared his retort. He then leant forward and beckoned Doug to come closer, which he did cautiously.

"Wade, you say? Are you sure? I don't know how I've missed her," John whispered conspiratorially. Doug looked astonished at first, then, tongue in cheek, continued in like banter.

"Are condoms cheaper here or in Spain?"

"I don't know. I never use them!" Doug shook his head. *I'm wasting my time! John is known as the master of repartee. What chance have I got? One last go.*

"I can see Mrs Langley coming into the station. I must go and ask her why you never use condoms!" Doug was peering out of the window towards the building entrance. John leapt to his feet and rushed to the window.

"Gotcha!" Doug shouted as he left the room in a hurry.

CHAPTER 13

"**Who**?" Maurice exclaimed when Jeremy Cook told him he was wanted on the phone. He had been entering a new client's details and requirements on the computer system he had installed.

"Sean Anderson, I believe he said. Is he a possible client?" Jeremy repeated the name.

"Sorry, no!" Maurice paused to recover from the mental blow he'd received. "He's the former priest, whose... life-change resulted from the incident that imprisoned me." He nearly said downfall and quickly realised it would have been unnecessarily cruel. He reached for his phone as Jeremy transferred the call.

"Jenkins here," he announced, as formally as possible.

"Hello, Maurice. It's Sean Anderson. I'm back from Africa and I'm staying at the Red Lion in the Square. I wonder if you'd care to join me for lunch?"

The voice was flat, and delivered as if Sean was repeating a prepared sermon. There was no hint of delight at being back in Houghbury.

Perhaps I'm silly to imagine there'd be anything between him and Helen. "Certainly. Will one o'clock be all right?"

"Could you make it earlier, say twelve-thirty, as I've only got today to look up some old acquaintances? Tomorrow, I've got to go to London to settle matters with the Missionary Society."

It was agreed, and Maurice, although noting that there had been no mention of Helen, decided to take the afternoon off to forewarn her. Nicola and Roger were on a half-term holiday and he would have the chance to play with them. Jeremy didn't mind as he knew of Maurice's concern for the Phillips family, and that he always put in excessive hours for their clients.

The lunch was brief and both men had difficulty in trying to restore the jollity of their meeting in prison. Sean narrated some of his adventures in Africa and enquired about Helen in a deliberately casual manner. Maurice detected the hidden depth in the question and struggled to hide his jealousy.

"They're all fine, I think. I'm able to help them when needed." *Perhaps letting Sean know that will reduce his concern for them and isolate his true feelings.* The silence that followed his statement caused Maurice to continue.

"Miguel Santos came here looking for you. He was worried when you stopped communicating with him."

Sean noticed Maurice's reaction and, though he was not very experienced in romantic emotions, he was sure it was jealousy. *What a fool I've been to imagine I'd be the only suitor for an attractive widow like Helen. Her letters helped fill the void left by Maria, yet... before Maria, I'd never considered having a female companion. Have I been using her because of my loss... or do I have a genuine love for her? I think she has feelings for me. Are they kindness, compassion, or something deeper? I'll have to visit her to find the answer.* "Miguel? OH yes, of course, Miguel! I'm sorry. I was daydreaming. I must be tired from all the travelling. I've been very selfish... wrapped in my own misery. I completely forgot to tell him about my Africa assignment. Did he leave any message for me?"

Daydreaming about Helen, I bet, thought Maurice, who replied coldly, "No. I told him about your new vocation and he left me his email address to let him know when I heard any more about you." *I'm damned if I'll tell him any details. He can find out for himself. I'm not his messenger boy! Not that I know much anyway.*

"I'd be grateful if you'd let him know. I'll contact him when I get to London. I don't think there's Wi-Fi in this pub," Sean requested, as pleasantly as he could. He was eminently aware he was asking a favour from a possible rival. Maurice's inherent obligingness overcame his reluctance to assist someone who seemed destined to hurt him at every turn. They parted with a handshake as tentative as at the start of their meeting.

Maurice left immediately to visit Helen. Dismay at her obvious excitement at the news was cut short by the kids dragging him outside to play. Bodily, he was relaxed at play; mentally, he was distraught and ready to snap.

As soon as Maurice went outside, Helen dashed to her room, put on her finest, most alluring dress, and refreshed her hair and makeup. *He may not come! If he does, it could be a friendly visit, not that of a potential lover. Lover! I can't tell him about Maria! Why should I? All's fair in love and war!* She paused to look out of the window. *Just look at Maurice playing the fool with Nicola and Roger. I wonder how Sean will be with them? A very good father, I imagine. Father? Father Anderson! Will he be different as an individual father compared to being a minister of God? Just look at the way those two are treating poor Maurice. He's got the patience of a saint... which is what he needed to survive the injustice he suffered. What'll Sean do now that he's left the Church and finished his missionary work? He'll need some employment if he marries me. We might have to move. In some ways, that'd be okay as it would remove the memories of Arnold. Who am I fooling? Arnold will be with me wherever I go. Staying here would be nice. After all the friends and kind people I've got to know, and the children are very happy here. Whatever happens, they'll always be my priority.*

The doorbell interrupted her thoughts and she started to panic. Opening the door, she was faced with a leaner, tanned Sean. They nervously shook hands and she led him to the lounge. Once seated with a cup of tea, their conversation started like a sparring match, as each sought an indication of the other's true feelings.

"Oh! I see Maurice is here. He's like an overgrown child, the way he's behaving with those kids!" *How could I have ever seen him as a rival for this beautiful, mature woman?*

"Yes, he's very good with them," Helen replied automatically as she turned to look out of the window.

"He tells me he has a new job as a financial advisor. I'm surprised. I think he'd make a fine teacher, if he's keen on children." Sean thought out aloud and then to himself – *Why on earth am I rambling on about him? If he's really keen on Helen, the last thing I should be doing is drawing her attention to him. How can I express my... my desire for her?*

Helen, still looking outside, thought – *Yes, Maurice is full of surprises. No wonder Arnold believed in him.* She turned back to face Sean.

"Do you like children, Sean?"

"Of course!" He returned her gaze and was reminded just how desirable she was. *She's a fine woman. A good catch for any man. She almost makes me forget Maria. Ah, Maria. Before her... yes, before her, I'd never even considered a female in such a manner. Everything started with Maria!* He made a minor display of returning his cup and saucer to the side table to cover his thoughts.

"As a priest, I was trained to care for everyone at every age," he recited, as his emotions were momentarily recaptured by Maria.

Helen caught the negative sparkle in his eyes, as if his thoughts lay elsewhere. *Is he reminiscing on his service with the Church or… or is he still obsessed with that Maria? Perhaps his experiences in Africa have turned his desires elsewhere; perhaps to Miguel. No! His letters were full of emotion, and he's someone I'm sure I can trust.* "You must meet Nicola and Roger. I'll call them in." She broke the silence.

"No. Not just now. It's you I've come to see. I can always meet them some other time," Sean responded quickly. *It's hard enough knowing what to say to Helen without kids muddying the waters. Why am I finding this so difficult? What is holding me back?*

Helen's heart swelled at the words… *'It's you I've come to see'. He's going to propose! Why am I not completely overjoyed? What's wrong? Is it something else he said? He was a bit abrupt when I mentioned my children. Perhaps he doesn't really care for children and they are my greatest treasures. They'll have to be agreeable to any man I marry. I may have misjudged him on that. After all, he's never had the opportunity to get to know them as my Maurice has. My Maurice? What* am *I thinking?* She moved the tea things away as she was reasoning. *There's something else. How could I marry Sean on a dishonest basis?* She tightened her lips. *He entered my life on the rebound and was desperate for a shoulder to lean on, even if it was by letter. He's slid into any relationship we might have.* The sound of uncontrolled laughter made her look into the garden once more.

Dear Maurice. He's had a real struggle to win my friendship. No! My affection! Nicola and Roger adore him. She swallowed hard and mentally slapped her cheeks.

What a complete fool I've been! I've been dreaming of Sean when… when I… when I belong with Maurice! He's been here for me all the time and I've treated his feelings with contempt. They say love is blind and nobody could be worse than I've been… here it is, right under my nose all the time. I must be honest with Sean even if I've not been with myself. She stood up very briskly and faced Sean.

"Sean. I've something to tell you, and I hope you won't hate me for not telling you immediately." Sean got to his feet and placed his hands on her shoulders.

"How could I ever hate **you**? You're the one who's sustained me throughout my time overseas." He squeezed her gently. She stared into his eyes and swallowed hard.

"Your friend Miguel told me when he visited me recently. The M Caballeros who died in the coach crash wasn't Maria! It was her mother!" Sean stared at her, open-mouthed, unable to breathe.

"You mean my Maria is *alive*?"

"Yes." He pulled Helen to him and gave her a kiss so passionate it surprised them both. At that precise moment, Maurice was facing the window where Helen and Sean were embracing, preparing to throw a ball to Nicola. The ball fell from his hand as he dashed down the side of the house. Tears were streaming down his face as he jumped into his car and left, gasping for breath as he drove.

"Why didn't Miguel tell me?" Sean released Helen and stood back.

"He only found out just before coming here. Apparently, she's had an offer of marriage from a senior doctor. She felt compelled to try once more to find out why you never contacted her, before making a decision." Sean slouched in despair as he listened.

"You mean she's married now?"

"No. She agreed to wait for Miguel's news when he returned from England. So now she'll know you didn't contact her because you believed her to be dead. In fact, I'm sure she'll be most flattered to find out the effect that her possible death had on you. I'm sure I would be."

"Thank you! Thank you, dear Helen. Forgive me if I leave now. I want to speak to her as soon as I can. You'll be the first to know how things turn out." He gave her a peck on the cheek as she opened the door for him. "By the way… it's none of my business, but I think Maurice is in love with you."

She smiled and gave a knowing nod. She stood there long enough to wave goodbye then returned to the back of her house, deep in thought. *I nearly made a gross mistake in looking far afield for my knight on a white charger. I hope Maurice's patience and, hopefully, his love will forgive me for being so wrong about him and about Sean.* She adjusted her hair and dress unnecessarily to compose herself for one of the most defining moments in her life. With a moment's pause, she opened the back door and stepped confidently into the back garden. She seemed to have lost the mighty weight from her shoulders, which had been there since Arnold died.

"Mummy!" Roger and Nicola cried in unison as they rushed up to her.

"What's wrong with Maurice?" Nicola demanded.

"Where did Maurice go?" Roger begged.

"One at a time! Nicola, why is Maurice not here?" Helen held a hand of each one.

"About ten minutes ago, he went pale, dropped the ball and ran to his car."

"He looked very upset," Roger added. Helen looked at each in turn and then at the house.

"Which way was he facing when he dropped the ball?" she prompted them. They looked at each other, then Nicola answered.

"He was facing the house. Why?" Both were puzzled by their mother's look of dismay. *Oh my god!* She took a couple of deep breaths. *He saw through the lounge window Sean kissing me!* She clenched her fists and screwed up her eyes. *He's got completely the wrong idea! What do I do? I'll contact him... first thing. For now, I mustn't alarm these two.* She opened her eyes and forced a smile as she looked at her angels. "I think he probably remembered an urgent engagement." *Engagement! That's the whole problem!* "I'll speak to him later. Meanwhile, you two scamps had better get cleaned up ready for dinner."

Later, when Nicola and Roger were in bed and she had finished her domestic duties, Helen sat with her late cup of red bush tea, contemplating the events of the afternoon. *How can I tell Maurice how I feel about him* now? *He's bound to find out that Sean is not marrying me but is going to Maria. That should tell him the kiss he saw was from gratitude. It'll also mean my foolish dreams for Sean are shattered. To show my love for Maurice now could mean I've turned to him on the rebound and that he's merely my second choice. He might love me enough to accept me under that illusion, but it could always be a nagging thought for him...*

To do nothing could be worse! It could mean I don't even consider him despite my disappointment. I must *tell him! But how and when? Sean's in contact with him and will certainly tell him about Maria, though I'm surprised Miguel never told him. If Maurice really cares for me, he'll contact me to offer consolation and more support. Then I can explain how I told Sean about Maria when I finally appreciated that Maurice is my real love. That's it! Problem solved!* Her shoulders lowered as she relaxed.

"I **will** tell Maurice." She spoke her solution aloud as she rose to go to bed. "When **he** next contacts **me**!" she added positively. Worn out by the emotional events of the day, she was soon in the arms of slumber, dreaming of her new shining knight.

Sean never contacted Maurice about Helen. Was it a fit of pique, which made him avoid Maurice? Did he consider it an eye for an eye? As Maurice had not told him about Maria being alive, why should he tell Maurice about Helen's real love? Probably it was simply that in his haste to contact the person he worshipped above all others, he forgot, or thought Helen would do it. The latter explanation is the more Christian for a former priest. History is littered with problems caused by misunderstanding and a lack of communication. So it was with Helen and Maurice, with her waiting for a contact he never made.

He didn't contact her, believing she was betrothed to another. Such was his anguish he immersed himself in his new profession to the exclusion of everything and everybody. The longer the separation, the harder it became for each of them. It was possibly worse for Helen as her children could not understand Maurice's absence, and she found it increasingly difficult to make excuses.

CHAPTER 14

The wedding was intended to be a quiet affair in a register office, then the guest list took over. Birdie and Terry reasoned mutually that they had to invite those people who had played a part in the dramatic events of the past year, which had brought them together. Maurice, the prime mover, was first and already accounted for. Derek and his family were a joint decision, and the occasion was looked upon as a belated celebration of Sonia's good health news. Then Birdie felt duty-bound to invite her younger brother, David, who was a tour guide in Portugal and Spain, even though neither she nor Derek had seen him for years.

"I'd forgotten you had another brother!" Terry exclaimed.

"So had I – nearly! Since our parents died and he went abroad, we've had no news of him. I'll try to contact him through his firm, but I doubt he'll come." *He was only a teenager when he went. He could've changed jobs or got married or anything. He was always a fly-by-night.* Birdie kept her thoughts to herself.

Terry's list included Eileen, his secretary; Mrs Gumbrill *(just for a laugh, I was going to say and then thought it too cruel)*; Judith Donnelly with Charlie and Sid; the Phillips family and a couple of fellow professionals. Birdie never hesitated in agreeing to Sid, her much-changed would-be attacker. He had probably saved her life and had become a major item for her new friend, Judith.

Birdie's list included Tyler, Langley and Bennett with their wives. She limited those from her former workplace as she had not done any socialising apart from with Ivor. From the local police, they jointly agreed on Watson, Pollock and Baxter, and their wives.

"That's about thirty guests! It's a bit many for a hotel reception. I remember a few years back, a friend of mine had his reception in one of those community halls. It was quite successful as they'd a sort of disco for everyone to dance to." Terry looked from the list to Birdie.

"Sounds good, but I don't fancy a disco as some of our guests are, to put it politely, rather more mature. We could have party games and quizzes," Birdie mused.

"I'm not sure about games. I know what you mean about a disco. I saw an advert for barn dancing in the local press. I had a go once and it's great fun. You don't have to be able to dance, just follow instructions, and when things go wrong, as they usually do, everyone has a good laugh."

"Would it suit all ages?" Birdie was apprehensive.

"Yes, and the music is more country-style."

"Sounds hopping good to me."

"Very funny! I'd better get hall and caller booked immediately. Fortunately, I've made some useful contacts while I've worked here."

Terry pulled out all the stops. He got a recommended caller with a free date, who was able to provide a suitable venue as well. Luck was with them as there was a vacancy for a wedding at the register office on the same day.

"We're all set for three weeks from Saturday," Terry announced proudly.

"I can't believe it! It's too good to be true! Something must go wrong!" Birdie shook her head in disbelief.

"You of all people shouldn't be pessimistic. Life's thrown you enough disasters this past year, without you wishing for more."

"But getting with you has more than offset the bad things." She snuggled up to him suggestively and fluttered her eyelashes. He put his arms around her, breathing heavily into her ear.

"You know what I'd like to do now, my sensuous bride-to-be?"

"You're insatiable – my gorgeous husband-to-be." She put her arms round his neck.

"What I really want to do right away…" he whispered and then drew back and spoke aloud "…is send invites over the internet, or our guests won't have time to book the date." He just managed to dodge the full force of the blow as she swung at him.

"And I thought you were intent on leading poor, innocent me astray." She became serious. "I guess you're right. It gives them less than four weeks."

Maurice received the news of the wedding date with much satisfaction. Jeremy had advised him to take a couple of weeks' vacation as it was a quiet time of year for their business, and he sensed all was not well with Maurice's private life.

I need to get away from Houghbury for a little while. I need to fully recuperate from my time inside and to try to forget – or at least lessen –the loss of Helen. I need… there I go again, thinking of myself! Dammit! Why shouldn't I? What do I really want to do for a holiday? I know. I'll go walking. It'll be good to be on my own, enjoying as best I can the English countryside. It must be different and physically testing. The Lake District. I'll book one week to start with.

As it was the low season there, he found suitable accommodation quite easily. When he arrived, the weather was horrendous, with both strong winds and heavy rain. *This is just what I need! Walking in these conditions will be perfect. It'll limit the number of folk on the trails, and tax me physically, to reduce the pain in my heart. I love this rain beating on my face. It's more than a pleasure; it's exhilarating. It's better than a cold power shower! It's nature's own massage.*

Once, on the very top of a mountain, he spread his arms into the wind and rain and stood like that for several minutes, a miniature Angel of the North. Though his landlady was accustomed to the eccentricities of the many ramblers who had stayed over the years, Maurice was an original. He often returned from a day's hiking soaked and shivering, yet not once did he complain! She decided he was either mad or a masochist. He was her only guest, so she tried to chat with him when she served his meals.

He was not rude, but he was very restrained, and her experience of people made her recognise that he was suffering psychologically. It brought out her maternal instinct, much to the annoyance of her husband, who adopted a distinctly negative attitude to Maurice.

"I think he's on the run and has come here to hide!" the landlord growled.

"Don't be silly! He wouldn't draw attention to himself the way he goes tramping the hills. I think he's suffered some great loss and has come here to try and forget." They debated about their unusual guest, and any person less wrapped up in his own woes would have noticed.

One day, Maurice returned early from a particularly wet walk. The drenching had washed thoughts of Helen from his mind; only his current discomfort occupied him. The earlier time caused him to pass the village school as the children were leaving. Immediately, the memories of Nicola and Roger came flooding back. Passers-by would have been hard-pressed to realise the water on his cheeks was tears and not merely the rain. Trudy, the landlady, saw! When he had dried and changed into dry clothing, he went to the dining room for the offered cup of tea.

"It's not really my business, but you've been crying, Mr Jenkins. A trouble shared is a trouble halved, they say. I'm only a stranger, but I'm discreet, so treat me as your confessor." That word was the last straw. Maurice started to cry again and it gave Trudy the opportunity to comfort him. Although she was not that old, she reminded Maurice of his mother, and he opened his heart to her. Trudy listened in amazement to his experiences of the past year.

"No wonder you're upset. I vaguely remember my husband mentioning your case. You must put the past behind you and look to the future." She remembered the advice from some TV programme, but she could not remember which.

"Thanks for listening to my woes. I know I must look to the future, but what future is there for me without the woman... and kids... I love?" He blew loudly into his hanky.

"You had a life before all these incidents. You'll have one again. Who knows, perhaps your lady friend's had a change of heart. Keep an open mind and try to see everything as new." She was getting out of her depth, so she stood up briskly, as if setting an example. "I must get your dinner ready. How about another cuppa?" He nodded agreement and sat back. When she returned a few minutes later with his tea, he was sleeping peacefully.

At the end of the week, he considered his options. *I could easily stay for another week. There are dozens more trails for me to explore from here and the weather is much better. I feel a bit awkward with the landlady since that episode two days ago. I could take her advice, face up to my heartache and visit Helen. I'll go back early.* Friday was his last day in the Lake District. Having thanked the woman for her good service, and advice, he headed home.

He arrived outside Helen's house when it was dark. Sitting in his car, he stared at her drawn curtains for several minutes. *If I call on her now, out of the blue, what excuse can I give? I'd tell her how I love her. She probably knows that already. She's probably got Sean there right now – and the kids will be in bed. I'm very tired… so I'll sleep at home and decide in the morning.*

Waking very early, he thought through his main choices in facing Helen. *She won't want to see me. I'd add to her stress. It's – too soon. Yes! It's too soon. I've still got seven days' holiday. I'll go to the coast. I could do part of the South West Coast Path.*

CHAPTER 15

He left Houghbury as the sun began to rise and by noon he had obtained accommodation in Lyme Regis. After a light lunch, he went for a walk along the nearby cliffs. The sun was warming and there was a waft of sea air to inspire him. *What a change from last week. The turf underfoot is springy. I feel I could march to the ends of the earth. Better get back, though, as dinner is in less than two hours. Gosh! This place has altered my outlook! I'm actually thinking about food!* A ball landed close by, and he instinctively retrieved it and looked for the owners.

It's Roger and Nicola – no! It's a couple of kids just like them. He threw the ball to them, turned away and walked to the very edge of the cliff. *I can't free my thoughts of them. Is it always going to be like this? A nobody going nowhere is what I used to think, and it's equally true now. Look to the future, she said. Well, I've tried and it's not working.* To add to his depression, an ominous cloud covered the sun, and the ensuing gust of wind caused him to sway on the cliff edge. As he found himself staring down at the rocks below, his thoughts darkened further. *Why not? A few seconds' physical pain and I'd have the relief I seek.* He stared below and leant over a degree further. A hand gently caught hold of his elbow and a soft voice insisted firmly, "Better step back a bit, sir. The cliff edge is very crumbly here and these wind gusts are dangerous."

Maurice did as instructed obediently, all dark considerations thrust from his mind temporarily. *This savage wind has a tender touch* and *a sweet voice. No, it is human. The police? No, it's some interfering busybody!* He turned to gaze with wonder at a slight red-haired girl, a few years his junior. He had been about to tell his rescuer to mind her own business. Instead, he paused and then held out his hand to her.

"Thank you very much. It's silly of me to stand there like that. I was totally engrossed with distant thoughts. Come to think of it, you probably just saved my life. How can I ever repay you?" He managed to smile as he spoke. The girl returned his smile with an enchanting sparkle in her green eyes. In a photo, she would be described as attractive rather than pretty. In life, her eyes and facial expressions made her completely captivating. Behind her, an elderly man hobbled towards them with the aid of two walking poles.

"It's Mr Jay you should thank. He noticed you dangerously close to the edge and insisted I warn you." She lowered her voice to add, "He's my employer." Maurice caught the slight change in her expression, indicating she needed him to understand her relationship with Jay.

"I believe I have you to thank for rescuing me." He walked over to Jay and gave a small bow.

"Glad to be of service. Megan's a godsend for me. She reacted instantly when I pointed you out to her. She's my carer while I'm recuperating here," he announced clearly while shakily hanging on to his poles.

"We were on our way back to town when we saw you. Perhaps you'd care to join us for tea at my hotel?" Megan had gone behind Jay to assist him, and her face lit up as she nodded agreement.

"I'd be delighted to. You're most kind." *Usually, I'd decline such an offer as being merely a courtesy and not fully intended. This girl's bewitching me! There's something about her that brings out the animal in me! I've got to know her further.*

The short walk was very slow and would have been tedious but for the alluring presence of Megan. The taking of tea was most formal, and Maurice could hardly wait to leave. As Megan showed him from the hotel, they were able to converse privately. *This is all wrong. I'm in love with a wonderful woman who's rejected me for another man. Yet I have to see more of this seductress! What does it matter if I find solace elsewhere? It feels wrong, but what the heck? I'm fed up with always trying to do the right thing.*

"I'd like to see you again, Megan." *There, I've said it! She can only say no. She must have a legion of boyfriends and admirers.* His thoughts were interrupted by her stopping, turning towards him and grasping his hand with a suggestive squeeze.

"I'd like to see you too. Old man Jay goes to bed very early, so I could meet you in the hotel bar at nine o'clock. Unless you've somewhere better in mind. Now I must get back to him before he gets suspicious." She came so close to him as she turned back into the foyer that he could feel her warmth and her enticing scent; it was not the scent from a bottle!

"See you at nine then."

He barely noticed what food was put in front of him at his guesthouse. His mind was full of Megan and his need to satiate his growing animal lust. He had to exercise maximum restraint to avoid arriving early, so he forced himself to walk painfully slowly to her hotel. He hardly recognised her when she came to join him in the bar. She must have been wearing some form of uniform while on duty, because she had become even more desirable in a pale green evening dress, which matched her eyes and showed every curve of her figure to best advantage. As he stood up to greet her, she floated towards him, never taking her eyes from his. She stopped when their bodies were just in contact, then she reached up and gave him a quick peck on his cheek. With his right hand still poised to shake hers, he pinched himself with the left one.

I must wake up soon! This vision, this ultimately desirable woman, kissed me. No! She's just a tease, out to torment me. There has to be a catch. What could she possibly want from me? Am I another sucker in her nefarious plot to ruin all men? His mind reflected on the themes of the numerous TV series he had followed as a form of escapism from his old, lonely bachelor pad. *Does she want me to perform some criminal act; even to kill her employer? What else can it be? I'm neither rich, famous nor god's gift to the fair sex.*

"What would you like to drink, Megan?" He held out a chair for her, which she refused.

"It's too crowded here. Get a couple of bottles of Devon Red cider, or what do you fancy?" She grasped his hand.

*You, my little vamp! All I want is you, you and **you**!* He coughed to cover his licentious thoughts. "I'll have whatever you have." He lowered his voice and made it as suggestive as possible.

"Devon Red cider is a good drink for a promising friendship. They stock it here and it's not too expensive." She squeezed his hand once more. The pressure of her hand combined with the proximity of her body set off a time bomb inside him.

Expensive? She's thinking money! She could be a whore! What do I care anymore? I desperately want sex and she's available and, *I think, willing.*

"Nothing's too expensive for you, my dear. Where *can* we drink it?" *That's the naked truth of the problem! Naughty! Naughty! I'm letting my imagination get ahead of events. It would be too cold to drink outdoors, and my little B&B is certainly off-limits.*

"No problem. I've a room right here in the hotel. It's not large and is tucked away from the luxurious suites like Mr Jay's. Ask for a couple of glasses as well."

By the time she finished, Maurice was almost perspiring with anticipation. The bar staff hardly blinked at his order. He followed Megan to her room on the top floor, beyond the reach of the lift system. He could see nothing but her heavenly shape leading him to a possible paradise. Her divine legs moved from one step to the next with supremely crafted care and lightness. The looseness of her dress was unable to disguise the taunting vibration of her perfectly formed posterior. Reaching her room, she bent to undo the lock and must have known the effect that her curved back, silhouetted even more through her thin dress, would have on the now rampant male behind her. She would also know he was forced to resist by the drink and glasses he was carrying.

Oh, for god's sake, open the bloody door before I do something I'll regret. Nothing is going to stop me having carnal knowledge of this siren tonight! What am *I thinking? If something is too good to be true, then it's almost certainly not true! Hold your horses, Maurice. Try and restrain yourself.* She opened the door and they went inside. She turned to him and offered him a seat, which he took as he surveyed her in detail. *Well, I can* try *to – exercise restraint!*

"Take your coat off and relax while I open the cider." She used a bottle opener borrowed from the bar, as he obediently removed his coat.

"Do you often entertain men in your bedroom?" He immediately regretted speaking his thoughts aloud.

"**Pardon**?" she exclaimed.

"Sorry, I shouldn't have said that. It's just that I'm not used to this sort of thing!" *Oh hell! I should just shut up and leave.* He started to rise, but she stopped him and handed him a glass of cider. She noted his embarrassment and smiled knowingly as she seated herself opposite him.

"What *sort* of thing are you referring to?" She tried to look indignant.

I've nothing to lose, so I might as well tell her all. Perhaps she'll reciprocate. He explained why he had been so depressed on the cliff; how he had been so grateful for her intervention; how he'd been so attracted to her.

"So you see, my dear, you're an angel sent to rescue me, but you became an object of my…" he coughed "…lust. In my wildest dreams, I'd never have considered being in such a tempting situation with such a beautiful woman like you!" He gulped a large mouthful of the cider and nearly choked. The sincerity of his statement and his fraught face nearly stopped her from teasing him further.

"So!" She paused. "You want to have your wicked way with me?" She leant forward and peered into his eyes, which he averted. Instead of replying, he took another swig of cider.

"You love another woman, yet you want to make love to me?" She reached out and turned his face towards her.

"Yes," he answered hoarsely as her touch reignited his passion.

"Snap!" she retorted.

"What do you mean – snap?" Her exclamation bewildered him.

"I mean I too love another, but I'd like *you* to make love to me. You see, my love's been working abroad for more than a year, and – to put it crudely – I'm missing my oats!" He gazed at her in astonishment.

"Have you been unfaithful to your boyfriend before?"

"No! Have you?"

"I haven't got a boyfriend," he joked as he relaxed.

"No! Your lady friend!" she retorted, giving him a mock punch.

"Ouch!" He winced in mock pain. "She only… well, she was never more than a friend. Then she chose to bestow her love on that damn priest. It only happened about two weeks ago. So you're the first one I've wanted."

"I've caught you on the bounce!" She placed her hand over her eyes and bowed her head. "You're just making do with me as the first available female."

He stared at her for a few moments. *Hell's bells! Why can't I explain myself better? My need for this girl is scrambling my mind. I can think of nothing else!* Then he noticed a faint smile on her lips, so he got on his knees in front of her. Clasping her arms, he tried to pull her hands from her face.

"Oh no, sweet Megan. It's more – much more than that. I'd never remotely considered sex with anyone other than Helen until I met you. You saved my life in more ways than one. You reminded me that life *is* worth living." As her hands came away from her face, it was revealed with a broad grin. "**Right**! You can explain yourself now," he insisted.

"Well, I've sexual desires that I've managed to suppress so far. When I saw you on the cliff edge, it triggered something inside me. Somehow, I felt responsible for you and – I had to have you." She paused to study him. "Now I know you better, I see you more as a friend and kindred spirit."

Her careful selection of words calmed his primeval urges for a while. *She's right! Does this alter things or – gosh, that cider is certainly having an effect on my loins!* "You took the words out of my mouth. I did see you solely as an object of overpowering lust. Now I've real respect for you."

"Oh! You didn't respect me before?" She returned to her taunting.

"Of course I did, but in a different way." He was pressed against her knees and he released her arms to run his index fingers gently down from her forehead to her shoulders. Then he brushed her breasts very, very slowly and continued down to her waist, which he encircled, pulling her to him. The movement obliged her to open her legs so he could embrace and kiss her. Their lips touched ever so gently at first, then parted, and their tongues performed a time-honoured battle as they endeavoured to encompass each other totally. Finally, they separated in an attempt to breathe once more. Silence!

They remained facing each other, resembling spectators in a gallery, studying works of art. Still pressed between Megan's knees, Maurice put his hands under her dress and very, very slowly caressed her with his fingers on the outside of her silken thighs. To Megan, it was the sensation of gossamer wings fluttering towards their ultimate goal, the honeypot at the apex of her thighs, almost quivering in agonising anticipation of the delights to follow.

"Quick," she breathed huskily.

"Slow, slow," he whispered back, continuing his progress millimetre by millimetre.

"Quick, quick."

"Slow, slow."

"This is no foxtrot," she giggled.

"No. More of a morris dance for two, and I'm the fiddler," he announced as his fingers slithered behind her panties. She gasped, pushed him away and stood up abruptly.

"You're right. This is not something we should rush into." She put one hand on her hip and wagged the other at him. He was too embarrassed to stand, as it would have revealed the size of his manhood.

"Does this mean I should go?" He tried to hide his disappointment. She leant towards him.

"No, no. I mean you're right not to act quickly. This must be performed as slowly as possible and with as much grace as we can muster." Her cheeks were flushed as she leant over until she was able to lightly run her fingers over the obvious bulge in his trousers. Kneeling before him, she painfully and slowly began to undo the zip to reveal black pants struggling to contain his erection. He gulped awkwardly.

"Oh, Sir Jasper! Are you trying to conceal something from me in your underwear? I'm only an innocent lass from the backwoods, you know, and I can't imagine what treasures you have concealed there." She hung her head and fluttered her eyelashes.

Jeez! She wants to play-act! I know I started slowly to arouse her, but I'm now so aroused I don't know how I can constrain myself. Wicked Sir Jasper, eh? Right, I can fill that role as well as I intend to fill her.

"Don't play innocent with me, my girl! As your lord and master, I'll do what I want with you. Now take all your clothes off so I may judge your suitability." He pushed her over as he stood up.

"My suitability for what kind, sir?" she whimpered coyly.

"Why, for a physical conjoining which will leave you fulfilled and enriched for life." he castigated her.

"You mean you'll pay me for my labours, sir?" She gazed up at him as if in awe.

"Not in terms of money but in terms of the most beautiful

orgasm." She frowned and, turning her head slightly, she looked at him out of the corners of her eyes.

"Can I choose the colour myself?" It was his turn to frown.

"It's a very personal thing and I'm not sure if people see any colour."

"Do you mean it'll be a white dress, sir?" She had a faint smile as she asked.

"What the hell's a dress got to do with anything?" He pretended to rage at her.

"The dress I'll be making from this organza you're giving me." She fluttered her eyes again.

"Not organza, you silly girl! Orgasm!" he enunciated carefully.

"But, sir, what good is that to me? Where I live there are organisms everywhere."

"No, no! The word is… oh, what the heck! Was it pleasant when I stroked you with my fingers?"

"Oh yes, sir, very pleasant. A real pleasure, sir, to be sure, a real pleasure." She raised her face to him and beamed happily, causing him temporarily to lose his stern look.

I'm actually enjoying this role-playing. I shall have to be careful I don't get carried away and hurt her as my character would've. He resumed his Jasper expression. "Well, this dance I am going to teach you will be a thousand times more pleasurable. Now get those clothes off, before I rip them off!" He made as if to grasp her dress and she backed away with her hands crossed over her for protection.

"I'm not undressing until I've seen what you're hiding in your pants… sir." She came close and undid his belt. He placed his hands on her shoulders, pretending to try and stop her as she pulled down both trousers and underpants.

"Oh, poor Sir Jasper, you must've been in such pain with

this hard thing squashed in your pants. Let me stroke it better."

Aargh! Damn restraint! All I can see or feel or think of is this gorgeous woman. He reached down and lifted her across the room onto her bed. She devoured his head and shoulders and tried not to giggle as he fumbled to undress her. As he prepared 'to have his wicked way' with her, she pushed him off.

"Why, Sir Jasper, I noticed you hobbled across the room. Won't we enjoy the dance more if you remove *your* clothes completely?" He complied, and finally they were able to satiate their overwhelming desires.

There was no more taunting; no more play-acting; no more speaking as they explored each other's bodies in some horizontal gymnastics requiring their full mental, physical and spiritual concentration. Gone were any thoughts of their erstwhile partners and possible recriminations. Gone were thoughts of neighbours, landlords or employers. Gone were cares about any biological consequences. All that mattered was the very noisy here and now! Climax followed climax until they became aware of someone banging on the wall. Reluctantly prising themselves apart, they smothered their laughter with the bed covers.

"Uh-oh! It's nearly midnight! I'd better dash back to my digs." Maurice started to dress.

"That's it! Have your wicked way with me, and then abandon me." She gave a highly artificial sob.

"No, Megan, it's not that. I'm thinking of your reputation." He continued dressing.

"And yours," she responded.

"I won't deny it." He pulled on his coat. And continued. "I've had a fantastic, life-changing experience tonight. One I'll never forget." Megan slid out of the bed, crossed slowly to him, pressed her naked thighs against him and wriggled.

"Same time, same place tomorrow then?" She breathed the words huskily as she reached up to kiss him. Spent force though he was, Maurice felt a stirring, gulped and nodded.

"Okay. Same cider, my little innocent rustic," he joked, and reluctantly left.

His landlady was none too pleased at being roused to let him in.

"I did tell you we lock up at eleven, Mr Jenkins!"

"Yes. I'm very sorry. I met an old friend and lost all sense of time. It won't happen again. I'll make certain I'm in before eleven tomorrow."

Five more nights! Those nights of tempestuous sex filled his mind and drained his body. *Six nights of lovemaking is almost poetic as the Latin for six is, of course, sex.* For Maurice, his plan to walk the South West Coast Path was forgotten as he used the daytime for recuperation – lazing on seafront benches or grassy banks. He found himself counting the minutes until he was with Megan again. The only blemish in his temporary heaven was when he closed his eyes; he pictured Megan with Helen's face. *Time will heal. It must heal.* For Megan, her age advantage was lost in seeing to the needs of Mr Jay. Fortunately, he thought her increased slowness was in deference to his age.

Friday night came much as the others, until it was time to part. The moment of their final farewell brought an awkward silence. *I've lost Helen. Do I want to lose Megan as well? How do I know if we've something deeper and potentially long-lasting?*

"Ships that pass in the night or a simple holiday romance? What do you think this has been?" She spoke jocularly, intervening in his thoughts, yet there was sadness in her eyes.

"More. Definitely something more. Much as I hate to leave you, we must look on the favourable side of this parting."

"Favourable side?" All pretence of jollity was gone as she protested loudly.

"Yes, we've had a fantastic week – well, I've had one. I've loved your company and, of course, our erotic evenings. If there is even greater depth to our relationship, absence will help to prove it. Much as you might have replaced Helen in my heart, I have to be certain. I don't know how you really feel about me, if indeed you do have any depth of feeling for me. If you do, then you'll need to know if it replaces your love for your absent boyfriend."

"I suppose you're right." She paused to examine his face. "It's been a kind of magical week and we need to know if that magic will last." She pulled at her earlobe as she thought. "I'm only with Mr Jay a little longer, then I return to London. Perhaps I could call in on you on the way back?" she implored.

"It's a bit soon for a real test, but a passing visit shouldn't hurt."

He agreed with minimal reluctance and nodded. *I'm weak. I should've refused. I'll just have to steel myself for the visit. Again, looking on the bright side, I'll be able to see her on my own patch. See how she'd fit in.* Fit in? *What* am *I thinking?* With a quick kiss, they parted reluctantly.

CHAPTER 16

Doug left for Spain with advice from every quarter fermenting in his mind. *Cheeky but understandable, I suppose – Birdie Lee sending me a request through my guv to check on her long-lost brother. If she'd trouble finding that he's in the Málaga area, I doubt if I'll be able to help much while I'm checking on Masood! Then there's Miguel. He's the key to my personal quest to understand my true nature. What do I feel about him? What should I feel?*

He stretched his legs as much as he was able to on the plane. *How do I behave when I meet him? He's really… really what? Upset me? It's more like he's destabilised me! I've been in strange situations and always had confidence in my ability to cope before.*

"Coffee, please." A stewardess invaded his self-contemplation.

Was Miguel just being friendly? Perhaps all gay men are like that when you meet them face to face. If I am attracted to him, does that make me gay? Or could it be… friendship? Fellow souls in a mixed-up world? What does he think the reason for my visit? Can I trust him if I tell him my real purpose? Will he think less of me? Do I care what he thinks? Well, yes, I believe I do care. I'll have to test the waters, so to speak, before I make any decision. He drank some of his coffee. *There's always this David Lee. He'd have his finger on the pulse of any lowlife in the* region – *young men abroad often know more about the shady side of life than they ever would at home.*

He paused to scratch his beard. It had started as designer stubble, then some classical paintings helped him decide to grow it further. Even after several months, it was still enough of a novelty to make him keep touching it. Colleagues noticed, and called him everything from Don Juan to the Thinking Man or the Professor. Soon, coupled with the way he always seemed to be deep in thought, the last became his nickname. As he swallowed the remainder of the coffee, he tried to concentrate his thoughts on his official task. *Masood! Did he leave England simply because his contacts had been exposed? He could've been due to be replaced in some cunning plan to confuse us. If he'd been considered a failure or expendable, he'd have been eliminated as the Turkish chief was...*

Unwittingly, he clicked his fingers and inclined his head. *Hang on, Doug! Why was the Turk killed in England? He could've been killed in any country. Was it in England because that's where the decision was made? That'd make Masood not only the UK boss but the overall headman! That's why he's in southern Spain, where Interpol reckon the criminal HQ is. Should I tell Bennett and Langley? No! They already believe me to be over-obsessed with Masood. I need to let somebody know, in case anything happens to me. I'll send myself a letter detailing my suspicions. If anything does happen, someone's bound to open it.*

He glanced around the aircraft at the other passengers. *Hello! Why's that pretty girl with the auburn hair smiling at me? Oh my god! I automatically smiled back in politeness and she's raised her eyebrows rather suggestively. It must be the beard.* Doug had always returned smiles to people. He had never considered that women could have an ulterior motive until this blatant passenger. He quickly turned to look out of the window. *I'm slipping! I actually feel embarrassed! This hasn't happened to me in years. I've always been master of any situation. Something's changed! Are my basic emotions ruling me? Jeez, this seat's cramped. My own fault, I suppose. I should've made this an official trip and had the Force upgrade me to business class. On the other hand, if someone on this flight recognised me, they'd be more suspicious. Slow down, Doug! Plan! As this is primarily a vacation, I'll start with Miguel. Right! I'll greet him as just a new friend, and grateful for his hospitality. I'll see what follows.*

His relief was visible to anyone observing him, as it was to the buxom girl with the long auburn hair. Damn! I must've turned as I was thinking, and that woman thinks I'm looking at her. Doug turned his head and read the provided newspaper for the remainder of the journey.

Once landed, Doug rushed to escape the femme fatale, but she was too quick and engaged him in conversation as they were processed into Spain. Even the baggage was against him – theirs came off almost together.

"You're here for one week and I'm here for a week and our bags came out together. This must be an omen." She breathed the words suggestively as she blatantly leant against him.

Momentarily lost for a more suitable retort, he muttered, "Quite a coincidence." He lengthened his stride towards the exit. Undeterred, she kept pace.

"Where are you staying?" she asked determinedly.

"With my friend over there," Doug replied with relief as he spotted Miguel waiting for him. The Spaniard was even more flamboyantly dressed than usual and waved effeminately at him.

"Oh… I see. Have a good time," she muttered in

disappointment as she moved away from him. Miguel advanced on Doug with arms outstretched.

"Nice to see you again, Miguel," Doug announced as breezily as he could, and offered his hand. Miguel took it in both of his in true presidential style, but with genuine warmth. The touch caused a ripple like iced water to run down Doug's spine. *I should never've come. I'm totally lost! I feel... I feel I want to hold this wonderful man tight in my arms.* They gazed into each other's eyes, and Doug squeezed Miguel's hand as if it was the most natural thing to do. They remained like statues as others swirled around them.

Miguel showed Doug around his villa, with some emphasis on the comforts of his own bedroom. His maid had provided them with a light lunch, which they enjoyed while Doug's bag was still in the entrance. *He's not said, yet I know he's waiting for me to decide where to sleep. It's the moment I've been dreading. I'll just have to trust him and tell him where I stand... or sleep.* "Miguel, it's time I tell you about myself. Firstly—"

"Don't tell me **you're** a priest," Miguel interrupted despondently. Doug frowned at the accusation and continued.

"No. Firstly, I'm a detective with the London Metropolitan Police."

"Oh! The Met."

"Yes. I had to tell you, and I'm trusting you not to tell anyone else," Doug entreated. Miguel leant forward and squeezed Doug's knee.

"I'm disappointed, but your secret is safe with me. It sounds exciting." He looked around as if seeking interlopers. "Are you on an undercover job now?"

Doug placed his hands on Miguel's. "Partly. This brings me to point two, which is the main reason I'm here."

"Which is?" Miguel questioned hopefully.

"A voyage of discovery!" Doug announced grandly as he sat upright. "I've always been a bit of a loner; I've never had many close friends." He paused, seeking the right words. "Until I met you, I never had any reason to doubt my sexuality."

"And now?" Miguel tightened his grip on Doug's knee.

"You have stirred something within me that I didn't know existed. I know you're gay. I've never been homophobic, but I never *ever* considered that I might be gay. I'm still not sure. I want to…"

Miguel put his other hand on Doug's other knee. "Want what?"

"That's just it! I'm not sure. I want to be your friend and to be with you, but I'm not sure about anything deeper," Doug blurted out.

"You mean actual sex."

"Er… well… yes."

"As you 'ave opened up to me, Doug, I shall do ze same," Miguel announced calmly, but Doug noticed the lapses in his previously almost perfect English. "I 'ave 'ad many friends. One was an Englishman I thought might be special. 'E is still a good friend, although 'e chose a woman instead of me. When I met you in 'Oughbury, I thought you were the partner I 'ave always dreamed of. Back 'ome, I try to forget you as… as the song says… as an impossible dream. Now you are 'ere and my dream could be real. I think this could be special for both of us, so you're right in a way. We mustn't rush things. You'll 'ave ze guest room and we shall be the best of friends. I'll do my normal routine and we'll meet at other times. I'll 'elp you with your duties, if I may, and I'll show you my beautiful country." Miguel finished, gave a final squeeze to Doug's knees and stood up. "Now I'll take your bag to your room."

Doug's shoulders dropped as he finally relaxed and he got to his feet. "Don't tell me you can cook as well?" he laughed. Miguel feigned injured pride and raised his eyebrows quizzically.

"You mean ze way to a man's 'eart is through 'is stomach."

"I suppose so," Doug replied awkwardly.

"Yes, I can. If I 'adn't gone into 'airdressing, I was going to be a chef. Now," he put down Doug's bag and turned to face him, "can you cook?"

"Being on my own, I've not had much opportunity to demonstrate my skills. I can do many traditional British dishes, and because I enjoy dining at good restaurants I attended a French cooking course for a time. I had to give it up when it clashed with my work."

"So! Ve should be able to reach each ozer's 'eart," Miguel stated, adding with a note of alarm, "Don't step in zat dog mess!" Doug quickly stepped aside, saw there was no mess and clutched his knee.

"Aargh! Twisted my knee." Miguel dropped the bag and reached to help Doug, who burst out laughing.

"Touché, my Miguel."

"My Miguel! I like zat." He reached up and kissed Doug's cheek.

Later, after dinner, Miguel posed the question that had been troubling him since learning of Doug's official reason for being there. "'As your vork 'ere got anysing to do viz zis man 'oo 'ates ze Met zat I found out about?" Doug decided to tell him the full story, including his personal reasons.

"No wonder *Señor* Jenkins warned me to steer clear of this Ali Parouk, though I don't know vat 'e looks like. Vy is 'e 'ere, do you t'ink?"

"Parouk was head of the criminal organisation in England,

so he may have retired here or come to take charge. Do you know what the flats are like?"

"Some are very big, but zey 'ave a nice position on ze seafront. I can show you it if you like?"

"No, better not. For your safety, it'll be best if we're not seen together."

"You're ashamed to be seen with me!"

"No! No! These are dangerous people. If I'm recognised, I could be in danger, and so would anyone they thought was working with me."

"I don't like ze thought of you in danger. Can't I 'elp you in any way?"

"Yes. I'll need your local knowledge. Don't worry about me. I've been in many a tight spot, but I don't believe they'd risk harming me, in case it draws attention to their presence here. I'll try and act like a normal tourist."

"Von't zey trace you back 'ere?" Miguel was becoming alarmed.

"Perhaps I could get back here by a hidden route?"

"Very difficult, for two reasons. One, zis villa is well away from bus routes yet is very prominent. Secondly, I may be compromised already, as I'm quite well known and lots of people saw us togezer at the airport."

"Damn! I was so busy worrying about what I was going to say to you that I overlooked that possibility. To not be seen together now would look more suspicious." Doug stroked his beard and Miguel pursed his lips as they each sought an answer to their dilemma.

"If you vouldn't be too embarrassed, ve could be seen together as… dare I say it… as lovers," Miguel suggested tentatively.

Doug stared at him. *Lovers? That's a bit presumptive! What* would *anyone think who knows me? I'd never live it down! Hang on! What would they think? They'd think I'm a closet gay here to meet my secret lover. Besides, if I truly have a strong affection for Miguel, I should welcome the chance to be seen with him.* His face blossomed into a warm smile.

"You're a genius… **my** Miguel. If anyone does recognise me, they'd think I was here for you." Miguel rose and started to clear the table. Passing Doug, he leant over and gave him a passionate kiss. Doug was startled but did not object.

"A reˋearsal, my dear Doug. You'll 'ave to accept my affection more naturally in public."

Doug looked at his potential lover and said sincerely, "I'd be honoured to."

The next day set a pattern for the rest of the week. Miguel drove to his salon with Doug, where they embraced, kissed and went their separate ways. This became a ritual when they met for lunch and for the journey home. The second morning, Doug tested the waters by trying to find David Lee. He was dressed in the required fashion to mingle with holidaymakers. His only link was the travel company David worked for. They checked their records and found he had left a few years ago. He was leaving their office when one of their employees spoke.

"I've seen him around town recently. He may be living at his old address." Doug noted the details and checked them on his map. Miguel advised him at lunch the best way to get there.

A pretty young man with almond-shaped pale brown eyes and short blond hair answered the door.

"Can I help you?" he asked bluntly as he surveyed his visitor.

"David Lee?" Doug questioned laconically. *What a sight! He's so delicate and attractive he could be a woman. Help! I'm starting to measure the looks of a* man. *Miguel has a lot to answer for. Pretty he may be, but he also looks gormless!* The object of Doug's appraisal had his mouth open and was regarding Doug from head to toe in an insolent manner.

"Lee? I t'ink...."

You certainly do! Doug thought as he caught the pungent body odour emanating from the man.

"I t'ink 'e was 'ere before me." Doug covered his mouth to suppress his laugh, turning it into a cough.

"Do you have a forwarding address for him?"

"No, if I meet someone 'oo know 'im, do you 'ave message I give zem?"

This local yokel's English is poor, but I'll tell him Sergeant Lee's news so at least I can say I tried. Doug hurriedly explained about the wedding and left for some fresh air. As soon as he had gone, the blond lad made an urgent phone call.

"I've just had a large British tourist asking for me. I put him off by pretending to be someone else. I think he believed me, because he didn't press hard." He listened to the reply and continued. "It seems my sister is getting married soon and I'm invited." He paused to listen again. "She's a sergeant with the London police, Birdie Lee. What's wrong, boss?" He listened intently. "Okay, I'll be there soonest."

Making sure he was not followed, David Lee took a roundabout route to his appointment with his boss. Meanwhile, the latter had referred the problem to a higher authority and received instructions. David was amazed at how seriously the incident was treated. He was given instructions.

"Pack essentials and move to this flat in Alicante. There you are to contact your sister on the grounds you have received third- or fourth-hand news of her wedding. El Herrero's associate has been very upset by her. How close are you to your sister?"

"She's nothing to me. She's just a stuck-up, self-opinionated goody two-shoes. I hate her guts, and I'd rather not have anything to do with her."

"El Herrero wants to test your allegiance and your potential. How far are you prepared to go?"

"As far as it takes."

"Would you kill your sister?"

"Yes! Yes! With pleasure!" David never hesitated.

"We'll be in touch soon. Now pack and move quickly."

That evening, Miguel could see that Doug was troubled, so he pressed him about his worries. Doug explained his visit on Birdie's behalf.

"You've done your duty, so what more can you do?"

"It's that young man."

"Oh, are you trying to make me jealous?"

"He was certainly pretty, but he smelled horrible and appeared to be a trifle stupid."

"So what's the problem?"

"I'm not sure. I've been casting my mind back and… that's it! It's what he said! The first thing he said to me was 'Can I **help** you?' When I asked for David Lee, his demeanour and his speech changed."

"'Ow?"

"The rest of the conversation was that of a local trying to speak English."

"So?"

"Don't you see? Before I mentioned David Lee, he said *help* with a positive '**h**'. Afterwards, he didn't pronounce a single one. I'll have to visit him again."

"You take care. Sounds serious to me. Do you vant me to come vit you?"

"No. I'll be okay."

The next morning, Doug went to the address again. He knocked. There was a slight pause, as if someone was observing him through the security glass. The door opened and a large swarthy man grabbed Doug's arm and tried to pull him inside, where another thug was waiting. Doug's training and fitness produced an immediate response. He grabbed the door jamb with his free hand and wrenched his assailant into the street. He stepped aside as the second man attempted to grapple with him, and pushed him over his fallen buddy. He was about to run when a hand on his shoulder spun him round. Quickly, he lashed out and was barely able to stop hitting a policeman.

"*Qué está pasando aquí?*"

Doug nearly answered in his schoolboy Spanish, which might have been out of keeping with the holidaymaker image he was trying to portray. "Ah, Officer. These men attacked me. I'm glad you rescued me."

"*Una momento, señor.* I must speak to ze oders." He went to the thugs who were now standing. "*Por qué atacas a este hombre?*" He pointed at Doug.

"El Herrero *lo quiere,*" one replied curtly.

"*Ah,* El Herrero! *Deja esto a mí.*" He turned back to Doug; he smiled reassuringly. "Deez men 'ave made mistake. Zay are sorry. For your protection and to record your 'urt, I take you to *comisaría de policía.*" He took Doug's arm and guided him away from the thugs.

"Thank you," Doug replied humbly. *My Spanish is not good, but I reckon this Herrero person controls this officer as well as the thugs. I'll play along for now.*

One part of his training, which he had developed, was map reading. Thus, before he looked for David Lee, he had memorised important features of Málaga including, through force of habit, the police station. He quickly realised he was being led in the wrong direction, which confirmed his lack of trust in the policeman. *This is awkward. I can hardly tell the officer he's going the wrong way. I can't assault him, but I can't allow myself to be put in unwarranted danger. If this person, El Herrero, is prepared to use force to meet me, he probably has evil plans for me. On the other hand, I think it'd clear the air and verify my position as a genuine tourist. I'll have to risk it.*

"Excuse me, sir, I'd like to cut through this next street and tell my boyfriend where I'm going."

"Your boyfriend?" The officer regarded Doug with some surprise.

"Yes. You probably know him – Miguel Santos, the hairdresser."

The officer stopped and stared at him. "Miguel Santos is **your** friend?"

"Yes. He's the reason I'm visiting Málaga on my vacation."

"Vy vere you at ze 'ouse vere zey attack you?"

"I was asked by a friend of a friend to find her brother. His old employer said he used to live there. It's the last time I do a favour for someone I don't know."

"So you're 'ere on 'oliday visiting your friend Santos? You're lucky not to get 'urt by dose men. Are you frightened?"

In for a penny...! The truth may cause ripples or, if the criminals already know who I am, it'll be the best option to back my story. "I'm in the London police. That's why I admired the way you dealt with the situation back there."

"You are viz ze London police! Zat explain vy you 'andle yourself so well. Let's go see *Señor* Santos."

The change in attitude was very marked. *Either he thinks he has enough information to satisfy this Herrero character or he's not bent enough to put a fellow policeman in danger.*

When they arrived at Miguel's salon, Doug went in boldly before the officer, winked at Miguel and gave a sign, which prompted Miguel to hug and kiss him.

"Miguel, I'd like you to meet this kind officer who rescued me from an assault by a couple of thugs." The officer had watched with amazement and some embarrassment. He now found his hand being shaken vigorously with a light grip by Miguel.

"*Usted ha sido muy amable en el rescate de mi amante. Si puedo ayudar a usted o los suyos, sólo házmelo saber.*"

"*Encantados de estar de servicio, Señor Santos. ¿Este caballero queda con usted.*"

"*Sí, vive conmigo. Yo me ocuparé de él ahora y tratar de mantenerlo fuera de problemas.*"

"*Señor*, I leave you vith your... friend." The officer made a slight bow and prepared to leave.

"May I speak with you outside for a moment, please?" Doug requested, and walked outside with the officer. "I have a great favour to ask you. Can you make sure the London police do not know about my relationship with *Señor* Santos. They don't know I'm gay, and it'd be very embarrassing if they found out. As one policeman to another, can I ask you this favour?"

"*Señor*, I understand. I keep it secret." He nodded and strode away.

If he's associated with Masood's gang, he'll tell them, but it'd reinforce my cover story. He returned to Miguel for a translation of his conversation with the officer, which had been too fast for him to understand. Miguel gave him a rough idea of what had been said, emphasising that he had told the officer they were lovers.

"Blimey! No wonder he smiled so salaciously when I asked him to keep our friendship secret. Still, it'll help to reinforce my reason for being here. Thank you for playing your part."

"Playing, Doug? I wasn't playing! I vas expressing my love for you. You said ze officer and ze ruffians mentioned El 'errero! Even I've heard of 'im. 'E's some sort of top criminal who uses the nickname because 'e thinks it makes 'im sound… grander or more sinister. In English, ze name means 'ze smith', in ozer words, one 'oo forges metal."

"The best I can do now is play the tourist and await developments." Doug's impatience showed.

"In zat case, ve can 'ave ze 'ole day togezer tomorrow, and I'll show you ze sights," Manuel stated emphatically.

That night, after liberal amounts of Rioja, they retired to their respective rooms. Some time later, Miguel slid into Doug's bed and embraced him gently. Doug found himself returning the caresses until their rising passion reached a climax. They spent the remainder of the night in an entwined slumber.

Dawn, and Doug woke first, disengaged himself from his new bed partner and went for a shower. *My life thus far has prepared me to feel guilt, even disgust, after such an experience. I feel neither! I… feel fulfilled! Until now, my existence consisted of striving for success in my work and mental and physical attainment outside.* He left the shower and grabbed a towel.

I have climbed to the peak of a happiness that I never knew existed. There is no void in my life anymore. Miguel has filled the emptiness left by the death of my sister. Whoever said it was right: a life shared is a better life.

CHAPTER 17

After a morning driving round various points of interest, Doug and Miguel had lunch in a tapas bar overlooking the sea. As they exited, a hand tapped Doug's shoulder.

"Evans? Is that you?" The familiar authoritative voice froze Doug and he slowly but obediently turned to face his inquisitor. It was Thwaite!

"Yes, sir," Doug replied from habit.

"What brings you to Málaga?" *Thwaite, you evil shite. I owe you for Kowalski!* Doug paused, ignored the question with difficulty, and turned to Miguel.

"Miguel, may I introduce you reluctantly to my former boss, Thwaite, who was sacked for bribery and corruption."

"There's no need for that, Evans. It was all a mistake and it's all water under the bridge now."

"It may be for you, but not for those who knew Kowalski."

"That was **not** my doing!" He changed the subject by looking at Miguel. "Who's your friend?"

"This is Miguel Santos, one of Málaga's top hairdressers. I'm spending my holiday with him. How come you're here?"

"I've a small apartment in that block over there. Now I'm retired…" he gave Doug a meaningful look "…I spend more time here, and I expect you will too." He gave Doug another look, but with a different meaning, and glanced towards Miguel.

The latter responded quickly. "I sincerely 'ope so!" He reached out and squeezed Doug's hand. Doug's heckles were aroused and he returned the squeeze.

"I'm sure your colleagues in the Met will be interested," Thwaite said with menace.

"As you said earlier, Thwaite, there's no need for that. As we could bump into each other again, I suggest we act civilised and keep our own knowledge to ourselves."

"Agreed. I bid you good day, gentlemen." He gave a mock salute and departed.

Doug watched him closely. *For a man who's been shamed, he's mighty unrepentant. They say honesty has its own rewards. In his case, it seems to be dishonesty. I bet his flat was given or at least loaned to him by Masood's crowd. I must find out how big it is and who owns it. I have to check on Masood – and then there's El Herrero.*

"Penny for zem, I t'ink the expression is." Miguel terminated Doug's thoughts. "I understand you do not like zat man and zat 'e was your superior."

"Yes," Doug replied pensively. "I think he could show some remorse."

"Remorse?"

"Yes! Shame." Doug was abrupt. Miguel frowned and tried to placate him.

"There is corruption everywhere in this world."

"Agreed, but his corruption killed one of my colleagues and nearly killed another!"

"Zen you vill be interested to learn zat ze building vere 'e lives is ze one Parouk lives in," Miguel announced softly, so no one could overhear. Doug's eyes widened.

"Do you know how big his apartment is and who owns it?"

"No, but I can find out. Now let us enjoy ze rest of ze day.

I'll drive you to Parque Natural Montes de Málaga. It will be cooler among hills."

The next day, Doug had to entertain himself as Miguel was very busy. He decided to visit Thwaite in his lair, and advised Miguel accordingly, as a precaution. The doorman at the apartment block looked every bit a bouncer. He conveyed Doug's request reluctantly to another gorilla-like guard, over 6 feet tall with a red face and long black hair, in a side room. For the few seconds the door was open, Doug noted the room contained CCTV screens and other electronic devices. He also saw a third man further back in the uniform of a superior. He was very slim and short, yet seemed even more menacing with his long, gaunt face and cropped grey hair. The foyer was standard for the building's age, but the doors into the rest of it looked impenetrable. When Doug asked to see Thwaite, the second guard studied him for a full minute, as if discovering a new species, and growled.

"'Ave you ze appointment?"

"No."

"Zen 'e vill not see you!" He indicated for his fellow gorilla to show Doug out.

"Tell *Señor* Thwaite that Doug Evans is here to ask a favour," Doug stated quickly. The guard retreated to the inner office, where some chamber music covered his conversation. *Music for the inner chamber*, Doug joked to himself. *I can't stand those violin pieces; they grate on my ears.* The guard returned after his discussion with the occupant and used the internal phone.

"Very sorry to disturb you, sir. I 'ave a Doug Evans 'ere. 'E say 'e vants favour." The guard listened intently and kept nodding his head. Then he turned to Doug once more. "Okay. You vait over zere. 'E be down soon." Doug took the indicated seat and laughed internally at the guard's attempt to be gracious.

Thwaite appeared through one of the doors, momentarily revealing its thickness and strength.

"To what do I owe this dubious pleasure, Evans?"

"Sergeant Lee is getting married and asked me to find her brother David. I tried the address given by his former employers and was attacked."

"Why do you think I can or would help?"

"The men who attacked me work for someone called El Herrero, who could be an associate of your friend Masood—"

"He's no friend of mine. He was simply my useful nark," Thwaite interrupted.

"I thought you might redress the wrong you did – intentionally or not – to Sergeant Lee and help find her brother."

"I might. Who's she marrying?"

"Some lawyer in Houghbury."

"I haven't had an invite." Thwaite attempted a joke to warm the atmosphere between them.

"Well, well. She's invited most of our old crowd. She must've forgotten you!" Doug forced a slight smile. *I mustn't be hostile or he won't cooperate at all.* "If you're successful, here's her contact number." Doug had hoped to meet Thwaite in his apartment, so he could learn more about both the man and the building. He had to be satisfied that he had done more than could be expected to find David Lee. He walked away without looking back. As soon as he was out of sight, he dashed past a few shops in a row and found a vantage point to observe Thwaite's building. He kept an eye on the entrance, waiting for Thwaite to leave, without success.

Studying the building, he noted it was rectangular with the long side towards the sea, as with most seafront establishments in Spain. It was ten storeys high with a flat top, and the penthouse seemed to have mirror windows. *I reckon those windows have a protective film, which helps prevent breakage and anyone from looking in. Strange! There's no construction on top for water, elevator or other services. They must be hidden behind the extra-high wall above the penthouse. If the top floor is used by the crime syndicate's headman, the roof could have a helipad. I wonder where Thwaite's flat is?*

Years of undertaking observation duties meant Doug instinctively noted vehicles coming to and from the building. A white Mercedes coming in the direction of the building appeared ninety minutes later. Doug quickly focused his pocketable binoculars. Thwaite was the passenger and the driver was either the human gorilla or his brother. The car disappeared behind the building and did not reappear. It was time to join Miguel for lunch at his favourite tapas bar. When he arrived, Miguel was already seated at a table, with a slim bronzed man and a pretty woman. Miguel rose to greet Doug.

"Doug, I'd like you to meet my very good friend Sean and his fiancée, Maria Caballeros. This is the gorgeous man I've been telling you about." Handshakes all round. Sean spoke first.

"Miguel has enlightened us about each other's situations. Therefore, I'd like to point out that **all** our current relationships result from a small boy falling off his scooter." Doug looked puzzled, so Sean explained further.

"Ah! The Houghbury connection, which incriminated Thwaite and Jeffrey and involved me."

"Yes, and my outburst at the Houghbury incident led to me meeting Miguel and my beautiful Maria."

"A happy ending for all," Maria added softly.

"Almost!" corrected Doug. "The evil Masood and his organisation are still operating." There was bitterness in his voice, which caused them all to look at him in silence. Maria reached out and laid her hand gently on Doug's.

"*Sí, Señor* Doug. You can never forget your sister. Miguel told us some of the details. Is that why you're here?" Doug looked at each of them in turn, with a slight frown at Miguel.

"Yes, partly." He reached out and patted Miguel's hand. "I'd like you all to not tell anyone!"

"You're right, darling, but Doug must not allow it to colour his whole life," the former priest asserted.

"I'll make certain it doesn't." Doug looked from one to the other and swallowed the lump in his throat. *What's happening? Where's all my emotional control? But I have never felt so relaxed in the presence of others before.*

"I've always been a loner." He swallowed again. "Now I know how rich it is to have friends," he admitted as his voice trembled. It became obvious that the stress of the morning, broken by the compassion of the other three, had brought him close to tears. The effect stunned the others, and Miguel was the first to react as he placed a comforting arm round Doug's shoulders. The cold, ruthless detective was showing a soft centre, which Miguel had foreseen. Sean and Maria rose to leave.

"If we can help in any way, Doug, do let us know," Sean requested as they bid farewell. Doug told Miguel about his meeting with Thwaite.

"I've got news for you," Miguel announced triumphantly. "My contacts at the town 'all gave me lots of information about ze building. It belong to an unusual property company 'oose directors are a mystery. It vas built vit an underground car park."

"That explains it!" Doug interposed, and explained about the white Mercedes.

"Also, it 'as 'elipad on ze roof," Miguel continued.

"Thought so."

"Also, each floor 'as two or three apartments, except ze top, which 'as just one. Ze only residents registered as locals are three employees who live on ze ground floor." He paused as he started counting the points on his other hand. "Finally, and most interesting, is zat none of ze apartments appear to be leased or rented. All ze occupants seem to be partners or friends of ze owners. Zey pay taxes on ze actual building, but it 'as no income."

"Where is Thwaite's apartment?"

"Zere's nothing official, so I checked back via ze cleaner. T'waite 'as one of ze three on ze next-to-top floor. One she's never been in, but ze third she cleans for a Pedro Gonzalez. My client gleaned this information over a long period, as ze cleaner is frightened to talk about it."

"Does anyone live on the top floor?"

"Yes, but zey've never been seen. Zere 'ave been signs of activity yet nobody knows 'oo it is. Sometimes a 'elicopter lands and eizer leaves or takes people 'oo cannot be recognised."

"Aren't the local police suspicious?"

"Not really. No crimes've been committed and zey 'ave plenty zat do need investigating."

He gave Doug a peck on the cheek and returned to his salon.

Doug went for a walk by the sea, striding out as he considered the possibilities of the criminals' building. *Being in a fairly prominent position, it can hardly be their secret headquarters. It could be a grace and favour residence for… for what? For retired or vacationing lawbreakers like Thwaite.*

He grinned at the thought, causing some passers-by to smile back. *Like a home for recuperating soldiers, which, in a way, I suppose it is. Why have such a mysterious penthouse? Perhaps it's a communications link or staging post. If it does house crime workers from further afield, perhaps that's why Masood is there – if this Parouk is our Masood. – I wonder where this self-styled El Herrero operates from? It could be there, but if it were, any honest police would have an interest in it. If the mob owns it, wouldn't Interpol be paying attention to it? Perhaps they are, in secret. On the other hand, with a helipad, which is a requirement of the mega-rich, it could belong to one of them, and Thwaite may've done* them *a favour at some time. What if... what if! I could go on ad infinitum!*

He noticed he had travelled far and should be meeting Miguel soon. A quick about-face and he retraced his steps with alacrity. *Masood! I must find Masood.* The thought of his arch-enemy put renewed vigour into his stride, and he failed to notice the faint plop of a bullet hitting the water. He glanced at his watch. *Shite! Less than ten minutes to meet Miguel!* He broke into as fast a run as he could manage and turned away from the shore to try a short cut. There was a nasty stinging sensation in his left shoulder near his neck. *Jeez! That was a bee and a half.* His pace scarcely faltered as he plunged into the cool shade of a side street. Several people stared at him as he passed. *They're probably thinking mad dogs and Englishmen. They don't expect to see anyone running flat out at this time of day.* He arrived at the salon to find Miguel standing outside.

"What's wrong?" he spluttered as he gasped for air. "I'm only a couple of minutes late!" Miguel was staring at him in horror.

"Your shoulder!"

"Oh that! Some bee stung me as I was running."

"That's no bee sting! You've been shot. Come inside while I call for an ambulance."

Now the pressure on his lungs was subsiding, Doug became aware of the pain in his shoulder. Putting his hand to it, he saw that the dampness was blood, not sweat. *No wonder people were staring at me.*

Sean was waiting for Maria at the hospital and saw Doug being assisted from the ambulance. He dashed over to join Miguel alongside Doug.

"What's happened?"

"Doug's been shot and didn't notice it! Vat a guy. 'e was in too much of a 'urry to meet me and t'ought it vas a bee sting!"

"I'll catch up with you both in a few minutes. I'm collecting Maria."

In the emergency operating theatre, the surgeon found the bullet had gone straight through. It had just managed to miss artery and bone. Maria, still in uniform, was able to get in to see Doug. He gazed at her in wonderment.

Ah. My ministering spirit comes to comfort me. Boy, she looks even more beautiful in uniform. I bet she's broken many hearts, and here she is, come to comfort me.

"You're very naughty!" She wagged her finger at him and frowned deeply. "Ve try to tell you to stay out of trouble at lunchtime."

Doug grinned at her ferociousness. "Aren't you going to comfort me, Maria?"

"No!" Then she beamed positively. "On ze other 'and, Sean'll not be giving you ze last rites."

He laughed with her just as Sean and Miguel entered. They looked from the laughing couple to each other. They both killed any trace of a smile and adopted a sterner look.

"What is your Doug doing with my Maria, Miguel?"

"Oh no, Sean. Vat is your Maria doing vith my Doug?" Maria glanced at the pair, winked at Doug, then bent down and kissed him.

"I'm cured! I'm cured!" He tried to get up. "You really are an angel, Maria."

"He's cured. Maria's worked a miracle!" Sean exclaimed. He hugged Miguel and poked out his tongue at Maria. She adopted her matronly attitude.

"Until ze next bullet!" Some time later, when Doug's three friends had left, still joking, a policeman came to see him. *I don't know if this cop is honest or not, so I need to be guarded in what I tell him.* He explained to the officer how he had been strolling on the beach and felt the shot as he started to run back into town.

"So it could be an accident or a mistake, *señor*?"

"I guess so. Same way those two men working for El Herrero attacked me by mistake." He had to explain the incident and guessed the original officer had reported to El Herrero and not to the police station. *If this Herrero person's had me attacked and shot, what does he hope to gain? Or is Masood behind it all? I've seen neither gentleman, so I don't know… yet*! After repeating his questions and correcting his notes, the policeman left.

The following evening, Doug was discharged from hospital, and he and Miguel were entertained to dinner at Sean's.

"An excellent meal, Maria," lauded Miguel as he finished his coffee.

"Hear, hear! Worth getting shot any day," agreed Doug.

"No, *señors*. Not me. It vas Sean." Maria extended her arm to acknowledge the chef.

"But I t'ought…"

"You t'ought vat, Miguel?"

"Zat you two vere living togezer," Miguel answered bluntly.

"*Cómo pudiste! Mi familia está aún sorprendido de que yo le visite solos.*"

She blushed as Miguel interpreted for Doug. "'ow could you! 'er family don't even like 'er seeing h'm alone."

"**And!**" Sean added very pompously. "What would her priest say?" They all looked at him in astonishment until his face lit up and they all laughed.

"Did you cook when you were a parish priest, Sean?" Doug enquired.

"Yes. I'd an exceptionally good housekeeper. Being interested in science, I watched her carefully and experimented with dishes. A bit like chemistry, I suppose. Then in the short time I've been living here with Maria… er … um." He looked around, feigning guilt that someone might have overheard. "Er… I mean visiting Maria…" Miguel and Doug pretended to be shocked "…I've been practising—"

"Don't say any more, Sean." Miguel clasped his hands to his ears. "Ve can imagine vat you've been practising!" Maria flushed and lowered her head.

"If you'd kindly let me finish, Miguel. I've been practising my Spanish recipes."

"Oh!" Miguel looked disappointed, and Doug pushed him with his good arm.

"Stop it, Miguel! You're embarrassing Maria."

"Not so embarrassing as 'aving to admit Sean is a better cook," Maria admitted.

"No difficulty for me, Maria. Miguel is a good cook, although I can make a delicious cheese and marmalade sandwich and a decent cup of tea." The evening continued in the same light-hearted and friendly atmosphere.

I've got to return home and to work in a couple of days. It's going to be hard leaving Miguel and these new friends. At least I've some news for Langley and the others. Miguel noted the change in Doug's demeanour and they bid their farewells.

Was El Herrero thinking along the same lines as Doug, or was it another example of inside information? A representative of the alleged master criminal made a statement to the police defending his boss. He claimed the attack on Doug by his men was a case of mistaken identity; they thought he was David Lee, who owed El Herrero some money. They wanted him to meet their boss, but Doug attacked them. El Herrero had made enquiries about the shooting and provided the police with the gunman's name. The man had a new rifle and was trying it and accidentally hit Doug when he altered course and started running. The police arrested the gunman, who submitted meekly and recited the facts as presented by El Herrero.

Doug had been ordered to take it easy and allow his wound to heal. Nights with Miguel were a problem, as they had to curb their passion. However, days were different as Doug decided a shoulder wound was no excuse for not pursuing his surveillance of the Thwaite building. Realising the front entrance was not used by anyone of importance, he concentrated on the entrance to the underground car park. Fleeting glimpses of cars entering and leaving made the identification of drivers and passengers very difficult. Doug used a digital camera with a good telephoto range and snapped every car. He hoped enlargement of the photos would provide faces to recognise. A few times, he had to move on when other people passed. He found a café with pavement chairs from where he could just see the car park exit. More importantly, it was on the route all the target cars had to take. He became so obsessed that Miguel had to join him there for lunch.

One day, he insisted on getting there much earlier and staying later. Miguel was worried about him but pandered to him with the excuse he could use the extended hours to check on his staff and catch up with his accounts. The extra time paid off. Not only did Doug see a chauffeur-driven man he labelled as Mr X leaving three times, but once on his return he had company. *Masood! Jackpot!*

CHAPTER 18

"It's been an eternity!" Birdie yawned and stretched as Judith woke her with a mug of tea.

"I'm sorry if you've been waiting for your tea, milady," Judith retorted.

"No, no, dear Judith! It's the wedding. I seem to have been waiting ages for it, and now the day's finally dawned." She stretched again.

"Considering this is your first night away from your betrothed for ages, what *are* you waiting for? The ceremony, the jollity or the title of Mrs Schott?"

"I don't really know whether I'm looking forward to the event or dreading it. It'll be nice, I suppose, to see so many old friends, though I was never one for socialising. Then, of course, I'm very pleased that David is here."

"That's not what Derek thinks!"

"What do you mean?"

"He spoke to me when he dropped you off last night. He doesn't trust David, even if he is his half-brother."

"That's my big brother! He's so mistrusting and unforgiving, it's a wonder **he** didn't join the police." She shook her head. "No! David may have been wayward, but I like to think of this as the return of the prodigal."

"What happened to the ruthless career woman I heard about?"

"Circumstances." Birdie nodded as if approving of her own thoughts. "Let's call it the Houghbury syndrome. There's Terry and Derek and you and Charlie and Sid and, of course, Maurice. You've all played some part in changing my life." *Uh-oh, Birdie! Don't start reminiscing on your wedding eve.*

"And then… there's all that sex!" Judith wiggled her eyebrows in a suggestive manner.

"I don't know what you mean. I'm an old-fashioned girl. I believe in honouring the old rules."

Judith opened her mouth in total disbelief. "Pigs may fly! Honour? Well, at least you're honouring the tradition of not seeing the groom on the day before the ceremony."

"True. It's kind of you – and your family – to let me stay here and prepare."

"Nonsense! We're only too proud to have you. It gives me the chance to give you a maternal lecture about the facts of life and the *evils* of men." She paused to try and pull a stern face.

"Methinks you're the one who needs the lecture, or would lecher be nearer the mark?"

"Me? Sweet, innocent me?"

"Yes, you! A divorced woman living with a sexy single man."

Judith grinned and spoke playfully. "I hope you're not referring to Charlie!"

"Incest was not what I had in mind, sweet, innocent Judith."

"Oh dear! You mean my patient."

"I certainly mean Sid. As for being a patient, I expect he can look after himself by now."

"Oh, he can. He really can."

"You mean you and he…?"

"Cleanse your mind, Miss Lee. There's none of that hanky-panky here!"

"I **thought** you looked as if you needed your oats."

Judith disregarded the last allegation and continued. "Apart from being his nurse, I'm merely his teacher."

"Teaching him the *Kama Sutra*, no doubt," Birdie breathed, with a salacious look.

"No! But I can dream. Well, to be honest—"

"That's what crooks say when they've been lying!" Birdie interrupted.

"Stop it! You're embarrassing me again. Both Charlie and I like having him here, but my parents don't. So whenever they come, I put Sid's arm in a sling and make him sit with his feet up. The rest of the time he helps around the house and with Charlie, who adores him, and then he draws or paints. I put some of his portraits in the Houghbury Artists' Exhibition, and he now has a commission for a portrait of the mayor. Speaking of which, you might care to open your wedding gift from us."

She handed Birdie a carefully wrapped package about 75cm square. Birdie opened it to reveal a framed portrait of herself and Terry. The faces were easily recognisable. The cartoon bodies showed Birdie with hands on hips and standing legs apart, before a humble kneeling Terry. The feature that most captured the attention of the viewer was the eyes!

"The eyes! Such expression! It makes me appear to be trying to dominate, yet with an underlying sense of humour. And… it makes it look like Terry is trying to look subservient, yet with the same touch of humour. This is a gift we'll both cherish. The last time I saw eyes painted with such depth of expression was in a Rembrandt. Where is Sid? I'd like to thank him as well."

"Tut tut! Did you really think I'd let my beau into the bedroom with a bride-to-be?"

"Right!" Birdie slipped a lacy dressing gown over her scanty nightdress. "I'll go and thank him now, before I get too busy."

"Not like that! He'll be mortified!"

"Have confidence in yourself and Sid. A little awkwardness on his behalf is a small price to pay for proving who he really cares for."

"Oh, all right, but don't push it too far."

"I bet you say that to all your men." Birdie's innuendo made Judith's jaw drop, then she retorted.

"All my men? I've only got one."

"So you say to him." Judith dashed over to Birdie and slapped her on the right buttock.

"Ouch! Kinky. Now the left one, please." Judith pushed out her rear and wriggled it suggestively.

"You're incorrigible! Let's find Sid."

The ex-convict was laying table for breakfast when the two women found him. He looked up with astonishment as the provocatively dressed Birdie advanced towards him. He was about to turn away in embarrassment when she reached him and grasped him tightly round the waist.

"Thank you for the wonderful portrait of Terry and me. We'll treasure it as a marvellous work of art, and as a reminder of the courageous man who saved my life." Her head was against his broad chest with her face turned to one side, and she could not see his reaction. Judith noted it well from the doorway. He raised his arms in consternation, unable to know what to do with them. There was an expression of terror and embarrassment on his face. He looked desperately at Judith for help. She indicated for him to put his arms around Birdie, which he did delicately, as if she might break. Birdie felt his gentle touch and pressed harder against him. That was too much for her former would-be assailant and he pushed away.

"No, Miss Birdie! It's..." he struggled for words "...it's a small thank-you for saving me." She gazed up at him. Suddenly she became aware of her appearance in front of another man and on her wedding day. She tried to cover herself.

"What do you mean, Sid?"

"Because of you, my life's changed and I met Maurice and..." he looked adoringly in Judith's direction "...and Judith." His voice and whole being altered when he said her name. Judith was overcome with the relative eulogy from her overgrown childlike admirer and went to him. She gave him a grateful yet loving kiss, and neither noticed Birdie had fled back to her room.

"Don't you think we should go round the block one more time?" Derek beseeched his sister. "After all, it's almost traditional for the bride to arrive late, or it makes her seem overkeen."

"To hell with tradition! I *am* keen and I don't care who knows it. Ice Maiden is a thing of the past. Anyway, if it *was* traditional, we'd have the ceremony in a church and not the register office."

"Our dad wouldn't have approved! He had very firm views about tradition and religion. Still, I know he would've approved of your choice."

So they entered the register office only a minute late, and Birdie joined Terry in front of the registrar. He turned to look at her and was on cloud nine. *This vision, this beautiful creature, is soon to be my wife!*

"Can I have your attention, please?" the registrar asked. There was a ripple of laughter among their friends, and Terry realised he had been gazing at her in awe for some time.

Formalities completed, they all proceeded to the hall Terry had booked. The caterers had prepared the tables in a circle at the request of the – Schotts. Now it really was a case of Birdie Schott! The place cards were arranged as planned, except Diana Gumbrill arrived early and changed places with Helen so she could sit next to Maurice. He had not dared to speak to or even look at Helen. This was partly due to his immense feeling of loss and partly from guilt over his week with Megan. Birdie noticed the switch and was about to protest when Terry stopped her.

"Mrs G is forceful, but Maurice can handle her. He'll have plenty of opportunity to sort matters with Helen later. No doubt Helen's kids will help." His prophecy was correct to a point. One of the loudest laughs came from the Metropolitan Police contingent during Terry's speech.

"I've been advised by my wife's colleagues – I'll repeat that as I like the sound – my wife's colleagues that I must be a cool guy to be marrying the Ice Maiden. Well, I've got news for them! I've set the thermostat in my... our... apartment to high for a really hot time!"

The tables were cleared and the barn dancing started. Guests were slow to join in until they realised that making mistakes was all part of the fun. Nicola approached Maurice and persuaded him to partner her in a dance. The wine, the child and the dance helped him to relax, and he even managed a meaningful smile at Helen as he passed her.

I must speak to her now. I can't keep putting it off. When the dance finished, he walked towards Helen and was distracted by a face peering through the glass section of the door from the entrance lobby.

Megan! *Aunty Mary! I'd forgotten she said she might look me up on her way back to London, but that's not for two weeks!*

Why is she here now? I'd better see her immediately, though without talking to Helen, I don't know what I want.

Helen was astonished when Maurice changed direction, as he appeared to be coming to her, and disappeared through the lobby doors. In the lobby, thinking he was out of sight, Maurice greeted Megan with a hug and a lasting kiss. They separated and Megan began to explain why she was early, when a man passed them and hurried outside. Megan, who had been facing the glass into the hall, spoke urgently.

"That man just put a backpack under the drinks table and fiddled with it before leaving!"

Maurice looked through the glass panel and realised only they were in a position to see the pack. Something was very wrong! He brushed past Megan, through the doors and pushed aside Helen, who was coming to speak to him. He raced to the table, grabbed the pack and, shoving everyone aside, he dashed through to the outside. Megan followed him closely. He shouted after David Lee.

"Here's your backpack!" David started to run away rapidly in terror and Maurice knew his original instinct had been correct. He threw the pack as hard as he could, but it was too late! It exploded, smashing both him and Megan against the wall of the building. David was knocked over but remained conscious. The bomb shook the hall, and several guests dashed outside. The police guests were the first to react, and one phoned for the emergency services while the others checked the wounded. David Lee told them haltingly how he had tried to stop Maurice from setting off the bomb, and that the woman must be his accomplice.

"I doubt he'll live to stand trial," muttered Tyler, who was examining Maurice.

"Nor will this woman," added Langley. Helen, who had seen Maurice kissing Megan, heard what the policemen said.

"He can't! He wouldn't!" she almost screamed, before Joe Baxter led her back into the hall. Terry and Birdie had reached the lobby and asked what had happened.

"Seems your brother's a hero. He stopped Jenkins and some red-headed woman from blowing us all to kingdom come. Can you look after Mrs Phillips, please? She's very upset." As they led Helen to a seat, they looked at each other quizzically.

"I can't believe Maurice could do such a thing," Terry mumbled.

"Nor my brother, even if he is the black sheep of the family," retorted Birdie, defending her kin. There was a strained pause, then they changed tack.

"Who's the woman?"

"His lover!" gasped Helen between sobs.

"Can't be," argued Birdie. "I **know** he **really** loves you."

"You know more than I do. Just minutes before the explosion, he was kissing a red-headed woman..." she sobbed again "...with passion, not friendship."

"I can't believe it." Terry frowned. "He never talked of anyone but you. You must be mistaken." Birdie nodded agreement with her new husband.

"I may be a rustic, but I know passion when I see it," Helen reaffirmed.

"But how's it possible?" Birdie asked.

"It's all my fault! I've only myself to blame." Helen shook with anguish as she told them about her dream for Sean. How she had discovered her true feelings for Maurice; how he had seen Sean kiss her in gratitude. "He must've thought I'd chosen Sean, because he left very suddenly and hasn't spoken to me since."

"Perhaps you also have the wrong idea when you saw him kiss this other woman," Terry suggested. Helen wiped her eyes and looked at them in contemplation.

While they comforted her, the ambulances arrived and rushed Maurice and Megan to hospital. David was patched up as he gave his statement to the police. He gave them the address of his lodgings and left. The wedding reception was definitely terminated, and county police interviewed the departing guests. Everyone's memories of events were hazy due to alcohol and the chaotic fun of the barn dancing.

"Did the fireworks go wrong, Mummy?" pestered Roger.

"What happened to Maurice?" Nicola added, only to make her mother cry once more. The underlying tension of her potential meeting with Maurice and the subsequent events overcame her natural reserve.

"Don't bother your mother now, children. She's had an unhappy experience." Birdie tried to quieten them.

"How?" persisted Roger, despite a nudge from his sister.

"Let's just say the wedding went off with a bigger bang than expected. Oh, and there were no fireworks – planned." Birdie had been about to say a bomb, but realised that it would have created more worry and questions. Helen was allowed to leave early because of her distressed state and her anxiety for her children.

"Sidney Cracken," the former convict announced as his place in the line of the Schotts' departing guests reached the officer operating a police laptop. There was a slight pause, then the officer indicated for his colleagues to seize Sid. The commotion caused by Sid's struggles involved Judith, who momentarily abandoned Charlie to help Sid.

"Stay calm, Sid! I'll—" Her words were cut short as one of the officers trying to hold Sid shoved her away. This was the ultimate offence to Sid's abnormal psyche, and he pulled free and lashed out at the offender. As other officers rushed to arrest him, the bride and groom and Joe Baxter prevented them. There was slight scuffling until everyone noticed the object of the affray was gently helping Judith to her feet.

"He's a prisoner on parole and he assaulted a policeman! Arrest him!" shouted the man with the laptop.

"*No, you don't!*" Birdie stepped in front of Sid and Judith. The officer, who had come in from a neighbouring force, looked at her in amazement.

"Who the hell do you think you are!" he continued shouting. There was a stunned silence during which DCI Watson moved forward, approached the shouter and showed him his ID.

"I'm sorry to interrupt you, Officer. Can I have a few words with you in private?" The officer passed the laptop to another and followed Basil to a quiet corner, while the throng left behind tried to relax. "The man you want to arrest is on parole for the crime of trying to assault my sergeant, the woman who you enquired about."

"But—"

"We now know that he has a psychological problem and is harmless…"

"Harmless!"

"Except when his lady friend and mentor is assaulted. If anyone is going to be charged here, it is your colleague who pushed her to the floor! We don't want the publicity that would bring – do we? So I suggest you apologise… no. There is no need for you to be embarrassed further. You carry on with your line-up and I'll do the apologies. You can explain to your overaggressive colleague later." After the situation had been fully resolved, its hidden benefits became apparent to Birdie and Terry. Sid was still holding Judith closely, as if she were delicate china that might drop and break. Charlie had joined them and was clinging to Sid's leg.

"Why have you pinched yourself, darling?" Terry observed his new wife's strange action.

"I had a moment's recollection of how I met Sid, and could not associate that… monster with this… family man." She stared at the mirage before her. Both Judith and Charlie were clinging to Sid, resembling some romantic group sculpture of old.

Not once in my marriage did I ever feel this secure. I could… eat him up. Forget the outer manifestation. This man is pure – gold? No, this man is a diamond! He's more than that; he's… he's my man! And Charlie thinks so too. Judith hugged Sid even tighter as she glanced down at her precious boy. The last guests were processed, and Sid became aware of his benumbed position. He looked around and realised he and his 'wards' were the centre of attention. Instantly, he was nonplussed and tried to break free.

"What's wrong, Sidney?" She held on.

"Look! Look!" he muttered awkwardly. She did look, and the former hippie turned into a shy mother as she pulled Charlie away with her.

"Thanks, Sid. I'm feeling much better now," she said over-loudly to cover her embarrassment. Birdie and Terry turned to each other and winked. Judith noticed and confronted them.

"What's that supposed to mean?" Behind her, the great mass of Sid was trying to hide.

"You know what people say, Terry?" Birdie's attempt to cover a grin failed miserably.

"What do people say… my lovely wife?" His attempt at a straight face was also unsuccessful.

"They say..." she paused for greater emphasis "...that persons who bond at weddings inevitably finish up plighting their troth."

Sid leant forward and whispered in Judith's ear. "What's she mean... Judith?" He had never lost the thought that he was somehow honoured to be allowed to use her name. With a shake of her head and a final glare at the newlyweds, she turned to her white knight.

"She is insinuating that because you helped me when I fell, I will marry you." Sid's eyes widened so much the others thought they would burst from their sockets. His entire face was gleaming red and his mouth gaped. Then he tried to speak, but no sounds emerged. Judith spun round to confront the others, who had become very serious at the tableau before them.

"I-I-" Sid tried to speak and swallowed loudly. Judith wheeled round to find him shaking his head in disbelief.

"There you are, Miss – no, **Mrs** Cleverclogs. He won't marry me!" Sid's head-shaking was now so vigorous they were all alarmed.

"Y-y-yes!" he managed to say. Judith was stunned and frowned at him.

"Sidney," she articulated carefully. "You mean yes, you would **never** marry me?" She reached up and grasped his shoulders to calm him. He started stammering and then took a deep breath.

"YES. I would marry you if…" His explosion of sound died away completely. There was a stunned silence, with Judith frozen in the middle. There was no more joking by Terry or Birdie as they glanced from one another to the subject of their former mirth. Beauty and the beast. The newlyweds' minds worked in unison. Judith's mind was in a whirl. *They were joking. So was I – in a way. Just look at the great lump. Who on earth would ever want to marry him? Oh dear! I think he's going to cry. I should comfort him.* Despite her thoughts, Judith was still transfixed. *Only minutes ago, I wanted to eat him. Could he ever be… a lover? Could he mean more than a brilliant artist… and a little – no – big – boy to me?* She was aroused from her stupor by a hand grasping her arm.

"I'm sorry, Judith. We didn't mean to cause you both such embarrassment," Birdie reassured her. They were saved from more awkwardness by the arrival of the hall's steward to lock up. The two groups parted at the door, and Terry took his bride to **their** apartment.

"Good job we're not going away until Monday!" Terry whispered as he carried her over the threshold.

The only conversation in Judith's car was a few words with Charlie, who soon fell asleep. It seemed like hours before Judith was able to sleep. She tried the alcohol she had so assiduously avoided at the reception. She tried to think of anything except Sid. She resorted to watching Charlie in his innocent slumber.

"Mummy! Why are you here?" Charlie shook his mother, who was asleep beside his bed. She stared at him through bleary eyes then leapt into action. Sid was already up and dressed, so he attended to Charlie's needs while she prepared herself for the dreaded day ahead. All the time, her thoughts swirled without structure. *They were joking… Sid wasn't. Was I joking? The whole idea is ridiculous… He's a fellow artist… I don't need anyone… Charlie loves him… I don't… He's good with Charlie… He's… he's been in prison! He's putty in my hands. He's got a low IQ… He's learning fast. He'd be a liability. He's learning to turn his hand to anything. He's almost ugly. He will almost certainly become famous for his art… I don't want someone famous… It would just be trouble. If he does become famous, he will have his pick of women. He'd be unfaithful… Unfaithful like Tom. He's clumsy… He was so gentle when he helped me yesterday. Yesterday! It was only the occasion speaking… He was overcome by the occasion. He's a… a romantic. He knows it could never work! That's it! He's not a proper man. Nice though he is… and to have here to help Charlie and me…he could never be a… lover! I need a lover! I really, really need a lover. End of argument! He can stay here as our help until I do find a lover… I'm too young to become* hors de combat.

CHAPTER 19

Late on Sunday morning, DCI Watson went to visit Helen. He was accompanied by Joe Baxter, who volunteered, as the friendly face she would know. When she started rambling on about the noise and vibration caused by the bomb, Joe calmed her and spoke gently.

"Did you talk about anything with Maurice Jenkins?"

Helen paused, pulled herself erect and stated calmly, "No. I thought he was going to, but he seemed to change his mind and head for the lobby doors. Through the glass in the doors I saw him hug and kiss a red-headed girl."

"It was a planned meeting then?" Watson suggested, giving a knowing look at Joe.

"I don't think so. He seemed to be coming to speak to me and abruptly changed direction to the entrance doors." She reflected on the scene. "She said something to him and he turned and looked through the glass of the doors. Then he dashed in and pushed past everybody, including me. Then he went to the drinks table, reached underneath and produced a backpack. Then he dashed out again, pushing more people aside, and the last I saw was the two of them hurrying outside." She reopened her eyes, which she had closed while she pictured the scene.

"And then?" Watson urged her.

"Moments later, there was that explosion, and I dashed

out, along with several men that I don't know, and saw the two on the floor."

"What two would that be, Mrs Phillips?" Watson queried bluntly.

"Maurice and the girl, of course!"

"You didn't see anyone else?" he continued.

"I wasn't looking for anyone else!" she snapped back at him. After a few formalities, the policemen left.

"Jenkins and Mrs Phillips have seen a lot of each other since his release from prison," Joe reminded Watson.

"So she could be biased in his favour?"

"Possibly, but I can't believe he'd want to blow up all his friends."

"What about his red-headed girlfriend? Perhaps she persuaded him to do it and he changed his mind at the very last moment."

"Or! Perhaps it was her plan and he found out and tried to stop her."

"She's the unknown factor in this."

"Don't forget Sergeant Lee's brother. He was outside when it happened."

"True, but Mrs Phillips never mentioned seeing him," Watson pointed out.

Meanwhile, at the hospital, Megan had recovered enough to be interviewed by the police. She gave her name and address and explained how she had stopped at Houghbury to see Maurice on her way home.

"How do you know Maurice Jenkins?" Sergeant Pollock asked the question she had dreaded. She grimaced as a new ripple of pain hit her. A doctor moved to stop the interrogation, but she determinedly struggled with an answer.

"We met on holiday in Dorset."

"Why go out of your way to visit someone you met on holiday?" he pressed her.

"We became very good friends." Her agitation caused her to close her eyes and her head rolled slightly towards the two cops. This exposed the terrible disfigurement to the other side of her face. One cop put his hand to his face to cover a gasp of horror. The sergeant steeled himself to continue.

"You were lovers?" he asked bluntly.

"Yes," came the croaky reply.

"Where... did... you... get... the... bomb?" he intoned carefully, aware that her pain could be affecting her mind.

"The bomb?" She gurgled and screwed up what was left of her face. "It was put under the drinks table by a blond man." Her whole body started to convulse, and the cops were ordered out.

Back at the police station, Joe and Basil Watson were joined by the group from the Met, who explained their interest in the case. They proposed that the explosion bore all the hallmarks of the Masood organisation.

"Why would they be interested in a wedding reception in Houghbury?" Watson countered.

"Revenge! Pure and simple revenge!" Bennett narrated how it was the Jenkins incident in Houghbury that caused the downfall and removal of a corrupt judge, cop, and the former head of the criminals' British organisation. "The persons responsible for their downfall, particularly the new Mrs Schott, are all here, except the one they've already killed and the one who's joining us later." Bennett remembered Doug was meeting them there to avoid any moles left in their London office.

Soon after lunch, Doug joined them at the police station and reported his findings. Langley told him about the drama at the reception.

"So David Lee came then?"

"Yes. He seems to be the proverbial hero!" Tyler muttered sarcastically.

"Why proverbial?" Doug asked.

"Phil's right in a way. We've only Lee's word at the moment of his heroic efforts," Bennett agreed.

Doug looked around at his colleagues. *I wonder if this Lee is the good guy?* "Can you describe him for me?" Doug looked at each in turn.

"I can do better than that! I've got a photo of him in my camera. He was standing with his brother and the newlyweds. I don't think he knew I'd taken it," Langley remarked as he produced a camera and scrolled through for the photo in question. When he found it, he enlarged David Lee's face and passed the camera to Doug.

"Thought so! He's the sod who denied being David Lee when I met him. He then mysteriously disappeared and was replaced by a pair of thugs who tried to grab me. I think he works for ZEBEC!" Bennett leapt to his feet, sought Basil Watson and warned him about David Lee. **Too late!** David had already left the country on the earliest flight to Spain.

Mr and Mrs Schott were leaving the hospital at the same time that Helen arrived. She assured them that she was better and in full control. Her children had been left with the Browns.

"I don't want them to go through the anguish they suffered when Arnold was dying. They're very fond of Maurice. He's… he's almost like a second father to them." Her voice trembled as she recognised the parallel drama now unfolding. She noticed their silence and tried altering the line of conversation, only to tread on other painful ground.

"Who's the woman?" she asked them directly.

"Megan Davies. Someone he met on holiday in Dorset." Terry tried to sound offhand.

"Oh! I see!" She bit her lip.

"I'm sure she meant nothing to Maurice," Birdie assured her, thus pouring oil on a smouldering imagination instead of on stormy waters. Helen decided she would rather have news, good or bad, from friends rather than strangers.

"How are they all?"

"My brother's fled the country. It seems he was sent here by criminals to plant the bomb. Derek did warn me that David was not to be trusted." The distasteful words poured from Birdie and she took a deep breath, which allowed Terry to continue gently.

"Maurice is still in a coma, and the doctors describe his condition as extremely critical. He may not live long, and if he does recover, he could be a vegetable." Helen started to cry and forced herself to speak again.

"And the woman?"

"She has a slightly better chance of living but is horribly disfigured."

"Poor girl." Even through her jealousy, Helen was able to show compassion. "Can I see them?" she begged.

"I'll take her up, darling, as I know most of the staff. You wait in the car. I won't be long." Terry took Helen to them and she was allowed to visit Maurice first. He looked like a corpse! With the nurse's approval, she was left to sit beside him for a few minutes. Minutes in which she clutched his hand and unleashed her true spiritual and physical passion for him. She told him how it had taken the meeting with Sean for her to recognise where her love really belonged. How Sean had embraced her on hearing that his Maria was alive, and she had immediately sought out Maurice, but he had left. She squeezed his hand as she promised that she and her kids would pray for his full recovery.

"We all need you," she whispered in his ear as a nurse interrupted her, so she went to see her rival. Megan was temporarily conscious and noticed Helen approach her cautiously.

"You must be Helen." Megan's voice was very croaky.

"Yes, I'm Helen."

"Maurice told me all about you."

"I know nothing about you." Helen dampened her intended retort to a flat statement.

"You've not talked to him since his holiday?" Megan sounded surprised.

The question made Helen feel guilty. *It's not my fault we've not spoken... well... perhaps. It's not my fault he got the wrong idea about Sean...*

"Are you okay?" Megan's croaky intrusion forced reality upon her.

"No! I mean yes, I'm okay. No, I haven't spoken with Maurice." The planned restraint of her emotions collapsed in the face of the genuine enquiries of her injured rival. Megan peered at Helen in silence, waiting for amplification.

"It's my fault! I know Maurice saw Sean kiss me and he got the wrong message. I should've gone after him immediately. I was – am – a dreadful coward and dreamer when it comes to matters of the heart. I don't know why I'm telling you this, but in the circumstances I have to tell someone." She lowered her head slightly after the outpouring of her confession.

"You're no coward!" Megan insisted firmly. "To be able to carry on with life as you've done, after the tragic loss of your husband, demands great courage." An extraordinary feeling of empathy, not mere pity, for her rival welled inside Helen, and she managed a friendly smile.

"Not really courage, more maternal instinct."

"I'd love to have children. At present, my life is spent caring for old folk."

"You must meet my two, Nicola and Roger. They're both a worry and a blessing. Maurice has been like a father to them. I know they love him, and it's helped them recover from Arnold's death." She had a sad smile as she pictured them. "How do you know Maurice?" She posed the question that had been troubling her since the reception.

"Put crudely, we had a rather passionate holiday romance." Megan shakily reached out and grasped at Helen's hand. "Why it happened is what you must understand. I first saw Maurice perched on the edge of a cliff. He looked totally depressed and desperate, even suicidal. I went and talked to him. I felt I wanted to mother him – to protect him. I met him later when my duties were finished. We had a few drinks and one thing led to another. He **is** a good lover." She managed a faint squeeze of Helen's hand.

"You must comprehend fully that he was with me physically, not mentally. That's how I found out about you. I had to enjoy the moment, so to speak. I've been apart from my boyfriend for a really long time. On reflection, I was using Maurice to satisfy my physical and maternal needs. After he left, I discovered the affair had gone further than I intended, and I think I'm in love with him. I knew there was little possibility of him loving me in return as he only turned to me for comfort on the rebound from you."

"Then why did you come here yesterday?"

"Hope! I just had a slim hope that you'd reject him. I only knew him for a week, but that was enough to realise he **would** make a full confession to you." She paused to grimace as she shifted slightly. "I can see now why he really loves you.

You **have** to be a person of great courage and compassion to visit a potential rival. In other circumstances, I'm sure we'd be very good friends." She coughed scratchily and intense pain showed on her face. "If I survive…" she coughed again "…I'll be lucky to have any friends, let alone lovers. Who'd want a woman with this face?" Tears trickled down her good cheek. "I'll be an object of pity and I… I'd rather **die**." Her face screwed up with pain and she emitted a partially suppressed scream. Helen called the nurse and left quietly.

Driving home, she had time to reflect on Megan's news. *Jealousy's eating my heart. I know it's wrong! If Maurice could wait all that time for me, while I was mooning over Sean, and he could tend so well to another man's kids, then I must understand and forgive… Forgive? What's there for me to forgive? He's not mine to forgive! That girl! I can't hate her.* She concentrated at a tricky junction. *What about the girl? I find I actually respect her… she's been so honest with me… She's in immense pain and might die –* and *she's horribly disfigured – for life – if she lives – and she thinks she's lost Maurice.*

For the remainder of her journey, she weighed up her rival's prospects. She stood still after alighting from her car and watched her kids run towards her. *I **want** to help Megan. I **must** help her.*

CHAPTER 20

Doug's visit to Spain had established that Zebec used their building, where they allowed Thwaite to live, as an HQ; that Masood lived in the area; that El Herrero was their local boss, and that the 'Zebec tower' had been designed as some kind of fortress. Miguel had discovered that a small subcontractor had been used to make internal alterations and install CCTV security around the building. He also found out that the contractor and the plans had perished in a mysterious fire!

A council of war attended by Bennett, Langley and Tyler listened intently to Doug's news and discussed their options.

"We know Zebec has infiltrated the local police, so we should avoid using them," Bennett declared, looking round at the others.

"Agreed, but we can't send Doug back on his own," advised Langley.

"True! Where can we find someone suitable and reliable?" Doug questioned his superiors, dreading the thought of having to nurse some less-than-adequate colleague.

"We can't send one of our own as it could lead to a diplomatic *faux pas*," Tyler reminded them.

"How about someone from Interpol? I could use contacts to get a suitable person," Langley offered.

"What sort of accomplice do you want, Doug?" Bennett raised his pen, ready to make notes.

"I've given the matter a lot of thought and used some… **constructive** doodles…" Doug gave his superiors a knowing look, as if inferring their habit of doodling was a waste of time "… to plan our strategy. Basically, we want two things; one is to find out who else is housed in the Zebec tower; more important is to find the purpose of the all-important top floor. If the penthouse is being used as the Zebec organisation's HQ or international communications centre, then we should destroy it. That would terminate or, at the very least, obstruct their activities."

"Destroy?" Tyler queried anxiously.

"Figuratively speaking, yes. With their ability to land helicopters on the roof, any delay would allow the mastermind, if he's there, to escape with the information we need to close them down completely."

"Okay. You still haven't told us what sort of person you want to help," Bennett reminded him.

"Right, guv. To break in and chart the Zebec tower, I'll need a small locksmith who is also handy with electronics. He'd have to be able to handle himself in a tough situation."

"Does he have to fly as well?" Tyler joked.

"No, but it'd be useful." They all laughed.

"Leave it to me. I'll see who Interpol can provide." Langley had the last word.

The next day, Doug was called to Langley's office.

"Interpol are pleased to help and have provided two possible officers. Both are highly trained as you requested; a male and a female. Read these CVs and choose one." Doug returned to his own desk and scrutinised the files.

Oh dear! Heads or tails? Technically, there's little to choose between them. Physically, she's smaller and lighter, and he's the stronger. My problem is the sex – oops! Good job I'm not thinking aloud. If I choose him, my colleagues, except Tyler, will think nothing of it. In Málaga, Miguel could prove awkward and the locals might think it's a ménage à trois. *Me arriving with a man could alert Zebec – but, then, so could a woman. Arriving with her'd seem strange to all who know Miguel and me – and it'd provide grist for the debased thoughts among this lot here. What to do?*

"Still deciding, Doug?" Langley enquired as he passed Doug.

"Yes, guv. Weighing up their advantages and disadvantages." Langley nodded and moved on. Doug placed the CVs side by side and perused them once more. *Everything points to the man, who's also fairly fluent in Spanish. The odds are definitely in his favour – but I feel I've missed something. It doesn't mention her ability in Spanish! Why?* He started to read her CV again. *Bloody hell! How did I miss it? She **is** Spanish! There's still the problem of us arriving in Málaga. Of course! That's the answer! We travel separately. She'd be going to visit a friend – Maria! I'm sure she'll help.*

Doug arrived at Málaga Airport to be greeted by Sean and Maria, and a petite dark-haired girl. *The lads in London'd be really jealous if they could see my new partner. A* señorita *to die for – if you like that sort of thing, but will she be any good on this assignment?*

"Lovely to see you again, Doug. This is my friend Esperanza Mariona. She's here on holiday and staying with u... er... me, much to my relatives' approval," Maria announced as she kissed Doug's cheek. Doug shook hands with Sean and then Esperanza, who reached up and kissed his cheek.

"*Buenos dias, Señor* Doug. I sorry my English not good."

Oh dear! Did I overlook something in her CV?

"Maria and I are busy with our wedding plans." Sean talked as he helped Doug with his luggage. "We wondered if you'd show Esperanza around Málaga, as you know much of it now. Also, she'd be safer with you than trying to ward off those tourist Romeos."

"I'd be honoured, but what'll Miguel think?"

"We've cleared it with him. He sends his apologies for not meeting you himself. He has a girl off sick and has to cover for her. Ah, here's my car." They stored the luggage and Doug sat in front with Sean.

"You're right to be cautious, Doug. We were followed by a couple of lowlifes all the way through the airport." Doug whipped round to find it was Esperanza talking in perfect English. He grinned and mimicked her in the highest pitch he could manage.

"I sorry my English not good." They all laughed. Relaxed in friendly company, Doug continued. "Esperanza! You're better than I dared hope!"

"Hope? Esperanza! Bit corny, Doug. You'd better mind your Ps and Qs with Esperanza. She's a black belt at karate," Maria warned him.

"So am I, 8th Dan."

"I think we'll make a good pair. Back to back!" Esperanza leant forward and ran a finger down his neck. A shiver ran down his spine and he sat forward abruptly, locking his seat belt. "Aha, *Señor* Evans! I've found your Achilles heel." Doug was forced to laugh with the others. They parked near Miguel's salon and he joined them for lunch.

Esperanza whispered in Miguel's ear when they were seated, "*Señor Doug es cosquillas en la nuca!*" (*Señor* Doug is ticklish on the back of his neck.)

"*Cómo lo sabes?*" (How do you know?) Miguel was jealous.

"*Lo toqué cuando estaba sentado detrás de él en el coche.*" (I touched it when I was sitting behind him in the car.)

"Doug, have you been playing fast and loose with this young lady?" Miguel tried to sound stern.

"We haven't had time." Doug winked at Esperanza. Miguel thumped Doug's shoulder and both laughed. Doug sat next to his partner from Interpol and whispered explanations as he showed her his plan. The other three knew the pair were on a dangerous mission and covered for them. Doug had obtained construction plans of the Mercedes most often seen entering and leaving the Zebec tower. He needed to get Esperanza into the car's boot and thence into the building. Doug had discussed the problem with a mechanic friend in England. The mechanic had instructed him how to get out of the locked boot and how to use a tiny webcam through a hole they could drill in the rear parcel shelf. So he had the accomplice, the tools and the wherewithal; all he needed was a means of getting Esperanza into that boot. She appreciated the danger involved but already had faith in Doug to assist in any eventuality.

"Do you know where the car is parked when it's away from the Zebec tower?"

"No!" Doug felt foolish for not having found out earlier.

"I suggest a homing device. I'm not known to the crooks, so I'd plant one when the car stops at traffic lights," Esperanza suggested, as if putting something on the weekly shopping list.

"Yes, of course." Doug clicked his fingers, and added, "to make it easier for you, I'd walk across in front of the car and stop and peer into it. It only needs one of the occupants to recognise me, or consider me suspicious, for it to distract them."

Doug grinned as he pictured the scene. "Perfect – how can I let you in when the whole building is surrounded with CCTV?"

"That's my job. The original building plans show the mains electric entering the building through the underground car park. I'll show you where on the plan. They've a standby generator housed in a small compound alongside the main building. I intend to fix the oil sight gauge so it doesn't change, and then empty the fuel. That way, they'll only be able to operate the generator for a couple of minutes after you cut the mains."

"Sounds good, but the generator area is covered by their CCTV." Doug delayed his reply while they were being served by a waiter bringing the paella speciality of the café.

"I hope you'll all enjoy this. I think it's one of the best in town," Miguel assured them.

"I agree. I 'ave been 'ere before," added Maria.

"With anyone special?" Sean enquired.

"Vell, I t'ought 'e was…"

"Oh, did you?" Without the protection of his church, he had fallen prey to the evils of jealousy.

"If you'd let me finish, my love…" she leant across and kissed him "…I t'ought 'e was special until I met you." She paused as she watched Sean's face light up, and added with a wicked glint in her eye, "And zen I knew 'e was special!" Sean grabbed her and pretended to slap her face.

"You wicked hussy! You've been leading me astray."

"Vat is 'ussy?"

"A woman of bad morals," Miguel answered, and laughed as the lovers glared at each other and then kissed passionately. The light-hearted interlude and the food delayed further planning by Doug and Esperanza.

The afternoon for them was spent playing their parts as tourists. They were bouncing ideas off each other, while Doug would point out features of the town worth noting.

They approached the Zebec tower, so Doug stuck entirely to sightseeing aspects.

"I've heard tell they get sharks off the beach there." He paused to point towards a headland.

"Don't let him scare you, miss." An authoritative voice caused Doug to whip round. It was Thwaite! Aren't you going to introduce me to your charming companion, Evans?" Esperanza looked from Thwaite to Doug and back.

"Of course." He delayed to swallow the ingrained 'sir'. "This is Esperanza Mariona. She's the friend of my friends. They asked me to show her around for her safety, after all the recent assaults on girls by seaside 'Don Juans.'"

"Very wise, I'm sure. Pleased to meet you, Miss Mariona." He grasped her hand in an unusual display of gallantry and kissed it. "You couldn't be in safer hands than those of Doug Evans here."

"Do you live 'ere, *señor*?" Esperanza looked so innocent yet charmed by his gesture.

"I live near the top of the Zebec tower there – when I'm in Spain."

"'Ow do you know *Señor* Evans?"

God, she's marvellous. No wonder she was recommended for this job, Doug thought as he kept a straight face.

"We used to be colleagues in England." Thwaite threw a meaningful look at Doug.

"Colleagues? What jobs did you 'ave?" Her question appeared so spontaneous that Doug was mentally overwhelmed. Thwaite looked at Doug with surprise.

"You mean he hasn't told you? We were in the London police." Esperanza looked astonished and turned abruptly to Doug.

"Vy you not tell me you police?" Doug swallowed hard and managed a glare at Thwaite.

"I... er... I thought your friends would've told you."

"Are you ashamed of being police?"

"No, no. It's... it's just that some people can't... er... relax with policemen." She looked puzzled and turned to Thwaite once more.

"Eez zis true, *Señor* T'waite?"

"*Sí*. It's a cross we have to bear." Thwaite's answer was supposed to be conclusive.

"You play Lord Jesus?" Esperanza was thoroughly enjoying her role and unsettling these men. Doug looked as mystified as Thwaite and, having every confidence in her ability, promptly questioned her.

"How does Jesus come into it?" Thwaite nodded agreement and looked at Esperanza for an explanation.

"Vy you no understand? You bear cross like Jesus did!" The men's mutual loathing was forgotten as they both laughed. "Vy you laugh at me?" She looked hurt.

"No, no, *señorita*! Bearing a cross does not refer directly to Jesus. In today's language, it means being a policeman is like... like being handicapped," Thwaite tried to explain.

"Ah!" Esperanza nodded. "You London police are 'andicapped." Again, the men looked at each other and laughed.

"Let me try." Doug inhaled strongly. "Many years ago in Europe, black people were treated differently." Esperanza looked up at Doug, frowned for a moment then grinned in understanding.

"*Sí*, I understand. London police suffer from – *prejuicio*." Doug peered at Thwaite for an explanation.

"She said prejudice."

"In a way, she's right." Doug smiled at the implications.

"So are her friends in trusting her to you, Evans." Thwaite

turned slightly away from Esperanza and gave Doug a suggestive wink. There were a few moments of silence, then Thwaite clapped his hands as if in celebration of a good idea.

"Why don't you two accompany me to my apartment for a cup of **real** English tea? That way, Esperanza can enjoy the view, and you, Sergeant Evans, can satisfy yourself about my lifestyle." He grinned as he emphasised the word Sergeant.

What the hell? This might be some sort of game for him, and everything'll look clean and above board – of that I'm certain – but it'll increase my knowledge of the place.

"Zat sounds nice, *Señor* T'waite. Is it okay to go, Doug?"

"Of course. Most kind of you – *Señor* Thwaite." The disgraced superintendent took them into the entrance lobby of the Zebec tower. They were met by the two rather frightening security guards – the very large beings who had developed their muscles and neglected their brains. He said something to one of them, and they all waited while the guard went into the inner office. The door was opened by the man Doug had noticed in the office on his previous visit. The man, in a 'chief' security guard's uniform, was very thin, with a large head, sparse grey-brown hair, high cheekbones and piercing, sunken grey eyes. Thwaite went over to him and obviously discussed the reason for his companions' presence. *Still playing his blasted chamber music, though I vaguely recognise this piece.* Doug must have unwittingly grimaced, causing Esperanza to glance at him. The 'chief's' face remained stony as he nodded his approval.

"Looks like something from an ancient tomb," Doug whispered to Esperanza. Thwaite took them in the lift to the ninth floor. Doug made a show of guiding Esperanza through the door while noting its size and strength. Thwaite, ever alert, noticed.

"Friends of Masood rent this apartment to me for a nominal sum, so I don't query why there's such a solid door. Possibly all the flats have them."

"Who lives on the top floor?" Doug asked bluntly.

"Huh! That's the big mystery. There are lots of rumours. I've not seen anyone go in or out. Whoever it is must arrive and depart in great secret. My apartment is small and provides all I need, so I don't push my luck. You know what Masood's capable of. The man upstairs, as I like to think of him, is probably even more ruthless." He conducted them around the flat, and Doug noted a comfortable lounge with a hideaway bed settee, a small kitchen with all mod cons, a double bedroom and a very nice bathroom with a door leading off.

"Is that another bedroom through there?" Doug enquired.

"Not as far as I'm aware. I don't have a key to it; I imagine it's something to do with building services."

"You 'ave a balcony, *Señor* T'waite!" Esperanza expressed surprise as she looked through the glass door at one end of the lounge.

"*Sí señorita*. I'll get the key and you can see how good the view is." All three went onto the balcony and admired the vista.

"It's a heck of a drop from here." Doug leant over and studied the ground beneath. He noted that the compound containing the generator and the oil tank was directly underneath.

"Do you ever get out 'ere, *Señor* T'waite?"

"Yes. Particularly in the morning if there's a good sunrise."

"I don't think I could. I've never been good with heights," Doug admitted, while thinking, *Showing some weakness might relax him.* Unfortunately, Thwaite didn't believe him, remembering Doug's service reputation as being totally fearless. Doug produced a small digital camera from his pocket. "Will it be okay if I take photos of the view?" He switched it on and balanced it on the guardrail. Thwaite stepped briskly to his side and grasped for the camera.

"Please don't. The landlord's very strict about taking photos. Something to do with conditions applied when the building plans were approved." As his hand touched Doug's, the latter let go and the camera fell straight down and hit the roof of the building in the compound with an almighty clang.

"Damn! I thought you had hold of it," Doug cursed. "I'd better go down and get it." As he made a move into the lounge, Thwaite stopped him.

"Sorry. That's not possible. I'll call security and have them collect it for you. Meanwhile, I'll give you the tea I promised."

He doesn't trust me! Even if he's not working for them anymore, he's exercising extreme caution. Why does he think I'm here again? Does he believe dropping my camera was an accident? Doug was peering out of the window while observing Thwaite's reflection in the glass.

"Eez big pity you lose camera, *Señor* Evans." Esperanza patted him gently on the arm. "I 'ave camera you can use," she added.

"Not now, Esperanza. Perhaps later. Our friends can get me any copies I want, thank you." Doug was about to sit down next to her when Thwaite appeared from the kitchen.

"Could you come out here for a moment, Evans?" Doug nodded and wandered after Thwaite.

"Something wrong?" he muttered.

"Yes! It's you! You might've fooled the girl; you didn't fool me. You dropped the camera deliberately. Why?" Thwaite stood directly in front of Doug and assumed his superintendent stance.

In for a penny... Doug thought as he paused.

"Okay. You're right. When I was here before, I'm sure I saw your friend Masood."

"He's **no** friend of mine anymore! Remember, it was his abusing my association with him that cost me my job," Thwaite interjected angrily.

"Be that as it may. I saw Masood and you know how I feel about him." He paused to underline his dislike for Masood. "I told Bennett and Langley and they agreed I'd come back here and check. My friends' request for me to accompany Esperanza is a useful cover. I'd hoped that dropping the camera'd give me the opportunity to see if Masood's in this building," He paused and glared deep into Thwaite's eyes. "Now **you** can tell me. Does Masood live here?"

"He might. I did see him here once, but I don't know if he lives here or was just visiting."

"Why don't you know?"

"This flat was offered to me as some compensation for 'helping' them by arresting their competitors. No need to look like that, Evans. I don't expect you're pure as the driven snow. I have this flat at a nominal rent – provided I stick to the owner's rules, which include minding my own business. You could say this place is like a home for retired vicars." Thwaite appeared to be smug at his own explanation.

"More like a home for retired criminals," Doug retorted as Thwaite poured the tea.

"Let's get back to your friend before she gets suspicious."

"And we get to blows," Doug suggested with a grin. The conversation returned to small talk with Esperanza, mostly by Thwaite. This was a side of his former boss that Doug had never seen, knowing only that Thwaite had divorced his wife. After the tea, Thwaite escorted them back to the entrance, where Doug collected his camera. Esperanza, ever the country bumpkin, thanked Thwaite profusely, as though she was overcome with the honour of being allowed inside such a posh establishment.

"Yes, thank you, Thwaite, you've been very helpful," Doug said as a matter of routine. Thwaite grinned and shook his head.

"Always pleased to help the police, Sergeant Evans." Thwaite chuckled at the time-honoured remark by Doug, which was intended to worry the listener. When they were safely out of sight, Esperanza spoke first.

"Right! What have we learnt? As a stranger to you both, I think Thwaite doesn't trust you, and I think he's hiding something. Furthermore, I don't think the generator *is* in that compound." Doug listened to her in amazement.

"Go on. I'm fascinated to hear what else you learnt today," he prompted her. She pushed her hair back carefully and peered at him over her sunglasses.

"That enclosure is far more guarded and secure than is necessary for an oil tank. The store, or whatever it is, inside the enclosure looks almost bombproof." She was pleased with her deductions and Doug's acknowledging nods. "Have I missed anything?" she asked.

"Air vents and pipes," Doug announced, as a matter of fact that she might have forgotten.

"There are no air vents or pipes in the store building?" she suggested.

"Yes, but there's a pipe leading into the main building, and close by was an exhaust vent."

"So the generator's in the underground garage," she deduced.

"Precisely! And what do you think is the reason for such a substantial concrete road leading to the iron gates? And what about the two circular iron covers slightly below ground level just inside the gate?" He stopped walking and turned to her. She stopped, looked left, then at a passing cloud seeking an answer.

"It can't be for water or sewage; they'd have to be readily available for the local council. You need a solid road if it's for heavy vehicles. The emergency generator would not require much fuel... so?"

"There must be a larger fuel tank underground," Doug proposed.

"For heating the main building?"

"But that'd require more air vents, and the fumes would discolour the outer wall." Doug offered his reasoning slowly to get her feedback. "What else could they need a large amount of oil for?"

Esperanza looked baffled. "Could it be for fuelling their cars?" she conjectured suddenly.

"Possibly, but why go to all that trouble when there are filling stations nearby?" He tried to draw the answer from her. She turned and studied what could still be seen of the tower.

"The only other thing to need oil is..." Her jaw dropped and Doug finished her statement.

"...a helicopter."

"Why would they want to refuel a helicopter when it could readily be refuelled at any airfield?" Esperanza was accustomed to technical and logical solutions to problems. However, this conundrum required the flights (no pun intended) of fancy to which Doug was accustomed in matters relating to Masood.

"Did you notice anything unusual about the top of the building?" He took her arm and they continued walking.

"There are no structures for elevators, water or air conditioning!" she declared after visualising it. "They're incorporated on the top floor – in the penthouse!" she postulated. Doug shook her arm gently.

"Picture the building carefully." He waited a few seconds.

"Now picture the windows for each floor." She wheeled around to him and froze.

"There's a much larger vertical area between the top-floor windows and the roof edge than between any other floors!" Doug clapped his hands and bent down and kissed her on the forehead. "Why, Sergeant Evans! It's a good job I know you're gay, or I might think you have amorous feelings towards me." She fluttered her eyelids in false modesty. Doug overcame his reaction to her declaration by listing the facts.

"There are no service structures visible because they're hidden by a rooftop perimeter wall. The same wall could hide a small helicopter."

"Big enough for one or two people," Esperanza stated, and then frowned. "Or could it carry more?"

"The more the merrier but I don't think the roof space is capable of anything that big." Her nod of polite understanding could not mask her concern.

"If the 'copter is basically for escape and not regular arrival and departure, how does Mr Big get in and out of the building, let alone the top floor?"

"Getting in and out of the building is easy. It's by car to and from the underground garage. Mr Big, as you call him, could either be driven by a trusted chauffeur or bodyguard, or... he could disguise himself as a chauffeur. This I'm certain from my previous time spent watching the comings and goings. The enigma is how he gets to the top floor. Sorry! You understand enigma?"

"*Sí*. It's the same in Spanish. I checked the elevator carefully. There's no button for the top floor. There was a keyhole near the buttons, which could be for maintenance or to operate some override system."

"Good! It's…" He stopped in mid-sentence and frowned. "Something doesn't correlate!" He quickened his pace as he sought the answer, and she almost had to run to keep up. "CCTV!" he declared, and stopped dead, causing her to bump into him.

"CCTV?" she repeated.

"Yes. This Mr Big likes to hide his identity. To operate an override, he'd be noticed by the guards. Thwaite may have given the answer. If everyone minds their own business and only the top man knows exactly who lives in each apartment, then he could have stairs or a lift from one of the other three flats on the same floor as Thwaite. The guards'd have to treat all occupants as possibly Mr Big. He'd live on any floor and visit the ninth floor when he wants to access the penthouse."

"No!" Her repudiation startled him. "Too complicated and too open to deduction by guards and cleaners. It **has** to be someone on the ninth floor."

"In that case, Thwaite knows who it is."

"Why should he know?"

"He may've been a corrupt cop, but he knew his stuff."

"Knew his stuff?" she queried.

"Yes. He was a trained and efficient policeman. His weakness was his impatience. He couldn't wait to get promoted so exchanged information with Masood. So rules or no rules from Zebec, his natural curiosity would lead him to find out which neighbour is Mr Big." They were approaching Miguel's salon where they'd part until the next day.

"You need to determine our priorities if we do get into the tower, Doug. Do we seek Masood or Mr Big?"

"Or is it the same person?"

"Or it could even be your Thwaite, though I doubt it."

"Why do you doubt it?"

"I like to think I'm a good judge of people, and I can see that he **would** bend the rules, but I don't see him as a real criminal. In fact, under other circumstances, I'd be attracted to him as a handsome and very personable man." She ended her favourable character analysis with a note of defiance.

Women! No wonder I'm gay! She's allowed herself to be swayed by Thwaite's false charm. I just hope it doesn't affect her duties here. "Sorry, but I disagree!" he whispered in her ear as he kissed her cheek while she was getting into Sean's car.

Esperanza contemplated their progress. *His antipathy for Thwaite is making him blinkered. I hope it's not going to affect our mission. Thwaite is okay. I know he was coming on to me, but I trust him.*

CHAPTER 21

That evening, Miguel provided Doug with more information. Through contacts, he'd learnt that El Herrero's level of operation varied according to whether if there was a person of higher authority in town.

"There's no news of anyone named Masood. The only person who has arrived in the past year who could be associated with any change in El Herrero's status is your Parouk." Miguel spoke with resignation.

"That's very, very interesting." Doug compressed his lips in deep thought.

"In that case, you'll be anxious to know where he lives," he taunted Doug.

"Not in the Zebec tower?" Miguel pretended to walk away. Doug chased him and gave him a shake.

"If you insist on knowing," Miguel teased him further, "yes, he lives in the tower!"

"It gets better and better," Doug enthused as they relaxed with their drinks.

Doug woke early and used Miguel's desk to make notes. *Masood arrives here and the criminals adjust their local organisation,* and *he lives in the Zebec tower! The head of their Turkish branch was deposed when he visited Masood! Thwaite is compensated – no – rewarded with a nice flat in prime position. First, because he was a major influence in Masood's rise to power and second because Masood knows and trusts him. Masood has not been relegated to Spain! He's simply moved his HQ! We won't need to mess with the lower floors. We can go straight for the top. It should be an official police raid to collar him. Getting it approved and organised would take time and Masood's spies'd find out. Esperanza and I will have to grab him and worry about the rules later. I'd better let Langley know.*

Being given all his lover's facilities was a real bonus. Using Miguel's computer, Doug sent Langley an urgent coded email explaining the situation and his plan.

"Secretly contacting a rival for your affections, eh, big boy?" Miguel appeared as Doug pressed send.

"Hardly. I've just been updating my boss. Anyway, what have you got to worry about? I didn't know what love is until I met you. Whereas you've probably had lots of lovers before me." Doug rebuffed him angrily.

"Ooh! Temper, temper! You're deliciously magnificent ven you're angry. To ze vorld, you're my lover, but to me, you **are** ze vorld!" The altered quote had the desired effect, and a placated Doug kissed Miguel.

Later, meeting in a busy café for coffee, the police duo compared notes.

"So you see, Esperanza, our target is revealed, yet we've no way of getting closer." Doug shrugged despondently.

"Yes, we are! That's **my** piece of news. On the way here, I saw the Mercedes, captured in your earlier photos, being left at a service garage. I stopped to browse a shop window opposite and saw the driver walk away."

"Excellent work, partner. When'll he be back? He may have collected it already."

"No. I wandered down the road and back and then went into the garage and asked."

"You asked when the driver would be back!"

"No. I told them my brother has a Mercedes like the one I could see in their workshop, and it's due for its annual service. I asked how long such a service would take. They said a basic annual service only took a few hours, but for a job like the one they'd got in, it'd take all day. I checked their hours of work as I left and found they close at 5pm." Doug was ecstatic and tapped the table gently before adopting a more serious face.

"Are you're ready for this? It's a golden opportunity, and we would have to assume that the car is kept in the underground car park. After all, with Zebec's obsession with security, they would ensure the car was serviced near where it was stored. And where else around here could provide such tight security as their own tower? It's a chance we will have to take, but there's much danger involved."

"You getting cold feet, Doug?" she smirked.

"Not for me. It's putting you in danger that's the worry."

"Look, Daddy! I'm a big girl now. I volunteered for this. You get the equipment ready for me."

At 4pm, they took up a vantage point with a clear view of the garage forecourt. The target Mercedes came out soon after they arrived, and they prepared to move closer. They checked the whereabouts of all the staff, then Esperanza concealed herself behind a bin near the car. Doug ambled over to the car and openly inspected it. Eventually, a mechanic came and asked what he was doing.

Doug ignored the question and enquired, "*Que es dueño de este coche.*" His Spanish showed he was a foreigner.

"*No es asunto tuyo!*"

I don't know what you said, but I presume you're not going to tell me the owner of the car, Doug surmised. He opened the driver's door and pulled the boot release. The mechanic was joined by another and they pulled him away from the car. Doug walked along and closed the boot as he passed it.

"*No toque el coche.*" Doug shrugged to indicate he still did not understand, and looked in his English Spanish dictionary.

"*Sí. Espero conductor.*" He strolled to the public pathway and leant against a post. When the driver arrived, Doug advanced again. Two mechanics restrained him while the driver signed some papers and quickly drove away. Doug walked away until he was out of sight and then started running at a steady pace to the Zebec tower.

Esperanza lay in the boot of the car, pressed against the back of the rear seats. She had found a few loose items there, which helped cover her in case anyone glanced inside. She was aware of each change of speed and direction, and knew when the car was entering the underground garage. Clenching large wire cutters, she prepared to launch a surprise attack on anybody opening the boot. She lay tensed, physically and mentally, in her personal mausoleum.

After hours – well, several minutes – of complete painful silence, she dared to move. With a compact hand drill, she made a small hole in the car's rear shelf. She paused every few seconds and listened for any other sounds in the garage. An eerie gushing noise made her stiffen, and even though she was in darkness, she automatically closed her eyes to interpret the sound. Liquid! It was a waste pipe. She finished her hole and slowly eased a small webcam through it. Turning and raising it at the same time, she was able to see most of the garage in the light of a couple of emergency lamps.

Assuring herself there was nobody there, she quickly worked on the boot lock and opened it. She inched it up and slithered out. Shielding the screen on her cell phone, she sent a message to Doug – Clean boot

She stashed the phone back into a thigh pocket in the all-embracing black hooded outfit she wore under her now-discarded street clothes. Knowing that the security guards may have CCTV to watch for any movement, she inched her way across the floor face down. Reaching the incoming power cable, she severed it with her insulated wire cutters. She paused, switched on her head torch and found the generator. Hastily, she severed the oil pipe and jammed the machinery with her cutters just as it kicked in. Dashing to the garage door, she opened the personnel door, letting Doug enter. As they headed for the stairs, a guard came down them, using a large torch. They ducked behind a car until he had passed, then Doug stunned him. Esperanza helped bind and gag the brute with tape.

"There's three guards on at this time. One will have to stay in their office and could've called for backup already. The other'll check on the one we've clobbered," Doug whispered.

"What about the residents? Many of them will be hard cases."

"Most should remain in their flats to protect their anonymity. As to the others... well... speed is our best weapon." They were nearly at the foyer when they ran into the second guard coming down. Something stunned him, and as they taped him, Esperanza looked at Doug in puzzlement.

"What just happened to this man?"

"I thought this might happen, so I picked up a couple of stones while I was waiting outside. I used to throw stones at targets on the beach as a kid, and it proved useful tonight."

They entered the foyer and found the security office locked. Esperanza picked the lock but the door was barred on the inside. A couple of attempts by Doug to charge it down failed, so they raced up the stairs with Doug in front wearing the second guard's cap and jacket. Twice they met residents who were deceived by Doug's appearance and returned to the safety of their apartments. Reaching the seventh floor, they were confronted by a hulk who could only be somebody's bodyguard. Doug indicated for Esperanza to hide and then he advanced on the guard, who produced a handgun. Doug raised his hands and continued to advance when a familiar voice came from the open doorway.

"Well, well! My old friend Sergeant Evans. Do come in," Masood sneered triumphantly. Doug walked slowly into the apartment with his hands still raised, followed by the gorilla with the gun. **Thud**! Doug stepped aside to avoid being crushed by the collapsing giant. Esperanza then used the fire extinguisher she had floored the bodyguard with to spray Masood, who was reaching for a gun. Doug grabbed the weapon and restrained him while Esperanza bound his arms behind his back. Forcing their captive onto a chair, Doug questioned him above the sound of police sirens outside. *That's rich. These criminals have a security alert with the police.*

"You're full of surprises, Masood. I thought you'd be living on the top floor."

Masood managed a grin and shook his head. "You're not as clever as you think you are. You really don't know who lives there! Well, I've got news for you—" Two gunshots caused both cops to duck and turn, Doug's gun raised. The apartment door was slammed shut. They paused to check Masood, who **was** dead, and then opened the door cautiously and entered the corridor. Empty! Listening carefully, they detected the sound of somebody climbing stairs.

Peering through the fire door, they saw that the corridor there was empty, so they raced up to the ninth floor. They heard some noises there, but the corridor was empty and all doors were shut. Crashing each one in turn with a fire axe, they found one empty and bemused occupants in the other, and no trace of guns or stairs to the penthouse. Finally, they assaulted Thwaite's door and gained access moments before the local police arrived. They were held at gunpoint until the police were satisfied that they were colleagues. Too late, they heard the helicopter depart at speed. Thwaite was out and Doug nodded knowingly.

"Typical! Conveniently for him! He was never there when I needed him in London."

"He won't appreciate what you've done to his door," Esperanza reminded him.

"Bugger his door. He must know who was in the 'copter, and will have a good idea who killed Masood." Back at the police station, they had to explain events to the *comandante*.

"If Parouk, or Masood as you call 'im, is not ze top man, 'oo is?" demanded the *comandante*.

"The person who should be able to answer that is Bernard Thwaite, my former corrupt boss. He must know, living just beneath the man. He pretends he doesn't, but he also denied knowing Parouk was in the building."

"Vere is zis T'waite now?"

"That's the problem! He was out when we got into the building, and I don't think he'll come back after what's happened."

"Do you 'ave any suggestions?" The *comandante* wanted to pursue the case to a better conclusion. For him to crack a major international crime syndicate would definitely help his career.

"I think we should search Thwaite's apartment very carefully. He'd not have been prepared for us breaking in, and there could be a clue to the top man there," Esperanza suggested, causing the others to remember her presence. So, the three of them, with a couple of trusted officers, returned to the Zebec tower. There were still some police there vetting the occupants. Nothing of any value to their investigation was found, and they only had the locked cupboard in the bathroom to check. Despite her best attempts, Esperanza was unable to pick the lock. A drill was obtained and nearly half an hour later they gained entry. When lights were shone inside, they all gasped. It wasn't a cupboard! It contained only one thing – a flight of stairs leading to the top floor. Doug didn't stand on ceremony as he dashed up the stairs, and the rest followed. There was a palatial apartment and a large office containing a computer and various communication appliances. Their unwelcome entry must have tripped some sort of self-destruct device, because there was much sparking and some smoke coming from the equipment. The policemen hastened towards the glass door into the office.

"Stand still!" Doug ordered.

"*Estarse quieto!*" Esperanza translated the warning with a shout.

"What's wrong, Sergeant Evans?" The *comandante* had frozen, along with his men.

"In Britain, we call it belt and braces. This mastermind appears to have thought of everything. So, not only will all information and links be destroyed, but there's probably a backup to destroy the whole apartment! There's nothing we can do for the equipment in the office now. I suggest we leave carefully and have explosives experts vet the place." Doug pointed towards the door where they had entered. Esperanza translated for the benefit of the others, and the *comandante* agreed.

"All evidence has gone, but at least *we* are here to continue the war against Zebec," Doug muttered.

"Perhaps you know who the top man is after all, Sergeant Evans?" The *comandante* smiled.

"You mean Thwaite?"

"Yes. 'E's not 'ere when we arrive and only 'e 'as access to ze top floor."

"Everything points to him. There's just one thing I must check with my London colleagues."

They left the building and Doug phoned Langley and asked for information on Thwaite.

"Yes. It's virtually certain that Thwaite is the top man. They've checked his personnel file and it confirms that he is a qualified helicopter pilot."

To think one of Europe's top criminals worked in the same office as me. Now I understand that Masood was merely a cover for the front man, Thwaite. The Turkish episode was decided by Thwaite, not Masood. When we captured Masood, he was about to betray Thwaite, who killed him first. Looks like I'll have to return and make my report just when I was really enjoying myself.

Esperanza, much shaken by her misjudgement of Thwaite, stayed in Málaga to clear loose ends and make her own report.

CHAPTER 22

Birdie and Terry left for their honeymoon. Many of their friends were surprised. *How could they leave the man who brought them together critically ill in hospital? There's nothing they can do to help at present, but they'd be available if there's any change in Jenkins's condition.* Thus ran the thoughts of their friends, though nobody voiced them aloud. To explain that they were only going as far as a small hotel in the Cotswolds would have defeated the mystery and possibly their privacy. They were less than an hour's drive from Houghbury, and they rang the hospital every other day to check if there was any change in Maurice.

The police circulated an international alert for David Lee, which resulted in his arrest in Spain. Conveniently, he was escorted to the UK in the custody of Sergeant Evans, returning to give his report. It was a dramatic meeting. Bennett, Langley and Tyler were joined by the commissioner, two other 'bigwigs' and two 'nobodies', who said nothing and were known only to the commissioner. As these strangers were not taking notes, it was reckoned that they were secretly recording the meeting. None of Bennett's team said anything about it but acted accordingly. Doug had taken personal photos of the Zebec tower, its surroundings and its interior, which he used to explain the events leading to Masood's death. His audience murmured when they were shown the cupboard with the stairs leading to the penthouse.

"You'd not get much up those," one person commented.

"Thwaite certainly covered his tracks," said Tyler. When Doug had concluded, Bennett took over to explain the role of Interpol and the invaluable assistance of Esperanza. He assured everyone that relations with the Spanish police had not been damaged and the Málaga *comandante* was delighted to have been able to clear up the Zebec connections in his town, including a couple of corrupt cops. There was an international warrant out for Thwaite's arrest.

"How much information was found in the Zebec tower?" asked the commissioner.

"Nothing of great importance, sir. Paper records were mostly destroyed, and any computer records were removed in the helicopter," Doug replied.

"How many people were in the helicopter?" The commissioner made a great show of taking notes himself as he enquired further.

What's he trying to prove? Doug thought. "We're not certain. There may have been two but no more, sir," Doug answered, with a hint of disappointment. The two nobodies looked at each other with quizzical frowns, which Doug noted. After a few more questions and explanations, the meeting was closed by the commissioner.

When the others had departed, Bennett and Langley held Doug back.

"The commissioner's authorised your immediate promotion to inspector, Sergeant Evans," Bennett said very formally, and added jocularly, "though John and I can't think who on earth would recommend you." They both shook his hand and patted his shoulder. Doug gave a sad smile.

"Thank you, both. However, it'll only be for a month or so as I'm tending my resignation." The two men looked aghast at him.

"Why?"... "What're you going to do?" they asked in astonishment.

"I've achieved my ultimate target with the fall of Masood. Now I'm going to have a new life in Spain." Tyler walked into the room at that moment.

"What's the problem?" he asked as he saw the look on their faces.

"Doug's been promoted yet is giving a month's notice," Bennett declared, raising his eyebrows.

"He's moving to Spain!" Langley shook his head in disbelief.

Tyler peered at Doug, who winked at him. "Good for you, Doug. I'm sure you've thought deeply about this, and I hope it turns out all right for you."

"Hope what turns out all right for him?" Langley demanded.

"His future life, of course!" Tyler retorted, and winked back at Doug.

"It's going to take me most of my remaining time to complete the Masood report and to tie up various loose ends. Plus, I've still got some leave owing."

At Bennett's suggestion, a joint case conclusion and retirement celebration would be planned. Later, Doug went to see Tyler.

"Thank you for not saying anything."

"Are you officially out of the closet, Doug?"

"I never knew that I was in it. You're right, though. I am gay and I'm going to live with my partner in Málaga." Doug's face brightened at the thought.

"Should the others be told?"

"At first, I thought no way! Now, I've decided people should be allowed to make up their own minds. If you agree,

I'd like **you** to tell them when I've gone. Then they can decide for themselves whether to keep in touch or not." Tyler agreed, they shook hands and parted.

Helen was extremely frustrated by her inability to help Maurice. Deeply moved by Megan's plight, she saw helping her as a way of relieving that frustration. *Megan said she'd not be able to confront the pity or horror her face would cause. Perhaps I could show her that neither need apply. How can I show her? **The kids!** She'd believe them… I'll have to prepare them, but I'll need help. Who? Perhaps the Browns know someone.*

Luck was with her; Rachel Brown had been very active in amateur dramatics for much of her life and was skilled at makeup. Rachel changed Helen's face, giving her a truly horrible appearance. Nicola and Roger were frightened when they saw the changes. Then they all talked it through, and the kids understood that they should not accept people at 'face' value. Helen further discussed Megan's plight and emphasised two facts. One, that the woman was a good friend of their best friend, Maurice, and second, that the woman was really young and beautiful.

"You don't dislike your thigh because it has a scar, do you, Nicola?" Helen patted Nicola's hand and regarded her earnestly. The girl pulled up her school skirt and looked at the mark.

"Of course not, Mummy!" Roger answered for her. "It's still Nicola, who's just as dreadful as before!" His sister thumped his arm. Helen was so thankful for their attitude that she released the tears conserved for Maurice. The kids were dismayed, thinking they had done something wrong. She put her arms around them and gave them a hug, which Roger, in his concern for her, forgot to fight. When she had her emotions under control once more, she explained how delighted she was by their attitude. She implored them to show the same good sense when they met Megan, for all their sakes.

The next day, on the pretext of visiting Maurice, who was still in a coma, they did visit Megan. She had physically improved but was still mentally depressed and turned her face away when they entered her room. Helen indicated for the kids to go round and sit on the other side so they'd see Megan's disfigurement.

"You're looking better today, Megan," Helen said breezily.

"Unfortunate use of words. Are you **trying** to be funny?" Megan replied gloomily.

"You're sitting up better and you're not so pale," Helen assured her.

"You mean you actually noticed my pallor?" She opened her eyes and as she turned to look at Helen she saw the kids. "Ooh!" she exclaimed, and tried to cover the scars on her face. Helen nodded at her progeny.

"I'm sorry, ma'am! Did we startle you?" Nicola spoke boldly. Megan removed her hands slowly from her face and peered directly at them.

"Who are they?" she asked Helen.

"She's our mummy and we came to visit Maurice," Roger piped up, as calmly as he could.

"Yes, and he's still in a comma—" Nicola started to explain and Roger interrupted.

"It's a coma."

"Same thing." Nicola glared at her brother.

"No, dear. A comma is what you use in writing. A coma is when somebody is unconscious," Helen corrected her.

"Told you!" gloated Roger.

"No, you didn't," said Nicola, and pushed him. He pushed her back.

"Stop it, you two, you're upsetting Megan." The patient had watched the episode with some amusement, completely forgetting her woes.

"No, no. What lovely children you've got, Helen. No wonder Maurice was so proud to know them."

Before Helen could acknowledge the compliment, Nicola intervened. "I'm lovely. He's horrid."

"The word is handsome, not horrid," Roger replied, and they started pushing each other again.

Helen was forced to separate them and made Roger sit on her side of the bed. Megan clapped her hands in delight and then spoke directly to Nicola, who was peering at her face.

"Does my face frighten you?"

"No."

"Then why are you gazing at it?"

"Nicola! It's rude to stare at people like that."

"It's okay, Helen. Let her tell me what she sees." She held out her hand to Nicola, who gingerly held it and leant closer.

"I see a pretty woman who's had a terrible accident. I was looking at the scars and wondered if they'd heal, like those on my leg." She paused to pull down her trousers and reveal her thigh, which Megan could just see with difficulty. "People used to stare at my leg and it made me unhappy at first. Then I forgot all about it and so did they. Mummy says you must be a very nice person to have made friends with our Maurice." The two women looked at each other and both swallowed hard.

"What did you tell her, Helen?"

"I explained how I hurt him deeply and you cheered him up." The women laughed together and it irritated Roger.

"What's so funny?" he demanded.

"You're too young to know," stated Nicola. Both women

looked at the girl, then Megan turned back to Helen and gave her a questioning look.

"And so are you, Nicola. Now, Roger, what do you think of Megan?" Helen changed the conversation.

"I didn't know I was an exhibit," Megan protested.

"I think that..." Roger stood up and, walking sloth-like with his hands behind his back, as he had seen his teachers do, he examined her from head to concealed toe. "I think she's okay, but she'd be a **lot** nicer if she talked to me instead of my stupid sister." The outburst brought a protest from Nicola and laughter from the women.

"If Megan agrees, next time we come, you can spend time with her separately," Helen assured him.

"I'll look forward to it. They're the best medicine I've had since the explosion."

As they left, Roger dodged back into the room and whispered in Megan's ear, "Can I show you my magic tricks?"

"I'd love to see them." She turned and kissed his cheek as Helen returned to collect him. He glowed as he left and Helen popped back briefly.

"He's always hated being kissed until you did it. I'm *really* jealous now." She grinned and waved farewell. *The visit's gone far better than I ever imagined. Megan seems shaken out of her self-pity; Nicola's maturing fast; Roger too is growing up; and myself? I'm on cloud nine with pride in my children. If only Arnold – or Maurice – could've seen them today!* A tear crept down her cheek as she drove home.

Thursday already! The newlyweds could not believe how fast their week in the Cotswolds was disappearing. Birdie's anxiety about Doug Evans's mission compelled her to text Phil Tyler for news. This was surprising, yet welcome. Phil, thinking she would not be able to attend Doug's retirement party, told her about Doug and Miguel and asked her to keep it secret. Her action prompted Terry to text Derek for information. Derek hated texting and reluctantly replied.

M Davies better. M Jenkins dead

Birdie checked the message to ensure Terry had read it correctly.

"Should we phone him?" Birdie wondered.

"Yes. From the look of his text, Derek had difficulty sending it." It was his normal office hours, so Terry phoned there. His secretary, Eileen, answered.

"Ah, **Mr Schott**!" She seemed even more cool than usual.

If she weren't such an efficient secretary, I'd get rid of her, Terry thought, but adopted as pleasant a manner as possible.

"Can I speak to Derek, please, Eileen?"

"**No**! He's at Carter's, making the arrangements. He is a *real* friend!" she said, implying Terry was not, then burst into tears.

Terry was amazed and waited for a few moments. *Carter's aren't the undertakers I'd have chosen. Still, it's good of Derek to do it for us.* "When is the funeral?" The crucial question was posed with reluctance.

"Next Wednesday, 11am at St Peter's. Lot you care!" She voiced her thoughts aloud.

She's very rude. She should be more understanding of my position. There's nothing I could've done for him. Why should I feel guilty?

"Tell Derek we'll be back on Saturday in plenty of time to make any more arrangements and to attend the actual funeral."

"All right," she replied bluntly, and rang off.

Terry turned to Birdie. "There's nothing we can do, and we've only a couple of days left. Let's do that special walk we've been considering all week."

She tried to force a smile to mask her sadness. "Let's. At a time like this, I'd rather be alone with you and nature than sightseeing."

The walk was more like a forced march as each strained for muscular pain to overcome the pressure in their hearts. Reaching the summit of the hill, they sat on a fallen tree to recover their breath. For several minutes, they sat there in silence, gazing mindlessly at the beautiful scenery. Terry became aware that Birdie's eyes were moist from... from what? Sorrow or the pace of their ascent?

"What is it, darling?"

"It's the injustice of life! Maurice was nobody special, yet he affected the lives of so many without ever reaping the rewards he richly deserved."

"He didn't just affect lives, he saved them." They sat in silence, remembering their departed friend.

"How **should** we weigh up his existence in the annals of human history?" Terry mused.

"That's what **we** can do," Birdie replied abruptly.

"Do what?"

"We can measure his life. I'll start." She cleared her throat. "I've just got some news from Phil Tyler which ties up matters stimulated by Maurice. **So** – to the reckoning. On the negative side of Maurice's life is the fact that without his incident with Charlie, Ivor Kowalski'd be alive. On the positive side, Masood, an extremely dangerous criminal, is dead, and a corrupt policeman and judge have been exposed. Bennett and Evans have been promoted and the latter is leaving the force to join his... er... lover in Spain."

"His lover?"

"Yes. It's that gay hairdresser who visited Houghbury."

"Did you know Evans is gay?"

"No. Neither did he until he was smitten by the Spaniard. Continuing my list – corrupt police have been exposed in Málaga and an international crime syndicate's been dealt a heavy blow. A perverted inspector in Houghbury's been uncovered, and dear Joe's received the accolades he always deserved. Oh yes, I nearly forgot. The physio who helped Ivor has joined the police, and the Malayan girl is marrying an RAF pilot."

"Are you quite finished?" Terry hugged her to him. "Now it's my turn. On the negative side, Arnold Phillips is dead, as is his anticipated replacement, Maurice."

"That doesn't count. Leave Maurice out, as he's the one we're judging."

"Okay. Also on the negative side is the redhead scarred for life. You've covered the Houghbury police. So, on the positive side… a priest has totally altered his life and is to wed a previously embittered nurse. Judith has escaped an unhappy marriage."

"As has **your** Diana Gumbrill," Birdie interjected, and Terry pretended to ignore her.

"And… Judith is reconciled with her parents, and then – there's Sid."

"Oh yes! There **definitely** is Sid," Birdie emphasised salaciously, to Terry's astonishment.

"What do you mean?"

"I mean Judith and Sid will be an item, if not so already."

Terry stared at her in amazement. "What **I** wanted to add on the positive side of the equation was that Sid's conversion from a thug to a portrait artist of growing reputation is a crowning achievement for anyone's life."

"Don't forget Diana Gumbrill." Birdie dug him in the ribs.

"Who **could** forget her? Did you notice she changed the place settings so she was next to Maurice?" At any other time, they would have laughed at the woman's antics, but the mention of Maurice dampened their conversation again and they sat in silence once more.

"I forgot one!" Birdie suddenly announced. "My former inspector, Phil Tyler's part in the Masood case, as stirred up by Maurice, resulted in him finally adopting the child his wife had always wanted."

"Therefore, Mrs Schott, all in all, the life of Maurice Jenkins has had a very positive effect on that of many others."

Birdie leapt to her feet. "Aren't you forgetting something?"

"What?" Terry replied bluntly.

"**US!**" she shouted, scaring some nearby birds. "Married less than a week and you've forgotten me already! Maurice brought us together!"

Terry jumped up and seized her to him. "How could I ever forget? I was just being unselfish and thinking of others."

After a long kiss, they separated to gaze across the countryside.

"The influence of Maurice Jenkins on the world'll not appear on any cold stone but in the warm hearts and minds of those who knew him or whose lives he touched." Terry summed up their thoughts as Birdie rested her head against him.

"Mmm. He's certainly the spark that lit our fire," she murmured.

CHAPTER 23

Doug's retirement function surprised him. Not only was it enjoyed by all participants, it almost made him regret his decision to leave. As he returned to his desk to collect his few personal items, a colleague passed a phone call to him.

"Who is it? he asked, covering the mouthpiece.

"Don't know. Chap said it's private."

It'll be a last minute joke, I'll bet. "Evans here." He spoke abruptly into the phone.

"Doug. It's me, Miguel. Tvaite contacted me. 'e said 'e needs your 'elp to prove 'is innocence. Should I tell ze local police or vill you deal vid it?" Miguel sounded worried. " 'ello, are you still zere, Doug?"

He wants me to prove his *innocence? He's joking! Yet.. Why do I hesitate? It must be the alcoholic conviviality of the moment.*

"Yes, I'm here. Leave it with me and don't tell anyone. I'll be with you in two days. *Todo mi amor.*" He closed.

His innocence! What's he up to? Is he trying to lay a smokescreen? Is he mocking me? Why make contact through Miguel? Oh! That's easy! It was to prevent me getting a trace on him... The facts all *point to him... How could he be innocent? It's so unlikely! Why ask for* my *help? He knows my attitude to his organisation. Does he know I've resigned? I could play along with him and make sure the swine is captured ASAP.*

"'Ask not for whom the bell tolls, it tolls for thee' as Hemingway wrote," quoted Esperanza in her best English. She smiled at Sian and Maria outside the church where they had just been married.

"Why, thank you, Esperanza, an apt quotation," said the new bridegroom, beaming, as the whole group moved to the shade of an almond tree at the behest of the photographer. As various combinations of family and guests were set up, Doug stood by Esperanza and whispered in her ear.

"The original words were written by John Donne in England in 1624. Hemingway part used them as the title of his book about your civil war."

She looked up at him and grinned as she slapped his arm. "You're smarter than you look!"

"Vat are you two up to?" queried Miguel, moving beside them.

"Esperanza thinks I'm smarter than I look," Doug repeated despondently.

"Rubbish, he… he's…" Miguel noted Doug starting to glow in anticipation of praise. "He's not smart either!" Doug wheeled around to note the wink Miguel gave the petite *señorita* before they both laughed at him.

"What are you two sniggering about?" Sian demanded as he and Maria changed positions for the umpteenth time at the request of the photographer.

"We were mocking Doug for being too proud," Esperanza informed them. Miguel explained the episode aloud in Spanish for the rest of the guests with some elaboration. This caused the natural smiles and laughter all round that the photographer had laboriously attempted to achieve.

I'm not letting them get away with this! thought Doug, and proceeded to act so wounded by the jibes that he actually managed a few tears. These were largely due to the effort of suppressing his own smile at the thought of the reaction by the female guests. This was more than he anticipated as nearly all the women flocked to him in a competitive mob to try and console him. Despite some covering perfumes, he was overpowered by the scent of women and realised where his true desires lay. Noticing Miguel's look of concern, he decided to seek amicable revenge and he started kissing each lady's cheek in turn. This was too much for his lover, who pushed through the throng and put his arms around Doug.

"*Te importa a señoras. El es mi marido!*" There was an audible groan from the women as they retreated. Then everyone began talking or laughing at once, and a real party mood conveyed them the few hundred metres to the restaurant reception. A gust of wind from the direction of the sea made Esperanza realise she had left her shawl in the church. It was not in her pew. She looked about and saw a bent old man in the shadows holding it towards her. As she reached for it and thanked him, the man spoke softly.

"Don't make a sound. I'm trusting you with my life. **Everyone** is hunting me!" It was Thwaite. Her training gave her control and she remained calm and silent. "I've been tricked by Zebec. They used me as the fall guy. I must see you and Doug in secret and explain fully. I'll meet you both right here same time tomorrow. When you've heard the facts, you can arrest me or help me. Do **not** tell anyone else! My life is in **your** hands." He handed her the shawl and disappeared into the interior of the church. This was something her training had not prepared her for! She was in Málaga at that time for three reasons. To attend the wedding; to debrief Doug about their mission; above all, to trace Thwaite. Instead, her prey had found her and she had let him go!

Why? I was perfectly capable of arresting him. Am I getting soft? Has the jollity of this afternoon's proceedings weakened my resolve? No! I may be very wrong, but I stand by my first impressions... Thwaite is not an evil man. Opportunistic, self-centred, blinkered even, but not a master criminal. How can I tell Doug? He's not a policeman much longer, yet he was so personally involved in the Zebec case that he will want to see the loose ends tied up.

The waiters were starting to serve the guests when she arrived at the reception. She took her place and waited until the proceedings were completed and the newlyweds had left before approaching Doug. Miguel allowed her to borrow Doug for a few minutes to 'talk shop'.

"I know you are retired from the force, but I must ask you how you feel about Thwaite?" She peered up into his eyes for his reaction. Doug paused and then swallowed hard.

"Why have you brought this up now? I thought we were going to have a proper debriefing in a couple of days." he said with a frown.

"Something has arisen that can't wait," she emphasised.

"Okay. Well, Thwaite. Initially, I hated the man and held him responsible for the death of a colleague and for being a traitor. I was astonished when you arrived at a more moderate view when we met him at his apartment. And my dislike was reinforced after the events at the tower. But..." He paused. *Should I tell her how Thwaite had contacted Miguel? Yes! A second opinion could prevent any bias I still feel.* "You're not going to believe this. Thwaite contacted Miguel and told him he wants me to prove his innocence! I thought—"

She interrupted him. "That's what I wanted—"

He interrupted her and continued. "I thought we could

play along with him and capture him!" She looked closely at him for some time and frowned slightly.

He returned her gaze and queried, "You wanted to say something?" It was as much a statement as a question.

"Is there **no** possibility that he's innocent?" She inclined her head slightly.

"Innocent of what? Betraying his colleagues? Helping Zebec? Being a criminal mastermind?"

"Why would he contact Miguel and ask for your help to prove his innocence?" she reminded him.

"To help him escape?"

"**No**. He'd be better off not making contact!"

"Perhaps he is not the top man and wants me to prove it."

"What is definitely proven against him?" she persisted.

"That he gained advancement in the police through his contact with Masood and gave the latter information leading to the death of a policeman and the severe beating of a policewoman. And… he helped Masood avoid capture. Is that enough for you?" He became angry. There was an awkward pause and Esperanza gazed into space.

"Suppose he was the victim of circumstances?" she reasoned aloud. Her quiet reasoning made Doug calm down. He took a deep breath, tightened his lips and raised his eyes to the ceiling, as if seeking an answer.

"You give me **one** good reason for even considering his innocence."

"He asked me to ask you to help him!" Doug clapped his hands to his ears as if to block out her words.

"When? Where?"

"Recently. He wants us to meet him so he can explain," she said cautiously.

"Where does he want to meet?" Doug tried to appear neutral.

"**Oh no**! In view of your closed mind, I'll keep that to myself." Doug glared at her.

There are only two things people can accuse me of that really upset me. One is being dishonest and the other is having a closed mind. If almost anyone else had said that to me, they would be on their backs now. I have great admiration for Esperanza, but I think her judgement is definitely lacking here. I will try to keep an open mind if she can give me some shred of evidence that his case is worth looking into. Doug forced a smile and spoke with as much constraint as he could muster.

"How did he contact you?"

"In person." She noted the change in his manner after his long silence.

"Why didn't you arrest him?" His eyes were cold, yet the smile was still there.

"I was tempted to at first, then I considered why he **had** put himself at risk when he could be living in hiding courtesy of Zebec. He was heavily disguised and emphasised that his life is in danger. As the EU does not have capital punishment, it means the criminals must want him. He wants to see us with information, which, he thinks, will prove his innocence."

"Innocence! Innocence of what?" Doug interjected.

"You must know better than I do which of his list of crimes has some doubt involved. For instance, if his life is in danger, he can't possibly be the head of Zebec. During the reception, it occurred to me that there could have been another person in the helicopter. Thwaite could have been just the pilot and once they had escaped, he would be surplus to requirements and then **he** knew the headman's identity."

"Pos...sibly... possibly. So it's more than mere female intuition. Aargh!" He failed to see the dig in his ribs coming.

"I know you will be retired in a few days, but could you consider helping Thwaite? Your knowledge of both him and the Zebec case could be vital if there has been any... misunderstanding."

Misunderstanding! Misunderstanding? This is Thwaite we're talking about!

"I will take you to meet him tomorrow if you can give me your word that you **will** keep an open mind and listen to what he has to say. And **not** arrest him unless we **both** agree. Will you help him if he can genuinely cast doubt on his guilt?"

There she goes again – open mind! Well, on those terms, what have I got to lose? "It's a deal. Except I need your word that if he does **not** cast doubt, **you'll** agree to arrest him."

"You have my word on it. I will pick you up here at noon tomorrow."

They parted and Doug returned to an increasingly jealous Miguel. There was an unproductive silence between Doug and Miguel until they were in the haven of his villa.

"Are you 'eterosexual, Doug?" Miguel enquired with hands on hips.

"I don't think so. Why do you ask?"

"*You 'ad more zan a few minutes vith your former partner! Vy?*" the Spaniard demanded loudly.

"Oh, you are so wonderfully attractive when you're jealous!" Doug smiled calmly.

"V*y*?" The tone became more threatening.

"Thwaite." The one word with a long, meaningful pause served to placate Miguel enough to remove hands from hips and sit down, waiting for more information. "He's contacted Esperanza and wants to meet us to..."

Miguel's face changed from jealous anger to deep concern.

"**You can't! I von't let you. 'e's too dangerous.** 'e killed Masood."

Doug went to Miguel and clasped his hands in his own. "That may or may not be true. The point is, he has now contacted both you and Esperanza when he should be in hiding or in another country. We will meet him to..." *I can't tell him when or his concern for me might make him do something rash, like tell the local police* "... to hear what excuses he has. If he is unable to throw any doubt on his guilt, we will arrest him." Doug spoke with finality, meant to close the subject. Miguel's anxiety forced him to pursue the matter.

"Ven and Vere are you meeting T'waite?"

The question I dreaded. I don't want to start this new life and relationship with an outright lie. I will twist the truth, as I would've done in the Met. "Esperanza is arranging it. It has to be kept secret because, if he is innocent in any way, the criminals could be after him and they may still have influence in the local police. Where's that DVD you got for our quiet night in?" Doug leant forward and kissed Miguel to smother any further protest. *I came here to relax and find I'm treading a tightrope with Esperanza and Miguel. I'm enjoying it! I've only had a short period of inactivity, yet I really welcome this challenge. I almost wish there was a reason to help Thwaite.* He sat back with one arm round his partner and a glass of wine in the other as the film started.

Miguel was at his salon. Doug had told him he wanted to go for a long walk so would not be there for their usual lunch date. He arrived at the restaurant where the reception had been held and had to wait nearly fifteen minutes for Esperanza.

"Sorry I'm late. I think I was being followed, so I took evasive action. Let's go quickly," she breathed in his ear as she took his arm and led him away. She pulled herself tightly against him and gazed up at him in a sexy manner as she tried to match her stride to his.

My god, she could make me fancy her. Am I heterosexual? I just hope neither Miguel nor his friends see us!

"Where are you taking me, my pretty maid?" He tried to joke to cover his discomfort.

"It's not far, but I think it's better to risk Miguel's anger than to alarm any Zebec spies. Try to look more loving and holy as we are going in this church." She gave a blatant wriggle against him as they climbed the steps to the building.

I'll play the part and it had better be worth it. God help me if an acquaintance sees us.

Inside the church she detached herself from him and went to the corner where she last met Thwaite. Doug followed with trepidation, looking in every direction for signs of their quarry. They stood there for several minutes and only a priest passed them. *This is ridiculous! He's just got us on a wild goose chase – and at the risk of my relationship with Miguel!* An old bent monk was shuffling past them.

"Don't say anything! Just follow me at a distance." It was Thwaite! They did as he asked and followed him through a small side door, which led into a garden with hedges and flowers. He stopped at a semi-hidden arbour and sat down. They joined him, and Doug was forced to admire his former boss's disguise.

"We don't have long, so I'd like you to listen, make notes if necessary and question me later. I admit that I benefitted from information supplied by Masood. I didn't even know it was **him**, until, like Kowalski, I realised who gained from my efforts. In effect, he was just my informant. He gave me what I now realise was false information about 'Masood' establishing a new sphere of influence in Norwich. As you were the expert on the man, I decided to send you."

"Why didn't you tell me that?" Doug was most indignant and doubting.

"I had strong suspicions about a mole in our offices long before Sergeant Lee. Masood's ability to always be one jump ahead was the reason. Who could I trust? That's why I had Bennett keep me up to date with matters. I never gave him any information, and it was a mystery to me how he got it. That was why I welcomed Sergeant Lee's investigation. She said she'd have positive evidence by the end of that week. I—"

"So you told Masood, and that led to Lee's kidnapping and torture and Ivor's death!" Doug burst in.

"**No**! I never ever contacted Masood until Bennett made me. I've had plenty of time while in hiding to review the situation." He swallowed hard. "I was a complete idiot! To avoid contacting me through the official phones, I received a cell phone, which was upgraded with current advances." He paused and waited for Doug or Esperanza to say something. Doug was having trouble accepting what he was hearing. Esperanza clicked her fingers and stated,

"The cell phones were bugged! I've had to do it for Interpol." Thwaite nodded.

"Where is your current cell phone?" Doug demanded. *He's had time to fabricate these lies so as not to uncover his stupidity!*

"This is one of the reasons I need your help. I left it in the locked middle drawer of my desk in my Sussex home. Here are the keys to the house and the desk for you to check." He gazed at them both for some positive reaction.

Doug stroked his beard as he pondered. *It all fits together too neatly. He really has woven a credible tale of... innocence? Or ignorance? If we fall for it, he will disappear once more.*

"If we believe your account of events and have the cell phone checked, how will we be able to contact you again, or will you just vanish again?" Esperanza held Thwaite's arm and peered into his eyes.

Is she reading my mind? She's certainly not letting female intuition sway her.

"I will meet you here, same time next week." He looked at Doug's quizzical visage. "I have already placed myself in your hands when I could have continued to lie low."

"Why have you?" Doug's blunt question made Esperanza sit back.

"That's where my third point comes in. I wondered why they offered me that apartment, and near the top of the building. After all, they owed me nothing, and not being in the police anymore meant I couldn't help them there. I didn't know about the contents of the bathroom cupboard until that fateful night. A man from a neighbouring apartment burst into mine and forced me at gunpoint up those hidden stairs. When we eventually reached the roof, my purpose in the organisation became clear. I was their helicopter pilot for just such emergencies. Still at gunpoint, I flew my neighbour to a little airfield where he boarded a small jet plane. Sixth sense caused me to duck behind the 'copter as he fired at me. After several attempts to kill me, the plane left. It may still be possible to check the airfield for the bullets. One last thing – the information Masood gave me did help put away lots of villains," Thwaite explained.

"Can…" Doug started to ask slowly. *I've lots of questions to fill the gaps in his picture of events, but he's getting up to leave.*

"Is that why you're in fear of your life? Zebec are after you as well as all the police forces." Esperanza spoke briskly as Thwaite adopted his former bent position and started to depart.

Doug seized his arm and Thwaite turned to face him. Here was the man who had held power over him for years, now with a look of genuine fear. Esperanza reached for Doug's arm as he let go of Thwaite's.

"You won't regret this, Doug, or you, *señorita*. Thanks and good luck." As he disappeared into the church, Esperanza turned to look at Doug. He spread out his hands palms up, as if to signify he couldn't understand why he'd let his erstwhile enemy leave freely.

"There **is** room for doubt, isn't there, Doug?"

"Yes, and danger."

"He's survived this long, so another week should be okay."

"I'm not talking about **him**! I mean **us**! We have two problems to worry about. One is if a friend of Zebec saw us go into this church together."

"And the second?" She shook her head.

"Is if a friend of Miguel saw us!" He bit his bottom lip as he considered the consequences.

"Sorry. I was too wrapped up in Thwaite's position to think of ours." They sat in silence for several minutes.

"Got it! Provided I can convince Miguel that it is strictly platonic, we can pretend we are having a fling and that will provide a cover against both sets of 'friends.'" (He made inverted comma signs.)

"What is fling? Esperanza queried.

Doug referred to his English-Spanish dictionary. "*Aventura*," he declared.

"Ah *sí*! It is also fortunate that I recently separate from my boyfriend. He was the jealous type." She made a show of fluttering her eyelashes at Doug.

"Hmm. I wonder what might have happened if I hadn't found out I'm gay!" He made an hourglass shape with his hands as he tried to leer at her. "Anyway, I suggest we leave here separately."

"What about Miguel? Won't he object?"

"I'll phone you with Miguel's answer later. Tomorrow, if he agrees, we will go to Sussex and check Thwaite's phone. I'll book us on an early flight." He stroked his beard as he considered the various possibilities.

She then voiced her thoughts aloud. "Pretending to have a fling is one thing; flying to England for a night together is surely too much!"

"We can each stay with one of my colleagues for the night to keep them informed and return the next day."

"*Aventura! Aventura*! 'ow do I know it vill only be *farsa* and zat you do not *hacer el amor*?" Miguel's-half controlled jealousy caused him to mix English and Spanish. Doug quickly looked up the interpretation.

"There is only room for one love in my life and that is you. It will be a pretend flirtation, and in England we will be staying at different houses with two of my former bosses. We **both** have to go to investigate properly and to explain to those colleagues what is happening. There is no need for you to worry, and all you need tell anyone is that I've gone back to clear my old work." He gave his lover a gentle kiss.

"You lied ven you said you vere going for a long walk! You vent to meet T'waite!"

"Yes. I had to. If you had known, you might have tried to stop me or have told the police. You must trust me, please."

Miguel swallowed hard and clenched his fists. "You're right. We have a life to look forward to together, and I know Esperanza and… and if you were to be unfaithful, it would not be so open." They were reconciled and Doug proceeded to make the necessary arrangements.

CHAPTER 24

"Are we going to the studio or shall I clear the gutters?" Sid asked Judith, trying to sound normal without looking at her. It was several days after the wedding, and the atmosphere in the house was still a bit different, although the adults tried to pretend nothing had passed between them. She looked outside and saw how windy it was.

"We'll all go to the studio. It's not fit to work outside." She relaxed her shoulders and prepared to follow her two 'men'.

Judith's parents visited in the afternoon and looked after Charlie in the house. Judith maintained the distant tutor-pupil relationship they had before Sid's release from prison. He was perplexed and tried to concentrate on the art, with poor results. This caused her to become impatient and snap at him. During a particularly low point in the session, the build-up of the psychological barrier was halted by a cry of pain from outside. They both rushed out into the rain to find her father lying awkwardly on the path, with a tray and broken cups beside him.

"I slipped on the steps. I think I've broken something," he gasped agonisingly. The rain was torrential and, without a word, Sid gently picked up the injured man and carried him towards the house. Judith hesitated then rushed ahead to open the door. Sid placed the patient gingerly on the sofa, moving the limbs as little as possible. Judith's mother and Charlie entered to see what the commotion was about while Judith was phoning for an ambulance.

"What have you done?" demanded Judith's mother, half looking at Sid.

"I... I slipped on the steps... to the studio! It's... pouring! Sid kindly brought me indoors!"

"The ambulance will be here in about ten minutes. They said we should move him as little as possible and keep him warm," panted Judith as she got some blankets to cover her dad.

The ambulance men calmly took charge, inspiring everyone with confidence. After examining Mr Donnelly and listening to details of the accident and the aftermath, they looked at the people gathered in the room.

"He's a big man! How on earth did you manage to bring him indoors without displacing his hip any further?" The junior medic smiled almost flirtatiously at Judith. She returned his gaze for several seconds, noting his dark hair, dreamy brown eyes and chiselled good looks, before noticing how her mother was frowning at her. Then she looked around and noticed Sid was absent.

"Just a minute, there's someone I think you should meet." She went to the kitchen where she found Sid seated at the table, looking decidedly morose. *Talk about chalk and cheese! Look at this... lump of a simple man compared to the medic. I know which one I'd like to... Jeez! The atmosphere created by Birdie's wedding has made me... like a woman on heat!*

"Did you want me?" Sid looked up and saw her frowning at him.

Want you? After meeting the man in the lounge! Her smile was forced and he noticed. "Yes. The medics want to meet you." She spoke over-abruptly. Like some chastised dog, he followed her to the lounge. Beaming at her new idol, she thrust Sid forward, never taking her eyes off the medic.

"Sidney here carried him in," she declared. While she continued to exchange amorous stares with one medic, the senior one pushed forward and grasped Sid's hand, deliberately turning his back on his colleague.

"Well done, sir. Carrying such a large man indoors out of the rain with such little disturbance requires real expertise. Where did you train?" Sid was too engrossed in looking at Judith and the other medic to reply. Judith's mum came to the rescue, breaking the fraught atmosphere.

"Sid's not trained. He's just naturally… kind, considerate and… helpful." She spoke loudly and very deliberately, causing everyone to regard her with surprise. Judith flushed and peered disapprovingly at her mum. The medics returned to the patient and carried him to their ambulance. The junior one returned.

"Who's coming to the hospital with us?"

"I am!" Judith and her mum spoke together. The medic looked at them and paused.

"There's plenty of room. You can both come." He looked meaningfully at Judith.

"What about Charlie?" Judith's mum reminded her.

Without taking his eyes off Judith, he replied. "Of course he must come! I'm Ken, by the way." He shook Judith's hand as if they were alone. Sid stood unnoticed in the background. Even with his limited experience, he recognised the flirtation taking place. The two women and the child hurriedly donned their coats. As they were shutting the door, they noticed Sid.

"Will you be all right, Sid?" Mum enquired.

Judith looked back at him. "He'll be fine. I don't suppose we'll be long. Help yourself to a snack. I'll do a meal when we return," Judith added as she left.

On the way to the hospital, Ken sat close to Judith while her mum held her dad's hand and made small talk. *Is it the excitement of this afternoon or the motion of the ambulance – or is it just the closeness of this highly desirable man beside me? Whatever it is, I'm feeling more randy than I have for a very long time. That's not the ambulance. It's this Ken! He's deliberately pressing and moving his leg against mine. Every time he reaches forward, pretending to attend to Dad, he rubs his thigh along mine – a little harder! Oh, he really knows what he's doing. And it's working. I want him! I must have him! To hell with propriety! I need...* **Sex**.

"What's wrong with Grandad?" The piping voice of her Charlie cut through her lustful thoughts.

"He's broken one of his bones and we're taking him to hospital to get it fixed," Ken said impatiently, continuing to make suggestive movements against Judith. Charlie's little face began to screw up and Judith reached for him and sat him on her knee nearest Ken.

What the hell am I up to? The first Don Juan to enter my life since... college, and I go to pieces. He *fancies himself more than I do. I should have realised what he's like when he left it to his mate to congratulate Sid. My god! Sid! What must he be thinking? I virtually ignored him as I mooned over this...* she slowed her train of thoughts to study the man beside her... *this... jerk. Sid would never speak to Charlie as this idiot just did. Bloody Hell! He's started to press against me again. Well, he's asked for it!*

"Please **stop** crowding me. You'll make Charlie sick, *and* me, you arrogant Romeo!" While she glared at him, her mum turned and smiled with a slight nod of approval.

Once, when they got into traffic in the town, the driver sounded his siren, and it made Charlie very happy.

In A&E, they were attended to swiftly. The doctors advised them to go home, as Mr Donnelly would not be awake for a long time, preparing for a hip replacement. As they left, they bumped into Ken, who offered them a lift home.

"No, thank you, we've got a taxi coming," Judith insisted, linking hands with her mum and son. Her mother gave her arm a gentle squeeze of approval. In the taxi, Charlie soon went to sleep.

"I realise you must still have normal desires, my dear, but you can do a lot better than that Lothario!" Giving her daughter maternal advice relieved the tension she had been under since the accident, and she released a muffled sob as a tear crept down her cheek. Judith put a comforting arm around her.

"It's a damn shame Sidney is not a complete man," Mum suddenly sobbed. Judith pulled away and turned to face her.

"Why, Mummy! I always thought you and Dad just tolerated Sid for my sake." She widened her eyes in mock surprise.

"He may look like an uncouth gorilla, but he's a true **gentle** – man, in thought and deed. It's very true in his case that you must never judge a book by its cover." She gazed into space and spoke dreamily. "If I hadn't met your father..."

"**Mother**!" Judith was genuinely shocked, and suddenly remembered, "We should've asked about Maurice in the hospital. He's the man who brought Sid into our lives." They remained silent for the remainder of the journey, each engrossed in their own thoughts.

Sid? Even when joking with Birdie, I never truly contemplated a more serious relationship with him. If he could fulfil my... body's needs... she swallowed as if to cover her guilty thoughts *...he'd be perfect. Well, not quite. He'd still* *not be an attractive escort. Does that matter? Look at Tom! While stimulating Sid mentally, I've been learning too. Perhaps I could stimulate him physi... Thank heavens we've arrived! Down lewd thoughts.* She chuckled and her mum gave her a quizzical look.

Mum paid for the taxi and Judith carried her sleeping son in and straight to bed. When she went to the kitchen, her mum had made tea and a sandwich.

"Where's Sidney?" Mum preferred to call him by his full name. "I've not seen him." She looked for him in his bedroom and the rest of the house. Both women started to worry.

"I'll check the studio." Judith noted the rain being driven against the windows and donned her coat. Struggling in the dark against the wind and rain, she reached her studio. There were no lights on, but she looked inside just in case he was there, before struggling back once more.

"He's not there, Mummy, and his sketch book and some pencils are missing!" Judith cried, dashing back into the house from the studio. "Wherever can he be?"

Her mum gazed at her pensively and frowned. "I hate to play devil's advocate, darling, but I think you made him very jealous when you flirted with the ambulance fellow."

"But that's no reason to... run away!"

"Isn't it? He is far more sensitive than people imagine and he depends on you – and he's madly in love with you!" She faced up to her daughter as she had done when Judith had been naughty as a child.

"Just because, out of the kindness of my heart, I helped the man, does not make me responsible for him. I don't own him and *HE DOESN'T OWN ME!*" she screamed at her mum, who promptly slapped her face. Judith started to cry and had to hide her distress as Charlie entered the room.

"What's wrong, Mummy? I heard shouting. Where's Sid?" The erstwhile centre of her life asking for the very person she was trying to reject was too much, and all the earlier mental stress broke free in a strange wail of despair. Her mother and son stared at her in alarm then rushed to comfort her.

"What **have** I done? Why do I lie to myself? I do love him. What have I done? I've been thoughtless. No! I've been cruel. I don't deserve any man, let alone one who… worships me. Where can he be? It's **terrible** outside and he has no transport." She became less hysterical and her voice reduced to a mere mumble as she reasoned with herself. Her mum left her and put Charlie back into bed. When she returned, Judith was curled up asleep on the sofa.

"**Stupid bugger!**" Terry exclaimed as he swerved just in time to miss the man bent over against the torrential rain. "I'm sure I missed him," he added as he pulled to the side of the narrow lane. They were returning from their honeymoon in quiet contemplation of the sadness that awaited them. He had to drive slowly and extra carefully because of the rain. Even so, he had only seen the dark shape of the walker at the very last second. Birdie was first out of the car as she already had her coat on. She bent into the storm as she approached the stranger leaning against the hedge.

"Are you all right, sir?" She touched his arm. The dripping shape slowly straightened up and turned to face her. They both blinked in surprise and due to the force of the rain. "**Sid!**"

"Hello, miss," he muttered, trying to stop shivering.

"What on earth are you doing here? And on a night like this. Look, darling, it's Sid!" She pulled Terry closer as he joined them.

"Get into the car, both of you! We'll catch our deaths out here." He caught hold of Birdie's arm while she pulled Sid with them. Once in the car, they made a protesting Sid remove his saturated coat and wrap up in an emergency blanket.

"Now then, Sid. Where are you going to?" Birdie had got into the back with Sid.

"I don't know, miss," he mumbled. She looked at Terry and shrugged.

"J-Judith d-don't w-want me no more," Sid rambled on.

"I don't believe you," the solicitor said, cross-examining him. Birdie took Sid's hand in both of hers and rubbed it.

"What makes you think that? Has she said so?" she asked gently.

"She's in love with this other bloke."

"Did she actually say so?" she insisted. There was a pause while he stared at the rain on the window.

"Well… no. B-but I could see the way she looked at him." Birdie gesticulated at Terry and he started the engine and drove on towards Houghbury. En route, Birdie was able to get a more complete picture from Sid. Midnight was fast approaching when they arrived at Judith's, and the house was in darkness.

"Have you got your key, Sid?" Birdie asked softly.

"No. I left it on the kitchen table as I weren't coming back." He peered through the downpour at his home. "I fink we oughta go!" He lapsed into his former thug speech.

"No!" Terry and Birdie spoke in unison, then Terry indicated for her to continue.

"They'll be worried about you. We will have to wake them up." She dashed to the door and rang the bell a couple of times. Eventually, lights came on and Judith opened the door.

"What's wrong?" She saw it was Birdie and pulled her inside. "It's very late! What's happened?"

"Have you lost anything?" Birdie interrupted, noticing her friend's eyes were red, and not from sleep.

"I don't think so, why?" Her question was answered by another ring from the doorbell. Impatiently, she opened it and found Terry pushing Sid towards her.

"**Sid**!" She threw herself at him, pulled his head down to her level and began kissing him fervently.

At first, he just let her, then he responded and returned her kisses with more passion than any of them would have believed possible. There were tears streaming down his face, mingling with the rain there. They separated for air.

"But what about the ambulanceman?" he gasped. Just then, Mum arrived.

"Tell Sidney the truth, Judith!" she ordered. Her daughter's joy at the return of her man was dampened by her mother's demand and the realisation that Terry and Birdie were watching.

"We must go. It is late and we've much to do tomorrow, which is why we've come back a day early." They left quickly with an excess of gratitude following them to their car.

"Now! You can explain yourself to Sidney while I go back to bed. I'll want you to take me to see your father first thing tomorrow." The warning was wasted as Judith geared up for the dreaded explanation.

"I'm sorry, Sid. I've been a fool!" she began tenuously.

"You can never be a fool in my eyes, Judith." His sincerity was reinforced by the unexpectedly bold way he sat down beside her on the sofa and put his arm around her. Her astonishment made him pull back. She saw the change in his expression and moved close to him, forcing his arm around her once more.

"I did flirt with that man – for a while. Something I've not done since my college days. Then I suddenly understood a feeling I've been hiding from myself for some time now."

The cultured woman, and former hippie, studied his face for several seconds before continuing in a small husky voice. "I… love… **you**, Sidney Cracken."

His acceptance of this unbelievable fact caused a metamorphosis, which astounded her. The cover of the book that was Sid almost glowed with confidence and love, reflecting the contents. It was a voyage into the unknown for him. Nobody had ever said they loved him in his whole life. Youths had admired him in his 'thug' days, but not one single person had ever really loved him. Despite his damp clothes, he was warm from some internal glow that spread throughout his body. His chest was bursting with pride and love; a tingle ran up his spine, bringing a lump to his throat and moisture to his eyes. There was another stirring he had never experienced before.

Sid reached for her and kissed her eyes, her ears and her neck, while he ran his fingers up and down her back, gently massaging her. The lump in his throat prevented speech, so he leant back, smiled and nodded as the moisture forsook his eyes for his cheeks. He cupped her face in his hands, kissed her forehead then her nose, her lips and her throat. His hands traced the shape of her face, her neck and shoulders, and finally came to rest on her breasts, which he caressed with the touch of butterfly wings. She gasped and closed her eyes, dampening his unaccustomed behaviour. He pulled back with concern and became awkward once more.

It is Sid! For a moment, I was transported to the very gates of paradise. Why did he stop? His face! He thought he was… doing wrong. If there is any wrong, it's the opinion I had of his abilities – and I don't mean art! Go for it, Judith! It's now or never! I'm being shameless and I don't *care!* She lunged forward, pushing him back on the sofa. She forced her tongue into his mouth and held him like that as her hands ran over his great frame, until one reached his groin. He had remained limp with surprise, but she recognised the stiffening where it mattered most. He half heartedly tried to stop her, and she used her other hand to guide one of his hands to the zip on her trousers.

Bloody hell! Do I have to rape him? Stop, Judith! There I go, talking to myself. He's a true virgin, and this has to be done properly. We can continue this in the proper place to avoid interruption. And to check that he is a real man... that this wasn't some aberration. She reluctantly separated their bodies.

"Come with me, Sid. We have to get you out of those wet clothes. We can go to my room, we won't be disturbed there!" She pulled him to his feet as best she could and half dragged him, collecting a towel on the way. "Don't do a thing. Leave it all to me," she commanded as she closed and locked the door to her bedroom.

"Yes, Judith," he managed to whisper, and remained petrified, partly from fear of the unknown and partly in anticipation, as she slowly removed his damp clothes. All the time, his eyes never left her and he felt no shame, somehow realising that the circumstances were the most natural thing. His body was his sole source of what little pride he had, and Judith was stunned by the magnificent muscles and sinews she was lovingly drying. He began to protest when she gently blew on his twitching penis and then kissed it. She pushed him onto the edge of the bed and removed his socks.

Standing in front of him, she dropped her arms. "Now it's your turn to undress me." He was very slow and clumsy to begin with, gathering pace with his growing manhood. Desperately, she helped him with the last items, and thrust him back on the bed. Then she completed his education – to **her** ultimate satisfaction.

CHAPTER 25

Superintendent Ron Bennett met Doug and Esperanza at Gatwick Airport. They had contacted Ron directly on his private phone and given him a brief explanation for their visit.

"Fortunately, **Inspector Evans**, you are not officially retired for another twelve days. I know you gave a nominal month's notice, but you had so much leave owing that we've been forced to keep you on the payroll a bit longer." Ron grinned as he gave Doug the news. Esperanza waited a moment then made a mock curtsy.

"**Inspector**! You never mentioned you'd been promoted, Doug."

"Aha! The famous Esperanza. The inspector here led us to believe you were **quite** a different person."

"I—" Doug was drowned out by his inquisitive partner.

"**Just what has he told you, Superintendent?**" She directed her remark at Ron while placing her hands on her hips and glaring at Doug.

"We asked about you after your success in Málaga, and he said you were a plain old-fashioned Spanish woman." She quickly checked the description on her electronic translator.

"*Claro anticuado!*" she read out. "I know I not pretty but you have been nasty! Why?" While Doug struggled for an explanation, Ron took her hand and held it to his lips theatrically.

"My dear *señora*, you are not **pretty**." Her eyes widened as he paused. "You are *preciosa*." She glowed as she reached up and kissed him on both cheeks. Meanwhile, Doug had been watching in amazement with his mouth open. He finally managed to speak, cutting in to Ron's romantic dreams.

"What is *preciosa*?"

"It means beautiful, Doug. A word I learnt as a young single man on holiday in Spain."

"Your superintendent is very gallant; you are not, Doug. Why did you say those things about me?" Doug swallowed hard as he grasped for an explanation.

"Before I admitted to being gay, I did not want the staff here to know how attractive you are because they would have teased me too much."

She checked her translator. "Ah, *burlase*," she announced. "Why, Doug, I thought the only sensitive part of you was the back of your neck." She reached up threateningly and he backed away.

Ron was enjoying Doug's discomfort. *So the man of iron has an Achilles heel. This is too good to let go.*

"Are you really gay, Doug, or are you using it as a cover for your philandering?" He winked at Esperanza, who understood and continued the assault on Doug. She briefly checked for the word she required.

"Why, darling, I'm sorry. I not realise you keep our affair secret. But why you tell them you are gay? You are good lover!" She breathed the words seductively as she moved closer to Doug, who shook his head vigorously. He clapped his hands loudly at each in turn to cover his annoyance.

"I shall treat all your remarks with the contempt they deserve. Have you arranged transport and accommodation for us, guv?" Ron tried to disguise his mirth by extracting his notebook and reading from it.

"We have received a message from the Málaga police for you, which I don't understand. It simply says – bullets found near abandoned helicopter." Doug and Esperanza looked at each other and nodded.

"Of course, Thwaite could have planted them." Doug was not convinced.

"Yes, but that would be too much forward planning at such a time," Esperanza reasoned.

They explained to Ron what the message meant. He rubbed his chin as he digested the information. "To avoid any leaks, I will take you to my home. We don't know how yet, but Zebec is still getting information from someone at our station. You can leave your luggage there and collect the car I've arranged for you. When you return from Sussex, you collect your bags and spend the night at John Langley's house." He winked at Esperanza again. "He has a double bedroom prepared for you both."

"That's wonderful. Isn't it, darling?" She reached for Doug's hand, which he started to snatch away then took her hand and pressed it firmly to his lips. He had spotted the last wink.

"That is marvellous. Now the truth is out, we can make the most of this opportunity." Then he leant down and whispered in her ear. "Have you got your pills? I don't have any condoms." She was taken by surprise and instinctively stepped back.

"W… what about Miguel?"

Ron noted the reaction and decided enough time had been wasted on horseplay. "Right! To serious business. Esperanza will stay at my home. Doug will be at John's."

By mid-afternoon, Doug and Esperanza had arrived at Thwaite's house near Midhurst. It was a nice three-bedroom modern house in a good location, surrounded by high hedges, helping to obscure it from the other properties on the small estate. Parking the unmarked police car on the short drive, they got out and quietly closed the doors.

"Good for privacy but not for security." Doug appraised the site as they approached the front door. He noted the burglar alarm by a firm called COPONE. Unlocking the door, they entered cautiously, pushing it firmly and partway against the pile of junk mail and tapped in the code on the alarm system. Preventing his partner from advancing further, Doug appraised the narrow hallway and listened for any sounds.

"What's wrong?" she whispered.

"I don't trust Thwaite yet, and this could be a trap." He listened once more and looked around the hallway intently, before letting her enter a fraction. Pointing at leaflets on the floor, he continued. "Notice how it's arranged. I was careful to open the door slowly and only enough to get at the alarm. Someone's been here before and pushed the door the whole way. Hence, the second pile against the wall." Esperanza looked from door to floor and nodded. They moved tentatively to the lounge, checking every footfall, floor, ceiling and furniture. Doug made her stand behind him while he scrutinised the contents of the room.

Nothing seemed amiss and he was about to go further when an alarm sounded in his head. *The desk is in the bay window just as Thwaite said it would be, so what is wrong with it?* Esperanza moved alongside him and opened her hands questioningly. He put a finger to his lips and pointed at the desk. He gestured for her to remain where she was and then moved very slowly to the desk. He selected the correct key and bent to insert it. He gesticulated for her to leave the room, which she did reluctantly. Gingerly, he grasped the handle of the middle drawer and, fraction by fraction, he opened it without using the key! When it was fully open, he called out.

"I think it's okay for you to come in." She moved beside him and regarded the empty drawer.

"Where's the phone?" Her voice was hoarse with the tension.

"There isn't one. If there ever was one, it's been stolen."

"You mean there has been a burglary?" she deduced.

"No. Look around. Nothing of real value has been taken. That cabinet is full of the very expensive china I heard he collected, and there are various silver items a burglar would've taken."

"Why did you make me leave the room?"

"I noticed that the top of the desk was laid out exactly as he had it at work. He was a creature of habit and liked everything to be in its proper place."

"So?"

"He had a blotting pad because he insisted on using a fountain pen. It was some kind of status symbol for him. The pad was always exactly in the middle. This is off-centre. Also, he had a Freudian thing about a photo of his wedding, which he kept upside down on one corner…"

"I didn't know he's married!"

"He's divorced. She got fed up with his dedication to the job and went off with another man. That's why he kept it upside down, to remind him of her infidelity, and for other people not to mention it."

"But it's not upside down!"

"Precisely! The robber or robbers must've thought they'd moved it and put it back the right way up. In fact, there must have been more than one, as a single robber would know he hadn't touched the photo."

"Judging by the small scratches around each drawer's locks, they had no keys and had to pick them. They could've done the same with the front door, but how did they silence the alarm?" Esperanza was on her knees, examining the desk.

"If they were part of Zebec, they would have had either the necessary expert or other means of disabling the alarm. Also, as the phone was in the obvious place on the desk, did they search the rest of the house?" Doug pondered aloud.

"Perhaps they had to check if he had any other evidence that could be used against them."

"Correct." He snapped his fingers. "We will have to tell the local police. They can look for fingerprints and so forth."

"What is fourth?" She was so alluring when she questioned his use of English he almost wished he was not gay. Before he could answer, the door swung open and four policemen entered.

"**Police**! Stay where you are," the sergeant instructed. They had been informed by a suspicious neighbour about intruders.

"It's all right, Sarge, we are police," Doug announced, reaching in his pocket and then remembering he had handed in his ID when he left for Spain. Esperanza recognised his predicament and produced her Interpol ID. The sergeant examined it and asked for Doug's.

"Can I have a word with you alone, Sergeant?" Doug requested, and moved into the hallway, closely followed by the suspicious policeman.

"This house belongs to my former boss, the disgraced Superintendent Thwaite. You've probably heard of the criminal organisation Zebec—"

"Yes. I recently read about the case in the *Police Gazette*. Major bust! Done by a man from the Met and a woman from Interpol," he quoted with pride.

Do you remember the pair's names?"

"Er... Evans and Mari – something."

"Very good. I'm Evans and took early retirement, but they brought me back from final leave to check new evidence. If you check the lady's ID again, you'll see she's the Mariona on the case." Doug proceeded to explain why they were there, what they had discovered and what they would like the local police to do. After rechecking Esperanza's ID, he agreed to collaborate.

"One thing that bothers me is how you got past the alarm." The sergeant scratched his head.

"Thwaite gave us the code. When he told us about his phone."

"But how did the robbers get in?" the sergeant asked. "This type of alarm is tamper-proof and is online to our station."

Esperanza had been quietly digesting the substance of their conversation. "How long has that particular alarm been installed?" Both men turned to look at her.

"About six years, I think. At least that's when it was linked to us."

"Would the firm that fitted it know the code?" she pressed the sergeant.

"No. Only the householders would know." Esperanza looked at Doug and directed her next question to him.

"How long has Thwaite been divorced?"

"I think it was four years ago. Of course, unless he was doubly careful, he obviously had the new door lock installed but wouldn't bother with the code. Being a very busy man, he would not want the trouble of trying to learn a new code." Doug clapped his hands in delight.

"You mean the robbers could've got the code from his ex-wife! Would she do it willingly?" The sergeant had picked up their train of thought.

"Zebec are experts at getting information. That's almost

certainly where they got it. And they'll have experts at picking locks," Doug assured him.

"How can we help now we're here?" The local man was keen to get involved and noticed his men getting bored. Doug considered the possibilities.

"Thwaite is a very tidy and methodical person. Could you have the rest of the house checked for anything unusual, broken, or just out of place. Check locks for signs of picking or forcing. Check potential hiding places for papers or valuables – or anything they consider worth mentioning. They should confer among themselves and bring it to our attention." He noticed Esperanza put a finger to her lips. "Finally, I must ask you all to keep this search and our presence secret. This mob has already killed several people, including a colleague. You may have seen his funeral on TV a few months ago."

"You mean Kowalski. I remember joking about it being a good old English name for a cop in the Met, and being severely reprimanded by our inspector," one of the other policemen butted in. Doug nodded and began to scrutinise the rest of the lounge, causing the rest to do their bit. Nothing untoward was found. Doug gave the sergeant the private phone numbers of Ron Bennett and John Langley and, with a final warning about the need for secrecy, Doug and Esperanza left the locals taking fingerprints.

"With your obvious dislike of Thwaite, I suppose you are more certain than ever of his guilt, as there was no phone." Esperanza stated wearily as they drove back to Ron's house.

"On the contrary, what we found actually supports his version of events."

"How? If there was a burglary, they could have just taken cash from the desk. There might never have been a phone." She played devil's advocate.

"True. However, nothing else of value has been taken, and the drawers have definitely been opened by picking the locks. Then there was the absence of anything suspicious and no signs of a safe."

"How does that support him?"

"He claims he got no financial gain from his relationship with Masood. The only assets he had according to the internal investigators were that house and a one-room flat near the office. Had he been getting money, he would've been careful enough to secrete it somewhere handy, like a safe."

"There wasn't one!"

"Precisely!"

"What do you suggest we do next?"

"Are we thinking along the same lines? You tell me what you would do."

"Interview his ex-wife," she said bluntly.

"Exactly. But that can wait until tomorrow." They separated at Ron's. Esperanza explained to him what had happened at Thwaite's house and their contact with the local sergeant. Doug did the same for John.

"Paul Tissier? He sounds French," Doug remarked when John traced the new husband of Thwaite's ex-wife, Marilyn. "Do we know anything about him?"

"Only that he visited this country regularly on business."

"What kind of business?" Doug questioned his former boss.

"Antiques. Though that covers a multitude of possibilities."

"How did he meet Marilyn?"

"Hang on, Doug, I'll consult my crystal ball," John retorted. "Fortunately, Immigration do have a copy of his passport photo, and they're sending it through on this computer."

Ron dropped Esperanza at John's house on the way to work. It would have caused suspicion if both men were absent. Doug brought her up to date.

"Where do they live now?" She got straight to the point.

"He has a flat in London but spends most of his time abroad," John replied, and checked incoming mail on his computer. Loading his printer, he handed them a photo of Tissier moments later. They all studied it, seeking inspiration, and Esperanza was first to react.

"If I can use your computer, John, I'll forward the photo to my boss at Interpol. He'll trace him to an address or criminal record if possible." John agreed and the two men retired to the kitchen for coffee. When they rejoined her, Esperanza had a disappointed look and was doing a pencil copy of Tissier's face.

"They have no knowledge of the man, but they have passed our enquiry to the French Ministry of Justice. I presume you two have had your police records checked." She looked up at them and smiled at their consternation. They each dramatically pointed a finger at the other, and John took over at the computer and forwarded the photo to his office.

Meanwhile, Doug kept looking at the photo and then closing his eyes. *I think I do know that face. Perhaps Thwaite had a picture of him with Marilyn. This is ridiculous! He may just be someone I passed in the street. I may not have a photographic memory, but that face has definitely got some associations for me. Huh. I'm getting paranoid. The only faces I remember from work are all connected with... Masood? No! It couldn't be.*

"Tell your men to check for a likeness among the pics in my old file on Masood," he instructed John.

"You will need more evidence that serious criminals are involved before Ron can authorise you to go to France," John reminded Doug.

"I agree." Esperanza startled them. "As you British say, we mustn't close the stable door before the cart," she continued, causing much amusement, which hurt her feelings.

"Good try, Miss Mariona, but you've mixed two sayings. The one that is correct in this case is don't put the cart before the horse," Doug explained. "And you are right, that's just what I was doing."

"Perhaps your local police will find something." She quickly recovered her composure, to John's admiration.

"I'll check when I get to the office and keep Ron up to date. You two can wait here and use my study and computer. We're still worried that there is another mole at the station. The suspected new boss of the UK branch of Zebec definitely has inside information, so we don't want them to know about you, for as long as possible."

When he had gone, Doug and Esperanza set about producing a spreadsheet on the computer in an attempt to clarify the facts and aid lateral thinking. Doug loaded all the negative facts against Thwaite's innocence.

"There's no mobile phone; no neighbourhood warning of burglars; only a few scratches to even hint at a burglary. Why was he in an apartment next to the top of the Zebec tower, and with hidden stairs to the top? Was it merely a coincidence that he is a helicopter pilot?" He looked at her defiant.

"The phone was stolen, at night, by professionals. He was given that apartment **because** he's a helicopter pilot. The secret stairs were a… how you say – braces and belt security."

"Why belt and braces?" he butted in.

"I've thought about what we found during our uninvited visit there and decided the lift **does** go the whole way to the top. It had a special locking device to prevent minions from going to the top floor. It would have been essential to get all the equipment installed. If there was an emergency, the top man could escape with the pilot up the secret stairs, delaying any pursuers, which is what happened. Using the lift would have been obvious and possibly allow quicker access to the top floor," she explained.

"Well reasoned, but it doesn't mean that Thwaite isn't the top man." He slapped his forehead as a new thought occurred to him. "OR that either of them is."

"How do you work that out?" His lateral thinking had lost her.

"If such a vast crime network could plan for so many eventualities, they could easily have made the helicopter escape a decoy. There were other unknown persons of dubious background staying in the tower." He paused for breath.

"Or even someone with **no** background." Her agile mind took his deliberations to the limit. "Anyway, such arguments mean you **are** opening your mind to the possibility Thwaite is telling us the truth." There was a note of satisfaction in the suggestion.

"On the other hand…" Doug smiled at her "…he could be the brains behind it all. He has contacted us to take the pressure off him while the organisation regroups. He could've arranged his house to make it look like it had been burgled, to back his story."

"How could he know you would spot the upside-down photo and the misplaced blotting pad?"

"Simple! He knows my ability to observe the smallest detail, and I may despise him for the way he got promoted, but I would never underestimate his abilities." Doug stroked his new beard thoughtfully.

"As he is a wanted man, he couldn't come to Britain to arrange it, and his ex-wife wouldn't help. He would've had to trust somebody else." Her voice trailed off as she considered the permutations.

"I'm not convinced that Thwaite's tale has any foundation – yet. We will have to wait for the local police or Interpol to provide something definite. Meanwhile, we can do some individual brainstorming and list possible heads and any new headquarters of Zebec," Doug suggested. Esperanza quickly ran through mentally all the people she knew to be associated with Zebec in any shape or form. She almost closed her eyes as she pictured the ones she had encountered.

"There is one person who should know *ze* top man," Esperanza thought aloud.

"**Who**?" demanded Doug.

"The zombie in the security office."

"How... of course! Anyone going to the top floor in the lift would be on his CCTV!"

"Or the CCTV cuts out when the special key is used," she countered.

"But he would still be seen using the key. We'll see if the local *comandante* knows the system."

"What about the *espia* at your police office?" she pondered aloud.

"*Espia*! What's that?"

"You know – person giving information to the crooks." She hastily looked the word up on her translator. "You say spy!"

"Right. If Thwaite didn't give them information, who did?"

"Or what?" she suggested.

"What?"

"Yes. There could be a bug in the office," she reminded him.

CHAPTER 26

"It was so sudden!" Eileen croaked, and began crying. Derek comforted her and indicated for Terry to go into his own office. A few moments later, he joined him and carefully closed the door.

"Sorry about that, Terry. I don't know why she's making such a fuss. She hardly knew Maurice," Derek said quietly.

"How'd she mean it was sudden? We thought he'd a good chance of recovery when we left."

"That's just it. His last visitors were Helen Phillips and that Megan girl, who's now staying with her."

"**Staying** with Helen!" Terry expressed surprise.

"Yes. It seems she has taken pity on her rival for Maurice's affections, in view of her nasty disfigurement. Though neither will win Maurice now. Anyway, they visited him together and came away full of hope, as he appeared to be making a total recovery. The very next day, they were informed of his death, and the undertakers removed him before anyone could pay their last respects." Derek shook his head in puzzlement.

"But Eileen told me you arranged the funeral!" the lawyer said, cross-examining his assistant.

"I told her that to stop her moaning about your absence."

"She has every right to moan. Birdie and I should've been here. I—"

"Don't **you** start! There was absolutely nothing **anyone** could do. Wherever he is now, I'm quite sure he would agree you were right to go." Derek held Terry's arms tightly as he interrupted. Terry, deep in thought, sat down at his desk.

"If you didn't make the arrangements, who did?" he finally enquired.

"That's another strange thing. It was the police. They had been guarding him ever since the incident and took full charge. I reckon they were afraid of reprisals against Maurice for saving the intended victims." Derek shook his head and frowned as he reflected.

"They announced that the sudden removal was due to them finding traces of polonium in the bomb residue and in Jenkins. However, it couldn't have been much because nobody else tested positive for it." Terry considered Derek's statement as he doodled on his notepad.

"Perhaps Birdie… er… Mrs Schott" he corrected himself with pride "can find out more. Meanwhile, it occurs to me that **this** is Saturday. What are you, and particularly Eileen, doing here?" He forced a smile.

"Devotion to duty, sir." Derek gave a mock salute. "We knew you would come in today, so we decided to be here for you." A movement at the door revealed Eileen bearing a tray of coffee for all of them, and they spent the next half-hour in small talk before going their separate ways.

"Mere words can't unlock the gratitude in my heart for all that you and your brilliant kids have done for me." Megan had a catch in her voice as she comforted Helen when Nicola and Roger had gone to bed. It was the time when she had always enjoyed Arnold's companionship. His death had turned it into a time for unwelcome loneliness. Now she had also lost his potential replacement.

"He would've chosen you... if only he'd lived," Helen sobbed, and hastily added, "I wish he was alive, even if he would choose you. I'd rather he be living even if it meant I'd lost him."

"**No**! He'd have chosen you as his one true love."

"No! No! Knowing him, his choice between us would've been determined by his sense of duty to you for what you have suffered." They simultaneously reached for their wine glasses.

"Allow me as your guest – for which I'm extremely grateful – to clarify the situation in case we start debating during the funeral tomorrow. What you say is partly true. He would've been sympathetic about my disfigurement, but that would not outweigh his greater love for you **and** for your kids. As for me, I still have feelings for my Danny, though now he wouldn't want an unfaithful woman, particularly when she's lost her looks."

"Maybe you're being unkind to Danny. If he loved you truly, he would accept minor defects," Helen assured her.

"Nice of you to say so, but I've lost all contact with him, so we'll never know." Megan's eyes focused on her innermost thoughts and memories. *He should be back about now. Will he try to contact me? Where and how would he contact me? If he finds me, how will he react to my face, let alone my fling with Maurice?* Unwittingly, she stroked her disfigurement, causing Helen to wince in empathy.

"I will have to move on, though I don't know where." Megan voiced her thoughts. "Will my current employer still want me? After all, can you imagine the effect this face would have on anyone I was assigned to care for?" Helen leant back and examined Megan carefully. She examined the horrific scar on Megan's left cheek and temple. These were currently emphasised by the shaved hairline above. Then she used her hands in a combination of positions, helping her imagine how to disguise the problem.

"They could give you blind people to care for." She laughed and gave Megan a mock punch.

"Thanks a lot! That's all I need to cheer me up." She grinned back at Helen. In the comparatively short time she had known Helen, she recognised her genuine qualities of kindness and consideration for others.

"Seriously, though, as time passes, you **will** become much less conscious of your scars. That in itself will rub off on strangers. You could have some plastic surgery. The easiest method would be to let your hair grow back even longer and have it loose over that side of your face to make the scars less visible. In fact, that would make you a real temptress. Blimey! If Maurice were here, then I wouldn't stand a chance." Her imagination had collided with her original jealousy of Megan. Then the mention of his name caused them a melancholic remembrance of their lost love.

"I could always get a mask of… Elizabeth Taylor… or would Boris Karloff be better?" she joked, to break the sombre mood.

Helen pretended to consider the two options and then continued. "Look how Nicola and Roger have accepted you as… a normal member of our family. If it comes to that, why can't you live with us on a more permanent basis? You're a great help with the house, the garden and definitely the kids. It would give me more time for my paid work and for my studies." She kept tapping the coffee table as she reasoned.

"Oh… I see… you want me as an unpaid skivvy… a domestic slave!" Megan tried to look hurt and threw a mock slap at Helen's face. The latter ducked back and clasped her hand to her cheek.

"Ouch! So that's all the thanks I get for offering you sanctuary." They both giggled like immature girls, reinforcing the bond that had grown between them. Megan retired for the night, leaving Helen to her thoughts. *I really like this girl. Well, I like her now. Would I have liked her as much – if at all – if Maurice had recovered to be the man he was before the bomb? Ah well,* she sighed and her eyes dimmed with moisture, *we'll... never know!* She hugged one of the sofa's cushions and slowly surrendered her state of abject desolation for that of slumber.

"I must remind you of the Official Secrets Act," Basil Watson, Houghbury DCI, instructed Birdie as he led her into his office. They sat either side of his desk and he checked nobody could hear them. "It's your fault he died," he announced dramatically. "If—"

"I beg your pardon. How do you work that out?" Birdie interrupted. A smile began to play on his lips, which he quickly covered.

"You must **not** tell a soul... not even your new husband... and you must remain desolate about what I tell you... Maurice Jenkins **is** dead. That is what you **must** bear in mind at all times."

"Yes, I know that!" Birdie was impatient. "What I want to know is why the police have organised the funeral with such haste and not left it to his friends?" Basil glanced through the window in his door to ensure nobody was watching, then leant forward and grasped Birdie's hand.

"Maurice is alive." He spoke softly, tightening his grip on her hand as she tried to withdraw it.

"**What?**"

"Remember! This is **sad** news I'm giving you." He shook his head and frowned deeply to create the image of imparting dire news. "He was making a full recovery. Only one doctor and a single nurse knew. Ron Bennett told us there was a potential threat against Jenkins's life. Due to the current shortage of our staff, we could not continue to provide a guard." He stopped, released his grip on her hand and wagged his finger at her. An officer had just knocked and entered. He left a file on Basil's desk and grimaced in sympathy at Birdie as he left.

"So you understand you weren't here to release an officer to cover the hospital, so we decided Jenkins had to die. This way, he is now being cared for, apparently under the arrangements scheduled for your colleague Kowalski, and the Zebec mob will lose interest in him."

"But the funeral! How has that been engineered?" Birdie struggled to play her part in the unfolding tragedy.

"The spur to the arrangements was the death of a John Doe tramp at the hospital. This means he will get a proper ceremony, not one for the pauper that he was." They stared at each other while she digested the information.

"How many people know the truth?" Birdie donned her official mantle.

"One doctor, one nurse, one mortician and us two, and, of course, Ron Bennett. I'm ashamed to say that we used the death of your Kowalski to impress on them the consequences of not keeping this secret."

"What about the people at the air base?" Birdie remembered the original plans.

"They think he's a war victim suffering from post-traumatic stress disorder." He opened the file he had just received, scanned it quickly and passed it to her, as she quietly digested the information. "I'd like you to investigate this case. It's very minor compared to what you were doing at the Met. There is an ulterior motive." He waited for her to open the file. "It involves thefts from the hospital and will give you a reason for being there. Then you can also check on the security of our

Jenkins arrangements. It will underline the need for secrecy to the three members of staff I've mentioned, and you can check whether there are or were any undesirables there. Naturally, you will be attending the funeral – in uniform. There will be a police guard of honour to mark the vital role he had in saving so many police and others' lives." She rubbed her eyes in mock grief. "Okay, okay. Don't overdo it. You didn't know him that well."

"I'll get straight on to it, guv," she said as she left his room. *He's right. Maurice may have played a big part in my life, but I didn't really know him. Terry did. Even his staff knew Maurice better. And what about those poor grieving women, Helen and... er... Megan? Then there are the kids. I believe they were particularly fond of him. Oh, and the French family. It's going to be very difficult to keep this secret from Terry. I must remember to ask Basil when I see him next how long this charade will last.* She opened the file again on her allocated desk and studied it, making a few notes of her own. *Perhaps my secondary investigation can hasten his return to life. I must contact Ron Bennett.* Ron was away from the office, so the telephonist put Birdie through to John Langley.

"What can I do for you, Sergeant Lee?"

"Schott!" she replied bluntly.

"Who's been shot?" John was alarmed at her statement.

"**Nobody!**" She expressed her annoyance. "You've forgotten already. I am now Mrs Schott."

"Oops. Sorry, Sergeant Schott. What do you want?"

"I need to speak to Ron."

"Can I help at all?"

"Sorry. It's something only Ron will know about." Basil Watson could be correct in his list of those acquainted with the Jenkins facts. However, although it was unlikely that Ron had not confided in Langley, she decided not to risk it. She tried another tack. "What are Zebec up to now their bomb plot missed its targets?"

"Ron will probably fill you in with more data, but briefly – that plan came from Spain. We think it was a knee-jerk reaction to our part in forcing Masood from the UK to their headquarters in Málaga. We further believe they have a new boss operating here as their known minions seem to be more controlled and more circumspect in their activities. The problem is, we still have leaks, so talk to Ron outside work." After a few pleasantries, the conversation was terminated.

"*Buenos dias.*" A young woman's sensuous voice answered the phone when Birdie rang Ron at his home.

"Sorry! I must have the wrong number." Birdie prepared to end the call.

"'Oo did you want?" The voice became mature and serious. Birdie hesitated before replying.

"Superintendent Bennett," Birdie replied abruptly.

"'Ang on. I pass you to him." Perplexed, Birdie kept the phone to her ear and heard sounds of laughter in the background.

"Bennett here. How can I help?" She vaguely recognised his voice despite an obvious attempt by Ron to cover his mirth. She decided to test him.

"If you really are Superintendent Bennett, you will know the first name of the man who uncovered your predecessor, and that of the woman he worked with." She heard him clear his throat, then he paused to consider if he could divulge the information to an unknown caller.

"Ivor and Birdie. Before I say more, I want to know who you are and how you got my home phone number."

"This is Birdie." She knew it had to be Ron by the very precise way he questioned her. "John Langley gave me the number." However, in view of the ongoing investigations and the unknown mole, he tested her further.

"Have you seen Basil, Sergeant… **Lee**?" He emphasised her maiden name, as he knew well the response of the real Birdie.

"The name is **Schott** now! Yes, I have seen Basil. Can anyone overhear me there?" She dropped her voice.

"No. What do you want, Sergeant?" He indicated for Doug and Esperanza to move away.

"Basil gave me news about Jenkins, and I'm investigating thefts from this hospital as a cover to check on any Zebec members. I want to know the reliability of the information that there's a threat and where it came from. If Jenkins is threatened, what about me and the Ramas girl, guv?"

"We think the initial threat could've been a piece of unauthorised vengeance by members of Zebec left in Málaga after the death of Masood. We are falling in with it to set a trap for the mole in our office, and to discover the *modus operandi* of Zebec's new UK head. We think they have one because there has been some more disciplined activity by them recently. Once we have the information, we will bring pressure to bear to safeguard Jenkins and the rest of you," he reassured.

"That's good to know. Not just for myself but for all the unfortunates who are currently grieving over Jenkins's death." A slight smile played on her lips as she imagined the effect of the good news on Helen and her kids, apart from all the others. *The more I think of it, the more grievers I can name, including Mr Cook he had started working for. Bugger! If this is kept secret for too long, Cook will have the replacement for Jenkins that he needs. Oh dear! It might seem a remote chance at present, but both his lady loves could meet and marry – as in the best novels, where the hero returns to find his sweetheart in the arms of another. Still, that's not my worry. I've enough on my plate with this hospital assignment.*

"Are you still there, Birdie?" Ron's enquiry broke her thoughts.

"Yes. Sorry, I was just imagining all the people Jenkins's death has affected."

"As you are privy to our biggest secret, I think I can trust you with some startling news. Are you alone and is your phone secure?"

Birdie made certain nobody was within earshot. "Yes. You have my full attention."

Ron then told her about the latest developments concerning Thwaite.

"Aha! So it was Doug's Spanish partner who answered. Why the seductive greeting?"

"Sorry. That was just a joke. We were expecting John Langley to ring."

"Does John know about Jenkins?" She recollected her caution earlier.

"Yes, and Doug and Esperanza." The news tickled Birdie's newfound sense of humour.

"I **hope** for **'evan's** sake, they are to be trusted." She forced a small laugh to help Ron understand she was joking.

"Why, Sergeant… er… Schott, married life has changed you." He laughed.

She finished the call and returned to her case notes. *Something niggles me. It's not this case, it's Thwaite. If they think there are grounds for believing Thwaite was not guilty, is it possible* he *didn't have me kidnapped? Was there another mole? But I only told Thwaite in private about my news. If he never told Masood, then… how did the crook find out? A* bug!

She rang Ron again and this time he answered himself. "Ron, if Thwaite **didn't** tell anyone about my pretend breakthrough, his office could be bugged."

"Many thanks, Birdie, but the room was supposed to be swept for bugs before I moved in, and they didn't find any. Thanks again, your thoughts on the matter are always welcome."

The charade of Birdie being at the hospital to investigate pilfering spread like a plague via the grapevine despite only the senior management supposed to know. Therefore, she actually had to make that part of her assignment very thorough. This completely disguised the ulterior reason for her presence but built a wall of caution between her and the hospital staff. One ward had been closed for a year for economy reasons and had recently been reopened. To give staff time to lower their shields, Birdie decided to check the inventory for that ward, before closure and after reopening. Quite a few items had been temporarily reassigned to other wards. Small high-value items had been removed to secure storage.

Her former 'Ice Maiden' dedication returned and she thrived on her twin roles. She used the excuse of very basic stocktaking to trace items physically, with as much help as possible from 'passing' staff. By observing members of staff and their interaction, she built a reasonable picture of their relationships. Using this knowledge, she would drop confidential asides to interviewees about other persons. Thus prompted, the interviewee usually relaxed more and in pursuing the gossip would often divulge information that was either directly relevant to Birdie's investigations or could be used with other interviewees.

Two of the very expensive beds from the closed ward had been sent for servicing but were not available when the ward was reopened. In the turmoil surrounding the reopening, new beds were installed and nobody appeared to have checked on the missing pair. Birdie's dedication pierced her post-nuptial euphoria. *I anticipated the theft of minor items, such as towels, rubber gloves and even headphones, but beds costing thousands of pounds each? Surely not! It would need someone in a very senior position to cover it up. If they* have *been stolen, who would want them? No! It's too ridiculous! And yet…? Such a major theft would also require very careful planning and the right sort of customer. In fact, this needs more than a few individuals… it requires an organisation! No! I'm counting my chickens! It's probably just poor bookkeeping or stocktaking. Y-e-t. I must have a word with the hospital CEO. He's only been here for six months, so he can't be involved but may be able to point me in the right direction.*

She contacted the CEO's office and arranged a meeting for the next day, as he was currently visiting another hospital. *I can't wait until tomorrow. I must do something now. Paperwork! I just wish I had someone like Joe I could delegate it to. Let's see – stock movements. Ah! Here it is! Two beds from Spire Ward to supplier for service. Looks okay. Damn! They only went four months ago, so they could still be coming back. I'm just wasting time. I'll just confirm the current position with the suppliers.*

"Can you tell me the current position of the two beds returned to you from Houghbury Hospital four months ago, please? You've **never** had any returned? No. It's all right; joker here's been having me on. Sorry I troubled you." Birdie could not put the phone down fast enough. So it definitely looks like theft. And it's happened since the new man arrived! Lucky I found out before I see him.

She took photos of relevant documents with her pocket camera and returned to the police station. Basil arranged for the photos to be downloaded and printed while Birdie checked the background of the CEO, Art Tompkins.

CHAPTER 27

Maurice settled into his new quarters on the air base. Briefly, he inspected the room where he sat. Briefly, because there were no decorations or objects there to either attract more attention or give any clue as to the room's purpose or previous occupants. Nothing to distract him from the mental exercise he wanted to avoid.

It's very nice being mollycoddled by a beautiful Malayan woman, but I'd rather be back in Houghbury, whatever the risk. I wonder how Helen and her kids are taking my demise? And what about poor Megan? Her looks were ruined because of me. But what about Helen? I feel pity and a sense of responsibility towards Megan, but I really love Helen. Perhaps it's best that I am officially dead. Jeez! I'm soon back in my sheep's clothing. No, it's downright cowardice. Perhaps if I'd been braver when I was alive, I wouldn't be in this dilemma now. That I've failed to carve my name for posterity doesn't really matter, I've left disaster wherever I've been. Except Sid, so perhaps I did some good. Being here reminds me I am taking a place originally destined for a dead policeman. I can't be here for long as the air base is closing soon. Part is to be used by the army as a supply depot and the rest is being sold off... to help balance the nation's books. To think I used to bemoan my boring life. Should I have appreciated more what I already had? No! Some of it has been exciting and stimulating. I hope I'm not going to be dead for long or I could lose Helen... or Megan.

"Are you in pain, Antony? Or are you daydreaming?" Suzy had knocked and entered his room without Maurice noticing. He rose awkwardly to his feet and studied his bronzed carer, remembering that here they only knew him as Antony.

"Ah…y-y-yes," he stammered, caught off guard.

"Yes, you are in pain, or yes, you were daydreaming?" She grinned at his non-committal answer.

"Yes. I was," he muttered vaguely.

"You were daydreaming and you **still** are!" she exclaimed, prodding him gently in the ribs.

Fully alert now, he twisted away and wagged a finger at her.

"Naughty, naughty! What would your intended say if he found you molesting your defenceless private patient?" he admonished her, rejoining the present. *I would be very jealous if you were mine. What am I thinking? Gorgeous as she is, I already have two very attract… – well, Megan? – women I… love.*

"You're dreaming again! You **must** get out. Go for a walk. Talk to the airmen or anyone you meet. Broaden your horizons. You will have to come back to life sometime. You're retreating into your shell. Find out about others' problems. Perhaps you'll meet someone on the base who needs cheering up," the porcelain-like Asian woman instructed him sternly. He gazed at her blindly.

"What's the point? There's nothing out there. It would just be exercise for the sake of exercise!"

"Dear oh dear! You **are** in the dumps. There's a presentation of the plans for the base in the officers' mess. I'll get my fiancé to take you. As a would-be financial advisor, you could find the process interesting." (He had told her what he hoped to do when he was fit again). "It will give you the exercise with a purpose you want **and** be good for you."

Toby? I've never seen anyone so misnamed! It's a name I associate with dogs or those collectable jugs, not with a rugged, immaculately dressed RAF officer, Maurice ruminated as he tried to keep up with Suzy's fiancé. *He's the sort all women want, not a non-entity such as me.* His self-pity had grown when he was introduced to Toby, and now his lack of fitness became apparent as he strove to match his guide's pace. Crossing from married quarters to the officers' mess, the deep draughts of cold fresh air forced into him made him feel exhilaratingly alive. *I'm curious to know why on earth I will be interested in the future plans for this base. Still, I am enjoying the outing in a sort of masochistic way. Perhaps young Suzy does know what she's doing.*

"Here we are," Toby announced as he led Maurice into the mess.

They went down a wide corridor with a polished oak floor and panelling, and entered a very large room or hall with a high ceiling. There must have been nearly fifty people there.

"Are these all airmen and women?"

"No. Most of the non-uniformed people are here to apply for the lots being sold. If you're interested in history, the large table under the plans was used during the war for plotting aircraft movements." Toby ushered Maurice closer to the huge structure.

The representation of the RAF site was divided into sections. One shaded in red was for the army and included most of the hangars, some service buildings and part of the married quarters. It had obviously been selected for its secure location. Further away, some large buildings with their service roads had been designated for an industrial estate. Large open areas were designated for agricultural use. The main runway and many perimeter roads were another lot. This left a few remote buildings with small parcels of land.

As they worked their way through the throng, Maurice listened with interest to the various conversations, many of which were hushed and secretive. Many potential bidders were making notes, which they hid as Maurice passed. Through the melee, one word captured his attention – 'Megan'. *Megan? Yes, it was definitely Megan. Hold on, Maurice! There must be lots of Megans about. Still – there's no harm in checking. How can I ever find the person who said it in this mob?* He looked around the table and tried to find the speaker. Nobody looked obvious, so he backed out and walked slowly around the edge of the crowd. Nothing!

Round he went once more, listening for the voice. *I'm being stupid. First, it could be any Megan. Second, I won't recognise the voice again after just noting one word. Bugger!* He cursed inwardly as a man backed out and nearly knocked him over. The bump would have been of little concern but for his current fragile state.

"Why don't you watch where you're going, boyo?" the man snarled at Maurice. Then, as the stranger noticed the look of pain on Maurice's face, he grabbed his arm. "Are you all right, man? We didn't bump that hard!"

Toby arrived and intervened as Maurice desperately tried to breathe. "I've got him, thanks." He put his arm around Maurice and held him erect.

"What are you trying to do? Work an insurance claim or something?" The man got angrier.

"For your information, sir, he is here to recuperate after being blown up in the service of his country." Toby spoke slowly but very precisely as he issued his half-truths. The stranger stared from the towering officer to the gasping object of his derision.

"Oh. Is that so? Well... well, tell him to be more careful in future," he added in his strong Welsh accent as he calmed down a little. He then stormed off with an elderly man in pursuit trying to reason with him. Toby found a seat for Maurice to rest on, despite the latter's protestations. Moments later, he was able to speak once more.

"Toby, I have to speak to that man!" he urged breathlessly.

"Calm down, Antony. He's gone now. You mustn't upset yourself further."

"You don't understand. It has nothing to do with what just happened. I need to ask him about something completely different."

"Okay. You wait here. I'll see if I can catch him." Toby left at speed and came back several minutes later with the older man.

"You wanted to speak to my son? Why? If it's an apology you want, you won't get it in his present state, so I'll apologise on his behalf. He's so upset he's driven off without me, but he'll be back. He's a good boy really—" The father rattled on until Maurice interrupted him.

"It's nothing to do with our... bump. Anyway, it's probably me that should apologise. I wasn't concentrating on where I was going. All I wanted to know was his name as I thought we might have a mutual friend." He looked questioningly at the man.

"His name – well, I suppose there's no harm in you knowing. His name is David Edwards. Is he the one you were thinking of?"

"No. Thanks anyway. Why is he so upset?" Maurice was mystified how somebody could be aroused by a set of plans.

The father visibly relaxed and seemed keen to talk to anyone about his son's problem.

"Well, you see, he had these big plans for his lady love. Now he's inspected what's on offer here and heard what the price could be, he knows it's only a pipe dream."

The last phrase triggered a memory for Toby. *I suggested to Suzy that I should leave the RAF when my commission finishes at the end of the year and start a small business we could run together. I explained how my father had been in the air force and my mother had an unsatisfactory life until he retired, and I didn't want her to suffer the same fate. At the same time, I didn't want to be away from her as I would be if I became a civil aviation pilot. When I couldn't give her details of an actual business, she told me it was just a pipe dream!*

"What is his dream?" Maurice and the father both looked at Toby in surprise. The older man glanced around to ensure nobody could hear him then gesticulated for them to move closer.

"You realise this is a very attractive part of the country. One that many would like to visit for holidays." The two listeners nodded and also looked around, as if they were about to be privy to a state secret.

"Some distance from the main base is a satellite airfield with an old farm and outbuildings, which has been used for some storage. There is also a small hangar for light aircraft, which are the only ones allowed to use the grass runway, except in an emergency. The rest of the lot consists of five acres of flat, well-drained but stony land."

"I know it very well. I used to go there to help with training the university air squadron. It's been closed for a few years because the surrounding woods had been allowed to grow."

Toby smiled nostalgically.

"That's it," the father continued. "David thought it would make an ideal site for a cottage rental business plus a campsite." He looked around to see if they could be overheard. "The old farmhouse would be more than enough for a home and possibly a small hotel. It would take a lot of work, which he was more than willing to undertake. He worked out the costs of doing each part of the enterprise, stage by stage. What he did not allow for was the suggested price for the site." He paused and shook his head in defeat.

"How much?" Maurice asked bluntly. The man turned to regard him and cleared his throat.

"Over half a million!" He shrugged his shoulders to emphasise the improbability of his son ever getting such a sum. "I'd better go out and wait for him. He'll soon be back once he's calmed down." He started to leave as the other two reflected on what he'd said.

"He will come tomorrow for the actual bidding, won't he?" Toby asked quickly.

"What's the point? It will only mean more heartbreak."

"You tell him to come. I'll make enquiries and see if I can help him," Toby instructed the dejected man.

"I will. I don't like to see him give up so easily. Nor will his girl if she finds out." He forced a smile.

It's the wrong name, but they are Welsh. Perhaps they used the name Megan. No harm in asking. "What's his girl's name? Perhaps I know her." Maurice was as offhand as he could be.

"It's Megan. Must go. I can see him coming now. Thanks for the chat, we'll see you tomorrow." He left.

"Do you know his girl, Antony?" Toby watched the older man disappear.

"No. The one I know has a boyfriend named Danny, not David." They wandered back to the chart table, and most of the potential buyers had departed. Toby led Maurice around the plans then stopped and pointed to a separate sheet.

"That's the area he's interested in." He studied it closely and ran his finger over the paper, bringing back more memories. *My god, there's a lot of work needed to meet his dream. It's too big for just two people to run. He'll have to get* – "partners!"

Maurice stared at him. "Pardon?"

"I just thought his project is too grand for just him and his friend. He'll have to get some partners."

Maurice studied him closely. "You mean you and Suzy!"

Toby looked up from the plan and half smiled at him. "Why do you think that?"

"I noticed the way you reacted to the words 'pipe dream', and immediately showed a greater interest."

"True. I have considered it, except for one major hazard."

"What's that?"

"Partners have to be agreeable to each other **and** trust each other. We know nothing about David, apart from his quick temper and his pleasant father. His lady friend could be…" He searched for the words. "A bitch?"

"No. I was thinking more along the lines of a complete slag. I wonder if he has put his name down for the bidding? Here we are – David – Alan – Norman – Edwards. Why does he need so many Christian names?"

"That's easy. The Welsh tend to have few surnames, so some are given extra first names. Hence he is: D A N Edwards."

"Or Dane to his friends?"

"Or Dan – E."

"You mean Danny."

"Thunder and lightning! Of course! I'll check him with my Megan to see if he *is* the one." He made a note of the cell-phone number by Edwards's name. As soon as he arrived back at his quarters, Maurice phoned Basil Watson. *They told me that he was the only person I could contact – until I am reborn.* He was laughing at the thought when the Houghbury police station answered. Eventually, he was able to converse with Basil.

"This is Antony J." He used the agreed name. "Can you talk with me?"

"Yes, Antony, I'm alone. How can I help?" Basil ambled round his desk and shut the door.

I'll have to be careful what I say as someone could be listening on their switchboard, Maurice reminded himself, and gave him Edwards's cell-phone number, which he had obtained from the list of prospective buyers.

"Could someone find out if the Davies girl's boyfriend is David Edwards, please? If he is, could they find some way of letting her know he will be at this airbase tomorrow morning?" He tried to sound casual.

"Certainly, Antony. Sergeant Birdie Schott will do it for you. She knows you and she knows Megan Davies." Although he was preoccupied, Basil felt a sense of responsibility to the man he had 'killed'. He contacted Birdie immediately and explained.

"Hi, Helen, Birdie here. Can I speak to Megan Davies, please?" She recognised the voice as soon as Helen answered.

There was a pause, then the unfamiliar Welsh tones of Megan came on the line.

"Megan here. How can I help you, Birdie? Sorry, but I don't know your full name." She spoke warily, wondering what a policewoman would want with her.

"Is your boyfriend David Edwards?" Birdie plunged straight in.

"Yes. How do you know?" *I never even told Maurice his full name!*

"A colleague of mine was visiting RAF Bireham, an hour's drive from here, and overheard the man talk about Megan Davies. My colleague heard of your accident and wondered if it was you. He didn't speak to him but managed to get his details from a list of prospective buyers for parts of the base, which are being sold."

"How on earth would he be interested in buying property?" Megan butted in.

"That's something you'll have to find out for yourself." Birdie supplied the phone number and rang off. Megan replaced the phone and turned to Helen, who stared at her with concern.

"What's wrong, Megan? You look as if you've seen a ghost." Helen put her arm around her new friend.

"It's my old boyfriend. He's back in this country and was overheard talking about me." Megan stared, unseeing, out of the window. *Damn. Hearing his name has really upset me. How can it after all that's happened?*

"Surely that's good." Helen squeezed her.

"No! He's not contacted me for nearly a year." Megan then lowered her voice, as if in shame. "Which was why I had my fling with your Maurice."

"Well, he's nobody's Maurice now." A tear sparkled on Helen's lower lid.

"Even if he was talking about me, it doesn't mean he still loves me. Why didn't he contact me when he was abroad… **or** since he's been back?" she reasoned methodically.

"He could have been unable to contact you from abroad, and you don't know that he hasn't tried since he's been back," Helen persisted.

"True." Megan nodded her head slowly.

"And, Miss High and Mighty, have **you** tried to contact him?" She turned Megan physically to face her.

"Er… no, but—"

"No buts! You ring him now," Helen demanded.

"But my face!" Megan pleaded.

"Oh yes. Sorry, I forgot about your fading scars."

"So had I for a minute." She gently touched the offending marks.

"For a minute? You've not thought about them, except perhaps when you look in the mirror. The only material question is do you love him still?" Helen made Megan sit down.

"I think so. What other choice do I have?" She rested her head in her hands. Helen regarded her carefully.

"Suppose…" Megan swallowed hard. Helen lifted Megan's head. "Suppose Maurice was alive, what would you do about the two men in your life? Would you have chosen Maurice?"

Megan stared into space and tried to concentrate on what may have been. *Before the bomb, I would've… what? Stayed with Maurice? But then he would've found out that Helen really loved him. Would I have wanted a man who loved another? Would I have wanted him, even if he was a good lover, if Danny had been here? If he was alive, how could I want Maurice now I know Helen?* "No!"

"Pardon? What do you mean no?" Helen sat forward.

"I was reasoning out and imagining if Maurice was alive. The answer is no. I would not have chosen Maurice."

"Are you sure?"

"Yes. I couldn't choose Maurice for three reasons. One, he loved you. Two, you love him and I love you."

"And what's number three?"

"Three is the feeling I got when I found out I could meet Danny again," she admitted.

"Then, for goodness' sake, ring him now," Helen urged. Megan reached for the phone and abruptly stopped.

"Now what's wrong?" Helen was getting impatient.

"I don't know if he still loves me. I don't know how he'll react to my face. And… I don't know if he will forgive my unfaithfulness."

"You won't find out until you contact him."

"If I do, I could lose him forever."

"If you don't, you'll have lost him anyway." Megan gazed at Helen, seeking more hurdles to cross.

"Should I tell him about Maurice?"

"Yes. Definitely. He's a man with, I presume, normal desires. In which case, it's odds-on he's had a fling too. You can both start with a clean sheet. Now ring or else!" She raised her fist to Megan, who reluctantly dialled the number for Danny.

"Danny! Is that really you?" Her whole body came alive as she recognised his voice.

"Megan? Oh, Megan! I've been trying everywhere to find you, *cariad*." Calling her sweetheart in Welsh brought back all her old feelings. "How did you get my number?"

"You visited RAF Bireham today and somebody who knows me overheard you talk about me. Apparently, he got your details from some list. What are you doing there?"

"It was going to be a surprise for when we get married, but I think it's out of reach now."

"I don't think you will still want me now."

"Why won't I?"

"Two reasons. I had a brief affair when I didn't hear from you and thought you'd found someone else." She paused to let her garbled news sink in. She heard him clear his throat.

"Is it serious?"

"No. Ships in the night and all that stuff."

Again, he cleared his throat. "Neither was mine," he muttered softly.

She was going to react. *Ah well. What's sauce for the goose...*

"Can we forgive each other?"

"I can, can you? What's the other reason you mentioned?"

"I don't know how long you've been back in the country, but you may have heard about the bomb incident at Houghbury." She waited with anxiety.

"Yes. Terrible thing! It's not far from Bireham, where I was today."

"Well, I was caught in the blast and one side of my face is badly scarred, and you won't like me anymore!" The words coming in a torrent could not disguise the anguish in her voice. There was a delay while Danny tried to analyse his feelings at the news.

Should I be repulsed? Only meeting her can answer that. Now all I feel is overwhelming concern for her. And I'm really angry with myself. For not staying here and marrying her. I neglected her so I could make more money abroad. All right... he reasoned with himself *...perhaps the extra money was for our future together, but what future have we got now? The money isn't enough to get the life I had all planned out, and, anyway, our mutual desire may be a thing of the past.*

"Danny, are you still there?" She was close to tears.

"Yes, *cariad*. I'm here. Can you come to RAF Bireham tomorrow? I wanted to keep it as a surprise for you – when I could find you, that is. I had hoped to buy an old disused farm and some land to run as a holiday business. It's up for auction tomorrow and could be beyond our means. At the moment, I am at a loss as to where I can get the necessary finance. We can meet there and decide our future."

So it was agreed, and Megan was left worrying how her disfigurement would affect him.

"Told you it'd be okay!" Helen tried to cheer her up. Megan looked blankly back at her.

"We are meeting to decide our future… if we have one together." She went on to explain Danny's plans, and his problems with them.

"Let's contact Jeremy Cook. He's the financial advisor that Maurice worked for. He may be able to suggest a way to help Danny."

"Yes, even if we don't have a future together, it will be good to know Danny is doing well."

Helen rang Jeremy immediately and explained to his wife who she was. There was a short delay.

"Cook here. How can I help you, Helen?" He sounded very tired.

"I'm sorry to bother you, but the matter is urgent." She proceeded to give him an outline of the problem and how it affected a 'dear' friend of Maurice. Eventually, Jeremy was able to speak in very sedate, almost angry, tones.

"Thanks to the demise of your Maurice, I find myself overburdened with work, and with trying to find his replacement." He paused, took a deep breath and let fly. "**Damn Maurice**! He was just **too** good! I'm not only finding it difficult to cover work he started, I'm finding it impossible to replace him. You just interrupted my interview of another candidate!" he panted after his tirade.

"Oh dear, I really am sorry. Can I ring back later?" Helen asked in despair.

"No!" He lowered his voice conspiratorially. "He was just as useless as the rest. Leave it with me and I'll try to work something out. You say the sale is at the airbase tomorrow morning?"

"Yes, at ten o'clock in the officers' mess." Relief coloured her reply.

"Right. I'll cancel my morning's appointments. I'll call for your friend at about eight-thirty and take her there myself so I can meet this would-be leisure magnate. Is that okay?" Helen explained quickly to Megan, who nodded, and it was agreed.

CHAPTER 28

"Tompkins, the new CEO, has a very impressive CV, almost *too* good to be true. Bob Pollock checked some of the entries for me. As Doug Evans is in London from Málaga and that was the last place Tompkins worked, I asked him to check." Birdie's confidential report to her new boss was interrupted by him. Much as he appreciated her reputation and her work for him, Basil had enough pride to insert his 'pennyworth'.

"I've heard of Evans. Hasn't he retired?" Basil pressed her.

"Yes, but he's back temporarily doing follow-up on Zebec. Well, one of his friends in Málaga is a nurse at the hospital Tompkins allegedly worked in. Through the magic of the internet, we sent her a photo of Tompkins. She recognised him immediately as a 'falso' manager put in by the local crime lord. When the local police cleared up after Doug's interference, Tompkins hastily departed."

"Game, set and match!" Basil was exuberant. "You've found the spy **and** the thief!"

"I wish that were true. If he was able to steal a couple of complicated hospital beds only two months after arriving, he must have at least one accomplice, guv."

"Of course! How do you propose we find them?" Basil pushed her file back.

"We need to find out **who** bought the beds **and** who conveyed them to their new home. They couldn't afford to use independent transport. They might even have disguised their vehicle."

"Who would be prepared to pay anything like their true worth?" Basil pondered.

"It has to be a nursing home or private hospital. It can't be local, so where do we start, guv?"

"CCTV!" Basil exclaimed. "Unless they were prepared to drive a van… a furniture van… slowly down the back lanes, they could have been captured by one of the town's cameras. I'll see if the duty inspector can spare anyone to check for all suitable vans on that day."

"I can save them a lot of trouble. Apparently, the beds were collected very early in the morning before the night shift had finished. One alert nurse queried the need for such an early start and was told it was because they had a long way to go." Birdie grinned at her boss.

"Okay, Sergeant Schott," Basil addressed her formally, "how the hell did you come by that piece of information?"

"Gossip! Pure and simple gossip. I chatted with various members of staff like a confidante, spreading and receiving gossip. The nurse in question distinctly altered her demeanour when I casually mentioned the beds. Apparently, the removal had a knock-on effect, delaying her getting off duty. It so happened it coincided with her husband going away on business and he missed his train because he couldn't leave their kids." Birdie relished her success just a little too much, so Basil nonchalantly mentioned his grasp of local affairs.

"Ah yes! That would be James Walters, the civil engineer. Nice family. Sheila, his wife, assisted me once before. You may find out more 'info' from her. Just mention that you're working directly to me. What do you want to do about Tompkins?"

"I think we should leave him be until I find his accomplice," urged Birdie. Basil rolled a pencil between his fingers as he considered the alternatives.

"Agreed. Don't take any risks. That's an order! I don't want your new husband causing trouble."

"Basil Watson suggested I have a private word with you to discuss my work here," Birdie explained as Sheila Walters led her into her dining room. Birdie refrained from using Basil's rank as in her brief period working in Houghbury she had found such formality often unnecessary.

"Is it about those beds?"

"Partly," Birdie replied as she took the proffered seat. "As you've worked at the hospital for several years, I hoped you'd give me more background on the changes over that time. I've seen the plans of the building changes, which must've affected your job, but what about people?"

"Huh! The building changes affected everyone!"

Birdie nodded in sympathy at the uncalled-for reply. "I expect there's been staff changes as well."

"Yes. Several on the permanent staff, some better than others." Sheila shook her head as she pictured them. Birdie merely raised her eyebrows, encouraging her to continue.

"Even here in the West Country, we depend on quite a few migrants." She paused as she reflected. "Mind you, most are good at what they do, although it's often hard to understand them."

"What's Tompkins like? New broom, new systems, I suppose?" Birdie tried to sound casual.

"Funny you should mention him. He interferes less than any of our previous bosses. Almost a breath of fresh air…"

"But? I sense a but there, Sheila." Birdie laughed lightly.

"Well… he's always charming, but I sense that he's not a soft touch and may have a temper. Heard he was very short with one of the senior doctors who queried some action of his."

"I thought most of the staff liked him," Birdie said argumentatively, to press for edifying reaction.

"What's not to like? He doesn't interfere much and keeps mainly to himself."

"Keeps his secretary busy, I suppose?"

"Betty, his secretary, is a friend of mine, and she gets on well with him. Says he keeps his cards close to his chest. Only seems to have one person he chats with." She paused and Birdie inclined her head to show curiosity. Sheila drummed her fingers on the table in an effort to suppress her thoughts.

"You make it sound mysterious. Is it some woman he's having a fling with?"

"Oh **no**! And I don't believe the rumours anyway," she announced emphatically.

"Rumours?" Birdie prompted.

"Yes. They say Tompkins must be gay." She shook her head vigorously.

"Good heavens! Surely not!" Birdie fell in with the homophobic tone of Sheila's statement.

"You see, the person he chats with is Roscoff, a young, almost pretty, male porter."

"Is the porter gay?" the detective pressed her.

"I don't really know. He's not been here that long. He arrived about the time that policeman's funeral was on TV." Birdie's eyes imperceptibly twitched.

"How on earth can you remember that?"

"Though none of us knew the dead man, we all felt some degree of sadness, except Julian, the porter. I just chanced to see him in the background clench his fist in a kind of triumph as the coffin was lowered."

"Oh dear! A copper-stopper!"

"A what?"

"It's what I call people who don't like the police. I'd better watch out for him!" She widened her eyes and gave a look of mock fear.

Sheila laughed aloud as she shook her head. "From what I've heard about you over the grapevine, he's the one who'll need to watch out!"

"You shouldn't believe gossip, but I'll keep an eye out for him. I'd better get going. My new husband is meeting me for lunch and insists on good timekeeping." Her excuse for leaving was partly true. She was not meeting Terry for nearly an hour, so she had time to check on the porter in police files.

"Not much to tell you." Basil sounded flat as he gave Birdie news about the checks he had instigated on her behalf the previous day. "Only trace was through the passport office. Seems he was born in a place called Earlham in Norfolk. Nothing on police files at all. Could be an innocent relationship with Tompkins or possibly a gay one. It doesn't look a promising line of enquiry."

"Agreed, guv. Maybe it's marriage or this move to the country, but I would like to follow my... female intuition... even if it's just for today." *Hell's bells! My old colleagues wouldn't believe I'd ever say such a thing.* She clapped her hands to her cheeks.

"Okay, Sarge. I'll give you until the end of the week, then we will have to move on Tompkins."

I daren't tell him that it's as much about Sheila's intuition as mine. Doug Evans was in Norwich for quite a time, thanks to Thwaite. Perhaps he can provide background on Earlham.

"'Ello, Birdie. Doug's phone identify you. 'Ow we 'elp you? Doug is busy at moment."

"Ah! The sexy Esperanza. Your voice is not as seductive as last time I rang. Can you ask Doug urgently if he knows anything about Earlham in Norfolk? I need information about somebody who lived there. Do you understand? This link is not good." Birdie almost laughed at her mental picture of some Spanish *señorita* working with the now-openly-known gay Doug.

"*Sí*. You want Doug to tell you about Earl Ham of Norfolk?" Esperanza enunciated it word by word.

"Yes, please. I will send him a photo of the person very soon," Birdie replied in similar fashion.

An hour later, while Birdie was copying the photo of Julian from his staff file, Doug rang back.

"Now then, Sergeant Schott, I do not know a *Conde Jambon* in Norfolk, but I do know a place named Earlham." His deep chuckle almost vibrated her phone.

"That's the place I want to know about. What is this other thing you mentioned?"

"It's Esperanza. Ouch! Stop that! This could be serious."

"What's going on there?"

"A 1.65-metre Spanish female just assaulted a poor little Englishman of 1.85 metres."

"Well done, Esperanza. What is this *Conde* thing you mentioned?"

"She thought Earl Ham was a member of the nobility. I know Earlham quite well from the time I was in Norwich. It's near East Anglia University. Who are you checking on?"

"There's a young man working at Houghbury Hospital who may be a spy for Zebec. He's very friendly with the new CEO, who is guilty of thefts in the short time he's been here. The CEO is the Tompkins your contact told us was a bad lot in Málaga." She explained in a low voice in case anyone was listening outside the room she currently occupied.

"I presume the young chap has been checked through our system?"

"Yes and all we could find was that he originated from Earlham."

"You're in luck! Thanks to the efforts of Thwaite, I was assigned an area around the university with little chance of major crime. Earlham was part of that area. The only trouble with youngsters, apart from drunken students, was the local lads who resented their presence. I'll check immediately with the few contacts I managed to make in my time there. Your lad could've been in trouble but not gone to court or put on record. Send a photo on the police internet. It may be useful. Apart from his friendship with Tompkins, is there any other reason to suspect him?"

"He was noticed silently celebrating Ivor's burial and – nice to chat. We must do it again sometime." The change in her tone and volume told Doug that someone had joined her.

"Understood. I'll be as quick as I can." As the door had begun to open, Birdie slipped the file back into the cabinet and pocketed the tiny camera.

"**Hello, Inspector**," Roscoff announced in as friendly a manner as he could muster. "Can I be of any service?"

"I'm looking for the last month's duty rosters." Not a total lie as that would have been her next line of approach if she was not investigating the man in front of her.

"Wrong office. This is Personnel. You want Admin."

"Thanks." He blocked her exit as she attempted to make for the door.

"Now, now, Sergeant." His use of her correct rank revealed the extent of his staged entrance. "You knew very well the rosters aren't in here. And you rather obviously changed your voice when I came in." She allowed her mouth to go slack and a guilty look to spread over her face. "Just who were you talking to in such hushed tones?" She made as if to walk round him and he moved to block her once more. He misinterpreted her struggle to control an urge to overpower her cocky suspect as fear. He advanced on her in a manner he supposed to be threatening and she backed away.

"No need to get rough."

She pleaded abjectly. "It was all quite innocent. I came in here because it was empty and I wanted to make a private phone call." She averted her eyes from him and shrugged her shoulders, as if to make light of the whole business. He pressed her against the wall and she flushed in the effort not to flatten him. He gloated with satisfaction as she wriggled to get away.

"I don't believe you! Your stupid boss wouldn't be bothered if you made private calls in official time! Who were you talking to?" She twitched as he placed a hand on her shoulder, and he took it as another expression of fear. In reality, she only just stopped her automatic reaction for self-defence.

"It was an old friend," she admitted in a whisper. She contrived to gasp a little.

"An old friend! And you a newlywed!" Now he considered himself not just a man to be feared, but also a clever interrogator.

"How do you know that?" she exclaimed in panic. *I must be careful and not get overconfident as I'm really enjoying this. Perhaps I'll join the local amateur dramatic society. Jeez, his breath stinks.*

"Aha! So it's not your boss you're worried about; it's your new husband! The old…" he made speech marks with his hands "…friend is an old boyfriend, and you don't want hubby to know!"

"No! No! It was nothing like that!" she blurted out.

"If it's entirely innocent, why can't hubby know?" He put a hand on each of her shoulders and pushed his face so close into hers that his foul breath crushed her.

"Well, he… he wouldn't understand." Her face went red with the effort of not inhaling his halitosis. This actually enhanced the impression she wished to create. One of his hands started to slide meaningfully towards her breast. She protested and weakly tried to push him away.

"I could arrest you for assaulting a police officer." She pretended to push harder in desperation.

"But you won't, deary, as long as I keep our little secret. You can—"

His control over her was broken by the entrance of the personnel manager. "Anyway, Sergeant, I'm glad I could be of service to you. Anytime you need help, you know where to come." He had moved away from her and prepared to leave the room, with a nod to the manager.

I don't know if this man saw or heard anything. It is too soon to take action until I hear from Doug. I'm surer than ever that Roscoff is our man. I'd better stay in role for now. "Oh, thank you, Mr…"

"Call me Julian," he retorted as he finally exited.

"Your Julian Roscoff is not on the Norfolk police records due to… you ain't gonna believe this! Due to a mystery fire which destroyed his record and the computer file. There was an investigation but nothing was found, nor any culprit. Until my enquiry, they believed it was done to cover up for some local villains," Doug told Birdie over the phone.

"Why – 'until your enquiry'?" Birdie queried.

"Because Roscoff was never considered as the prime object. A couple of the older officers remember him from the photo I sent as a cocky little queer who was suspected of drug dealing. Every time they got close to a collar, witnesses changed their minds or disappeared, and strange alibis were produced. Sounds familiar, don't you think?"

"Definitely! All the trademarks of Zebec!"

"How are you going to handle this?"

"The DCI here is getting a search for the van or vans suspected of moving stolen hospital beds. Once we know the recipients of the beds, we will be able to act. Thanks for your help, Doug."

"All part of the job – Birdie. Are you able to speak freely?"

"Yes. That's why I got you to ring on my cell phone."

"Good. This is being kept under wraps at present, so this must be kept secret from everyone, without exception."

"Okay. Tell me. I'm by myself." She waited as Doug cleared his throat before confiding.

"You must've heard that Thwaite is the most wanted man in Europe."

"Hope they get the sod soon."

"Well, Esperanza and I have good reason to think he is **innocent**!"

"**What**! You're joking – or drunk!"

"That's what I thought when he actually asked us to prove his innocence. Yes, he gained rapid promotion on the basis of information from Masood, but we now believe he never knowingly gave information in return."

"But what about my kidnapping? He fell into the trap I set for a mole and…"

"That's the point! He did not tell Masood, **you did**!"

"That's ridiculous!" she blurted into her phone.

"**Listen**! We checked his story and have every reason to believe it. His office and his cell phone were bugged. The phone has been stolen from his house in Sussex by experts who took nothing else. And Zebec's UK gang were still getting information from our offices. The building has been swept for bugs yet again, and eventually one was found in Thwaite's old room."

"But what about the events in Málaga?"

"He thought the flat was a bribe for something. Didn't care after the way they'd used him and the service treated him. He never understood the real reason until he was forced at gunpoint to fly some man in the escape helicopter. They then tried to kill him, and are still after him. What do you think now?" Birdie held the phone away from her and stared at it in disbelief. "Are you still there, Birdie?"

"Yes. I'm trying to overcome my strong… aversion to the man. I-I'm having difficulty in accepting your facts. Having been in that position – at one time – I can see how the promotion ladder can be all-consuming. What does Bennett think?"

"Like you, he was very sceptical until we found the bug in Thwaite's office, which **he** now occupies. Like us, he assumed we still had a mole because some of his plans were obviously known to the new Zebec boss."

He paused in order to be fully understood.

"Instead of removing the bug, we used it to set a trap with false information. Only Ron and myself were privy to the details, and they fell for it. Rather than destroy the bug, we intend to use it again to catch them. Remember! Nobody had more reason to dislike Thwaite than me, and I'm convinced that he allowed his obsession with promotion to obscure his judgement." Doug paused.

"So what happens to Thwaite now?" Birdie demanded, as she was not wholly convinced.

"That's where the bug comes in handy! You're still okay to talk, are you?"

"Yes."

"Well, we'll let them think we have captured Thwaite. Then we will have a mock trial and sentence him to prison. News of the secret site of his incarceration will be leaked via the bug. A lookalike officer will take his place and will be under constant observation. To further safeguard the imposter, he will be isolated from other prisoners, allegedly for Thwaite's protection from them. This will last for a couple of weeks to see if any attempts are made to harm or even warn him. This will be in the prison holding your attackers. If nothing happens, we think it will be because they no longer consider Thwaite a threat."

Birdie found herself nodding in agreement. "Talking about threats, what do your colleagues think about letting Jenkins be reborn?"

"They told me he could come back once the problem at Houghbury Hospital has been resolved. After all, he was only an unwitting fly in their ointment. He suffered for his interference, and there are several more likely candidates for their wrath. We think, and don't take this personally, that our rustic colleagues at Houghbury have overreacted to the situation." He bit his lip, hoping she would not be affronted. Birdie took a deep breath and counted to ten.

"Don't you dare quote me, Doug, but I agree. They're a great bunch here and I love working with them. However, the bomb incident was completely outside their experience and shocked them into taking excessive precautions." She felt guilty as she said it but trusted Doug's integrity from what Ivor had told her about him.

"We should be arresting the Zebec duo at the hospital soon, and I would like some… er… perhaps… acknowledgement of our success from Ron. Plus, of course, a mention that there is unlikely to be any further Zebec interest in our area."

"Right! I'll let Ron know immediately. We'll let you know how the Thwaite affair progresses. Bye for now."

"Thanks. Bye." Birdie felt relaxed after the tension of controlling herself with Roscoff.

CHAPTER 29

To get onto the RAF base, Jeremy realised they would probably need some sort of official permission, as he did not know the rules for the forthcoming auction. He checked with Birdie, who passed the query to Basil. He discussed it with RAF Security and obtained clearance for Jeremy and Megan. Security advised Danny that Megan and her financial advisor had been included in his team for the auction. News of a financial advisor roused Danny's curiosity and gave him fresh hope for a solution to his predicament. Meanwhile, Toby discussed his idea for a partnership in Edward's holiday centre with Suzy. She viewed the idea favourably, subject, as Toby suggested, to their compatibility with Davies and Edwards.

"It's a nice idea and it would be nice to stay in this area. It would be nice to work together and it would be nice not to be stuck indoors." She nodded gently each time she said nice.

"Well! That is **nice**!" Toby mocked her while nodding his head vigorously.

"You know what I mean," she protested.

"Yes, darling. It will be... er... **nice**!" Despite all his military training, he failed to dodge her jab in his ribs.

"What about the money?" she asked, controlling her mirth.

"I've got that house I've been buying as insurance for my retirement. We could sell that and use the proceeds towards our share of the investment." Toby explained.

"Selling our future love nest…" she reached up and kissed him "…would be a gamble."

"But if we get on with them, and think that we would be able to work together and be very close neighbours, I think might be possible." Toby scratched his head in contemplation.

"That's the be-all and end-all." she interrupted.

"Right! We really need to meet them for a conflab before the auction."

In checking the contact details for Danny, Toby found two names added to his team. Remembering Maurice's interest, Toby asked him about the new people.

"Megan Davies is the girl who was injured with me in the bomb blast. I've not seen her since and understand a large part of her face is hideously scarred. I know she hasn't seen Danny, as he is called, in over a year, so whether he still wants her is anyone's guess. Jeremy Cook is the financial advisor I worked for before my enforced demise. He is a good man. Despite Danny's anger brought on by frustration and disappointment, I think he **may** be the son his father claims him to be." He paused, thought about the situation and prepared to leave them. "I can't be of any further help, except to say they must **not** know of my existence."

"Thanks. I'll arrange to meet them as early as possible before the auction, to test the waters."

Toby suspected there might have been more than mere friendship between Maurice and Megan. *If they had an affair, it could account for her presence at the bombing. My earlier curiosity about the incident and Antony's being here is paying off. I'm a fair judge of character and I think there will be no better time to judge this Megan and... er... Danny than when they meet after all this time and these events.*

Thus, when Megan and Danny met at the base entrance, they were secretly watched by Toby and Suzy. There was an initial, seemingly interminable, pause when Megan did meet Danny. Her regarding him sheepishly; him studying her carefully. Then Danny moved. He rushed up to her, embraced her with a tender passion and kissed her. First, he pressed his lips to hers, and then, to the surprise of the onlookers, he proceeded to gently kiss every part of her scarred face. One tough-looking guard was so overcome with emotion by the scene that he turned away and swallowed hard. Everyone witnessing the drama was affected, including Toby and Suzy. Megan continued to cling to Danny as if her life depended on it. The tableau was broken by an embarrassed cough from Jeremy. While Jeremy introduced himself to Danny, Edwards senior embraced Megan. Suzy, watching beside Toby, was the first to speak.

"What his father told you must be true. He must be a really good man to show such love and compassion for one so horribly disfigured." Toby gulped and nodded. She glanced at him and asked, "Would you do that?" He tried to cover a grin.

"I don't know. I've not been introduced to her yet. Ouch!" He bent as she poked him in the ribs again.

"Kiss me like that if I was all scarred?"

"No! 'Cos you might hit me again!" His laugh was cut short as she did hit him.

Danny's group was shown into a quiet room so they could discuss the forthcoming auction. He showed his plans with rough costings and projections to Megan and Jeremy.

"I realised yesterday that these are just a dream. I've not prepared accurately enough to go to a bank for the loan, which I now see I'll need."

"I love the idea, Danny, but I've not saved anywhere near the amount you're suggesting." Megan squeezed his arm.

"If only I'd known a few days ago, I might've come up with a solution. Trouble is, I'm supposed to be retiring and I've been very overworked since Maurice died," Jeremy started explaining.

"Who's Maurice?" Danny enquired.

"He's the one killed by the explosion that injured me," Megan said quickly.

"Perhaps I could invest my pension fund in your holiday camp," Jeremy mused tentatively.

"That's very kind of you, but I certainly cannot ask you to take such a risk as—"

"But you **can** ask me!" Danny was interrupted by Toby's authoritative voice as the door, which had been ajar, was pushed open by him and Suzy.

"Pardon?" Danny was amazed by their intrusion.

"You can ask me and my wife-to-be to take the risk!"

"H-h-how?" Danny spluttered.

"I'm leaving the RAF very soon and am looking for a new career."

"How would helping us give you a new career? We can't expect to make a decent living for some time, let alone repay your investment." Instead of being elated by Toby's suggestion, Danny looked puzzled, as well as despondent. Toby warmed to this erstwhile angry man.

"Before I explain further, can you tell me your intentions towards…" he paused as he turned and looked at Megan "… towards this beautiful woman here?" As Megan's mouth dropped open, Suzy clapped in approval. Danny looked from them to Megan, who managed to speak.

"I am **not** beautiful!" she protested with anguish.

"Real beauty is more than skin-deep, and a few fading scars won't hide it." He turned and pointed at Suzy. "You don't think I'm marrying this... person... for her looks, do you?" They all turned to look at the subject of his lecture, who was frowning in anticipation of further comments.

"No!" Toby continued emphatically. "It's because she's a good nurse and I need someone to look after me in my dotage." He jumped back with a dirty laugh as Suzy tried to slap him. The others understood the pantomime and laughed with them.

"Well?" The gentle enquiry closed the frivolity and everyone gazed at Megan.

"I beg your pardon?" Toby asked her.

"What **are** your intentions, Mr Edwards?"

Danny twitched his eyebrows as he glanced around the room. Everyone froze. Drawing himself upright, he placed his hands on his hips and spoke very officiously. "My intentions towards you... Miss Davies... are completely... dishonourable." The others mirrored Megan's look of surprise. "I intend... Miss Davies... to..." he looked from Megan to the onlookers and back "...to marry you and have my wicked way with you... *cariad*." As everyone laughed, Suzy fluttered her eyes at Toby.

"Will you have your wicked way with me, sir?" she breathed sensuously.

"Frequently, I hope," he replied.

"But not in your dotage!" she retorted.

The ice well and truly broken, Jeremy steered them back to date.

"As an outsider, I don't wish to harass you, but shouldn't you be doing some serious and speedy talking if any of you hope to participate in the auction?"

"I'll second that," Mr Edwards senior contributed.

"I... we... are prepared to join you in this venture as partners – fifty-fifty, that is," Toby offered.

"Oh! That's something I'd not considered," Danny replied hesitantly. Megan and Suzy smiled approval at each other, while Danny weighed up Toby.

"May I be the arbiter here, as time presses? If you two can agree to pay half the initial auction price each and shake on it, we can thrash out the other details later. You can have firm contracts drawn up by Terry Schott," Jeremy proposed.

"He's the solicitor whose wedding reception was bombed," Megan informed Danny.

"Do it, son! He's taking as big a risk in you as you are in him," Edwards senior urged. So it was agreed and they all hurried to the auction.

Though Maurice did not want to be seen by Megan or Jeremy, his curiosity about her appearance drew him to the auction. He concealed himself in a side corridor. The bidding for the various lots was much slower than expected due to a drastic downturn in the national economy. With Jeremy at his side prompting him, Danny bought their planned lot for slightly less than anticipated. Eventually, after all the paperwork was completed, they congratulated each other until Jeremy reminded them that the hard part of their partnership agreement was still to come.

Sombre-faced, they started to leave the building when Megan asked to go to the little girls' room. Toby told her how to get there and the others waited by the main entrance. Maurice went to peep round from his hiding place and came face to face with Megan. She inhaled noisily and fainted. All thought of concealment gone, Maurice tried to catch her. The disturbance attracted the others, who promptly dashed over to them. Danny grabbed her from Maurice.

"What have you done to her?" he shouted. Toby caught up with him.

"What happened, Tony?" he asked as calmly as possible.

"Unfortunately, she just saw me and fainted."

"Why **should** she faint?" Danny spoke without looking up as he nursed Megan and was joined by Suzy.

"Because she has just seen a dead man." Jeremy squeezed the words out as he stared at Maurice.

"How?" "What?" the others blurted out as Jeremy tried to continue, but words would not come. Toby brought a chair for Jeremy. Maurice was preparing to explain when Edwards senior interposed.

"You're the one who asked me about Danny yesterday!" Danny looked from his dad to Jeremy and back to Megan, who was beginning to stir.

"The police decided I was at risk from the criminals due to my actions with the bomb. They came up with this plan for me to die and be resurrected when it *is* safe. They haven't given the all-clear yet, so nobody else must know. Only Chief Inspector Watson knows in Houghbury."

"So **how** do you know Megan?" Danny demanded.

"Of course!" Maurice decided attack was the best form of defence. "You **wouldn't** know. She's the hero who spotted the man leaving the bomb and told me. Without her diligence, dozens of people would've been killed."

As he spoke, Megan sat up. "You… you're dead," she muttered.

"Sorry, Megan, as I just explained, the police pretended I was dead for my own safety! I was just telling your friend here what a hero you were at the Houghbury bombing. He's lucky to know you."

"Luckier than poor Helen and her kids, who think you're dead," Megan responded.

"**And** luckier than me with all the extra work I've had to do. Not to mention all the time spent on a fruitless search for your replacement," Jeremy added.

"Hold on! **Hold on**! Just what is this Maurice to you two?" Danny tried to unravel the connections.

"I'll answer that," Maurice quickly interjected. "Megan saved **my** life when I was in Dorset. I would've fallen off a cliff if she hadn't been there. Then she called in to see how I was doing on her way back to London. That's how she was there and saw the bomber. Jeremy was my kind employer, who I'd like to work for again when I'm permitted to come back to life." While he was explaining, Megan slowly sat upright. She continued to stare at him as though he were a ghost, until Danny caught her attention.

"Is that true, Megan?"

She looked at Danny and cleared her throat. "Er… well… yes… I suppose so."

"You suppose so! Is it true or not?" Danny demanded gently. Megan cleared her throat once more and took a deep breath as she glanced back at Maurice.

"It is true… except…"

"Except what?" Danny was exasperated.

"Except that I wasn't really that brave." Her astute mind was working overtime. "It was anything that anyone would've done in my position." Danny began to visibly relax until Maurice re-entered the debate.

"That's not true!" The whole group stared at Maurice, and Megan's expression froze.

"What's not true?" Danny was puzzled.

"It could **not** have been done by anyone! Only a person with the sharp eyes and quick mind of Megan." As Danny digested the praise for his beloved Megan, Maurice continued.

"If I hadn't been so seriously wounded and destined to die…" he made speech marks with both hands "…I would've given your lady friend a big kiss of thanks. Thanks for saving my life and those of my friends. Now you're together, I couldn't risk your anger again." Danny frowned, then he understood Maurice was referring to his outburst on the previous day.

His father intruded on his thoughts by putting a hand on Maurice's shoulder and asking, "Was it you who told Megan that Danny was here?"

"Yes. Through connections."

"I thought so! That's why you asked me about Danny."

"Yes."

"Who did you tell?" Megan was curious.

"Only Chief Inspector Watson. He told Birdie, who passed the message on."

Danny helped Megan to stand up and proffered, "Thank you, thank you **very** much. You've more than repaid any debt to Megan, don't you think, *cariad*?" He gazed lovingly at his betrothed.

"Definitely, my love," Megan was both happy and relieved to say.

"When can we meet to fine-tune the plans and get the contract finalised?" Toby enquired in the ensuing lull.

"Why not do the plans now – at least in outline – and then we can firm them up when we meet the Scott man?"

"S-c-h-o-t-t, Schott," Jeremy corrected.

"I'll arrange some sandwiches for lunch," Suzy promised.

"You won't need me," Maurice suggested, and they all spoke at once.

"Do come." "Yes, we do." "Please come." "You can help." "We do need you." "Come! You're the link." Maurice was overwhelmed.

"Okay. But remember that as far as anyone else is concerned, I'm still dead. Well, until Watson says otherwise."

"What about Helen and Nicola and Roger? They really ought to know!" Megan protested.

"I know it's unkind, but even they can't know. I'm just hoping she'll be there for me when I'm reborn."

As they proceeded to Toby's office, Megan explained to Danny about Helen and her love for Maurice.

CHAPTER 30

"We've traced the receiver of the beds... and some other equipment identified as coming from Houghbury Hospital. The local police got a warrant and found all the evidence needed to convict the owner of the care home and your supplier. The icing on the cake is the receiver identified Tompkins and Roscoff but was too frightened to explain who was behind it all. We think this could be part of a much larger operation as the inmates – sorry, patients – were mostly young illegal female immigrants. It bears all the hallmarks of Zebec!" Basil Watson announced triumphantly to Birdie.

"Marvellous! I trust *I* will be the one to make the arrests, guv?"

"Of course! I have men watching the hospital right now to ensure Tompkins and Roscoff don't leave before you arrest them. By the way, I've had a suggestion from Ron Bennett that Jenkins can be reborn as his team are satisfied that there is no longer any threat from Zebec. They have far more important targets. Sooo... perhaps you could deal with that, as you know him."

"By accident, the woman injured in the bomb blast bumped into him at the RAF station. I'll contact her and Jenkins now before I go to the hospital. Thanks, guv. This is one day I am really going to enjoy."

"One final thing, Sergeant. I know your feelings about Roscoff, but don't be too hard on him."

"I'll try. It's largely up to him. Must dash now. Cheers, guv."

I know it's wrong but I almost - no! - I do hope he tries something. I'd love to knock the smirk off his ugly face. It's wrong... yet... from a woman's point of view, it could teach him to show us more respect. Ah. Somebody's answering the Phillipses' phone.

"Ah, Helen. Can I have a word with Megan, please? It's Birdie here," she added as an afterthought, such was her eagerness to give the good news. *I wish I could be there when she's told, but duty calls.*

"She's not here, Birdie. She's moved in with Danny. It's great that they're back together, don't you think? Is there anything I can do?"

I'm certainly not going to tell her over the phone. I need to discuss it with Megan first as she must know Helen quite well by now. "No, thanks. I have to go now. Byeee."

"I'm very honoured that you asked for me to accompany you on this arrest, Sergeant." Constable Floyd was very sincere as he drove Birdie to the hospital.

"I admired your enthusiasm and I owe you for the trick I played on you with Sid. I've got a vital phone call to make now if you'll excuse me."

"What trick was that, Ted?" one of the officers in the back asked.

"If you must know, she led me to believe she was the accomplice of Cracken and I arrested them both."

"Ah. That's when Cracken got shot at the station."

"Yes. Best to keep quiet now she's on the phone." She dialled the RAF station and was put through to Maurice.

"Birdie here, Maurice. **You** are alive!"

"I know that, Birdie... what... you mean..."

"Yes. You can come out of hiding. I'll let you know the

arrangements later, but I'm very busy just now. Don't tell anyone just yet." She could hardly contain herself but tried to sound as formal as possible for the benefit of the constables listening.

"Ready and raring to go when you say so, **Mrs Schott**."

Arriving at the hospital, they were met by one of the officers on watch.

"Well, well! Young Pink Floyd! What you doing here, eh?" the officer mocked with a laugh as he nodded at the others.

"My name is Ted! But it's Constable Floyd to you."

"Stop it, you two. Listen, Constable. If you wish to insult my assistant, you're insulting me."

Birdie glowered at the officer.

"Oh yes, miss. And just who are you?" the officer demanded, giving her a withering look.

"It's not miss! It's Sergeant Schott," she announced calmly.

"Oh dear, a sergeant. I've not had the pleasure… Sergeant," he drawled suggestively. Birdie stared at him in amusement and shook her head. As she prepared to reply, Floyd intervened.

"Sorry, **Constable**! I should have introduced you." He tried to hide a grin as he continued. "This is **Sergeant Birdie Schott**." The officer frowned, wondering why this raw constable was trying to impress him. "Formerly known as Birdie **Lee**." The officer's expression was a joy to behold.

"You're the one that floored that thug Cracken!" The words tumbled out and his mouth remained open. Birdie smiled and was preparing to answer when Floyd interrupted again.

"I think you owe the sergeant an apology. Particularly for insulting the man who saved her life almost at the cost of his own." Ted Floyd drew himself up to full height and put on a very serious visage as he admonished the older man.

"Yes, yes! Sorry, ma'am. I've been on detachment and didn't know the full story."

"That's better. You should know better than to judge by first impressions." Floyd was enjoying himself too much so Birdie took over.

"That's enough, Constable Floyd. I seem to have heard that piece of advice before, haven't I? Thank you for the apology. Now we are in the hospital, you remain here at the main entrance," she instructed the object of her displeasure. "You two check the other exits while Constable Floyd and I arrest Tompkins in his office." Floyd stopped to check the Admin office as requested and Birdie walked to the corner of the corridor.

"'Ello, sweetie. Can't keep away from me, eh?" Roscoff slid round the corner.

"Just the person I'm looking for. I want—" Birdie was cut short as he grabbed her and tried to press her against the wall. Remembering Watson's instructions, she resisted her battle instincts and merely tried to free herself. "I've warned you before about assaulting a police officer in the performance of their duties. I have to arrest you and warn you that anything you may say—" He struck at her face, only to hit the wall as she twisted him round so *he* was now facing the wall.

"Do you want any help, Sergeant?" Ted rushed to her, having witnessed the encounter.

"No, thanks, Constable. I can handle this specimen quite easily." Roscoff tried to kick her and she simply stepped aside and shoved his arm further up his back. Two female nurses arrived in time to witness the manoeuvre and spontaneously applauded. Roscoff swore profusely and had to accept his inability to move.

"You forget, bitch, that I know about your secret phone call to your lover," he whispered venomously.

"Oh yes? That call was to a superior in London who gave

me background information about your activities in Norfolk. Quite the little bad boy, aren't you?" She spoke loudly for the benefit of the spectators. He made a final attempt to break free and was easily restrained by Birdie. "I am arresting you for the theft of hospital equipment." Floyd applied handcuffs and looked pleadingly at Birdie. "Read him his rights, Constable Floyd, and your colleague here will help you get him in the car." The two officers from the car had joined them. Birdie took the other one with her to the manager's office.

"Come in!" Tompkins called out lazily when Birdie knocked on his office door. "Oh, hello. What can I do—" He stopped abruptly when he noticed the officer following her. Quickly regaining his composure, he got to his feet and approached her. "Is there something wrong? As CEO, I have a right to be informed." Birdie's face eased into what her former colleagues knew as 'The Ice Maiden's Smile'. To anyone else, it was just a pleasant look.

"Quite right! I have to inform you, Mr Tompkins…" she paused, deliberately adding weight to her words *and possibly a little suspense for the thieving basket* "…as CEO, that we have just arrested Roscoff for theft of NHS property."

Tompkins's slight twitch was noted by Birdie before he spoke boldly. "How could he?"

Birdie took some delight in stopping him from continuing. "Because you are his accomplice! One might even call you the mastermind." She laughed inwardly as she continued to read him his rights. He tried to force a laugh and protest his innocence. Finally, when she had finished, he became more threatening.

"You'll never make this ridiculous charge stick. You have no idea who you're dealing with."

"Zebec." Birdie interrupted his tirade quietly.

"What did you say?" Tompkins demanded.

"Zebec," she repeated calmly. There was just a tiny pause in the guilty man's performance.

"Never heard of it. Is it the name of some car?" He skilfully relaxed his posture.

"The word originally comes from the name of a small three-masted Mediterranean boat. However, in this case, it is the name of the organisation you work for."

"Sorry, miss, but I work for the NHS."

"Allegedly." She paused for any response. As none came, she continued. "Due to an unfortunate development at the Zebec building in Spain, and the reorganisation of the Zebec structure in the UK, you are unlikely to get their help. Let's hope for your sake that they will just ignore your arrest." She studied him closely as he tried to keep a cool visage.

"I know nothing of these boat people, so what can they do except ignore this miscarriage of justice?"

"Well!" Birdie turned her head slightly down and to one side so she gave the air of taking him into her confidence. "A mere courier for the organisation was killed in prison. A former head in another country was eliminated and driven off a cliff in a burning car. The former head of their UK set-up was killed painfully in his retirement, et cetera, et cetera." She was enjoying embellishing her facts.

"So how should I be worried?" Perhaps she had overdone it, because he started to get cocky.

"I don't know. As they are nothing to you, it will be all right if we give court statements about your cooperation and press releases about where you'll be serving your time. We have lots of evidence already from the destination of the items you stole." She watched his face intently. "That place is now being investigated intensively. It seems the criminals running it are not very pleased with you for leading us there!" She raised her eyebrows and gave a look of feigned innocence. Tompkins was momentarily at a loss for words.

"I never did," he muttered to himself. "I know nothing of any organisation. It must be Roscoff, 'cos I don't know what you're talking about." He almost shouted over his shoulder as two policemen led him from the room.

I don't know who he's trying to convince. Unless it's my officers. I don't think there's anybody else in hearing range. She checked casually before leaving the hospital with an unsuppressed smile of satisfaction.

CHAPTER 31

"You bet I'll help!" Megan exclaimed to Birdie. "Helen and Nicola and Roger and that lovely old couple, the Browns, were so very good to me when I was so – dejected." Her face lit up as she remembered how they had virtually restored her flagging spirit. "Just how can I help?"

"It's bound to be as big a shock for Helen as it was for you to see Maurice alive. So I think it will be easier if we prepare everyone except Helen and then produce him when they are with her," Birdie proposed positively.

"How on earth can you arrange a meeting **without** making her suspicious?" Megan rebuffed.

"Yes. I admit that did trouble me. Then it struck me." She squeezed Megan's arm. "You'll arrange for them to meet Danny so he can thank them all for their help." Megan was silent so Birdie continued. "What do you think?"

By introducing my Danny to all those super people, it will show Helen that I'm really not a rival for Maurice's affections, Megan reasoned to herself.

"Sounds perfect! Danny has already asked to meet the people who helped me to recover. How will you let the others know in advance?"

"I could have a word with the Browns." Birdie hesitated and frowned. "The kids will be a problem as we mustn't tell them too soon or they might not be able to keep it secret."

"I could tell them just before Helen gets home from work, but—" Birdie interrupted her.

"How could you?"

"I might have moved in with Danny, but I'm still honouring my commitment to look after them 'til she gets home."

"That's excellent!"

"Is it? I was about to say earlier that I don't think we should tell them."

"Whyever not?"

"Having lived with them for several weeks, I think the surprise should be for all three."

"Why?" Birdie was mystified, realising she was going to have a lot to learn about children.

"Because kids are more spontaneous, and their reaction should cushion the blow for Helen."

"Why should she need it cushioned?" Birdie's considered plans seemed to be full of holes.

"Put yourself in her shoes. First, she lost the love of her life… the father of her children. Then she first hated and then loved the man she held responsible for his death. Then – **he** dies! Just **how** is she going to react?" Birdie was momentarily lost for words.

"As a once high-flying police sergeant dealing with human nature daily, I'm still learning. I think you're right!" Birdie admitted, without getting on her high horse as the Ice maiden would have done.

"Well, thank you, Mrs Schott. One more thing." Megan's confidence, with her Danny back, was enabling her to question a person whose impressive reputation she had heard of. "How will you be there?"

"I've just thought of that. You will need Danny's car. I presume he's got one and that you can drive… to get to Helen's for childminding. Then I'll bring Danny and Maurice. We should arrive about 6pm, giving Helen time to straighten out. Maurice will stay in the car while I bring Danny inside. At the right moment, I'll signal for Maurice to come."

Back at the police station, Birdie explained her plan for the reappearance to Basil.

"Sounds good to me," he agreed. Birdie went to the door and checked the corridor outside before closing the door again.

"Something for your ears only. Thanks to the efforts of Doug Evans and his Spanish assistant, who were following a lead from Thwaite, they have found the mole in their office. Thwaite's former office, which is now occupied by Bennett, has been bugged all the time! It substantiates Thwaite's statement that he never gave information to Masood. Furthermore, our ruse to bury Jenkins was known about from the beginning!"

"My god! Did they know where he's been hiding?"

"Yes. Bennett has played them at their own game and had the new Zebec chief's office bugged. He has retained their bug in his own office."

"So what's happened?" Basil chortled at the thought of it.

"Bennett held a prepared meeting with Inspector Tyler and Evans, et cetera, where they disclosed their top-secret plan to bring Jenkins back to life. The Zebec reaction was carefully monitored. They could hardly contain themselves!"

"Do you mean they are going to target Jenkins?"

"Quite the opposite! They were laughing about all our efforts to safeguard someone they had absolutely no interest in."

"But he ruined their plan with the bomb!" Basil almost protested, and Birdie smiled slightly.

"Apparently, that was one of revenge attack on behalf of

Masood when he was alive. All his enemies were gathered in one place. An opportunity too good for him to miss. It was agreed to because of his earlier work but was not within their planned use of resources. Now they are thinking more calmly and realise eradicating known enemies in the police would only bring unknown replacements."

"So Jenkins is totally safe now?" Basil nodded in understanding.

"Not quite." She sighed with impatience. "We still have to keep up the pretext of worrying about his safety so we don't betray our inside knowledge. Jenkins is to receive an award for his outstanding bravery. For safety's sake…" she made inverted commas with her fingers "…the actual presentation will take place in London."

"Anything **else** I should know?" He was getting irritated.

"Yes! All this has happened while I was gallivanting around the hospital. We've let them think we will be deploying undercover protection for Jenkins. This unnecessary use of our manpower caused further mirth among the criminals," Birdie explained apologetically. Basil sat back in his chair to consider the information.

Birdie studied him for a few moments, before adding, "This means I must act as if there could be some danger to Jenkins still. So I can't let anyone know otherwise?" she postulated aloud. "How about any undercover guards?"

"I'll see what can be done, but there's no need to alarm anyone unduly so only Jenkins can know we are keeping an eye out for his safety."

"Okay, guv."

"One more thing. Congratulations on the hospital arrests. Particularly in bringing them in alive." He laughed loudly.

"What do you mean?" She feigned a look of hurt innocence.

"You mean you don't know your new nickname?" He raised his eyebrows. She glared at him for some moments while he remained silent.

"Which is?" she demanded.

"Boadicea, the warrior queen! You've gone from the too-cold-to-handle Ice Maiden to the too-hot-to-handle Boadicea. After the way you handled Sidney Cracken, your colleagues even fear for your new husband should he dare to argue with you!"

"Why, you rotten lot!" She leapt out of her chair and pretended to attack him. Then stopped just as quickly and joined in his merriment.

CHAPTER 32

Eagerly, Birdie sought out Terry to give him the good news.

"You mean he's been alive all this time and you never told me!" Terry was delighted then angry when he realised she had known earlier that Maurice was not dead.

"Only four people in Houghbury knew. Basil insisted that I could tell nobody, not even you in case you had any further dealings with Maurice's existence. It could have affected your behaviour."

He considered her words carefully. "I suppose it makes sense. I hope you've not got any more secrets you're keeping from your new husband."

"Only that I love him more each day."

"Better not tell him then or he might take advantage of you."

"In that case, I will tell him." She posed suggestively on the edge of his desk. He regretfully pushed her away as there was a knock on his office door.

"Sorry to interrupt you newlyweds…" Derek tried unsuccessfully to keep a straight face "…but I need Terry's signature on these forms so I can catch the post." As Terry obliged, he looked questioningly at Birdie.

"We have some news for your ears only. Maurice Jenkins is alive and has been given the all-clear to come out of hiding." She proceeded to explain her plan to them.

"I'm sorry, I have to disagree with your plans! I feel that as I did so much for Maurice, I should be the one to tell him about the plan. And act as chauffeur to Danny and him to see the Phillipses." Terry looked at her cautiously, awaiting her reply, while Derek nodded his agreement.

Why, the cheek of them! Husband or not, it doesn't give him the right to take over. It's my plan and it should be me. I've earned it. She studied their faces with some hostility. *I've done... while he's... he's... he's spent months fighting for Maurice's freedom – proving his innocence and keeping his spirits up.* She regarded Terry closely as his earlier defiance melted, waiting for the inevitable storm. *My delight for Maurice and his friends has clouded my judgement. I mustn't give in too easily, but they're right. It has to be him.*

"Right!" she began vehemently. "Let's balance the books. You went into a most dangerous courtroom and let your client be sent to prison. I had a friendly meeting with the then master criminal in Britain. You endured dangerous visits to Maurice in the hostile surroundings of prison. I had a fun-filled party with a couple of gentlemen who made quite an impression on me and somehow managed to shoot my colleague. Meanwhile, you were having to endure the hostility of a corrupt policeman AND struggle to adapt prison rules to assist your client. Finally, you had to suffer the invasion of your private life by an unfriendly, lazy policewoman." She paused in her tirade to look from one to the other of her... opponents.

"Er..." They both struggled to speak while trying to disguise their crestfallen expressions.

"Well..." She pressed home her temporary advantage.

"All joking apart, gentlemen, and leaving aside my litany of occurrences, there is one overriding fact that determines who gets the honour of reintroducing Maurice." She smiled and savoured her moment as husband and brother were held in suspense. "You have been with Maurice Jenkins from the very beginning, while I was merely collateral damage. Of course *you* must do it! And **that** is an order!" She winked at her brother as she wagged a threatening finger at Terry.

"We'll do it together." Terry insisted.

"All right, but you must do the talking. I wouldn't know what to say." She fluttered her eyes demurely.

"**You**! That's a laugh! When have you ever been at a loss for words?"

"Actually—" Birdie started to reply but Terry banged her shoulder.

Later, Terry visited Pru Gravillons and knocked apprehensively on her door.

"*Bonjour*, Monsieur Schott, *comment*… 'ow are you?" She greeted him in such a friendly fashion that it was hard to imagine it was the same woman who had once vented her wrath in his office.

"I have some good news for you, Madame Gravillons," he stated in a matter-of-fact fashion.

"Come in, *monsieur*, please. I get you a drink, yes?" She stepped back.

"No, thank you. My wife is expecting me home for dinner. I have some good news for you and must ask you a big favour." She peered at him intensively and frowned. He waited for her to appear calmer.

"Good news! *Zoot alors*! Ze only good news you could 'ave for me is that poor Maurice is not dead, vich is—"

"**Correct**! He is alive!"

Pru sat down heavily. "*Ce n'est pas possible*! 'Ow can 'e be?" She threw her arms wide and shook her head vigorously.

"The funeral was staged... I mean, a pretend one. It was done so Maurice could go into hiding in case the criminals who planted the bomb sought revenge." She clapped her hands to her cheeks.

"Zis is marvellous. Ven vill 'e be back 'ere?"

"He should be back tomorrow evening. I must ask you not to tell anyone until then."

"*Mais oui*! Of course I vill. Vy ze delay? Is zat ze favour?"

"Very few people will know in advance. We want to prepare his lady friend so she does not find out from another source." He paused to think further about explaining Maurice's relationship with Helen.

"You mean the lucky Helen Phillips?"

"Yes, but how do you know about her?"

"Maurice is like one of our family and 'e reveals 'is 'opes and desires to me. *Naturellement*, she must know before ze public." Terry smiled inwardly at the thought of this petite French dynamo being such a good friend to his client.

"I have much to prepare tomorrow, including collecting Maurice from his hiding place. So I wondered if you could prepare his apartment for him?"

"But of course!"

"I'd pay you—"

"You insult me, *m'sieur*!" she exploded.

"I'm sorry. I didn't mean to. I just thought I was being cheeky in even asking."

"Vat is cheeky?"

"Asking too much. Expecting you to do something that I have no right to expect."

"So! You not understand 'ow much we valued... do value... Maurice and 'ow much ve vill do for 'im." She calmed a little.

"Exactly. I thought it would be a nice homecoming for

Maurice if his apartment was clean and tidy." *And possibly some plants or flowers to brighten it, but I daren't ask for more.*

"It vill be done. I forgive you for your affront and vill make sure 'is 'ome is really good for 'is return."

Birdie had a good laugh during their dinner when he narrated his encounter with Pru.

Megan phoned Helen early the next day to catch her before her school run and work. *I'll let her think any excitement in my voice is due to her meeting Danny.* "Helen. I just wanted to confirm that I'll be there when Nicola and Roger get home. When you get back, my Danny is coming to meet you all."

"That is nice, but I won't have anything prepared."

"Don't worry. I'll bring a cake and get the tea ready for you."

"That's great." Helen spoke with genuine relief and turned her thoughts to the centre of her world once more. "Thanks a lot. I must dash now or my kids will be late for school. See you all later then. Bye."

Terry drove out to the airfield with Birdie and collected Danny and Maurice. The former had spent most of the morning trying to calm Maurice. Such were his trials and tribulations over the past months that Maurice was very apprehensive about the coming meeting. Sometimes, impatient and excited. At other times, afraid and reticent. During the journey, Birdie added her support for Maurice.

"It's bound to be a shock for Helen and the kids. Once over it, their true feelings will take over and we will probably leave you with them. That's another reason for meeting Danny first."

"It sounds great in theory, but I've grown to expect problems where none should exist." He spoke aimlessly, as if voicing his thoughts.

Megan met Danny with Terry and Birdie at the door and escorted them to the lounge to meet Helen, who was standing nervously by her fireplace. The children were seated impatiently in a corner. They had been told to behave until the visitors left and then they'd be able to play.

"This is Danny! I'd like you to meet the wonderful family who helped me through a terrible period in my life. In fact, they were the ones who made life worth living for me. Helen, Nicola and Roger, I'd like you to meet my husband-to-be." They all shook hands with Danny, who was most effusive with his thanks. They all found seats, except Helen, who felt obliged to remain standing and handed out the tea and cake with some help from the kids.

I understand the Schotts acting as chauffeurs for Danny as Megan had his car, but why both of them? There's a strange atmosphere that I don't care for. Call it sixth sense, but I'm not feeling relaxed in my own home. I've noticed Birdie looking out of the front window. Why did she come in if she's so anxious to leave? Or is there some other reason?

Outside, Maurice was very impatient. He left the car and paced up and down, hidden by the hedge, his thoughts undulating rapidly. *It's… it's like… it's like waiting for an important interview. It's the woman – it's the family – I want! How do I greet them? Good evening, Mrs Phillips and children.* **No!** *That's just silly. Hello, everyone? No, too formal. I rush up and kiss her in a strong embrace. No, leave that to the movies. Should I wait to be introduced? That's silly as well. Talk to Roger and Nicola first? No! That's avoiding the issue. I'll just say hello, Helen, and wait for a lead from her. Damn! There may not be a lead. It's ages since the bombing of the reception. Any feelings that friends tell me she had for me may have been weakened or killed entirely by time and…*

my affair with Megan. She must know about Megan and me. Hell! How would I react in such circumstances? How did I react? Bugger! I'm probably here under false illusions. She'll want nothing to do with me. He stopped pacing as he neared the end of the hedge by the gate and peered round quickly. *Ah! I caught sight of the back of her head. That is **my** Helen. She is the very core of my being. **She** is my reason for living. I love her kids, but she means everything to me. Without her, I cease to exist. Think positively, I agreed with Arnold. Her Arnold. My Helen?*

He peeped round the hedge and saw Birdie run her finger along her nose in the pre-arranged signal. *Come on, Maurice Jenkins! It's now or never!* He took a deep breath and walked towards the house.

"More cake, anyone?" Helen moved round and deliberately positioned herself to see out the front of the house in her mirror. *There's nothing there, so Birdie couldn't have been looking at anything in particular. Hang on! Somebody just peeped around my hedge.* She stopped moving. *There again! He's coming up the path!* It's... it's **Maurice**!

She dropped the plate.

"Are you all right?" Megan dashed to her side.

"I've... just... seen... a ghost!" she gasped, over the painful tightness in her chest and throat.

"It's no ghost, Mrs Phillips. It *is* Maurice. He's not dead. He's been in hiding from the criminals," Terry hastily reassured her.

Maurice! Alive! Everyone knows but us! I've been through agony over his death. Now they spring him on me like some belated birthday present! This whole thing is a set-up! Well, I'm not playing! I don't want Nicola and Roger to suffer such a shock.

"*Will you all please leave and take your ghost with you*! I'm not prepared to play any part in this pre-arranged drama. *Leave,* **everyone!**" she almost screamed at them as they hurriedly got to their feet. Just then, the doorbell rang.

"Shall we get it, Mummy?" Nicola asked.

"**No! Stay here**! Our guests can answer it on their way out." The four visitors quietly made their way to the front door with Megan at the rear. She turned back to give Helen a questioning look.

"I'm sorry to be so blunt with everyone. I don't want to be rude but I need… time… and space to consider the shock I've just received." Helen opened her hands as if to reveal her emotions. Megan nodded and gave her friend a supporting smile.

"Don't worry. They'll all understand. That's what true friends are for. Just let me know when I can help. And **soon**!" Megan wagged an index finger at Helen while smiling warmly. Helen collapsed onto a chair, and her alarmed kids dashed to her side. They had not seen Maurice as they had been staring at their mother ever since her outburst.

"What's wrong, Mummy?" Nicola asked with apprehension.

"Why couldn't we answer the door and why did those people have to leave?" Roger gabbled.

"It was Maurice!" Helen breathed shakily as the extreme tension in her mind and body was released.

"What about Maurice, Mummy?" Nicola asked, as Roger frowned heavily.

"It was Maurice at the front door!" she snapped irritably, and immediately regretted it. She held their arms and explained. "Obviously, he is not dead and I – we – have mourned him for no reason. It was such a shock when I saw him through the window that I allowed my anger at all the pain I – we – have suffered to override my true feelings." Nicola and Roger gazed at each other and then back at Helen.

"Shall I run after him, Mummy?" Roger started for the door.

"No. They'll all be gone by now," Helen pointed out regretfully. "Can you both clear away the tea things and bring me a fresh cup of tea, please?"

As they obeyed, she sat deep in thought. *They say that the path of true love never runs smoothly. Well, in the case of Maurice and me, it seems particularly apt. Will his feelings for me – us – be strong enough to accept my outburst? I will call on him first thing in the morning… after taking these two to school.*

The nervous Maurice was met with an outpouring of people all trying to talk at once. Finally, the solicitor took control.

"I'm sure I speak for us all, Maurice, when I tell you that the shock of seeing you has been too great for Mrs Phillips. She has asked us to leave as she wishes to be alone just now." The other three nodded in agreement.

All the colour left Maurice's face. *They were wrong to bring me here. She doesn't care for me. In fact, she has probably returned to her initial thoughts of me as her husband's killer. That's it! If she really had even the slightest feelings for me, she would at least be glad that I am alive.*

Megan and Birdie took an arm each to lead him back down the path. He shook them off.

"Sh-sh-sh-!" They all stared at him in horror, thinking he was having a fit. "**Sugar**!" he finally managed to shout, with force, yet controlling his language. "I knew she would never forgive me."

"Forgive you for what?" Danny asked. Megan nudged Maurice's arm as a warning.

"Well, for not being there when she most needed someone… among other things. Thank you all for trying, but I'm afraid it's a lost cause." He regained temporary control of his emotions.

"Helen did say how sorry she was to be so abrupt. I think the shock of seeing Maurice alive was too great after all she's been through," Megan said to reassure the others.

Maurice quickened his stride back to Terry's car. *She's just saying that for my benefit… just to soften the blow.* He stared vacantly into space as Terry and Birdie helped him into their car. After parting handshakes, the two groups left in their respective cars.

Maurice remained silent and expressionless. *If she cared for me at all, she would have considered my feelings after all I've been through. This is what you get for helping people and trying to be a good citizen. I was better off in prison. There were no mistaken meanings or emotions in there. There was Sid! At least my life hasn't been completely useless. I did help Sid. What can I do? Where can I go? Eh? What?* Maurice suddenly became aware of Birdie talking to him. That was the first reaction she'd had from him on the whole journey.

"We'll drop you at your apartment, Maurice. Pru Gravillons has prepared it for you. I expect you have much to get on with. All your friends and acquaintances will be glad to hear from you."

Friends and…! I have none. I don't want sympathy. I'm not ready to go to… what? My home? Even the word sounds strange. I can't face Pru and her family in my current state. I just want to lose myself… in a crowd! He managed to clear his head before speaking.

"Could you drop me in the Square, please? I appreciate all you've done for me. Now there are things I have to do for myself."

"I'm not sure—" Terry was about to remind him that Pru would be expecting him, when Birdie butted in.

"Yes. Of course we can. Mrs Gravillons won't be expecting you at any particular time. Let us know if you need help with anything. Anything at all. After all, we owe you a lot."

"And don't forget Mr Cooper is waiting to hear from you," Terry reminded him. Terry stopped the car at the edge of the Square, and Maurice thanked them very quietly as he got out. After wandering aimlessly around the Square looking in shop windows, old habits found him back at the shelter for his bus. As he contemplated his surroundings, his mind switched on again.

*I'll be damned. This is where my whole… fatal adventure? – No! – experience began. What have I gained? Okay. So it's selfish thinking! I don't care! I've been rejected by the only woman I have ever really loved. I **am** all alone.*

He stopped to gaze around the rapidly emptying square as a binman passed. Looking straight at him brought back bitter memories, and he had to fight back the tears.

"Cheer up, mate! Things always get better, you know," growled the worn-looking old man. Maurice reacted as if he'd had an electric shock.

"I hope so," he muttered to himself. He took a deep breath and added aloud, "Yes. Thank you. I really **do** hope so!" The astonished binman paused in his trudging and looked at Maurice.

"D' you know, you're the first person to talk to me here since I took over this route—"!

"…From Arnold," Maurice interrupted.

"Blimey! 'Ow'd you know?"

"He was a very good friend of mine and he changed my whole life."

"For the better, I should 'ope. Though it don't seem like it when I first saw you" was the grudging reply.

Maurice paused to reflect. *I've had some terrible experiences but also some wonderful...* "Definitely for the better! You have a vital job and never forget it. You are an asset to the community."

"An asset?"

"Yes! Without you, we'd be swamped in rubbish and the germs that result."

"Blimey!" Binman repeated. "I never thought of that. Cheers, mate." He continued his route with renewed vigour.

"Yes. Cheers, mate," Maurice called after him. He left the shelter and went to some of the shops. There, he purchased flowers for Pru and some small gifts for her children. *Whatever else may happen, I'll always be grateful for the friendship of the Gravillonses. If they'd not been away, perhaps I'd never have gone to prison. Although... even that had its plus side. I met Sid. Actually, now I think about it, I introduced him to Judith. I believe they are quite an item now.*

He smiled at the thought of Sid and his beautiful art teacher. *Hmm! Oh, Terry! Good lord! I just treated him like a stranger. The man who fought for my release. What did Birdie mean when she said they owe me? Ah yes. They met because of my case.* He hastened back to his bus stop.

Damn! Just missed it! Oh well. I'll wait for the next one. He laughed aloud, causing others at the stop to look askance at him. *I'm definitely not walking with these gifts. You never know when some kid might bump into you.* He laughed again and people moved away from him.

Careful, Jenkins. Don't upset the mob again. Though there's only four or five now, remember last time. Last time! Last time, if I remember correctly, I was thinking about having my name carved in graphite for posterity. Forget it! Much more important I've helped some people here and now. Bugger what posterity thinks. He sat calmly for a moment as he regarded those around him.

Huh! Happy couples....

His whole demeanour sagged again, his temporary euphoria pricked by the thought of Helen. An elderly man approached him through the growing throng. It was the binman without his yellow jacket.

"Oi, mate! You still 'ere! Your kind words inspired me to buy a lottery ticket, and I've won a fasound pounds!"

"Well done! You deserve it and I'm pleased for you. Don't go gambling it away."

"I won't. Thanks again." He continued on his journey and the 'disinterested' bystanders resumed their conversations. *Good to know I can still help someone. Helen! Helen? I can't get her out of my mind. But for... Binman, I could have felt totally defeated Now? Now? Now, Maurice Jenkins, dream on!*

He gritted his teeth and moved with the rest towards the bus, which had just arrived.

"**It will get better**!" he said out loud, and shook his packages with determination, causing people around him to look in alarm!

CHAPTER 33

Thwaite was provided with intense security when he was 'captured' and returned to the UK with much publicity. He was held at a secure police location, where the swap with a substitute would be made. There was constant vigilance during all these manoeuvres as well as eavesdropping on the new UK master criminal. There was some discussion by the latter, but it seemed he had been instructed to do nothing yet. They were waiting to see if he was worth bothering with.

Keeping his Christian name as the surname, he was now Roy Bernard, and was given temporary accommodation in Southend, Essex, which was considered a backwater as far as the police knowledge of Zebec could make out. It was close enough for him to be called upon in future investigations into the criminals.

With days left until he was officially retired, Doug requested a meeting with Roy Bernard and Esperanza at Bennett's house. Despite having caused a major upset to the criminals' organisation, Doug could not forget the fact that he must have been very close to catching their mastermind. He had to know who 'Bernard' had flown from the Zebec tower.

"The security around Bernard has not been tested in any way." Bennett announced as he opened the meeting.

"Has there been any interest by the new Zebec boss here?" Doug asked hopefully.

"They must be worried about vat 'e is going to tell us!" Esperanza proposed. Interpol had agreed to her attending the meeting.

"That is what's so interesting. They don't seem very bothered!" Bennett frowned.

"Suits me!" Bernard said. He had deliberately kept a low profile on meeting his successor, though he was grateful for the work that Doug and Esperanza had done on his behalf.

"The big question is…" Doug stressed, tapping the table they were all seated at "…**who** did you have in the helicopter with you?"

"Your guess is as good as mine!" Bernard exclaimed. "He never introduced himself. Unless you count pointing a pistol at me and forcing me up to the roof and to fly the chopper!"

"Had you ever met him before?" Doug queried.

"Not met exactly, but I did see him going into one of the larger flats on my floor a couple of times."

"Do you think he could be the head of Zebec?" Bennett insisted. Everyone looked intently at the former superintendent.

"No!" Bernard replied hesitantly. "At first I did, but when I saw the accommodation in the penthouse, I asked myself why he was living on the lower floor when such luxury was available."

"Per'aps 'e was, and using a lower apartment was part of 'is cover." Esperanza suggested.

Bernard smiled at her almost affectionately and continued. "Funny thing is, I thought that possible, but something he said niggled me."

"What?" Doug was getting impatient.

"When he produced the gun and ordered me up to the roof, he said **we** are to escape in the helicopter." He looked round his audience for a sign of understanding. Each one of them was trying to interpret what he had just said, in their own way.

"So?" Doug asked as he tried to picture the scene. Bernard looked questioningly at each one in turn before explaining his thoughts further.

"If he was the boss, he should have simply ordered me to fly the chopper. He would not say we are to escape as if **he** was following instructions." Suddenly there were knowing nods of agreement all round, with Doug and Bennett realising that it was not just inside knowledge that had caused Bernard's fast promotion.

"What country was he from?" Esperanza followed up quickly.

"That's another thing! His speech was a bit guttural, and with his build and blond hair, I would say he is definitely Nordic."

"Zebec is a Mediterranean name, and most of their operations are based in that area," Esperanza added from the Interpol view.

"So! If your passenger was a decoy, it means the big cheese was still in the tower!" Doug had been unusually quiet while listening to the others. Now he was alert and, like his reputation as a bloodhound, he had got the scent once more. Abruptly, they all studied him, and even Esperanza recognised the glint in his eyes.

"What is this big cheese?" she asked.

"The top man," Bernard explained, looking at her with admiration.

"You three have all been there! Between you, you should be able to name **some** suspects," Bennett instructed them.

Lost in his thoughts, Doug tapped the table and peered

at Bernard. "This gun that was pointed at you by your passenger... had it been fired recently?"

"I don't think so. And he did hold it close to my face, so I should have smelled if it had been."

"You mean...?" Esperanza hinted.

"Yes!" Doug replied. "He was **not** the one who shot Masood..."

"As 'e was about to name ze cheese!" Esperanza gasped.

"Gorgonzola!" Bernard laughed, smiling at her.

"Be serious!" Bennett ordered. "Who *is*..." he glared at Bernard and Esperanza "...**the top man**?" Almost shouting the last words appeared to awaken Doug from a trance. In the ensuing silence, Bennett added, "If he was there at all!"

"**The Ghoul**!" Doug finally declared.

"Who?" Bernard was mystified.

"The head of security," Esperanza declared as a revelation. There was total silence as each absorbed the news. Doug explained to Bennett about the security arrangements at the tower and how he and his Interpol colleague had given the man the nickname. "This also solves the riddle of how anyone could use the special key to take the lift to the penthouse."

"And how he knew you were about to get information from Masood!" Esperanza added.

"And how he was able to disappear after shooting Masood. He would have the master keys and dashed into any spare room," Doug summed up.

"But there was someone who went up the stairs," Esperanza reminded him.

Doug thought back to the incident and clicked his fingers. "Of course! Everything was happening so fast he needed to instruct Bernard's passenger on the next floor. Then he would have waited to make sure the coast was clear before getting the lift down to the foyer in time to welcome the police."

"Possible, but I think Ron may be right!" Bernard declared cautiously. They all looked at him questioningly, and he continued. "In the past, criminal organisations, such as the Mafia, depended openly on the fear they created. Today's criminals, living in an era of mass communications, depend more on information. Particularly inside information! The Zebec tower may have been their communication centre – requiring technocrats – but why would the top man need to be there? From their inside information, they probably knew that it was only a matter of time before their presence in the tower was discovered." He paused for breath.

"So, if they had planned for any eventuality there, they would have had more than one decoy. As you point out, this is the age of the internet, so the top person does not have to be physically in touch with his minions. He could be any rich person!" Doug proposed.

"Why rich?" Ron retorted.

"Because any poor person enjoying even part of the fruits of his labours would immediately create suspicion!" Bernard answered.

"What is the Ghoul's position then?" queried Esperanza.

"As the only one here not to have the benefit of visiting this tower, I can answer that," Ron interrupted. "He must be the technocrat in charge of their communications. So he does have a vital position and would need protection. You say his security office appeared to have lots of electrical equipment. Well, he wouldn't require much in order to have full control over that in the penthouse."

"No ordinary technocrat!" Esperanza declared. "One who kills!"

"Or not!" Bernard smiled at her again, much to the annoyance of Doug. "How could he have got to Masood's apartment so quickly after you? I think you are right that he could have been in charge of the tower, but he would not be expected to kill people when there were many dubious persons already in the building who could do it for him," he continued. Ron nodded, while the other two reflected on their experience.

"You have caused the organisation a setback, but they were still capable of controlling their links here," Ron pointed out.

"I vonder 'ow difficult it vill be for zem to replace ze Ghoul if we find a reason to arrest 'im?" Esperanza asked quietly.

"Let's find out. You and I should return to the tower immediately with a search warrant. We can check the security office and question and hopefully arrest the Ghoul," Doug insisted.

"You only have three days before you are out of the police!" Ron protested.

"Would that be long enough for us, Doug?" Esperanza queried.

"Yes, definitely!" he confirmed.

"Okay. I'll make the arrangements straight away," Ron conceded.

CHAPTER 34

"Vy, are you not retired yet, my love?" Miguel demanded when Doug and Esperanza appeared at his villa. They had managed to catch a late flight to Málaga and take a taxi to Miguel's.

"*No te preoupes por eso. Se reterara en tres dias!*" Esperanza stated as she appeared from behind Doug. Miguel held his arms up in mock surrender and studied her intently.

"La la! You 'ave brought my rival to my 'ome." He reached out and took her right hand in his, slowly turning her round.

"**Hallo**, Miguel! It's nice to be home. What have you got to say for yourself?" Doug demanded.

"I must work on Esperanza," Miguel insisted, ignoring him and forming a ball with his hands.

She hastily took a step back and Doug looked mystified, so Miguel continued. "She is just ze model I 'ave been seeking for my new 'airstyle." Doug gave Miguel a quick kiss and they proceeded into the house with more banter and laughter. Before they retired for the night, it was agreed that Miguel would give them an early lift to the police station. Also, his new model agreed to let him perform his magic on her hair once the Zebec operation was completed.

Thanks to added pressure from Interpol, the necessary search warrant was waiting for them at the police station. The matter had been entirely handled by the *commisario* personally to prevent the occupants of the tower being forewarned. Doug and Esperanza were supplied with a select team of six armed officers from their investigation division at the last moment. The surprise visit worked, and the only delay was in breaking down the armoured door into the Ghoul's lair. The latter protested about being awoken so rudely.

"**How dare you break down my door!**" he shouted in a voice louder than he looked capable of. "I shall report you to the chief of police! Why didn't my security officers contact me?" He was clearly very shaken by their entry but spoke in perfect English, recognising Doug. "I-I-Why didn't you ring or knock?" He finished up spluttering and made to sit down at what appeared to be a control desk. Doug grabbed him and held his arms tightly until one of the policemen handcuffed them behind his back.

"We have a search warrant and are securing you to prevent any… misunderstanding," Doug declared officiously, while behind his back Esperanza was trying not to laugh. "We will be seizing your computer records and would appreciate your help in making them freely available." Esperanza coughed to cover her mirth at her partner's impudence.

The officer now holding the Ghoul looked questioningly at her, so she offered an explanation to him, which translated as "You are restricting this man because he was about to attack our little British colleague. Aren't you?" The officer looked from the wisp of a man he was holding to the formidable bulk of Doug. He screwed up his face to cover his incredulity.

"*Sí, Señora! I protejo a este pequeno ingles.*" He spoke slowly with a big grin.

"*Idiota. No sabes con quien estas tratando!*" The Ghoul almost spat the words at the man holding him.

"Who **is** he holding, sir?" Esperanza stepped in front of him.

"Christos Aetos," the Ghoul declared proudly.

"Well, Christos, we are following up on our last visit to find who killed Masood and who left in the helicopter," Doug informed him politely.

"**Mr** Aetos to you, Englishman!" Christos insisted vehemently.

"Yes… sir!" said Doug, taking a step back and mockingly bowing his head. Then he made the officer holding Mr Aetos remove him from the room while he and Esperanza searched it. There was a large array of screens revealing the whole of the outside of the building as well as the 'public' areas inside. There was a clear view of the roof and the part of the penthouse formerly occupied by the computers. The latter had been cleared and seemed ready for complete rebuilding.

"Why would they risk using this as a headquarters or even as a communication centre after its discovery and destruction, Doug?" She voiced her thoughts while watching the screens.

"There is the possibility that they thought lightning couldn't strike twice, but…"

"What has lightning got to do with it!" Esperanza demanded.

"Sorry! It's an old British saying meaning that the same thing is unlikely to happen in the same place twice," Doug explained, and continued. "This building and its function served its purpose and defeated our attempt to capture the mastermind or break into their communications. By restoring its function, they feel confident it will do so again."

"Ah! Then our sudden return might have upset the haycart." She spoke with pride in her use of English.

Doug realised that what she had intended was 'upset the apple cart', but, noting her pride, did not correct her. *After all, a word is simply a means of conveying a message, and I got her meaning!*

"I think we should study these screens to fully understand what is and what is not covered by them," he suggested. Esperanza nodded as she continued to stare at the changing views.

"One…" "None…" They spoke simultaneously.

Doug bowed and gestured with a sweep of his arm for Esperanza to continue. She beamed *like some model in an advert, from the idea Miguel had put to her*, he thought.

"Thank you – sir. One screen does not change and permanently covers the lift. This means to me that Aetos must be top man or at least know who he is." Her smile faded with the seriousness of her observation. Without a reply, Doug walked around the room, looking into any cupboards or rooms. Then he put his finger to his lips as she was about to comment. He held up his right hand and cocked that ear while gesticulating around the room. Then he pulled out his notebook and wrote briefly, 'If he's not top, he could be observed', showed it to her secretively and put it away again. They immediately did a tour of the room. Finding nothing obvious, they temporarily left the building and rang the *commisario* for an expert in bug detection. While they waited, they brought Aetos outside and interrogated him.

"Who is your boss?" demanded Doug. Aetos glared at him and said nothing.

"No, Inspector Evans! You are mistaken! Dis man is de boss!" Esperanza corrected him with a strong accent. Aetos looked from one to the other and smiled at Doug.

"The lady is wrong, Inspector! The boss, as you call him, left in the helicopter when you came here before." They both stared at him in disbelief. "I may be head of security, but I am only an employee!" He inclined his head to one side in a show of very false modesty.

"Then where did you sleep?" Doug enquired quietly after a moment's contemplation. Esperanza frowned thoughtfully while studying their prisoner's face.

"Why do you want to know?" Aetos narrowed his eyes almost imperceptibly and she noticed. "I have some rooms on the ground floor," he finally admitted.

A police vehicle arrived and a bespectacled man got out with a large carry box.

"Look after Mr Aetos, please, while we take this man inside," Doug instructed the officer who had been guarding their prisoner. Esperanza translated into Spanish then followed Doug inside once more. The security expert opened his comprehensive tool kit and checked Aetos's workplace so precisely that it caused Doug to start strumming his fingers with impatience. When the man had done a complete scan of the rooms, he maintained his frozen expression and gesticulated for them to follow him outside.

"*Fantastico!*" he exploded. An astonished Esperanza requested his report in English. "You were correct to call for me. There are two devices in adjoining walls that cover the entire room, including a view of all those screens. They are so well concealed in the actual walls that I doubt if the person working in there knew about them!" He took out a large pad and drew a sketch of the room, marking the bugs' positions.

The two detectives studied it carefully, making mental notes of what the devices covered.

"I didn't tell you about them in the room as I thought you might want to make use of them yourselves." the expert added, causing the others to nod their heads in admiration.

"We certainly might," Doug conceded. "What made you think that?" he added.

"*Señor*, I have much experience," the man said with pride.

"*Gracias, señor.*" Espranza shook his hand as he prepared to leave.

"One thing, though," Doug interrupted, "how can anyone see through blank walls?"

"Ah! They are a modern version of the old pinhole cameras. Just a very tiny hole is all they require to work." The two detectives pointed at each other as they both realised the implications of what they had just heard. The expert shook Doug's hand as he prepared to leave.

"Can you wait a moment, please?" Esperanza requested in Spanish.

"What's wrong?" Doug was surprised at her request, which she translated for him.

"The implication that Aetos was under surveillance in the security office could mean he also was in his own quarters."

"Satisfied, are you?" Aetos's voice from a distance broke into their deliberations. He had guessed that their visitor was some sort of specialist and had noted their reactions to whatever news they had received. Doug pulled Esperanza further away and turned his back to him.

"Just in case Aetos can lip-read," he explained. "He could very well not know about the bugs."

"I bet he doesn't!" she declared. "He might have a prime position in Zebec, but he definitely is not top man." Doug nodded and turned to look at Aetos, who smiled smugly at him.

"What have we got on the little shite?" Doug said angrily, turning back to his partner.

"You inspected the rest of the rooms around his office, so did he live there?" she asked.

"**No!**" Doug clicked his fingers as her enquiry brought his thoughts back to their task. "Then where did he sleep?"

He walked slowly back to Aetos. "For the record, Mr Aetos, where do you sleep?"

"I have some rooms on the ground floor, of course!" he replied arrogantly. Doug returned to Esperanza, who was beckoning him.

"The quickest way to find out, Doug, is to check all unoccupied rooms with the master key to see where he keeps his clothes. There can't be another 'mature' adult…" she made quotation signs "…his size in the building."

Doug looked at her with admiration. *Trust a woman to think of clothing and sizes.* Finding the master keys, they took a plan of the building's apartments and began a steady yet cautious check of them all. Those with absent occupants were inspected for suitable clothing. Nothing! This left the penthouse, and, yes, the set of master keys did include one for the lift. The whole of the business part had been cleared, so they tried the luxury suite.

"Fancy that!" Doug exclaimed. "The door is locked!" The appropriate key was on the bunch Doug held, so they very slowly opened it.

"You surely don't think this could be mined?" Esperanza was impatient to see inside.

"Why not?" Doug countered.

"Because there have been safeguards just to get this far and the occupant's patience can only extend so far," she stated firmly. For once, Doug was really irritated by his partner and impatiently stood to one side and gestured for her to take over. With a show of bravado, she tried to fling the door open but it hardly moved. Doug moved her to one side as he held his arm at full stretch and pushed the door fully open. Carefully, he peered inside.

"It's Fort Knox!" he announced. "Both door and walls were built to withstand the blast from the destruction in their computer room. Let's see what else we can discover." The apartment had every conceivable comfort, including the latest big TV and a CCTV unit that could duplicate each of the units in the entrance office.

"Look what I have found!" exclaimed Esperanza, holding up a small pair of trousers.

"Bingo!" Doug cheered. "I doubt if there is another adult resident of this tower as petite as Aetos." Esperanza examined them more intensively and showed the inside label to Doug.

"That clinches it! Tailor-made to order means they were for Aetos." Doug clicked his fingers in delight.

"And," she added, "his wages are more than those of a mere head of security. That firm is very exclusive and expensive!"

"So he might not be Mr Big, but he's certainly the chief round here and near the very top of Zebec." Doug pursed his lips in contemplation.

"The man who left with Bernard was a decoy, but we still don't know who killed Masood."

"The one who we heard running upstairs?" Doug frowned on recollection of the incident.

"That's a point!" Esperanza grabbed his arm. "Why would a murderer use stairs when there is a perfectly good lift?" Doug froze so she continued. "Why didn't we use the stairs?"

"Because they were already… being…" His voice faded as he remembered. "*Gilipollas*!" To her astonishment, he swore in Spanish.

"Who are you calling an idiot?" she retorted.

"Sorry. Only swear word I have learnt so far in Spanish. I'm the idiot! We all used the stairs because the power was off."

She smacked her forehead. "So much for my lateral thinking." She paused. "Though why did we assume the murderer was running **upstairs**?"

"To get to the penthouse." Doug thought that was obvious.

"Just suppose he was going downstairs because he had already been upstairs," she argued, and Doug shook his head in disbelief. "I want you to answer a few simple questions for me, Doug. First. How could the killer arrive a few moments after us?"

"Because he was right behind us?" Doug wondered where all this was leading.

"Yes, if he was very fit and very quiet, and started out immediately after us."

"If Aetos was in the security office, it would have taken him too long to check that we had left to be able to catch up with us that quickly. So it could not have been him," Doug reasoned.

"What time of day did this all happen?" she persisted.

"Early evening."

"What do most people do at that time of day?"

"Go home and have a meal." Doug answered as one being 'taught to suck eggs'.

"Precisely! Then where was Aetos likely to be?"

"Geronimo!" Doug almost shouted. "He was in the penthouse and must have seen something of what was happening before the power went off!"

"He checked as he went downstairs and saw us go to Masood. Killed him and then—"

"Then he continued downstairs," she finished conclusively.

"But how do we prove it? He has had plenty of time to lose the gun, and it's unlikely there were any witnesses." Elation turned to dismay as Doug understood he would not be able to close the case before retiring.

"Why don't we ask Bernard for his thoughts?" Esperanza suddenly suggested.

Bloody Thwaites again. Is she obsessed with him? Still, she has been very useful thus far. Doug bit his lip. "Phone him now! He did live here and might know something we don't." Doug tried to sound more positive than he felt. She did and fortune smiled as Bernard replied immediately. She explained their thoughts about the incident that led to his hasty departure, despite Doug holding his finger to his lips and shaking his head.

"I think you could be right. I never knew of Aetos, as you call him, eating out, and I think he did have food deliveries. I also know that he and his heavies were armed. One day, when the others were engaged elsewhere, he did produce his own handgun to threaten a belligerent occupant. I remember it catching the light sufficiently to read that it was a Turkish Canick. I always wondered who lived upstairs," Bernard concluded. She had put her phone on loud so Doug could hear it all.

"Did you ever see him go to the penthouse?" Doug asked, so Bernard could hear him.

"No. Though now it's obvious as it had to be him or someone he could see from his observation post. Stay safe, the pair of you. Remember, there is nothing more dangerous than a wounded animal."

"You too," they said in unison.

"Didn't you take his gun off Aetos when you grabbed him, Doug?" she enquired.

"Yes. I gave it to the officer holding him. Hang on. I'll go and get it."

While he was gone, Esperanza continued her search of the accommodation. No other guns. An enormous fridge full of ready meals. A king-size bed with the finest silk sheets. A bedside chest with a drawer containing condoms! Also in the bedroom was a small safe concealed by an original classic painting, and she left it uncovered for Doug to see when he returned. There were a few reference books and a couple of novels. The windows had a panoramic view and were both tinted and armoured. Doug returned in time to find her testing the swivel chair at a desk.

"Guess what?" He tutted as he entered the room.

"Well?"

"It's a Colt!"

"Then where is his Canick?"

"I asked him and he denied all knowledge of such a gun!" He waited for her prompt, which never came as she was becoming accustomed to his ways. "However!" He delayed deliberately to annoy her, but she just nodded. "However, the police officer did not understand much of my questioning, but he pricked his ears up at the word Canick, so I would like you to ask him what he knows… please." She smiled and prepared to return to the entrance. "One more thing. Could you bring our bug expert back with you?"

She did as asked, getting a lengthy oration from the officer. While she was absent, Doug examined the safe. When Esperanza returned with the expert, she had an undisguised look of triumph.

"It seems that a Canick was seized from some stupid young thug who tried to use it to hold up a *casa de cambio*. They resisted and pressed the alarm, and he failed to fire the gun as the safety catch was on," she translated briefly. Doug laughed as he visualised the scene.

"Could you ask him to contact the *commisario* and request a ballistic comparison with the bullet that killed Masood?" Doug became serious again.

"Already done… Inspector Evans," she announced with great satisfaction.

"What a partner!" Doug threw his arms wide to the alarm of the expert, so he held his hands up with the palms facing the man. "I – we – would like you to check this suite for bugs, and do you know anything about booby traps?" Esperanza translated and frowned at Doug as the man set to work. "I'd love to see what is in the safe but it could be…" He raised his eyebrows and inclined his head. "Booby trapped!" She nodded. "Although, if this suite is bugged, it would be more practical to have the contents destroyed than risk another explosion."

They continued to inspect the contents of the rooms while their colleague did his check. When finished, the latter read his notes to Esperanza, who translated.

"There are two devices in the main room, which are similar to those downstairs, but none in the bedroom where the safe is. He doesn't know if the safe is booby-trapped and suggests we fetch Aetos and stand him in front of it while we try opening it." She shook her fist in approval, and Doug looked at the expert with new admiration.

Aetos was placed very close to the front of the safe. Then the expert used a stethoscope device he produced from his box of gadgets to listen to the tumblers as he tried to open it. To everybody's incredulity, it was opened. Inside was a lot of money in various currencies and two passports for Aetos. One Greek and one American. There was also an envelope containing a letter authorising the death of Babur Demir, the Turkish boss who had been killed in the UK and driven off a cliff in Dorset. It was simply signed R with a considerable flourish. The postmark was blurred, but with the help of a magnifying glass, produced from the expert's box, they eventually decided it was Stranraer!

"Where on earth is that?" exclaimed Esperanza.

"It's in the extreme south-west of Scotland," Doug announced in amazement, adding, "If that is an authorisation from the top man, why the hell would he live in such a place?"

"What's wrong with it?" Esperanza demanded.

"It's not the sort of place anyone with the power and wealth of the top man would live. It does not have the facilities or weather anyone would seek. It's further south than most of the border with England, and, despite rarely having frosts, it tends to be very wet with a comparatively sparse population. Very little light pollution, though." Aetos had been removed to the outer office so they were able to talk freely. Esperanza made a mental picture of the area.

"What are its communications and transport connections like?" she said, voicing her thoughts.

"There is a ferry service from Stranraer to Larne in Northern Ireland. The trains go to Ayr and Glasgow and London at least. I think the nearest commercial airport is at Ayr, which must be about 80 kilometres away, but there are light aircraft airfields nearer." He stopped to scratch his head while he tried to remember. "Ah yes. There might be one at Drummore at the southern tip. An old buddy of mine was in the RAF regiment and trained there. So what do you think?" While he had been giving her the details as he remembered, Esperanza had made some notes with possibilities from lateral thinking.

"First thought is what better place to hide, as even we find it hard to imagine. Then, though, we know that a man in such a position would want to enjoy the fruits of his labour." As she considered her notes once more, Doug reviewed his own list of the area's attributes.

"As he is unknown, so to speak, the world is his oyster."

"What do you mean, his oyster?"

"I mean he can go anywhere in the world with his wealth and the area's transport connections. But that applies to many places. So why there?" He shrugged.

"Because it is home!" Esperanza exclaimed. Doug considered the suggestion.

"Then he is unlikely to be just a commoner!"

"How do you mean?"

"That is mostly cow country with a rustic population. He must be something like a local farmer or laird."

"What is a laird?"

"A Scottish lord or clan chief."

"I've heard of the Scottish clans. Are they something like the Mafia?" He looked at her in astonishment.

"No. In ancient times, they used to be fighting each other. The clan names are those of the main families," Doug tried to explain.

"So which one begins with R?"

"Could be dozens – but then it might not be a clan name."

"What else could it be?" she persisted.

"Nothing to do with a clan; it could be a *nom de plume*. After all, the person in charge obviously wants to keep in the shadows but needs a symbol of his authority. The R could be the first letter of his Christian name or his hometown." He glared at her and added, "Are you paying attention, Esperanza?" She looked up from her cell phone and stood to attention.

"Yes, sir! I am, sir! Suppose it is neither their name nor town but the area?"

"Why, what have you found?"

"Stranraer is in an area called The Rhins of Galloway! Spelled with an R!"

"Very good. Whatever it is, you have good reason to believe the head of Zebec has a home in that area," he summed up sadly.

"Why me? What about you?"

"Tomorrow is my last day. The trail, which started with a kiddie falling off his scooter, led to the downfall of much corruption and other criminal activities in Britain. It also resulted in Masood's death and, I am confident to state, in the capture of the one who killed him."

"And a major blow against Zebec. Oh! And I understand many innocent lives have been seriously altered, largely for the better."

"Definitely! Including mine. I found my true love and finished my career on a high note and with the best partner anyone could wish for." He opened his hands towards Esperanza as if giving her a presentation. She flushed slightly and stepped forward and kissed him just as the officer holding Aetos looked through the door.

"*Perdona por entrometerme pero que quieres hacer con este hombre?*" He grinned salaciously.

Esperanza glowered at him and snapped back that Doug was retiring in two days and she had congratulated him. Aetos was to be taken to the police station immediately.

"Why are you arresting me?" Aetos demanded in English, for Doug's benefit.

"For the murder of Masood for a start," Doug replied with a smile.

"Ridiculous! You have the wrong person and you won't be able to hold me!" Aetos growled.

"We have your gun, which fired the bullets, with your prints on. Special arrangements have already been made for your incarceration! R is not going to be very pleased with you. Is he?"

While he was saying this, Doug had his fingers crossed behind his back. He was gambling on the forensic results. Twenty-four hours later, at the very end of his career, the results confirmed his guess. He notified London of the result and that he would return the next day to hand in his full report and ID, etc. Tonight, he was going to celebrate with Miguel, Esperanza, Sian and Maria.

Now the pursuit of Zebec would be up to the MET and Esperanza.

CHAPTER 35

Cooper was very relieved to have Maurice back in harness, relieving him of both his worries and his backlog. This was welcomed by Maurice, and he threw himself into the task with gusto. It helped keep his mind off Helen slightly. Driving out to meet clients should have helped, but, despite his love of the whole area, he was unable to enjoy it fully as his mind turned to thoughts of Helen time and again. *When can I see her? Does she really care for me? Perhaps she was only friendly with Megan because I was dead. How should I approach her? What could I say?* These and similar questions plagued him incessantly.

Birdie felt responsible for the situation and invited him to dinner in her marital love nest. At the meal, the atmosphere showed little of the earlier kinship. Perhaps it was due to the Schotts trying too hard or because Maurice felt a sense of intrusion… theirs or his? Even an unaccustomed indulgence in alcohol did little to relieve the tension. They even tried introducing him to a simple card game known simply as Molly's Game. As he was looking distressed and they had all been drinking, they sent him home in a taxi.

He went to lunch with Sid and Judith and a playful Charlie. He was given a tour of their studio and tried to appreciate their paintings and drawings. He even felt obliged to play a bit with the little boy. Pleased as he was to see his prodigy and how successful he had been, the sight of the child brought back memories he was trying to suppress. To make matters worse, they had learnt of the fateful meeting between Maurice and Helen. Thus, they reasoned that they had to entertain him as much as possible. Naturally, this made matters worse, and Maurice felt obliged to make excuses for an early departure. This then made him feel guilty and his mood blackened once more.

"Why did he have to go so soon, Judith?" Sid was perplexed.

"I think it may have been our fault, Sid. We tried too hard to cheer him up."

"I don't understand. How did we try too hard?" He was still baffled by his erstwhile mentor's departure.

"Sit down, Sid." She sat facing him and grasped both his hands. "He is in love with Helen. I believe she loves him." She paused for him to consider the facts.

"Then where is the problem?" The psychology of people was still a bit mystifying to him.

"People were made to believe Maurice was dead, for his safety. This upset everyone who knew him, even more so Helen. She lost Arnold, the love of her life, and was ready for a new partner in Maurice. Then she thought she had lost him and was very upset."

"Of course she was!" Sid declared very seriously.

"But!" Judith emphasised. "He suddenly appears alive and everyone but her knew it."

"Blimey, that would be annoying." The situation was slowly dawning on Sid.

"So Maurice's eagerly awaited reunion with Helen is terminated by her apparent rejection of him." She held Sid's hands, willing him to see beyond the admiration he had for Maurice as his mentor.

"That must have really upset Maurice, but we were being nice to him. Why would that upset him?" Sid pulled her closer to kiss her. His all-embracing passion for her was something she never had before, particularly from her husband, and she relished it.

"Well!" she exclaimed, breaking free at last, "he is in a fragile state, like someone was when he thought I preferred an ambulanceman."

"That was me!" Sid explained to nobody in particular, and made to kiss her again.

"Yes. So he is trying to overcome his disappointment and return to a normal life, but his friends are unwittingly reminding him of his loss."

"What can I do? I owe him so much!" Sid now saw the pain that Maurice must be suffering.

"We all owe him so much. He saved Charlie, helped you and brought us together." This was the last straw for Sid and he grabbed her once more. Their embrace was broken by the arrival of Charlie. "We'll talk about it later, dear." Judith got up and went to her son.

Pru tried her best to comfort Maurice with the same results. As a last resort, she asked him to take her children shopping. She had had partial success when he took them to the park. She reasoned that the additional responsibility could concentrate his mind. It nearly worked. Until they came out of the sweet shop and Helen saw them from the middle of the Square.

Not knowing they were his **neighbours**' kids, her mind was in turmoil. *What have I done? Stupid, stupid me! I've pushed him away once too often and some other lucky woman has him… and her kids. Kids! Oh dear! After Nicola and Roger collected the seeds I wanted, I gave them money for sweets. I daren't warn them or he will see me. I'll sit on this bench and keep watch.*

Just as she thought, her two dashed into view and bumped into Maurice.

"Maurice!" they both screamed at the same time, much to the alarm of the French pair.

"*Qui sont-ils?*" they exclaimed together. Maurice was frozen to the spot while trying to think. Passers-by looked with some alarm at the bearded man surrounded by gibbering children.

"Er... Monique and Gaston, this is Nicola and Roger," he finally stated, and hurriedly explained further before the youngsters could interrupt. "Nicola and Roger, these are my neighbours' children, who I am looking after." Then, turning to the others, he said, "*Ce sont les enfants de la femme que j'aime.*"

While the French kids nodded in understanding, as Pru had told them about Maurice and Helen, Nicola spluttered, "Then why don't you tell Mummy that you love her?" She was learning French at school. All four gazed at Nicola in surprise.

Monique nodded and smiled at Nicola and said, "*Oui!* Why you not tell her, Maurice?" The boys glared at their respective sisters, united by a common bond of sibling rivalry and dislike of sloppy romance.

"I will when I can but she won't see me!" Maurice protested in a somewhat annoyed tone, as he was not used to being told what to do by children. Taken aback by the manner of his reply, the children all looked a trifle upset. This had an effect on Maurice, and all five stood in silence for a few moments until Nicola took a deep breath and spoke cautiously.

"You could tell her now." Even the boys sensed that something different was about to happen.

"How?" Maurice mumbled apologetically, realising how he had snapped at them.

"She is here in the Square, waiting for us." Roger was pleased to be involved in the conversation. He gesticulated for the benefit of Gaston.

"Yes! She is waiting for us by the memorial. Let's all go and see her," Nicola suggested, and added for the benefit of the others in her best French, "*Ma mère est dans cette place par le memorial. Voulez-vous la voir?*"

"*Je comprends qu'on devrait rencontrer ta mère,*" Gaston burst in, determined not to be left out.

Nicola and Roger took Maurice by his hands and led him into the centre of the Square, with the others following. Helen had watched the scene avidly, trying to guess what they were all talking about. She was very alarmed when the whole group started to come in her direction. *I must hide. No! Whatever it is, I have to be here for my angels.* When they reached her, she stood and faced them. Maurice started to shake, and four pairs of young eyes stared at him in awe and noticed the tears forming in his misting eyes.

Though Helen had been trying to avoid looking directly at him, the perplexed expressions of all the kids forced her to do so. She nervously put out her hand to greet him. Suddenly he fell to his knees and put out his arms to ward off the proffered help from the kids.

"**Helen, will you marry me?**" A question he thought he was never going to use poured from him as if it was the most natural thing in the world. Never would he have dreamed of proposing in the middle of a public square, but he had to seize the moment. The children all started clapping and a small crowd gathered to witness this strange scene. Helen stared at him. She was speechless. The silence was strained and people started shuffling their feet in anticipation.

I refuse to be forced into anything. Particularly in front of a crowd of onlookers. My instinct is to refuse.

"Yes," she whispered. *To hell with instinct! I do love him. And so do Nicola and Roger.*

"Pardon?" Maurice asked, to ensure he had heard correctly. The four kids looked from one to the other.

"*YES!*" Helen shouted, to the delight of all the spectators, who applauded vigorously. Maurice was so overcome that he rushed to embrace her, forgetting he was still on his knees. His moment of supreme ecstasy finished not in an embrace of Helen but a lurch into a Muslim prayer position. As he scrambled to his feet, the concerned looks of his audience turned to hoots of laughter, with which, to his own surprise, he joined in. No longer the loner frightened of ridicule. Now he was a confident member of the human race. Ignoring everyone – children and strangers – he stopped Helen's laughter with a passionate kiss and cuddle. They were interrupted by Monique.

"*Monsieur* Maurice! *Maman* will be worried about us!" She tugged at his arm. The amorous couple separated with gasps of rapture and gazed down at their French chaperone.

"Yes, we must get back. My dear, darling Helen, allow me to introduce Monique and her brother, Gaston. They are the children of my neighbour, Madame Gravillons. *Mes enfants*, this is Helen, who is to be my wife. I would like you all to come back with me and meet Pru Gravillons. Had she not been in France when I was arrested, I might never have gone to jail!"

As the jubilant six went to his car, Maurice looked round the Square, where all his adventures originated, and sighed contentedly.

You don't need your name carved in **graphite** *to be remembered. You just need friends and family to remember you!*

This book is printed on paper from sustainable sources managed under the Forest Stewardship Council (FSC) scheme.

It has been printed in the UK to reduce transportation miles and their impact upon the environment.

For every new title that Troubador publishes, we plant a tree to offset CO_2, partnering with the More Trees scheme.

For more about how Troubador offsets its environmental impact, see www.troubador.co.uk/sustainability-and-community